Clearstream Style

Mr. Lawrence Edward Holmes

ISBN-13: 9780615965512 (Holmes Publishing)
ISBN-10: 0615965512
Clearstream Style/Lawrence Edward Holmes — First Edition
1-Kidnapping & Murder-Fiction, 2-Terrorists-Fiction 3-Conspiracies-Fiction, 4-Banks & Financial Institution-Fiction

Library of Congress Cataloging-in-Publication Data LCCN: 2014902535

Printed in USA by Holmes Publishing

Chris —
Thanks you
Montana
Holmes

Dedication

I dedicate this book to my wonderful wife Glenda Holmes. She gave me the
motivation to start writing and inspired me daily.

Prologue

efore I begin on my odyssey, I need to ask you some very important questions. Where were you September 11, 2001 or perhaps November 22, 1963? You probably could tell me exactly where you were and what you were doing and the exact time you were doing it. How about going back even further in American history to December 7, 1941, where were you then? Instantly, like most people you recall where you were and what you were doing. You can't forget these dates because of their historical significance and certainly the tragedy of the events. September 11, 2001, remembered more by 9/11, appears to have become an enduring icon unto itself, as though the date were intentionally selected for committing this tragic event.

Unfortunately, when tragedies such as these take place, they remain indelibly engrained in our brains. Perhaps that is good. I certainly remember where and what I was doing on 9/11. Do you remember? I had a business meeting scheduled in downtown New York City with an agent. You see, I was a tennis professional just joining the Associated Tennis Professional (ATP), world tour. It was a Tuesday morning and I had just arrived at the world's busiest airport, Atlanta Hartfield Airport, to catch an early morning flight to New York's LaGuardia Airport. I was excited at the prospect of attending this much-anticipated meeting. However, I didn't make it. Suddenly at around ten o'clock in the morning, the Atlanta Airport shut down completely. No planes were arriving or departing. The atmosphere in the airport was eerie and daunting. Just a little earlier, I was in the Delta Air Lines Crown room crowded around a television along with many other frequent flyers, trying to comprehend the reality of what was unfolding before our eyes. It was surreal. All of us were transfixed watching the horrible sequence of events unfold. Even today, it seems like it happened just yesterday. Suddenly, we were informed all flights, no matter the destination, were cancelled for the day and that we had to claim our luggage and wait outside the terminal for all of our bags to be inspected. Fortunately, for all of the passengers and their guests, it was a beautiful fall day. It was clear, no clouds and very comfortable outside. We had to wait in long, long lines to claim our bags. Every bag had to be examined and inspected one bag at a time, including carry-on luggage. Each piece of luggage was hand searched, sometimes twice.

This was the beginning of the Transportation Security Administration (TSA). We were patient and most everyone accepted the inconvenience and understood it was required. All of us made it home in one piece that day. Unfortunately, just over 3,000 people didn't make it home on that heartbreaking, dreadful day. They were part of the blood bath that will live in all of our memories forever. I will get to the relevant nature of why this day changed my life shortly. To start with, let me give you some historical perspective of how events evolved to the here and now. At the turn of the twentieth century, the noted historical journalist and writer William James penned, "History is a Bath of Blood." He's regarded as one of the best journalists ever on the subject. "Modern man inherits all the innate pugnacity and all the love of glory of his ancestors. Displaying war's absurdity, irrationality and dreadfulness is of no effect on him. The horrors make the fascination. War is the tough life; it is life in extremis; war taxes are the only ones men never hesitate to pay, as the budgets of all nations show us."

Today, in the twenty first century, James' cynical observation couldn't be more appropriate. On Tuesday, September 11, 2001, less than one-hundred years since William James' essay appeared, the United States suffered the most mindless and outrageous act of violence on innocent men, women and children. Immediately following these most hideous barbaric acts of aggression, the United States set in motion a number of ways to protect itself and take the offensive. We were now engaged in a war, albeit without borders, with faceless cowards who exploited the weaknesses of other countries and people. They hide in caves like the scum they are. In addition, they wear masks to hide their identity, again like cowards. We Americans live in the freest country in the world; as a result, we are and will remain targets of radical thinking people pervaded with envy, prejudices and misconceptions. Unfortunately, this is the penalty we Americans pay to be free. That early Tuesday morning will live indelibly in all of our memories. The sky was a stunningly clear blue and accentuated with more than a few puffy white clouds. New Yorkers typically went about their demanding days and the many tourists began exploring lower Manhattan, for queuing in long lines to visit and see the Statue of Liberty and other famous New York landmarks including the well-known Twin Towers in downtown Wall Street. The massive World Trade Center development was located in the heart of New York City's downtown financial neighborhood and consumed over one-thousand acres of prime real estate. In an instantaneous moment, that tranquility was shattered, as was the apparent sense of security Americans felt in their own country. The now known hijackers deliberately and willfully piloted two jumbo jets, American Airlines Flight 11 and United Airlines Flight 175, directly into the Twin Towers of the World Trade Center Buildings. At approximately 8:46 a.m., the first plane, American Airlines flight 11, which had originated from Boston, was indisputably navigated into the north tower of the World Trade Center in Lower Manhattan.

Most onlookers interpreted this originally to be a freak accident involving a small commuter plane or helicopter. The second plane, United Airlines flight 175, also from Boston, struck the south tower 17 minutes later. The two Boeing 767 planes were fully loaded with jet fuel; deliberately with malice and without doubt, the terrorists were using these large commercial aircraft as missiles to explode on impact. At this point, there was no misinterpreting that the United States was under attack, these coincidences were no longer accidents but were premeditated murder on the grandest scale, and the targets predetermined. It is so difficult to conceive what the people on board these flights were going through just prior to impact. In addition, it is inconceivable to imagine what it was like sitting having coffee at the Windows on the World, located on the 106th and 107th floors in one of the nation's most prominent dining establishments. Just the thought of it creates nightmares. Each building structure was wrecked and damaged by the impact. Both buildings erupted into firestorms of utter hell. It was as if the world was experiencing an apocalyptic abyss so vividly real, it created a lasting impression in our minds of coming events and foretelling the end of the present age as we know it. Office personnel who were trapped above the points of impact, in some circumstances, hurdled themselves to their deaths rather than face the infernos now rapidly spreading uncontrolled within the tallest buildings in New York City. At least two hundred people fell or jumped to their deaths from the burning towers.

After burning for approximately fifty-six minutes, the South Tower collapsed, followed a half-hour later by the North Tower, with the attacks on the World Trade Center resulting in 2,753 deaths. According to some New York newspapers, "falling debris from the towers, combined with fires that the debris initiated in several surrounding buildings, led to the partial or complete collapse of all the other buildings in the complex and caused catastrophic damage to ten other large structures in the surrounding and adjacent area. Once all of the buildings had collapsed, the sky appeared as dark as hell with zero visibility. If you were fortunate to survive, you were now caught in this ominous black like cloud of tar falling from the heavens.

People were literally choking and gagging from the overwhelming haze of heavy polluted air. Everywhere you gazed, people were running aimlessly and seemed to emerge as zombies. The New York firefighters, police officers and emergency response teams looked like ghosts covered in debris and soot. There didn't appear to be a place to find shelter or to hide. The toxic cloud seemed to be permanent and would last forever. The stench was nauseating. Suddenly, there was deadening quiet and then finally it ended. Most everyone had to begin putting the pieces back together. The procedure of cleanup, recovery and healing at the World Trade Center location took eight agonizing long months. The 9/11 assault was both violent and brutal.

Make no mistake; this strike was extremely well executed with military like precision that had to be well financed. There were two other attacks that fateful day and unfortunately, for whatever reasons, these attacks have never received the same consideration as the attack on the twin towers. As reported in the Washington Post and witnessed on the ground, "A third plane, American Airlines Flight 77, that crashed into the Pentagon (the headquarters of the United States Department of Defense), resulted in a partial collapse in its western side, killing over one hundred twenty-five people including both military and civilians. The fourth plane, United Airlines Flight 93, originally targeted for the United States Capitol Building in Washington, D.C., but instead crashed into a rural field approximately eighty miles southeast from Pittsburg, PA. Apparently, in the last minutes leading up to the crash, some of the passengers unsuccessfully tried to overpower the hijackers." According to the headlines the next day, the New York Times reported, "In total, just over 3,000 people died in the attacks, including the 227 civilians and 19 hijackers aboard the four planes. It also was the deadliest series of tragic hellholes for firefighters in the history of the United States." How did these terrorists bankroll these attacks?

Where and how did these nineteen fanatics get the money to organize and execute such a provocative well thought out, extremely expensive undertaking? Al Qaeda alone couldn't afford to pull off a plan of this magnitude, especially one so sophisticated and elaborate. Osama Bin Laden and the wealthy Osama Bin Laden family are intimately connected with the innermost circles of the Saudi royal family. However, the Saudis have vehemently denied any connection, knowledge, or awareness and support of Al Qaeda. As reported on the MSN headline account, "The entire concept for the planned violence originated with Khalid Sheikh Mohammed, who first offered the idea to Osama Bin Laden sometime around 1995 or 1996. At that time, Bin Laden and Al Qaeda were in a period of transition, having just moved back to Afghanistan from Sudan."

The report continued, "The 1998 African Embassy bombings and Bin Laden's 1998 fatwa marked a turning point, as Bin Laden became intent on attacking the United States. In late 1998 or early 1999, Bin Laden gave approval for Mohammed to go forward with organizing the plot. A series of meetings occurred in early 1999, involving Mohammed, Bin Laden, and his deputy Mohammed Atef. Atef provided operational support for the plot, including target selections and help arranging travel for the hijackers." Furthermore, the same story indicated, "Bin Laden overruled

Mohammed, rejecting some potential targets such as the U.S. Bank Tower in Los Angeles because there wasn't enough time to prepare for such an operation. Bin Laden provided leadership for the plot, and was involved in selecting participants. Bin Laden initially selected Nawaf al-Hazmi and Khalid al-Mihdhar, both experienced jihadists who had fought in Bosnia. Hazmi and Mihdhar arrived in the United States in mid-January 2000."

According to more reporting from MSN, "In spring 2000, Hazmi and Mihdhar took flying lessons in San Diego, California, but both spoke little English, did poorly with flying lessons, and eventually served as secondary backups and ultimately were the muscle hijackers aboard the back of the hijacked planes. In late 1999, a group of men from Hamburg, Germany, arrived in Afghanistan, including Mohamed Atta, Marwan al-Shehhi, Ziad Jarrah and Ramzi Bin Al Shibh. Bin Laden selected these men because they were educated, spoke English, and had experience living in the west." In addition, "New recruits were routinely screened for special skills and Al Qaeda leaders consequently discovered that Hani Hanjour already had a commercial pilot's license. Hanjour arrived in San Diego on December 8, 2000, joining Hazmi. They soon left for Arizona, where Hanjour took refresher training. Marwan al-Shehhi arrived at the end of May 2000, while Atta arrived on June 3, 2000, and Jarrah arrived on June 27, 2000. Bin Al Shibh applied several times for a visa to the United States, but as a Yemeni, was rejected out of concerns that he would overstay his visa and remain as an illegal immigrant. Bin Al Shibh stayed in Hamburg, providing coordination between Atta and Mohammed. The three Hamburg cell members all took pilot training in South Florida." Moreover, MSN elaborated, "In spring 2001, the secondary hijackers began arriving in the United States. In July 2001, Atta met with Bin Al Shibh in Spain where they coordinated details of the plot, including final target selection. Bin Al Shibh also passed along Bin Laden's wish for the attacks to be carried out as rapidly as possible."

Repeatedly, the evidence has shown the money was already in place for many years even before Osama Bin Laden became a household word. Not one of the hijackers had the capital or resources to undertake the suicidal missions. Have you ever asked yourself, how does a group of rebel Islamic terrorists living like swine and rats in the desert mountains of Western Pakistan, get funding for their extreme religious hatred of the west? All or most of Middle Eastern Moslem African and Southeast Asian Countries, including Indonesia, deny any involvement. In addition, China and Russia both repudiated and totally rebuffed any connection in the financing or support of Al Qaeda.

Just consider the following information on how much money had to be available for these well-coordinated terrorist attacks. According to reliable sources, in total, terrorists took more than 500 commercial flights over a period of six to seven years. Moreover, they chartered private aircraft and rented their own planes. Terrorists traveled to and from Afghanistan, Pakistan, Iraq, Sudan, Saudi Arabia, Los Angeles, San Francisco, Chicago, Bosnia, Egypt, San Diego, New York, Munich, Spain, London, Paris, Brussels, Syria, Arizona, Miami and Zurich. They traveled to just about every country in Europe and the Middle East, several times, and then many more trips to the United States. Often they took multiple trips for different reasons. In addition, they received flight training and re-training. Housing expenses were enormous. Terrorist lived in a hotel for many weeks and in some cases, they were in hotel suites for many months at a time. They rented cars for weeks and sometimes months at a time. Not one terrorist worked or had a regular job. Finally, many of the terrorists enrolled in taking private tutoring English lessons. In fact, because they did so poorly, they were required to repeat several times. Some had large families to support. On average, it cost in excess of eighty-five hundred to ten-thousand dollars per month for each lowly son-of-a-bitch terrorist. What filth they are. Where in the world did they manage to find or get the capital? No one seems to know. Today, terrorism has transformed the playing field; as a result, there is more uncertainty. It is more difficult to determine who the enemy is.

Increasingly, intelligence collecting has become vital and necessary, not only to the western world, but also in developing third world nations because we are entering a new era of conflict with its own unique characteristics and requirements. Because of this major change, the world of intelligence gathering is in perpetual transformation.

Author's Note

John Style was just an average American citizen at the time of September 11, 2001. His life was turned upside down and like most Americans, life wasn't the same ever again. Style deliberated days, weeks, months and even years after the 9/11 tragedy occurred; often he would ask himself what could he do for his part to catch the terrorist. He felt regretful and needed to do something for his country and for himself. It took a while for Style to realize what he needed to do. In the very beginning, he thought too much like a reactionary die-hard by considering enlisting in the military. That certainly would help. However, he patiently waited sometime and then started to deliberate more, analyze and proceeded to ask himself the most logical and tough question. How does Al Qaeda get the money to fund their diabolical global terrorist activities? Ultimately, John Style made a decision to do something about the 9/11 tragedies but not the way he originally planned. This is the story of how he got involved in solving one of the greatest mysteries of the last one hundred years. John Style is the new Sherlock Holmes (Sir Arthur Conan Doyle), Perry Mason (Erie Stanley Gardner) and Hercule Poirot (Agatha Christie) all combined into one remarkable spy detective. John Style will become legendary all over the world because of his ability to solve complicated spy mysteries and for his razor sharp powers of observation, which he uses to solve perplexing terrorist crimes and mysteries. Style has determination, intellect, and an ingenious method of developing positive results. Style employs a Machiavellian approach for uncovering the truth of how world terrorism is getting their funding. He followed his instincts and eventually was recruited by the Central Intelligence Agency's (CIA) Clandestine Service (CS), to become a field agent and solve how and from whom terrorists have been receiving their financial funding and backing. Finally, we now have the answers to where the funding is originating to finance Al Qaeda and terrorism around the world. Follow John Style's odyssey around the globe and his unique intellectual manner of investigation in the discovery of the truth. He'll amaze you.

1

"Every gun that is made, every warship launched, every rocket fired signifies in the final sense, a theft from those who hunger and are not fed, those who are cold and are not clothed. This world in arms is not spending money alone. It is spending the sweat of its laborers, the genius of its scientists, and the hopes of its children. This is not a way of life at all in any true sense. Under the clouds of war, it is humanity hanging on a cross of iron."
Dwight D. Eisenhower
President of the United States

PARIS, FRANCE
Several years after the tragedy of 9/11, the professional tennis circuit was now in Europe. The second leg of the Grand Slams was in the city of lights - Paris, France. Springtime in Paris is beautiful and romantic. It was early June and one of the biggest events of the -year for all of France, The French Open Tennis Tournament, was just beginning its second week. There is no more picturesque and charming city in all of Europe to enjoy both the spring and to attend the second of four professional tennis' Grand Slam tennis events. The men's Associated Tennis Professionals (ATP) and the Woman's Tennis Association (WTA) tours combine to compete at Roland Garros, the

official name for the French Open, in separate events, namely the singles and doubles. The Grand Slams and a few lesser events are the only tennis tournaments where men and women play against each other in the mixed doubles. Roland Garros is less than five miles from the heart of Paris, not far from Right Bank and shopping within walking distance of the iconic attractions of the city such as Paris Opera Garnier, Place de la Madeleine, Place de la Concorde, the River Seine, the Louvre, Champs-Elysees and the iron lattice Eiffel Tower.

In the first days of the tournament, the weather was unpredictably chilly and rainy, but entering the second week that changed suddenly to delightful sunny days, and cool comfortable light sweater wearing evenings. During the first week there were no major upsets; as a result, going in to the second week, attendance was breaking records. Less than two weeks earlier in Italy, a protester covered with simulated blood, leapt onto to the tennis court during the women's Italian Open Final brandishing a gun, frightening the women's eventual champion Nadia Rolfe from Romania and creating near panic with the large capacity crowd, compelling a fast reaction from the Italian national military police Carabinieri and private security. As a result, the French Nationale Police were not taking any chances at the French Open. They carefully examined their security policies and procedures and made some dramatic changes for spectators. Although the new policies were demanding and time consuming, the French fans accepted the inconveniences without much fanfare. According to a pre-tournament published report, the French Open tournament security director stated, "We will reflect the current threat level and make certain all of our fans are safe and protected."

In the meantime, the quarter-finals evening session of the tournament was approximately thirty minutes from starting. The atmosphere was electrifying and exciting because of the evenings anticipated grudge match between two of the top ten men's ATP tour single players. As is the tradition, the French national anthem, La Marseillaise, was sung by Mireille Mathieu along with the over 15,000 French fans in Roland Garros stadium. Suddenly, out of the early evening sky, emerged a two-tandem parachute team descending on a trajectory to land in Roland Garros stadium. At first it appeared the parachute teams were competing in a thrilling four-way formation display of precision freefall.

Approximately two thousand feet from landing, all of the parachutist's colorful chutes opened, followed by the French national colors of red, white and blue smoke trailing behind each of the jumpers. All of the spectators were on their feet applauding, as the four parachutists gently landed directly on the center court stadium. All at once, the four men took out their AK-47s and started shooting randomly in to the crowd of spectators. All hell broke loose. There was mass hysteria. People were desperately trying to escape the carnage, but all exits were now blocked by mounting bodies of men, women and children. The terrorists were accomplishing their hideous, repulsive and shocking assignments to perfection. All you could hear was the most ungodly screaming and yelling. Suddenly, there was a massive explosion. One of the terrorists had set off a bomb. The suicide bomber was the bomb. Fortunately, the two professional tennis players, French favorite Giles Lefebvre and American John Style, were still in the locker room anxiously waiting to go on to center court, stretching and warming up. Usually on match days, you don't see the opponents talking to each other, but once they heard the enormous blast and witnessed the lockers falling over and the mirrors on the walls shattering, both players turned to each other to quietly converse. Immediately, security guards burst in to the locker room and escorted both competitors through the tunnel leading to the stadium rear emergency exit.

Once they exited the stadium, both players were hurriedly taken to a waiting limousine and taken back to their respective hotels. In the meantime, center court was a horrific scene; no matter where you looked, you saw unspeakable bloodshed. Within minutes, there was a full contingency of French Nationale Police on the scene eradicating the last of the remaining insurgents. All four terrorists were killed. Al Qaeda had once again done their senseless hideous barbaric acts of violence.

In the meantime, America's number one tennis player, John Style, was ushered back to his five-star hotel, The Hyatt Paris Madeleine. Style sat on the edge of the bed transfixed, watching the local news recount over and over the sensational events that Style was fortunate to have escaped. Channel after channel telecast the same horrific news story describing how over two hundred innocent people were murdered and countless victims severely wounded. It was surreal for anyone to watch the graphic videotape replay of the indiscriminate slaughter of human life. These supposed religious fanatics who were responsible for the butchery, aren't part of the human race. Instead, they are the lowest form of scum that exists. Style started to feel guilty he survived the bloodbath and felt he needed to do something. He was filled with outrage and disgust. Style didn't know what to do or who to call to ask for help. He was alone, lost, and depressed. At that moment, he made up his mind. After finishing the professional ATP tennis circuit this year and satisfying his legal obligations, he would definitely do something to fight Al Qaeda and combat world terrorism.

2

TLANTA, GEORGIA

Approximately nine months later after the dreadful events of the French Open in Paris, John "Montana" Style was just returning home to the United States, exhausted and consumed, after playing at the Australian Open, the first grand slam professional tennis tournament of the year starting off the tennis season. At one time, the Australian Open was the last scheduled event of the year. In recent years it was moved ahead a few weeks to accommodate the ever expanding tennis circuit schedule.

The tournament lasted a long grueling two weeks in the very hot, beautiful city of Melbourne, Australia. Style was in excellent shape and had no problem lasting in the scorching summer Australian sun. This was Style's sixth consecutive year at the Australian Open. Each year he successfully managed to get to the next level of the tournament. Unfortunately, he lost to the eventual winner Jaka Bombac from Slovenia in the quarter finals in a match that lasted five grueling and demanding sets in just over six exhausting hours with court temperatures hovering around one hundred twenty-five degrees. Fortunately, because of his splendid physical conditioning, Style managed to win the second and fourth sets in tiebreakers. Almost a decade ago, he graduated at the top of his class from Georgia Tech University, where he majored in International Law and Computer Science. He was the number one collegiate tennis player in his senior year and had won the prestigious annual NCAA tennis tournament held each spring at the University of Georgia, in Athens, Georgia. Prior to attending Georgia Tech, Style had been raised on a farm in the North Georgia Mountains not too far from Blue Ridge and Jasper and within a stone's throw of Tennessee.

Because of his unique knowledge of both international law and software engineering, he was highly recruited by the FBI, Secret Service and CIA. In addition, several major corporations including Cisco, IBM and Ernst & Young were very eager for him to join their ranks. Instead, he elected to try competing on the men's Associated Tennis Professional (ATP) tennis circuit. He'd managed to slowly rise in the ATP rankings to where he is today in the top twenty at number fourteen. Style was physically exhausted from the long twenty-hour non-stop flight from Melbourne, Australia. When he finally arrived at his beautiful townhome located in the northern suburbs of Atlanta, he flung his luggage and tennis equipment into the corner of the living room and collapsed on the leather sofa. Within minutes, he fell into a deep sleep.

At around three in the morning, a total stranger suddenly awakened him. At first he thought he was dreaming. Then swiftly he realized he wasn't imagining and was now more concerned about being robbed or worse yet, assaulted. Style promptly jumped to his feet, standing tall, creating an imposing figure at six foot three inches and just over two hundred pounds. The total stranger hurriedly introduced himself as Kent McIntosh, a field agent for the Central Intelligence Agency and in the same breath he tried to explain why he was in John Style's apartment.

McIntosh was handsomely dressed in an expensive dark blue pinstriped Italian Brioni business suit and was probably around forty-years old. In the next few minutes, Style's life would be turned upside down. Although Style was startled, he still managed to ask McIntosh how he got into his apartment and why.

McIntosh replied, "I used a credit card," and further explained "that this is the only way I could get your immediate attention to discuss a business opportunity with you. This wasn't exactly a business proposition but more of an opportunity for you to perform a positive and constructive initiative for your country and in addition, at the same time, earn a substantially comfortable living."

Style reacted instantly and asked, "How comfortable a living?"

"Please let me finish several other details first, and then I will get to the compensation, Mr. Style." McIntosh had this unique manner of talking with his hands. If he didn't say a thing, you could pretty much guess what he said by his hand gestures. Style's first immediate reaction was to shout or yell for help, but he didn't. He simply sat and tried his best to comprehend the minute. Finally, after pausing, he started to think more clearly. Once he was able to appreciate the circumstances, he came to his senses. Style observed with an almost arrogant tone of voice, "Why would I want to work for the CIA when I already make close to a half million dollars a year and have all my expenses paid for by the companies I endorse and sponsor? Furthermore, it is safe and I personally control my own destiny, not some well-paid bureaucrat sitting at a desk in Washington D. C. who literally has control of my life including where I can go and who I see. Frankly, I'm not sure I can compromise my freedom and independence. I would have to be crazy to ever consider this preposterous idea."

"In a little while, all of this will become clearer," said McIntosh. "Allow me to continue and I will explain. First, may I sit down and provide some details."

"Please sit down, Mr. McIntosh; I apologize for being so inconsiderate." Style was still flustered and confused. "Mr. McIntosh, for the life of me, what possible reason would the CIA have in a touring tennis professional?"

"Well, for one thing Style, from what we understand, thirty to thirty-five is about the age that most professional tennis players begin to consider calling it quits. Next year, you will be thirty. Is that correct, John Style?"

"Yes, it is," Style replied somewhat defensively.

McIntosh continued, "I could guarantee that you will make at least two million dollars the balance of this year and double that amount next year."

"Don't you mean if I survive first? Please forgive me if I'm being cynical and rude, Mr. McIntosh."

"Your attitude, John, is perfectly understandable and quite reasonable."

"I still don't understand, why me?"

"I would like to provide clarity to a number of important points. Most important and without doubt a very essential fact, Style, is that you don't have to leave the professional tennis tour either. On the contrary, we prefer that you continue playing on the ATP tour and that is one of the principal reasons we are interested in your services, talent and skill set.

Have you ever asked yourself since the tragedy of September 11, 2001, what you could do for your country?"

"Yes, repeatedly. However, I didn't do anything. I felt guilty and even to this day I continue with the guilt. What possible skill set can I offer the Central Intelligence Agency?"

"There are several reasons, but primarily your outstanding academic knowledge of International Law and software engineering application development. In addition, I believe you are in excellent physical condition. You are also a rated pilot with just over one thousand hours in both single and multi-engine props and jets."

"Yes, in fact just behind you on the wall is my FAA certification, displaying what types of aircraft I'm rated to fly and where I received my training to be a pilot. As you see, most of my training has been at local airports here in Atlanta and North Georgia."

"Style you have accomplished a lot. Moreover, now I understand you recently received your license to fly helicopters."

"Yes, I managed to obtain my helicopter pilot's license this past winter, just prior to the Thanksgiving holiday season."

"Yes, we know John. It appears you need something to keep you busy all the time. You understand I'm just joking with you, right?"

In a blurred voice, Style asked, "Mr. McIntosh, I'm now more confused than ever. I still don't understand. Can you explain why me of even more qualified people?"

"Allow me to continue, Style, with some more details. Your international travel on the ATP tour is exactly what we need for a field agent as a cover."

"Why is that?" Style asked with a completely bewildered look.

McIntosh reacted at once in a very calm voice, "because you will appear to be almost transparent while engaged in assignments," McIntosh said in a very calm voice, "and at the same time compete on the professional tennis circuit in Europe, United States and China and especially in the Middle East."

"The money offer seems extremely generous. What will I be doing?"

"Now that I have your attention, let me begin and explain the why, where, when and how you will fit in. First, I need to provide you with some background information on a sequence of events brought about by the bad guys. The bad guys I'm referring to are the radical Islamic terrorist from any number of Middle Eastern countries with a few even raised in the United States. I know it is difficult to comprehend that some terrorists are even home grown Americans. I'm sure you recall the first bombing of the 1993 World Trade Center where a group of terrorists detonated a fifteen hundred-pound truck bomb in the basement of the Twin Towers' parking structure. Instantly, the massive explosion killed six people, injured roughly a thousand men, women and children, leaving a substantial crater and enormous destruction. Approximately seven years later in October 2000, Al Qaeda proudly admitted to the suicide attack against the United States Navy guided-missile destroyer USS Cole while it was harbored and being refueled in the Yemen port of Aden. Seventeen American sailors were killed and many were injured. Not since the late 1980s was there a more deadly attack against a United States Naval vessel. Ultimately, the terrorist's organization Al-Qaeda claimed total responsibility for both attacks."

"Yes, I remember both of those acts of terrorism," responded Style. "Of course you remember the 9/11 terrorist attack that was a defining moment in American History, one that profoundly changed a shocked and dismayed America of the well-executed second World Trade Center attack in which over three thousand innocent men, women and children were brutally murdered. That unforgiving, vindictive act transformed the United States. All of these horrible tragedies became American travesties just like December 7, 1941."

"Certainly I remember. How can anyone ever forget 9/11," countered Style.

"Obviously the most recent controversial attack in Bengasi, Libya, that killed the United States ambassador Christopher Stevens and three other American officials was the direct result of a well-planned and executed attack by Al Qaeda. What is most distressing about the Bengasi attack wasn't only the brutal manner in which the victims were kidnapped and murdered, but then the terrorists viciously dragged the bodies of the four American diplomats through the streets of Bengasi. Within two hours after the initial attack, the terrorists also succeeded in confiscating over two hundred fully equipped ready to load missiles. It is easy to understand why most Europeans today are on edge going to the airport to catch a flight. Finally, the Boston Marathon bombing in which two Americans lost their lives and over one-hundred men, women and children were severely injured in another senseless terrorist's attack. It never seems to end. Obviously, the common thread in all these horrendous attacks is Al Qaeda. Have you ever asked yourself how does a group of renegade Islamic terrorists living in the middle of the desert highlands of Western Pakistan and the eastern mountains of Afghanistan get enough funding for their extreme religious hatred of the west? It is simply extraordinary how they exist. Just consider the constant training and movement of their troops, food, shelter, weapons, recruitment and training of young radical fanatics and perhaps one of the biggest expenses is their constant travel. They have successfully managed to deploy some of the world's most sophisticated computer hardware and software cloud based electronic military weapons. When they need it, they get it. Cost never seems to be an issue. China, Egypt, Russia and Indonesia all deny funding Al Qaeda. Certainly, Pakistan couldn't afford such an expensive involvement. Yes, there was no doubt Pakistan was providing a safe haven, but financial support never. Perhaps Iran, you may be thinking and no again. Their economy is in shambles and the political process is a fiasco. They couldn't afford to support such an ongoing financial burden."

"Mr. McIntosh, I need to interrupt you. The history you are providing is quite extraordinary and interesting but I still don't understand how I fit in to the equation."

"Mr. Style, let me please finish; you will then understand more of what I'm saying when you see the bigger picture."

"All right, but how much longer will you need?"

"Remember, Al Qaeda has been in the terrorism business for a long time. The origins of Al Qaeda can be traced to 1977, during the Carter Administration, when the Soviet Union invaded Afghanistan. Osama Bin Laden traveled to Afghanistan and helped organize Arab mujahedeen to resist the Soviets. There has been much speculation Al Qaeda could have existed prior to the Carter administration and earlier. Naturally, Saudi Arabia would be the ideal nation to fund Al Qaeda because of their very rich oil fields and strong government control over other major economic activities in the Middle East. The CIA had to give Saudi Arabia a thorough examination because of their history involving Wahhabism which has been Saudi Arabia's dominate faith for more than two centuries. It is an austere form of Islam that insists on a literal interpretation of the Koran. Wahhabi Islam counts among its adherents such names as Osama Bin Laden and Saudi Prince Nayef Again."

"I don't mean to make light of your explanation, Mr. McIntosh, but I have never heard of Wahhabism. It sounds like cannibalism."

"This extremist religion offers many a theological justification and mandate to kill those they deem to be infidels. According to Wahhabism, the vast majority of Muslims (over 99%) are also considered infidels, heathens, and enemies. In addition, Wahhabism has had a significant, yet unfortunate, influence on culture by stifling the creative arts, treating women badly, doing away with any sense of individualism or displaying any form of prosperity. After a substantial amount of energy and time investigating the Kingdom of Saudi Arabia, the CIA determined that Saudi Arabia couldn't be involved in financing world terrorism, because it would be too costly a sacrifice to mix their oil wealth with extreme religious beliefs such as Wahhabism. So, where does that leave us? Let me share with you something so unique, at first, you will think we are off our rocker. The CIA has a theory and is out to prove that just prior to the beginning of World War II, starting in 1937; the Swiss Banks collaborated with the Third Reich in hiding the gold stolen from the Jews."

"My God, now you are talking about World War II, Swiss Banks, Third Reich, gold and the Jews. I'm getting a little confused."

"Please allow me just another ten minutes or so and you will understand, believe me."

"This is beginning to feel like a history class, but please continue."

"Thank you. In 2001, the United States learned that the Swiss had protected an International Bank that handled finances for Osama Ben Laden. One of them, the Bahrain International Bank, had funds transiting through non-published accounts of Clearstream, which has been qualified as a 'bank of banks.' Ultimately, the United States Government and the CIA are now convinced and anxious to prove that the Swiss banks had many secret numbered accounts that contained the stolen 'money' taken from the persecuted Jews."

"Are you suggesting this is the money that is funding world terrorism?"

"Yes absolutely, this is indeed the money being used by Al Qaeda to fund world terrorism. In particular, the Central Intelligence Agency and its Allies in Western Europe are aggressively determined to prove that financing of Al Qaeda terrorism originated from the illegal confiscation by Nazi Germany from the beginning of the World War II in 1939 through 1944. There is an estimated nine hundred eighty million dollars of central bank gold, around one hundred billion dollars in today's values, along with indeterminate amounts of treasured arts and other assets during World War II which was kept under wraps by the Swiss Banks for over three generations."

"I'm now becoming more interested and curious; please continue with the story, Mr. McIntosh."

"These goods were stolen from governments and civilians in the countries Germany overran and from Jewish and non-Jewish victims of the Nazis alike, including Jews murdered in extermination camps from whom everything was taken down to the gold fillings of their teeth."

"You certainly have gained my attention. I'm definitely interested in moving ahead. What do I have to do next? Obviously, I need training and orientation."

"Your role would be to not only recover the remaining gold and other assets stolen by Germany during World War II, but to also prove Al Qaeda is using this money to fund its worldwide terrorist activity. Naturally we are anxious for you to get started, but first you will have to go to Langley for orientation, training and meet the boss. I understand that you will have some time before your next tournament. Is that correct John?"

"Yes, my next scheduled event is in Dubai, United Arab Emirates at the Dubai Duty Free Tennis Championships, I believe the end of April. I expect to be the number seven or eight seed."

McIntosh responded, "This is terrific. That will give us at least three months for you to receive the initial training and preparation. By the way, there are several other tournaments scheduled before then. Is there a reason why you elected to wait three months before your next tournament?"

"Yes" replied Style, "that is easy to explain, I'm exhausted and I need to rest both my shoulder and knee. In fact, I elected to drop out of Davis Cup, along with tournaments in Germany, Austria, Chile and Brazil."

"OK, that makes perfect sense to me, John. You sound really interested." "Yes, I'm definitely interested Mr. McIntosh. However, how do I explain to my family, friends, agents, fans, girls I date and the Associated Tennis Professionals (ATP) a sudden rash of income and wealth?"

"We have that covered. Georgia has a lottery, is that correct?" asked McIntosh.

"Yes, Georgia has had the lottery for twenty years," replied Style.

McIntosh further asked, "Have you ever played the Georgia lottery?"

Without hesitation, Style said, "just recently in fact, on the way through the Atlanta Airport I purchased a quick pick lottery ticket."

McIntosh said, "Yes we know. I have been following you since you left the tournament in Australia. We can arrange for you to win a large amount of prize money that will remain quiet until someone begins to ask questions".

"How can the CIA manage to do that?" Style asked with a bewildered look.

"Very easy replied McIntosh, we will make certain the money is deferred with an annuity, spread-out over a reasonable period."

"Mr. McIntosh, could you please clarify and explain to me why my skills are so attractive to the CIA?"

McIntosh replied, "As I said earlier, we feel the professional tennis tournament travel is ideally suited as a cover and certainly would not draw the suspicion or attention of our enemies, particularly Al Qaeda and the Russians. One day you will face the inevitable and will admit to yourself that it is time to call it quits and move on. At that point, it would be relatively easy for you to consider being a consultant or an adviser to the Associated Tennis Professional international executive organization or perhaps even coach an upcoming young tennis professional. In the meantime, let's stay focused on the mission at hand. Most important is your terrific knowledge of international law and your ability to write and read code no matter how sophisticated the software. That is just a sensational combination of skills. We also understand that you are fluent in reading and writing Spanish, French, Arabic, Farsi, Italian, Chinese and Russian. I'm curious Style, what possessed you to study such an eclectic choice of languages."

At first, Style's response was hardly discernible, but he acknowledged he could speak and write over six languages, and now he was just learning German. He continued, "Fortunately, learning a language came easy. As a result, both my parents encouraged me to learn as many unique languages as possible, and I did as you can see."

In finishing their conversation McIntosh added, "once you complete your initial training, you will be given one of the most valuable assignments in the history of both the CIA and the British Intelligence Service (SIS), commonly known as MI6 (Military Intelligence, Section 6. Personally, John, I can't recall in recent memory an assignment of this magnitude and importance. Ordinarily, Style, clandestine training is twenty-four months but because of your exceptional academic background, avionic skills, language proficiency, the training has been reduced substantially to allow you an opportunity to get in the field faster. However, because your training has been reduced in time, nothing has been compromised in your instruction and training. You will categorically be trained thoroughly and you will learn many important life-surviving procedures. Most assuredly, the training will prepare you as a field agent. Shortly, you will receive a package of information from the Central Intelligence Agency office in Langley, Virginia, outlining your daily training process and the educational routine you will receive. We know we selected the right person for this project and many more assignments to come. Finally came Style's enthusiastic reaction; "I look forward to the challenge and opportunity to start serving my country, Mr. McIntosh."

3

They that can give up essential liberty to obtain a little
temporary safety deserve neither liberty nor safety.
Benjamin Franklin

CIA HEADQUARTERS LANGLEY, VIRGINIA

Style arrived early at CIA headquarters, located in the Washington D.C. suburbs, on a very cold, dreary gray morning. It appeared to him the CIA compound was indeed an eerie place with all of the barbed wire fences, military police and security cameras everywhere. He was incessantly being stopped to produce an ID. Style, hesitated and thought, I could get paranoid around here.

Even its location———Langley, Virginia isn't what it seems. In fact, it doesn't exist. On his flight into Ronald Reagan Airport, Style did some research on Langley. He discovered Langley is the name of an estate that was acknowledged to be owned by a member of the family of Robert E. Lee who led the southern forces in the Civil War. Georgetown Pike and the Blue Ridge Mountains of Virginia border the estate. Later, Langley became a village and merged with the city of McLean. As a result, Langley officially doesn't categorically exist. This further adds more mystery and secrecy to both the history and all of the clandestine stories of the CIA.

Style was promptly escorted in to the office of Assistant Director, Bryan Nogaki. As Assistant Director for the CIA, he had all Global strategic responsibility for the agency. Nogaki was dressed like a banker, conservative and very professional, neat, not ostentatious. This was definitely not your typical U.S. government office with an old gray desk, bland worn shabby carpet, old faded photographs on the wall and re-cycled office furniture. Nogaki's office was tastefully decorated and conservatively furnished.

There were several photographs of a woman with children on the desk and on the credenza, perhaps his wife and family. There was a large photograph of the current President of the United States, prominently displayed on the wall to the left of desk. On the opposite wall was another large photograph of former President Ronald Reagan along with awards, certificates of achievement and a diploma from the University of Virginia. In the corner on a stand was the American flag. Nogaki was tall and lean, appeared to be in great shape as if he managed to spend extensive time in the gym. Bryan Nogaki was approximately forty-five or so with gray at the temples.

"Good morning John Style. I'm Bryan Nogaki, Assistant Director of Global Operations, including most of Europe, Russia, China, Southeast Asia, Africa and the Middle East. Please have a seat, Style. Would you like some coffee and perhaps a donut or muffin?"

"No thanks sir, I have already had two cups of coffee and I'm not hungry."

"O.K. John, let us get started. Prior to discussing the important subject matter, these next weeks and months are going to be intense and demanding. Since you are a new recruit, I would like to put you at ease and allow you to develop the right frame of mind for our discussions today."

"Yes, sir, that already makes me feel comfortable," said John.

"First, I would like to ask you something about your nickname, Montana. How did you acquire the name?"

"When my sister and I were young, my family would take trips to Montana and go fly fishing as often as possible, especially in the summer. As we got older, my sister became less interested. As a result, my dad and I would go together just about every year until I was about fifteen or so. Initially, my dad started calling me Montana because I just simply loved the beautiful big sky country, especially in and around Bozeman, Montana."

"I've been there many times, John, and I agree it's beautiful country. Please continue."

"You can't beat the picturesque scenery of State Road 191, which leads south out of Bozeman and winds its way along the Gallatin River, heading into magnificent Yellowstone National Park. The nickname continued throughout high school when I started getting serious about playing professional tennis. The name Montana stuck with me throughout college. Even to this day, many of my fellow ATP friends call me Montana."

"What would you prefer that I call you, John or Montana?"

"It doesn't matter to me sir; either would be just fine."

"Traditionally, when the agents are in the field we ordinarily communicate by their last name. This avoids confusion, especially under duress. However, for today, I will call you Montana."

"That is just fine with me, sir."

"Let me begin by sharing with you some very valuable information. Essentially, in life, two basic traits and characteristics motivate people - pain and pleasure. This is especially true for undercover field agents and specifically for the type of agent you will be. Your role as Non-Official Cover (NOC) is a term used here at the CIA for an agent or operative who assumes a covert role in the Central Intelligence Agency without official ties to the United States government, regardless of the position held. An agent sent to spy on a foreign country, some agency of their government or a business might for instance pose as a journalist, a businessperson, a worker for a non-profit organization (such as a humanitarian group), or an academic.

Style was fast to realize and thought to himself, "I'm going to be a sacrificial lamb." Consequently, he interrupted Nogaki briefly and asked, "Do you mean I'm a man without a country?"

"Not necessarily Montana; please let me explain."

"Yes, I'm definitely interested to know what a Non-Official Cover does."

"Great question and I will provide you an upfront honest answer. In espionage, agents under Non-Official Cover (NOC) are operative who assume covert roles without ties to the United States government. Sometimes these agents are known as illegals. Non-official cover is contrasted with official cover where an agent assumes a position at a seemingly benign department of U.S. government, such as the diplomatic service. This provides the agent with official diplomatic immunity, thus protecting him from the steep punishments normally meted out to captured spies, instead usually resulting in the agent being declared persona non grata and ordered to leave the country. Agents under non-official cover don't have this "safety net," and if captured or charged they are subject to severe criminal punishments, up to and including execution. Agents under non-official cover are also trained to deny any connection with their government, thus preserving plausible deniability, but also denying them any hope of diplomatic legal assistance or official acknowledgment of their service. Sometimes, entire front companies or strawman entities are established in order to provide false identities for NOCs."

"Are telling me that in no uncertain terms, I will be at a great risk and if caught, I could be shot for spying as a NOC. Wow! I never realized that would be the case."

"Montana, do you want to just quit and leave. As you are finding out and will discover, we don't mince words; we tell it like it is. If you want to leave, there will be no ill will."

"No. I never quit and never will. Please continue, sir."

"Some countries have regulations regarding the use of Non-Official Cover. The CIA, for example, has, at times, been prohibited from disguising agents as members of certain aid organizations or as members of the clergy. The degree of sophistication put into NOC stories can vary considerably. Sometimes, an agent will simply be appointed to a position in a well-established company which can provide the appropriate opportunities. Other times, entire front companies can be established in order to provide false identities for agents. An example is Air America, used by the CIA during the Vietnam War. Air America was the CIA's private airline operating in Laos, running anything and everything from soldiers to foodstuffs for local villagers and made famous by the late 1970's film, 'Air America.' Do you have any question so far, Montana?"

"Yes, Mr. Nogaki; I believe I was told early on I would be a Non-Official Cover (NOC) as part of my new job description. Now I certainly have a more clear understanding of my role."

"You are correct Montana. Your role as a NOC will be further explained in much more detail later once you begin your training. Obviously, you will be using two covers: touring tennis professional and financial business consultant. In addition, the financial business consultant and the entire company front we developed for you will also be further described in specific details at the 'Farm.'

"I'm unclear as to the meaning of the term the 'Farm.' Can you explain the meaning?" "Yes, of course. The term the 'Farm' developed over a period of time, going back to the original Office of Special Investigation (OSI) during World War II. The property that is now owned by the U.S. government here in Langley was at one time a farm. Over the last seventy years or so, the name "Farm" has evolved and has remained for every CIA graduating class. Does that make sense, Montana?"

"Yes, everything you say makes a lot of sense and I do appreciate you taking the time to explain."

"We got off track briefly, so we need to get back to where I left off; in life, there are two basic traits and characteristics that motivate people: pain or pleasure. Let me explain. For example, when you are in a relationship, you continue the relationship until one day you wake up and say to yourself, 'I'm no longer happy.' Therefore, you determine you must do something to fix it or leave. Why? Because you have arrived at a point where the pain is too much and there is no longer any pleasure, not just sexual or emotional, but you also feel psychologically robbed."

Style observed, "I'm not sure I understand completely, sir."

"OK, let me give you a more clear-cut, better-defined explanation and something that you can relate to. When you play tennis tournaments, travel and practice day in and day out, it can be quite exhausting. Is that correct?"

"Yes, absolutely without a doubt," Style admitted.

"Correct me if I wrong; I understand one of the reasons you elected not to play Davis Cup for the United States was that you were tired and had physical problems with both your shoulder and knee. Is that correct, Montana?"

"Yes, unlike most professional sporting events, tennis is twelve months of the year and that makes it difficult to get any sustained rest, especially if you have an injury."

"I understand and as a result, you just decided that the discomfort (or pain) was too much and you needed a long rest. In other words the pain, both physical and emotional, was no longer giving you the satisfaction to continue and wasn't providing you enough pleasure."

"Great analogy and now I understand totally, sir."

"I hope that you do, because the Central Intelligence Agency invests a lot of time, energy and expense in the training and education of all our agents. We depend and believe in all of our employees, especially the field agents. There is no proven scientific way to evaluate how well the CIA is doing in recruiting agents. Most times, we are very fortunate and lucky. Obviously, we know when an agent is successful in performing his assignments, especially when the results are productive. In addition, when agents submit their reports on time, with accurate information that can be easily substantiated and verified, then it is very straightforward in evaluating an agent's performance.

Sometimes the difficulty we have is when an agent must use his imagination and be creative in solving difficult assignments. This type of thinking outside the box allows him to get out of complex, potentially dangerous or life threatening and challenging situations. However, as is often the case they sometimes break the rules. Then, we must be some-what more objective, flexible and supportive, but certainly within reason. Do you know what I talking about?"

"Absolutely, what you are saying makes a lot sense and I do comprehend," replied Style.

"As I mentioned earlier, in the old days, during World War II and throughout the post-war 1940s, when the CIA was called the Office of Special Investigation (OSI) and especially during 1950s and early1960s, one of the major difficulties we were confronted with throughout the agency was quantity versus quality. Unfortunately, for the longest time, the more prodigious the volume of your reports you submitted, determined your success or failure as an agent. It also established how frequently you would be promoted. In other words, the more reports submitted, the faster the advancement."

"That is so difficult to believe, let alone accept," observed Style.

"Today, Montana that process has changed dramatically. We expect reports to be thorough and not just quantity. Instead, we demand excellence in the quality of all reports and nothing less. The reports should be brief, accurate, and contain all the vital information in the event someone suddenly needs to be replaced or is injured."

"Yes, I certainly understand. The puzzle is coming together for me, Mr. Nogaki."

"I want you to understand that I will give you my complete backing Montana. I will support you as long as you don't violate the CIA code. I'm sure you have memorized the code by now."

"Yes, it is very simple. I'm a member of the greatest team, I depend on the team, I concede to it and forego for it, because the team, not the individual, is the supreme winner."

"At times, Montana, you may be in a situation where a foreign agent would like to jump ship and become a double agent. I feel we have the natural advantage in the spy game business representing the United States. Foreign agents like the KGB are more likely to want to work for the U.S. than the other way around. Many people recruit themselves; they just walk in. In addition, I want you to recognize that you will be recruited, often and frequently, by the bad guys. So, be on your guard and be prepared."

"Yes, I'm very cognizant of that fact and completely aware of that potential, Mr. Nogaki."

"OK, let us get on with our discussion Montana. As stated in the CIA official personnel recruitment handbook in making assessments of potential agents, the CIA relies on four basic human drives and motivations illustrated by the acronym MICE: money, ideology, conscience and ego. There are several other agencies in the United States government and other international intelligence communities that don't realize that

MICE is already a plural word and they insist on adding an S to the end for 'sex.' However, sexual entrapment isn't a reliable method of attracting smart intelligent agents like you. Once you receive your assignments, you will immediately discover how sexual entrapment works, especially for Eastern European agents. Let me clarify what I mean. A blackmailed agent tends to be indignant, ominous, untrustworthy, most likely disposed to disloyalty and the creation of intelligence with total fabrication. His mind becomes a crossroad of contradictions and instantly becomes a storyteller with a very vivid imagination as though acting on stage. Russia and China, for example, have used sexual entrapment in their intelligence operations without hesitation. On the other hand, the relationship with an agent motivated by money is straightforward and more trustworthy. We give you cash and you steal secrets. That simple! Perhaps that is a little harsh description.

So, let me clarify and rephrase. Instead of steal, you either bargain or permanently borrow. I used a little twist on words. Does that make sense to you Montana?"

"Yes sir, I understand completely."

"The agent motivated by ideology, or as often as not, by the painful loss of ideology, may develop slowly over a period of time. This particular agent no longer believes in his government. He has been badly treated by the system and loathes his superiors who may have destroyed his entire career and his personal conviction. Many governments around the world, both past and present, take away hope and institutionalize despair; for example, Lenin and Stalin slaughtered millions of their people during the Russian Revolution and the Cold War of post-World War II. Another example was in 1976, the Cambodia communist Khmer Rouge genocide of millions of their people and then, of course, Saddam Hussein was notorious for not trusting his closest generals. Directly after dinning with them, Hussein would have them taken out and shot in the back of the head. Eventually an agent develops a neurosis and becomes paranoid. Unfortunately, the list is endless.

Why continue to support such a horrible political ideology? Now, the agent inspired by conscience is worth scrutiny. He may believe too much in the Messiah, too often favors the heavens for help, and often looks for ways to make amends for his sins or for the sins of his political system. Worse yet, he tries to apologize for all the evil of the world. The ticking of time and age also affects the remorseful conscience. With too much war or disloyalty, there could be sudden enlightenment, creating doubt and distrust. The spy game is a perfect subject for examining the human condition. Its specialists trade in trust and betrayal, hope and fear, love and hatred.

Today, our intelligence gathering needs to multiply in the rush to understand where and how Al Qaeda will strike next or how China and Russia will use both natural and liquid hydrocarbon gas to extend its reach, or how soon Iran will have nuclear weapons or what will be the next step out of Pyongyang, North Korea. Case officers around the world continue their work, trying to persuade people to become traitors and deploy tools as old as the trade itself. Today, Russia would do anything it could to convince an American informant turned spy, to stay and share as much information on the United States, especially someone who worked for the NSA, CIA or FBI. In World War II, there was a double agent for England's MI5 by the name of Eddie Chapman. Have you ever heard of the name Eddie Chapman, Montana?"

"No sir, I don't recognize the name Eddie Chapman. Should I know who he is?"

"Not necessarily. This is quite an extraordinary story Montana. Chapman was a thief who robbed banks in England sometime around the early 1930s to approximately the outbreak of war in 1939. Because he was so clever and cunning, he successfully managed to avoid being arrested for many years. Eventually, he was captured and sent to jail on the island of Jersey. After Germany was successful in conquering France, they invaded the Island of Jersey on the English Channel very close to France. Eventually they freed Chapman but recruited him because of his craftiness and greed.

The German spy organization, Abwehr, trained him to use explosives and to be a code breaker. Slowly, he started to bore easily because of the Nazi's constant harassment and distrust. Then again, what troubled Chapman the most was the Nazi's lack of respect for the British people.

As a result, he shortly became a double agent for Great Britain's MI5, and was one of the most successful spies in World War II. Eventually he inherited the name Agent Zig Zag. Without any question, Chapman was undeniably motivated by his loyalty to his country and the financial rewards.

His loyalty was extraordinarily high to the British people and it showed many times. Early on in our search, we did an analysis of your background and discovered how committed and determined you were when we watched several of your tennis matches in South America. Under harsh circumstances, you refused to give up and roll over, despite the discomfort and hostile surroundings. In particular, when you played Davis Cup last year in Argentina, your ability to withstand horrible, unfriendly and belligerent fans put your patriotism on display. That is when we concluded you were our man for the job. At that time, we were able to establish that your motivation would be patriotism followed by financial realization."

"Mr. Nogaki, I will not argue with your assessment because that is how I feel. That is me without any doubt. I have always been a patriot, despite not being in the U.S. military. I attribute that to my Georgia roots, I guess. Today, I'm the only male in the family who didn't make it to the U.S. military. More importantly is how my Mom and Dad have been an exceptional influence on my value system. The fact is, they are. Their integrity and their value system are relatively simple – country first and foremost, and then work hard with honesty and you will be rewarded well."

"That is a great attitude and very admirable, Montana. Your training will not begin for several days. As a result, I would like to continue our conversation tomorrow morning at 8:30 am. I have a very important staff meeting in a few minutes and I need to prepare. The delay also allows you an opportunity to process our discussions and then develop questions. Is that suitable for you, Montana?"

"Yes sir, absolutely; I look forward to continuing our conversations and will be here at 8:30 am."

Early the following morning, Style returned to Nogaki's office to carry on their discussion.

"Let's continue where we left off last evening and discuss your upcoming orientation. Of course, your training will be demanding and you will be busy six days a week with sixteen-hour days. We give you Sunday off; however, you will be too occupied with studies to realize its Sunday, so you will not be able to do anything other than study and do some physical conditioning. I can assure you it will be demanding and intense. I do trust you understand what is expected of you?"

"I'm prepared for the demanding schedule and training, Mr. Nogaki."

"In particular there will be much memorizing, many briefings, frequent trips to the weapons range, learning details of banking & finance, firearms handling, survival training, explosive instruction, interpreting and reading maps and espionage case studies. Obviously, this is just a very brief overview, Montana. Because of your unique academic background, much of what you will learn will be somewhat redundant, so in those situations we will simply provide an overview. However, there will be in depth learning of world banking and finance, computer science, code breaking, communication methods, photo interpretation, World War II and Nazis German history. In addition, you will learn everything you can about the Swiss Banking industry and European Union (EU) and their economic system, Al Qaeda, Islamic culture and the Moslem faith in Iran, Pakistan and Afghanistan. Because the primary source of law in these countries is Islamic Sharia law, derived from the teachings of the Qu'ran and the Sunnah (the traditions of the Prophet), Sharia isn't codified and there is no system of judicial precedent. Do you have any questions so far, Montana?"

"Yes, I'm a little puzzled. I'm trying to connect the dots and understand how and why World War II, Nazism, Banks in Switzerland and Al Qaeda are associated or connected?"

"Let me give you a brief overview on why we feel so confident that there is a definite relationship between the Nazis, Swiss Banks and world terrorism today."

"You have my attention," replied Style.

"Since the end of World War II, there has remained conjecture on just how the Swiss remained neutral and in what manner did this issue of dormant Swiss bank accounts, Nazi gold and terrorism get started. This is a really remarkable story, almost like a puzzle and certainly incredible, almost implausible."

"How do you mean like a puzzle and implausible, sir?"

"Let me begin by giving you a brief background and a little history, Montana."

"Yes, sir I'm most intrigued and definitely interested."

"Going back to the middle of the 1990s, United States Senator Alfonse D'Amato (Republican, New York) raised the subject of dormant Swiss bank accounts, Nazi gold and loot acquired during the Third Reich's reign over Europe from the early 1930s to the end of World War II. Senator D'Amato of the U.S. congress managed successfully to conduct hearings into the dormant Swiss bank accounts. As you probably know, the military neutrality of Switzerland has become well known, and that Switzerland hasn't been involved in any external tensions or conflicts since 1815. This can't be misinterpreted that Switzerland has been completely unbiased or objective when it comes to wartime economics and finances. It has been accused of assisting or abetting other countries, such as Germany, while still maintaining an appearance of neutrality. Under a number of treaty agreements, neutral countries still have certain legal and moral obligations during wartime, and Switzerland has largely succeeded in meeting those obligations, although some have questioned the country's understanding of neutrality."

Style observed, "That is almost cowardly, selfish and unquestionably self-serving; would you agree, Mr. Nogaki?"

"Not necessarily," replied Nogaki. "Switzerland remains militarily neutral largely because the country itself is especially vulnerable to invasion from any one of its powerful neighbors, especially prior to the 1950s, and principally from France, Italy, Austria and Germany. Refusal to take sides and to avoid political involvement for a small country with a limited military capacity is generally preferable to a hostile takeover from a confrontational and aggressive neighbor. As long as the country is officially recognized as neutral, no country can legally form plans to invade it or use it as a base of operations.

A neutral country can accept refugees or political prisoners, but it isn't obligated to join peacekeeping missions after the conflict ends. Finally, after nearly fifty years since World War II ended, the hearings succeeded to unearth the truth about the survivors' claims. Pressure from the United States had infuriated the Swiss, who sensed that this was an assault upon their reputation and character for the benefit of U.S. banking industry. Before long, questions concerning the morality of the Swiss during the war came into the public limelight when a security guard at a Swiss bank noticed in early 1997 a pile of documents relating to Nazi and wartime accounts waiting to be shredded. The Swiss claim that these were of no interest to the hearings. That same year, the city of New York considered boycotting Swiss banks and served notice of how serious they were about getting resolution to the whereabouts of the money, gold and treasures taken from the Jews.

Apparently, the pressure worked because approximately a week later, three Swiss banks announced that they would create a philanthropic and humanitarian fund of one hundred million Swiss francs (seventy-million U.S. dollars). Since most of the Jews who opened these accounts were murdered, there are no accurate figures about how much money Jews really placed within the Swiss banks. Jewish organizations believe there could be many billions, while the Swiss have only uncovered several million. Several years later, the Swiss government announced that it would establish another $5 billion humanitarian foundation. On the other hand, what about the survivors of the Holocaust whose families had their entire fortunes stored in Swiss accounts? In mid-1997, the Swiss produced a list of dormant accounts that was accessible to the public. Any person with a valid claim on these accounts had to go through an independent accounting firm and then an international panel decided whether there was reasonable evidence to award the claims. Finally, in 2000, Swiss banks anted up an additional ten billion dollars to reach a settlement for the last time."

"Mr. Nogaki, if I add that up, that is approximately $80 billion that is unaccounted for and still missing."

"That is almost correct replied Nogaki. The exact number is $85 billion in cash, gold, silver, jewelry and treasured art."

"Wow."

Nogaki further explained. "I think you are beginning to understand why the CIA needs someone like you Montana for this high priority assignment."

"Yes sir, I do."

"Montana, one last thing before you leave; your upcoming training will be very demanding and competitive. I know that you will do extremely well. In addition, your study will certainly include the political, economic and social culture of both Russia and China. We know you are up to the task."

At the last minute, Bryan Nogaki pulled up a chair and grabbed a sheet of paper. While drawing diagrams, he detailed how the whole process of intelligence gathering was an integral part of their everyday lives. Further, he explained how the "station" worked, listing the top agents and providing excellent detail about the tradecraft. He illuminated the idiosyncratic agent network and the challenge the station faced, outlined the station's relationships with the local liaison service, and gave details how the station served a broad range of U.S. policy customers. Nogaki answered Style's many questions with clarity and patience. Style learned more from him in that short briefing than any other training discussion.

"More than likely, this will be the only time we will meet for some time, Montana. Once you complete your orientation and training, you will be introduced to your case officer. I need to share one final observation."

"Yes, Mr. Nogaki; what might that be?"

"There is one aspect of being a field agent that sometimes will test your determination and commitment. I'm referring to diplomacy and politics. In each country, the United States has either a high-ranking diplomat or ambassador, who determines how business is conducted in that particular country. Please be mindful of that fact. Sometimes you can benefit and other times it can be a pain in the ass. It is politics. Good luck to you, Montana. Do you have any more questions or concerns?"

"I don't have any more questions, Mr. Nogaki. I know I've learned many important factors from our discussions. Your many anecdotes were very enlightening and for me personally - chronicles I have never heard of previously."

"Remember Style, our failures are known, especially when the press picks up a CIA failed attempt and, unfortunately, our successes are never known. This is an absolute truth. Montana, once more, we thank you for entrusting your future with the Central Intelligence Agency. I would like to wish you a prosperous career and success with this difficult assignment."

4

"The object of war is not to die for your country,
but to make the other bastard die for his."
General George S. Patton

*L*ONDON, ENGLAND
The flight from Ronald Reagan Airport was bumpy and certainly disruptive for sleeping. As a result, Style was exhausted, tired and somewhat agitated. In addition, it was early in the morning and he was naturally tense and eager at the same time. Just before landing at Heathrow, he started to become a little nervous.

Although he was trained thoroughly, there was still a certain amount of self-doubt and uncertainty. He was anxious and couldn't wait to get started. On final approach, he could see in the distance the London skyline accentuated by the rising sun. Big Ben, in particular, stood out, followed by Buckingham Palace and the River Thames. At last, the large jumbo Delta 787 jet landed.

Being a touring tennis professional and traveling literally over millions of miles, Style experienced many departures and arrivals but none like this one. This one was different. For one thing, he was no longer his own boss being in charge. Undeniably, there was added risk, certainly life threatening danger with more mystery in never knowing where it would take him. Nevertheless, in these last months he determined in his mind many times that he was qualified to be a loyal and dedicated CIA field agent and to be successful in completing this formidable assignment. He fondly remembered a saying, *"Every morning we are born again. What we do today is what matters most."* He felt strongly that America was the greatest country in the world and he was prepared to do as much as he could to solve the mystery of how terrorists were getting their money. While in flight, he had several opportunities to discuss and develop confidence in his new temporary cover as a financial consultant with other business passengers. Just prior to touch down, Style realized that flying business class did have many benefits and perks besides great food, wine and service and that included being able to exit at once without any delay. He grabbed his carry-on luggage and Dell laptop computer, hurriedly exited the plane and went directly to the Delta Crown room. Upon entering, he provided his membership card, passport and hastily signed the guest log. He remembered his instructions were to ask for the conference room as soon as he arrived.

The attendant replied, "Sir, the room is ready and you have a guest waiting for you in conference room two, located in the back off to the right with a great view of the runways and the London skyline. May we offer you refreshment, some coffee, a roll or some orange juice"?

"No thanks," replied Style.

Seated at the head of the mahogany conference table was a middle aged, stocky looking guy. He was dressed rather casually in a gray Ralph Lauren Polo knit sweater over a white dress shirt and no tie. Despite no tie or jacket, he appeared professional. As he reached out to shake hands with Style, he introduced himself. "I'm James DiSciascio and welcome to our team," he said in a slightly heavy, west side New York accent. "Would you care for anything else before we start, Style?"

"No thanks Sir." Assured and confident, Style added, "but thank you for the warm reception."

"Our meeting this morning will be straightforward and brief. I was very impressed with both your resume and the manner in which you graduated training from the Farm - first in class and exceptional in fire-arms, code breaking and explosive training."

"Yes, I was fortunate. At the Farm and at HQS, I not only learned the essentials of espionage, but also gained greater insight into my personal strengths and weaknesses as an unseasoned field officer. Believe or not, I'm also convinced the training will help me in competing on the Associated Tennis Professional tour. Learning field tradecraft, intelligence science collection and writing cypher code were brand new skills to me. Obviously, the one essential skill that I will need to develop is learning the nuances of recruiting foreign agents."

"I couldn't agree more, Style. Recruiting foreign agents is extremely critical and is without doubt one of the most difficult aspects of field assignments in different locations around the world. Once you arrive at your assignment, one of the very first things you will need to do is start assessing any recruitment possibilities. The reasons are numerous. Certainly, the more effective you are in recruiting, the easier and faster you will extract pertinent intelligence and promptly have an ally. Let's discuss hardware for one minute. How do you like the weapon of choice, the standard issue Sig Sauer P226, 9mm with fifteen rounds and Siglite night-lights?"

"Mr. DiSciascio, the weapon is great and easy to fire. The pistol is top of the line in all aspects. It feels good, the slide release and decocker are easily accessible with the thumb while gripping the gun. The accuracy is superb. The SIG P226 is similar to the Beretta 92FS in design. It has moderate weight, fast action, loaded for bear and I understand is very effective for protection."

DiSciascio adds, "It's the standard issue for U.S. Navy Seals. Without doubt, you sound like you know your weapons. What are you using for backup?"

Style replied, "I was informed Sir, when I arrived in London, you would recommend a backup weapon."

"You are entirely correct, Style. Each new field agent is given a small gift from our team, a Smith & Wesson Bodyguard, .380, six-shot mag, polymer light frame that you carry on your ankle. You will find out, Style, this will be handy when the time arises."

"Fantastic. Please thank the team for me."

"As you may know, historically as the cold war started to wind down, the CIA began concentrating even more than before on uncovering plans to develop nuclear, chemical or biological weapons one of the CIA's more traditional and most important roles. Perhaps, this would be a good point to ask, do terrorists have the bomb?"

"I have no idea, Sir."

"Forgive me, Style, my question was rhetorical. No, we are certain of that fact, at least not yet. However, we have discovered that Osama Bin Laden had reportedly been trying to obtain nuclear material since as far back as 1993, when members of his Al Qaeda network tried unsuccessfully to buy stolen South African uranium for a nuclear bomb. Just one month before the September 11, 2001 attacks, Bin Laden met in Afghanistan with several officials from Pakistan's nuclear program. Obviously, Bin Laden was seeking assistance in building or acquiring a nuclear weapon. There are many other times that he tried but was unsuccessful in purchasing nuclear, biological, and chemical weapons. Again, I repeat we have been extremely fortunate so far."

"That is most obvious. How can he possibly afford to do all of these things; aren't they expensive?"

"That is a wonderful observation and a thought-provoking question, Style. I will elaborate on the economics later. As a result, since September 11, 2001, world terrorism has become a major focus and less attention has been given to our more traditional enemies: Russia and China. Simply put, Al Qaeda terrorism, violence and lawlessness have no geographical boundaries, as a result intelligence gathering has become more intensified and complex."

"Mr. DiSciascio, how do you mean, intelligence collecting has become more intensified and complex?"

"Certainly with the advent of drones, world aggression and terrorism have been put on notice. Without doubt, the relatively new Unmanned Aerial Vehicle (UAV) has been at the center of focus for the Aerospace Industry and Department of Defense. Let me give you the finest example of where we are headed in using UAV technology. An American company, NorthFlex, has developed a UAV surveillance aircraft that employs

high-resolution synthetic aperture radar (SAR) and long-range electro-optic infrared sensors that are able to locate, follow, digitally film,
record and listen to people's conversations at a distance of 20 miles in
space. Simultaneously, it is possible to watch keystroke for keystroke
just as someone is on-line using his or her computer. In other words,
the moment you are connected with the outside world on just about any
device, whether wired or wireless we are there. This applies to just about
everything that transmits or is electronic and that includes a computer,
mobile phone, portable screen, etc. The SAR instantly tracks and images
the communications. It is happening today as we speak. We can track
and listen to conversations of people in the deepest caves, secured buildings and even in the oceans as deep as 2,000 feet. Simultaneously, UAV
technology allows for the use of laser synthetic beams as offensive weapons. These weapons are almost completely invisible. The new technology
allows both of these groups (Aerospace & DOD) to amplify system safety,
security, efficiency and interoperability. Quite simply, they work, they
are cheap, and drone technology is spreading, becoming very popular
and, no question, an absolute necessity. As such, we want to make certain
we have the right people for the right assignment and to match those
agents with the technological tools. In future assignments you will be
responsible for making decisions in the use of this type of very sophisticated technology."

"Thank you for clarifying and providing an in depth explanation
of how some of the new technology is being implemented. Now it seems
clear-cut and I do certainly understand why it is so essential."

"Well, Style let's get started. As you know by now, I'm your case officer and handler. I will be the person most responsible for your safety
and key contact for all of your assignments while in Europe and the
Middle East. We will communicate only when necessary and in some
cases, how and when we connect could be rather awkward, untimely and
unexpected."

"I think I understand Mr. DiSciascio."

"Style, always remember, nothing is what it seems. Have you ever
heard of the story of the Monuments Men?"

"No, I have never heard the expression until now."

"Well, let me give you a brief account of what they were about and what they achieved."

"OK," replied Style.

DiSciascio provided an in-depth story of the Monuments Men and the complete background starting with the beginning of World War II. The war was without doubt the most destructive war in history. Most, if not all, European cities were destroyed or badly damaged. The human toll was incomprehensible. Throughout history, spoils of war have featured objects of art, notably gold and silver, but also traditional sculptures and paintings, including arms, armor and bullion. Man has always justified the spoils of war and sometimes in their plundering and foolishness, they destroyed wantonly for no reason. However, in World War II, despite the horrific destruction and loss of life, one element of our human culture survived, almost as though through a miracle. For example, I'm referring the beautiful works of art at the Louvre in Paris and Leonardo da Vinci's

'Last Supper' that was on display in Milan and all of the splendid

paintings, sculptures, drawings and photographs throughout Europe and Russia. Adolf Hitler embarked upon a mission to acquire the greatest works of art and steal as much riches as possible. This was his master plan. The plan was conceived in the early 1930s and his generals carried out his wishes beginning with the invasion of Poland. Each country that Hitler's armies invaded, they stole everything of value, including famous art and artifacts. How did these many works of art survive this terrible war and Hitler's wanton greed?"

"To be perfectly honest with you, that is something I never considered. I don't know. Now, I'm a little bewildered and confused," replied, Style.

"Let me finish and you will understand." DiSciascio continued his story. "All of us are very familiar with the major battles of World War II; Pearl Harbor, D-Day, Battle of Guadalcanal, Midway, Iowa Jima, Battle of the Bulge, Leningrad, Anzio, North Africa and the list of stories seems to go on forever. However, there is a story, for whatever reason, that has never been told. There was a group of men who were on the front line who quite literally saved the world's culture, as we know it; a group that didn't carry machine guns, drive tanks or pilot planes. They were not authorized ambassadors but understood the serious threat to some of the greatest cultural, artistic and enlightening accomplishments the world had known. These anonymous heroes were branded as the Monument Men."

"That is quite fascinating and interesting, but how does this story affect me, Mr. DiSciascio?"

"Very simple, you are going to be our 21st Century Monument Man. Your orders are quite specific. First, you need to resolve where the Swiss banks have hidden the $85 billion and the estimated $3 to $5 billion

missing treasured art. Next, you must get evidence to prove that this money is being used by Al Qaeda to fund their world terrorism."

"That is exactly what Bryan Nogaki, the Assistant Director said when he introduced the subject to me when we first met in Washington D.C.," said Style.

"Furthermore Style, there are a couple of matters we need to conclude, mostly administrative. Here are additional passports; you will need them, along with multiple IDs, credit cards and cash. In each of the countries you visit, there will be an account established at the major banks and at the American Embassies. You will be informed of what banks and where they are, when you arrive at these different locations. As you know, most American Embassies are located in the capital cities of the respected countries. Therefore, whenever you need cash, it will be available. However, please be prudent and selective how you spend it. We don't want receipts either and for good reason."

Knowingly, Style commented, "I understand no paper trails or any records."

"You are absolutely correct, Style. Whenever, wherever, whatever destroy all receipts, including airline, auto rental, taxi, beverage, dining, entertainment and any expenditure."

"Yes, I will be extremely careful sir."

"Early tomorrow you are scheduled on a flight to Zurich. Tonight, you will be staying at the first class Intercontinental Hotel in downtown London. Your entire luggage, including tennis gear and equipment has been forwarded to the hotel. We arranged at the local tennis club for you to practice."

"Now that is terrific news."

"We want to make sure that you stay in shape and remain highly competitive."

"How long will I be in Zurich?"

"That depends; you will be there as long as it takes to finish the project. More than likely, you will be traveling in and out of Zurich many times. One of your covers is a financial consultant for a very large American corporation."

"What is the role of the consultant?"

"As consultant, you will be endeavoring to get a very large capital investment to allow the company, DeSoto Industries to expand operations into Slovenia, Austria and Switzerland. Austria and Slovenia are very close neighbors of Switzerland. Zurich is Switzerland's leading financial center, followed by Geneva. Banking in Switzerland is regulated by the Swiss Financial Market Supervisory Authority (SFINMA), which derives its authority from a series of federal statutes. The country's tradition of bank secrecy, which dates to the middle ages, was first codified in a 1934 law. Both Clearstream Finance & Banking, LTD and SFINMA will be one of your first major objectives to initiate your intelligence gathering. Without doubt, I believe they both are central to the overall outcome."

"I completely understand, sir."

DiSciascio continued to provide more background information on the Swiss banking industry. "As of the end of 2008, the banking industry in Switzerland had an average leverage ratio of 29 to 1 (assets to net worth); while the industry's short-term liabilities were equal to 260 percent of the Swiss GDP or 1,273 percent of the Swiss national debt. Very impressive and quite extraordinary, don't you think for such a small neutral country?"

"Yes, so it seems."

"What is more astonishing is that they have managed to continue this charade since the turn of the 20th Century, just prior, in fact, to the beginning of World War I."

"That is quite amazing. I recall that from one of the many discussions at Langley, we had lengthy debates on Swiss neutrality and national sovereignty. In addition, the Swiss have been long recognized by foreign nations that have fostered a stable environment in which the banking sector was able to develop and thrive."

"You are precisely correct, Switzerland has maintained neutrality through both World Wars, successfully remained out of the European Union, and wasn't a member of the United Nations until 2002."

"That is quite an astonishing fact and something I didn't know. I find that to be quite remarkable and inconceivable, Mr. DiSciascio."

"Now let us finish up. Here is an observation and just a couple of items for you to consider prior to wrapping up. As you probably know, the press, especially the liberal media, doesn't like the CIA. Both the media and politicians are constantly scrutinizing us. It is bad enough we have to contend with the motion picture industry image in how they portray us. In the last ten to fifteen years, there have been a dozen or more commercially successful spy movies that often suggest in their story premise, field agents for the CIA are robots that can't be trusted and are drug induced or alcoholics. Furthermore, Hollywood exaggerates the image that the CIA is pre-occupied with incestuous fighting. There is nothing more absurd and further from the truth. As a result, at all cost avoid any discussions with the press and certainly all politicians whenever possible; it doesn't matter what political party they represent."

"I will be extremely careful because a reporter already has wronged me when he totally overstated the facts and misquoted me. Believe me, I can relate."

"Before you leave today, my administrative assistant will provide you with a folder containing different documents. The first one is a letter of introduction to the chairman of Clearstream Finance & Banking, LTD and SFINMA, Ulrich Melmer. Please do your utmost to gain the chairman's confidence and trust. Believe me, this will take some doing on your part."

"Why is that, Sir?"

"Our preliminary analysis has determined he's emotional, extremely smart and always thinks he's right, resulting in his arrogance and defensiveness. As a result, Ulrich Melmer is a very difficult person to get to know. There is no doubt you will be pushed to your limits and it is going to take all the patience in the world to develop a business relationship with Melmer. You must employ your maximum skillfulness in the initial discussions. This will allow you to slowly gain his confidence in order to satisfy getting to the next level of penetrating their very secretive organization. Once you overcome the initial challenges, I believe good things will begin to happen. Additionally, the folder contains several more documents that are valuable, all of which will be highly scrutinized by his staff. The letter of introduction contains the letterhead of the corporation introducing who you are and what role you play as consultant to DeSoto Industries. Chief Executive Officer, William MacFarland will sign it. Before I continue, I would like to let you know that DeSoto Industries has been briefed on all aspects of our investigation. MacFarland and his executive staff do understand and have agreed to cooperate with us. Obviously, we elected to get their cooperation in the event someone at Clearstream Finance & Banking, LTD or SFINMA started to ask questions."

"What is the second document, Mr. DiSciascio?"

"The second document provides specific details in a spreadsheet of how much capital investment DeSoto Industries is seeking in order to satisfy their aggressive growth of international expansion into several different European countries. Melmer will probably query you why Austria and Slovenia. I know you can provide an excellent response. The third paper describes all of the particulars of how the funding will be used and the approximate size of each of the plants, including the number of people who will be employed, architectural drawings and renderings. To demonstrate our commitment and to show DeSoto Industries' good faith in requesting the loan, we are prepared to deposit twenty-five million U.S. dollars as collateral into the Swiss Bank Clearstream Finance & Banking, LTD. As a matter of fact, the first cover letter will elaborate the specifics of the collateral commitment with certain conditions along with the manner in which the money will be transmitted and how fast. Now, the last thing and probably the most important point in completing this very complex mission, are the resources. You will be given wide latitude in evaluating what assets you will need and how fast you requisite them. Also, at any time you feel contained or threatened, you notify the team; in return, they will then contact me immediately. I repeat, you notify the team as soon as possible when in jeopardy. Do you have any questions on how you need to contact me?"

"No, everything is understood and perfectly clear."

"Style, I hope so, because it is highly critical that you do you understand."

"Yes sir, I do."

"Perhaps the irony in trying to resolve the world issues and prevent terrorism is that we make more enemies out of countries when we provide economic aid and military support or supply military weapons. An excellent example is the United Nations or both Pakistan and Egypt. We literally send them billions of dollars in aid every year but guaranteed just about every day when you turn on the news in the evening, the lead story is: U.S. strongly opposed by U.N., Egypt or Pakistan."

"Where is the justice and it doesn't make sense sir."

"We believe in good and evil. We choose good. We believe in right and wrong. We choose right. Our cause is just. Our enemies are all around us. You stepped through the looking glass, Style. Today, as you are well aware, all of the American Embassies throughout the Middle East, stretching from West Africa to Indonesia, have been on heightened alert since Benghazi. In fact, some have even closed down for days on end. Unfortunately, these measures, although they are taken to protect American citizens, in reality, they serve the goals that the terrorist elements are seeking to achieve. One of the most hostile and unsafe countries in the Middle East is Yemen. Yemen has become the second strategic home to Al Qaeda in the Arabian Peninsula (AQAP), and one of the most active affiliates of the network established by Osama Bin Laden and where the United States uses drones to hunt militants."

"What about Pakistan, Mr. DiSciascio, and the role they played in hiding Osama Bin Laden?"

'That is both a timely and a great question, Style."

"Certainly, without doubt Pakistan remains the number one haven for Al Qaeda. Every day we intercept electronic communications between Ayman al-Zawahri, who replaced Bin Laden as head of al Qaeda, and Nasser al-Wuhaishi, the head of AQAP. These are the bad guys and the ones we need to get rid of quickly. How do we accomplish the elimination of assholes and trash? The answer is relatively simple; remove their bounty of cash and financial resources. That is how. Can America save the world? Certainly not, but when you examine the facts, just about every day the headlines read: terrorism, suicide bombings and genocide may make the world seem 'downright apocalyptic.' Actually, we are truly making the world safer. This doesn't necessarily mean we can relax and drop our guard. Much to the contrary; we must work harder and smarter to achieve more peace and spread democracy. To that end, we entrust to you, our field agents, all the confidence and encouragement we can. Is that completely understood, Style?"

"Yes, I do understand."

"Great. Now, once you determine successfully the connection between terrorism and their funding, we can then eradicate their supply of capital and support. I feel extremely confident that you will help solve this extraordinarily complicated and horrendous nightmare that we and the rest of the free world have faced since the mid-1970s or for that matter since the end of World War II. Then we can move on to a more secure

place...hopefully. Success to you and be safe."

"Thank you sir, I will do my very best."

5

The supreme quality for leadership is unquestionably integrity.
Without it, no real success is possible, not matter whether it is on a section gang,
a football field, in an army, or in an office
President of the United States
Dwight D. Eisenhower

URICH, SWITZERLAND
Style was out of bed early and ready to go at the break of dawn. He shaved, showered and dressed right away. Then he started to review all of his notes while enjoying a cup of freshly brewed Swiss coffee and a French croissant. He opened the curtains affording a splendid view of Zurich. Since he arrived so late and was exhausted, he didn't remember too much about the ride from the Zurich Airport to the hotel. There was a light dusting of snow overnight, enhancing the beauty of the city. While relaxing and appreciating the morning tranquility, it suddenly occurred to him that he was now somewhat independent in making critical decisions, just like when he decided to enter tennis tournaments and when to practice. Knowing he still was somewhat self-sufficient and independent provided him with a surge of confidence. This allowed him to maintain a strong sense of conviction and be composed. However,

he understood perfectly well what was expected of him. After finishing his breakfast, he hurriedly caught the elevator down to the lobby and managed to pick up a copy of the London Financial Times. He scanned through it quickly, looking for any possible information or communications from his contacts in both London and throughout Europe. He was hoping to find some additional information on the Swiss banking industry that could possibly assist in his early morning appointment with Ulrich Melmer, Chairman of Clearstream Finance & Banking, LTD. There wasn't anything to take notice of, which includes any possible scrambled or covert encrypted messages in the current soccer scores on the daily sports page. Style was instructed to check the *London Financial Times* on a daily bases for changed plans and/or updates. Upon arrival at the headquarters of Clearstream Finance & Banking, LTD. and SFINMA, Style was regarded as a distinguished high-ranking executive and, as such, was greeted with high protocol in the sphere of officially representing an American corporation. At once, he was escorted in to meet Melmer. Simultaneously, they both reached across Ulrich's massive antique desk to shake hands. His office was almost too majestic, to some extent imposing and ostentatious. The enormous windows were covered with heavy maroon curtains made out of velvet, accented with gold braids. All of the furniture, including the chairs and tables, were very heavy and considerable in size.

"Mr. Style I would like you to meet Hans Schroeder, the Vice President of Finance for Clearstream Finance & Banking. Hans has worked with our company for nearly twenty-five years. Is that correct Hans?"

"Yes, sir, in fact in two months it will be twenty-five years."

"Congratulations Hans," said Style

"Thank you, Mr. Style."

"Hans Schroeder will be available to assist you whenever you need a hand. Please have a seat, Mr. Style."

"Thank you", replied Style. He couldn't help but notice that Ulrich was a large man with thinning gray hair, approximately 60 or so and expensively dressed. He walked very erect and there was something distinctive about his mannerism, almost military like. Style made a mental note of his observations. At the same time, he also noticed how Hans

Schroeder was dressed and conducted himself. Hans wore a black suit with a vest, polka-dot tie and a very heavily starched shirt, all very conservative and typical of the international banking business. His mannerisms were extremely formal, especially in directing his conversation to Ulrich.

"Would you like some coffee to start, Mr. Style?" asked Ulrich.

"Actually, I would sir."

Ulrich further added, "As you know, the Swiss make some of the world's best coffee." He said this in an accent evoking of someone who is either German or Austrian. Undoubtedly, this accent wasn't unusual in Switzerland.

"Yes, I already experienced the exquisite aroma and wonderful flavor earlier this morning at breakfast when I was provided an extraordinarily tasteful cup of coffee in my room at the hotel Park Hyatt. Swiss coffee can certainly become addictive."

"I understand Mr. Style, the Park Hyatt is an excellent hotel, and I believe a five star resort offering supreme service and accommodations with a spectacular location directly on Lake Zurich."

"Yes, Mr. Melmer, the view and the hotel are first class with a central location for conducting business."

"As you know, I'm the Director of Swiss Financial Market Supervisory Authority (SFINMA) but my most demanding and responsible position is here as Chairman of Clearstream Finance & Banking, LTD, one of Europe's largest, most prominent and highly successful financial institutions dating back to the mid-19th Century."

"Mr. Melmer, very impressive credentials and these are exactly the reasons why we selected your bank. It was imperative that not only did the financial institution have a thorough knowledge of banking and finance but have a comprehensive appreciation for how American companies conduct business in Europe," reacted Style.

"Sensational John Style, that was perfectly said to get the meeting started on the right foot. You certainly know how to build up a partner's ego." observed Ulrich.

"I believe you received all of the necessary documents, Mr. Melmer; is that correct?"

"Yes, indeed we received all of the essential papers. We were very impressed with how thorough and complete the credentials are. We sensed a certain amount of urgency and apprehension. Are we accurate, Mr. Style?"

"Yes, to a certain degree Mr. Melmer. As you know the world economy is improving on a daily basis and DeSoto Industries, would like to get started before land prices start to rise too rapidly. In addition, I would like to make certain that all of our discussions are kept highly confidential, certainly for good reason. Finally, I request that the press be absolutely kept in the dark until we have completed negotiations and signed an agreement and broke ground. I'm sure you understand our position." Melmer reacted immediately and replied, "We are prepared to sign any necessary documents, including non-disclosure and confidentiality agreements. In advance of your arrival, Clearstream and SFINMA had several meetings to discuss the importance of confidentiality and we consciously limited our conversation and information regarding DeSoto Industries to just a few of our key executives, isn't that correct Hans?"

"Absolutely, that is right without question sir," answered Schroeder.

"Terrific," responded Style, "that puts me at ease. So, let's get started."

"How long do you anticipate being in Zürich?" asked Melmer.

"Without appearing to be abrupt, at least until we feel assured that we successfully completed and signed the contract. With that said, I also recognize that I need to be flexible, but hopefully we can accomplish all legal and business matters, anticipating signing a contract in less than 45 days or certainly not more than 60 days. Additionally, DeSoto Industries would like to incorporate visits to the three sites once an agreement has been successfully negotiated. Of course, I'm referring to the three separate commercial properties we are most interested in purchasing, located in Kranj, Slovenia, Salzburg, Austria and Enge, Switzerland. Furthermore, I have additional business matters while I'm in Switzerland, which may require me to be interrupted to allow travel to several other European cities. Consequently, that means undoubtedly I will be on the move traveling in and out of Switzerland on a regular basis for many weeks to come."

"We certainly understand, Mr. Style," responded Melmer.

"Is it possible that I can have a working office while I visit? I need the space so that I can be more affective in reviewing all the documents and resolve any issues without always using the telephone. What's more, most likely I will be staying late into the evening and sometimes into early morning. Does that create any difficulty for you or with the staff at Clearstream?"

"There is no problem, Mr. Style. We do have available an executive office for visiting senior managers located on the 20th floor. Financial operations, documents, personnel and records share the floor. Your office is located directly off the elevator to the right when you exit and the stairs are to the left. During the daytime, there will be available assistance from one of our many highly qualified administrators. Hans will definitely take care of all arrangements, including an executive dining pass, keys and an ID card. Is there anything else you may need?"

"Initially, I believe that takes care of everything Ulrich. May I call you Ulrich?"

"Certainly John. OK let's get on to today's agenda."

"Absolutely Ulrich, where do you want to start?"

"Would you mind sharing with me your company's philosophy and explain why DeSoto Industries made such a huge commitment to open facilities in Slovenia and Austria. I think I know why you selected Enge, Switzerland, certainly because of the beautiful city of Zurich and the spectacular location on Lake Zurich, with an abundance of skilled technical personnel along with easy access to the airport."

"You are absolutely correct Ulrich, all of the reasons you just amplified and there are certainly many more reasons," reacted Style.

After approximately three hours of discussions, Ulrich interrupted and suggested we break for lunch. Ulrich turned to Hans and proposed that he take Style to lunch at the Café Elan.

Hans replied, "Terrific idea Ulrich."

The Café Elan was just around the corner, so the two men walked and had a brief conversation. Hans was very open and unpretentious. He revealed that he'd been working with Clearstream since he graduated from the London University School of Economics. He worked his way up from accounts payable all the way to the position he held today. Hans mentioned that he was happily married with two children and today he lived on the east side of Lake Zurich. Just before they arrived at the café, he directed his attention to asking Style some questions. "Beside, being involved in financial matters and working as a consultant for a large

American corporation, what other activities are you interested in doing, John?"

Style replied, "I have a pilot's license and enjoy flying whenever possible.

I work out at the gym as much as I can and I enjoy reading mystery novels and world history."

It was becoming obvious both men were becoming more comfortable and relaxed with one another. As Style was making mental notes, he started to think to himself - "I need to be very cautious in what I say." They actually had a good time getting to share their respective backgrounds and interest. It also helped that lunch was outstanding and very satisfying.

Later in the day and after returning to his room, Style was primarily focused on his day's accomplishments and disappointments. He removed his notes from the briefcase and at once started scanning and doing an analysis, reflecting on his meeting with Melmer and Schroeder. His first impression of Melmer wasn't of him being the emotional man as originally described in the initial briefing at Langley, but instead more reserved and cooperative, at least for now.

There is no doubt Melmer is brilliant, arrogant and selectively defensive. As for Melmer's heavy German accent that undoubtedly added to the mystery of Melmer or could it be nothing at all. As fast as possible, he needed to get more personal background information on Melmer; with a bit of luck it could provide enough detailed data on his history. Certainly birth certificates would afford the preliminary information such as country, town, year born, parents, etc. Without any doubt, his instincts were telling him there was something about Melmer that didn't set right at this point. It was late in the evening, just before ten o'clock, but Style needed to become more familiar with the layout and logistics of the Park Hyatt Zurich located right in the city center of downtown Zurich. Consequently, he took a short walk from the hotel and discovered a stylish high-end shopping mall. Walking just a little further, he came across beautiful Lake Zurich. At first Style didn't realize it, but the lake was just out the backdoor of the Hyatt Hotel. There were several appealing attractions within a very short walking distance, Congress Hall and the Opera House. Both buildings were set beautifully aglow in a mixture of direct and indirect sparkling lights, majestically reflecting their glowing silhouettes on the lake nearby. The whole landscape seemed surreal and breathtaking. Since it was very cold and getting late, he decided to finish his brief walk, but just before getting to the hotel, he discovered that the metro subway or tram happened to be very conveniently located within a one-minute walk straight out the front door of the hotel. Upon his arrival back at the Hyatt, the hotel's Concierge greeted Style. Hello, my name is Marie and I'm the Concierge here at the Park Hyatt Grand Hotel.

She was very attractive with light brown hair, tall, and appeared to be in great shape. She spoke flawless English with a slight French accent. The Concierge provided him with a welcome package of information, including a map of the city, a set of complimentary tickets to the Opera and dinner at Piccolomini's Zurich, one of the best Italian Restaurants in all of Europe.

While looking at the map of Switzerland, Style suddenly realized that Zurich International Airport is just eight miles from the hotel, approximately 20 minutes by taxi. Some of the various amenities offered from the hotel included arrangements for a limousine, no matter the requirement or destination, and in the summer a captained sailboat, plus they could make provisions for a rental car. Of course, John Style wanted the best, so he specifically requested a Porsche Carrera GT Turbo to be reserved for the next morning after breakfast.

He couldn't help but ask the Concierge would she join him for the Opera and dinner?

She didn't hesitate and in a very sexy voice said she was married but she had a sister who was one year older and available.

"By the way, when may I use the opera tickets, Marie?"

"Just about any time you would like as long as you are staying at the hotel, sir."

"Marie, could you arrange for a date with your sister?"

"Ordinarily I would not but in this case I believe I can give her a call and ask."

"Wonderful! Would you first see if your sister is available two weeks from this Friday?"

"Hold on Mr. Style, let me give her a call to see if she is available."

"That would be wonderful," replied Style

Marie called her sister right away. She wasn't on the phone very long.

Marie turned to Style to say, "My sister is available that Friday night and her name is Zosa, meaning lily."

Style, responded anxiously, "That is terrific." He further confirmed, "The opera ticket reservations are for two weeks from this coming Friday evening, correct Marie?"

"Yes Mr. Style, as it turns out Friday evening is perfect for her."

"Will you please inform your sister, I will arrange to meet her here in the hotel lobby at seven p.m. if that is a convenient time for Zosa?"

"Yes, I will call her back and provide her with all the necessary logistics and schedule."

"Also, please tell her I look forward to meeting her that Friday evening." Before Marie left, she turned and asked Style if he had any questions or concerns about his accommodations or could she or the Park Hyatt Grand Hotel provide any better service.

Style said he was extremely satisfied and the room was splendid with a terrific view of beautiful Zurich. Service has been outstanding so far and he didn't have any more questions. He thanked Zosa for all of her help and said goodnight.

He was too tired to go out to dinner, so when he returned to his suite he ordered room service. Directly after eating, he decided to send several e-mails requesting additional background information on Melmer and to provide a progress report. As always, all communications are transmitted in top-secret encrypted e-mail code.

Just prior to calling it a day, he sat down on the edge of the bed and realized how lucky he was with the location of the executive office he was given at Clearstream Finance & Banking, LTD and SFINMA. The office location was in one of the best places to start his search and investigation.

This didn't necessarily mean this investigation would be a trouble-free, as he shortly would find out. The next morning, he was up early as usual; the first thing Style did was check for messages. There was one message from James DiSciascio.

Style:

"In our first background investigation of Ulrich Melmer, we didn't find any unusual problems. However, after receiving your request last evening we probed much deeper into Melmer's past. We now discover that he was born in Frankfurt, Germany in 1949. Both of his parents were members of the German Nazi party in World War II, but more interesting is the fact that Ulrich's father Karl was one of six members of the so-called 'Gang of Thieves.' I anticipate that there will be additional information with more details to follow...Be safe and continue with the excellent work."

Success,

DiSciascio

Upon arriving in the lobby and after first reading the *London Financial Times* for his daily updates, Style hurriedly checked in with the Concierge to see if his reservation of the Porsche had arrived. Immediately, the young man escorted Style to the front of the hotel where the Porsche was parked in the hotel-parking garage.

The Porsche 911 Carrera 4S Turbo was solid basalt black metallic with a sumptuous black leather interior. A seven-speed PDK transmission was standard on all 911s. Style was indeed very pleased with his choice of cars. Because it was early, he decided to take the 911 for a short spin around Lake Zurich. Right away, he became familiar with the car's ample number of digital displays and layout. The many Bose stereo speakers provided an ambient environment for pleasurable listening of fine jazz. He started it up and couldn't resist spinning out from the hotel parking lot. He drove the speed limit 120 km/h (75 mph), undoubtedly to avoid any possible legal problems that would compromise his status and cover. The scenically designed motorway was free of snow making it an easy challenge for the Porsche. Intuitively, Style shifted through the gears of the finely engineered Carrera transmission as though he were on the Grand Prix circuit. He cautiously negotiated the sharp curvatures of the road that followed the contours of the lake below. There were steep rises with gentle slopes covered with spectacular vineyards and orchards and breathtaking views of the Alps to the south. Since it was the middle of winter, the mountains were completely covered in snow and it looked almost like a fairy tale. He drove approximately ten miles, turned around and headed back to the hotel. When he arrived back at the Hyatt at around 8 a.m., he parked and returned to his room to get his suit jacket and put on a tie. At the last minute he decided to have breakfast. As soon as Style arrived at Clearstream headquarters, Hans Schroeder greeted him.

"Good morning John; did you have a good night?"

"Yes, as a matter of fact Hans the Swiss air does wonders for me."

"Security dropped off your executive dinning pass, card key and an ID card. I will you show you to your working office on the 20th floor."

When they finally arrived at the office, there was a very attractive blond woman waiting for them.

Hans introduced Hilda to Style.

"Hilda will be your assistant for as long as necessary. John, I need to run and take care of some business, but if you need anything, please call me."

"This office is exactly what I need. Once again, thank you Hans."

As soon as Schroeder was gone, Hilda turned to Style.

"Would you like some coffee, Mr. Style?"

"Yes, I would." First, she showed me around the office and then took me for a walk down the hall to meet some of the people working in operations, personnel and finance. After introducing me to several department heads, she departed.

Without delay, I settled in to the large leather chair, removed files from my brief case and plugged in my laptop. In a little while, Hilda returned with my coffee. She explained that her office was just down the hallway. She added, "Please call me if you need any assistance, Mr. Style."

Style turned and asked, "Is there a map of the building?" he explained that I had a phobia in tall buildings.

"Yes, Mr. Style, I will get a map from personnel. Is that all you need at this time?"

"Thank you. You've been very helpful, Hilda; I believe that is all I need for now."

Although the map was several years old, it provided me with the exact information I needed. I soon memorized all the exits, including the stairways and elevators. The map also stipulated the location of security and the executive offices. Because the building was over a hundred years old and most likely refurbished and enlarged several times over, I decided to take a walk to check things out. Much later in the day, Hilda returned to let me know she was leaving. I told her goodnight and thanked her for her assistance.

I remained in my office until I heard security walk past. After a while, I was able to determine the frequency of their routine and established it was approximately every 45 to 50 minutes. For at least a week or so every day, I would mentally make notes of everyone's activity, especially securities' daily schedule and routine. I decided to wait several more weeks before I would start my investigation and examination.

6

Don't be disappointed if people refuse to help you. Remember these words:
"I'm thankful to all those who said no. Because of them, I did it myself."
Albert Einstein

carcely a week later, instead of going out to lunch, Style decided to go to the local Zurich library to further his appreciation of the Swiss history, culture and language. He was surprised to learn that today the official Swiss language is predominately Swiss-German and the language most spoken by 70% of the population. Prior to 1950 almost 80% to 85% of the Swiss people spoke fluent German. Certainly, that would account for Ulrich Melmer's heavy German accent. While the French-speaking Swiss prefer to call themselves Romands from their part of the country la Romandie, the German-speaking Swiss used to refer to, and still do, the French-speaking Swiss as Welsche.

Nearly 70% of Switzerland is comprised of mountains, with the Swiss Alps covering close to 60% of the total mountainous area, thus making Switzerland the second most alpine country in Europe after Austria. As soon as he finished his brief Swiss cultural education, he headed back to the office.

At the last minute, on his return to the office, he stopped at a café for a late lunch. He was beginning to become a little uneasy that someone was following him. He had no idea why because he was extremely cautious. Maybe it was just his imagination. It seemed each time he turned around, he discovered the same person observing his every move. He decided not to make an issue out of it, at least not yet.

Back at Clearstream, to avoid any suspicion each night, he stayed until after midnight. So far, no one had questioned a thing and he wanted to keep it that way. He couldn't afford any type of compromise or create a situation that would be questionable. The damage would be irreparable. Finally, by late Wednesday afternoon, he decided he was ready to start his formal investigation and begin searching for some material evidence.

Style elected to initiate the investigation with the personnel department because of the relative proximity to his office, and from time to time, he discovered the office workers often left files on their desk in plain view. Furthermore, the security guard on duty most nights didn't walk through the personnel offices, which Style couldn't understand. Also, he discovered their security camera surveillance system was out of order because of a malfunctioning component.

So far, everything was going smoothly without any issues or problems. Of course, he was anxious and on edge. Style sat in his office reflecting on his personal abilities and what motivated him. He decided he would use all his cunning and sly tactics for uncovering how world terrorism is getting their funding. He was determined to get to the bottom-line and solve this complicated mystery surrounding the financing of Al Qaeda and every other radical organization.

His father always reminded him, "If you wanted something bad enough, you needed to remain steadfast and persist to use you intellect." Style's mother would interject and say, "John, use all of your resourceful talent, especially your razor sharp powers of observation, sheer determination, astuteness, and ingenious method of solving complicated problems." Soon he would discover he would need to use his entire god given talents. After the security guard caught the elevator, he closed his office door, deliberately leaving the light on and walked slowly down the hall. When he arrived at the personnel office door, he knocked on the door loudly to make sure everyone had left. He used one of the many tricks he learned at the Farm to pick open the door's lock. He walked in and headed directly for the files in the back of the very large office. There seemed to be over fifty or so desks throughout the office.

Finally when he arrived in the back of the office, there were file cabinet after file cabinet; there were literally hundreds of them in varying conditions. He soon discovered that the labels on the front of the drawers didn't mean a damn thing, especially drawers with the old files prior to the 1970's. His first reaction was, "Oh shit, I'll be here forever." He certainly didn't anticipate this mess.

Previous experience had led him to believe the Swizz were extremely neat, well organized and disciplined. When he started searching, he was looking for any evidence of anyone who was accountable for managing Clearstream Finance & Banking, LTD during the period from 1930 through 2000, a 70-year time span. He was able to determine there were at least twenty to twenty-five or so managers over the period directly or indirectly involved making critical management decisions, from the executive suite to department heads.

Of course, the primary timeframe would be 1935 to 1944 and 1946 to 1951. The post war period 1946 to 1951, is believed to be the time that the Swiss banks started to conceal and relocate files to different locations. In addition, there was some evidence they also shrouded and purged a very small fraction of the financial records.

Once he had a majority of the names, he could possibly shorten the time span, and then proceed to the finance department and start correlating the names with dates to a decisive sequence of events, possibly leading to locations of the most important financial transactions, mainly the years 1942-1943. Those two years were when the greatest number of mass deportation of Jews took place out of Poland, Czechoslovakia, France, Belgium, Netherlands, Austria, Germany and the Low Countries.

During the Nazi regime in 1933-1945, there was something like 8 million new accounts opened in Swiss bank accounts and approximately three-quarters were refugees from the war. This included Jews, Gypsies, Pols, communists, partisans and Russians or just about anyone who was displaced by the German occupation. At least three-quarters of all the total accounts were created at Clearstream banking.

Obviously, at the time, this was a major undertaking and a serious commitment for the entire Clearstream banking and financial organization. Coincidently, it is also believed 1942 is the year when the Swiss Financial Market Supervisory (SFINMA) was officially created.

Fortunately, Style knew he was headed in the right direction when he discovered, almost by accident, that most of the account records were cross-referenced, implying that if he could dig deep enough and find sufficient collaborative and trustworthy facts, it would lead to fine points that are more specific. This motivated and directed Style to believe that when he finally started on the files in the finance department, most, if not all, of the supposedly misplaced financial records would be within reach or at least provide some measure of evidence of their existence.

Without a doubt, that would include the Swiss Financial Market Supervisory (SFINMA) records. He started to speculate but believed sometime around 1943, when the greatest number of refugees and Jews departed their home countries, the Swiss bankers created a double and triple entry banking accounting system to allow the hiding of the appropriated accounts. In this manner, if someone produced enough proof to verify who they were, they would be allowed to withdraw their funds with relatively no difficulty or trouble. The bankers certainly were well aware of the fact that most of the poor persecuted Jews would never return or show up. As a result, the banks would hold onto the deposits under a different name and get away with embezzling millions and millions of dollars, if not billions of dollars. Subsequently it became literally impossible to question or suspect anything. The accountants created an easy solution for allowing the use of double and triple entries. Since most of the names on the files were either Hebrew or Jewish, the accountants would take the last letter of the last name, and then correspondingly match a Swiss-German surname with same last letter and apply it the file.

For example, the Jewish name Sapir was the original file name and it would be converted to Richter and then filed accordingly. Because Style was in the early stages of uncovering important information in the personnel department, he was very confident that he would soon uncover more details, considering that when he was initially briefed in London, he was told most, if not all, account records either disappeared without a trace or vanished without an explanation. As the story goes, around 1948 there was a serious and damaging fire. The press was told all or most personnel and financial files perished in the intense fire. However, the CIA and British Intelligence Service MI6 did their own investigation and as a result didn't buy into this fabrication and felt confident that most of the records were still in existence, somewhere. Style distinctly remembered that from one of his classes on financial banking at the Farm, the instructor thoroughly covered newer methods of hiding deposits and its history. The process actually started sometime in the 15th Century. As new technology was introduced, accountants and bankers alike started adopting newer methods of deception and avoidance of reporting transactions to the respective state governments. By being able to hide their accounts, depositors can circumvent reporting

interest income received on their deposits and avoid paying taxes.

Most western countries have a serious problem with unreported accounts in the banking industry, particularly banks in the Bahamas and Switzerland. In just about every instance, foreign deposits are never reported. Certainly, with the advances in financial cryptography, public-key cryptography could make it possible to use anonymous electronic money and anonymous digital bearer certificates for financial privacy and anonymous internet banking. This would enable institutions and issuers of such certificates digital cash and access to secure computer systems. Approximately five hours into his investigation, Style heard footsteps. He hid behind one of the files cabinets and the door opened slowly. He couldn't see and he naturally assumed it was security. The footsteps started to get closer. He was prepared to engage in a confrontation, if necessary. As the person got closer, he took out his weapon. He decided to play it cool and stay low. Apparently, whoever it was worked in the office because no sooner had they removed something from their desk, they were gone. Cautiously he continued his search. Each file that he opened he managed to take photographs and simultaneously secure digital recordings. In addition, on most of the files he clipped a tiny microchip that contained a Global Positioning System (GPS) memory chip.

It looked just like a small staple and if it were ever discovered, it would take an extraordinary effort to determine exactly what it was designed to do. Whenever Style was finished with examining a cabinet, he very carefully replaced everything to its original state to avoid any questions or potential problems. It was getting late and it soon became quite apparent he would need much more time and perhaps up too many more weeks to go through all of the cabinets in the personnel department. As soon as he got back to his room at the Hotel Hyatt, he assembled all of the material and submitted a progress report to DiSciascio. Two or three hours after sending his progress report, he received a top-secret message from DiSciascio:

Style:

Before I begin, here is some background information on World War II and the Nazi Party, both past and present. According to old captured German records from World War II, Karl Melmer became an adviser to Adolf Hitler after the Night of the Long Knives. As a result, Melmer's influence grew and in 1937 he was appointed by Hitler as Minister of Economics. In 1939, the Reichsbank was renamed as the Deutsche Reichsbank and placed under the direct control of Adolf Hitler, with Karl Melmer as the last president of the Reichsbank from 1939 to 1945. About this time, Melmer formed a relationship with Heinrich Himmler in stealing money looted from the Jews. Together, they literally murdered and robbed poor innocent victims of everything they possessed, down to and including their gold fillings. As you may know Heinrich Himmler was Reichsfuhrer-SS, head of the Gestapo and the Waffen-SS, Nazi Minister of the Interior from 1943 to 1945 and organizer of the mass murder of Jews in the Third Reich. In my last message, I indicated that Ulrich Melmer parents were members of the Nazi Party during World War II. It is now been confirmed that Ulrich Melmer has been the organizing force behind the right wing Neo-Nazi Group by name of National Democratic Organization (NDO) and is responsible for the resurrection of the "Gang of Thieves." Initial reports indicate the NDO is both violent and very aggressive. Apparently, the National Democratic Organization is very active in Switzerland, Germany, Austria & some Low Countries. As soon as I receive additional information on the "Gang of Thieves," I will forward it to you ASAP.

I don't have to tell you this, but remember, "The apple doesn't fall too far from the tree." In this case, the apple is apparently right under the biggest limb. I received your excellent progress report. Some of the information is an eye opener and certainly revealing. Continue with the excellent work. Best advice: be careful and keep on your toes at all times, no exception. More to come...Be careful.

Success,

DiSciascio

Style was exhausted and decided it was about time to retire. He had another very busy schedule for tomorrow and furthermore he was looking forward to his beautiful date.

7

What the horrors of war are, no one can imagine. They are not wounds and blood and fever, spotted and low, or dysentery, chronic and acute, cold and heat and famine. They are intoxication, drunken brutality, demoralization and disorder on the part of the inferior ... jealousies, meanness, indifference, selfish brutality on the part of the superior.
Florence Nightingale

The next morning, Style decided to relax a bit and take his time leaving for the office. He was enjoying his morning coffee when unexpectedly there was a sudden and massive explosion somewhere out in the street. He ran to the window and cautiously looked out to see if there was anything he could see. Off in the distance he could see a billowing cloud of smoke rising into the sky. As the smoke cleared, Style was able to establish the approximate location in downtown Zurich. It didn't look too far from the financial center, indeed within proximity of the Clearstream bank headquarters.

He hurriedly got dressed and immediately departed taking a different route to the office. As he got closer to the Clearstream financial facility, his suspicion was exactly right. Directly in the front of the Clearstream headquarters was a car bombing. Apparently, a new Mercedes Benz sedan was used to detonate the bomb.

The Zurich police were still milling around searching for evidence and questioning bystanders. Fortunately, there were only a few people injured, but not seriously. The few injuries can be attributed due to the early hour that the bomb was detonated; as a result, the number of casualties was minimal. In addition, the fire department was busy putting out a number of fires created by the bombing, especially the Mercedes used to detonate the bomb. It was completely demolished. Style stopped one of the police officers and asked, "What happened?"

The officer was blunt, obviously preoccupied and justifiably so, but indicated that it was a high explosive bomb containing both shrapnel and incendiary meant to cause substantial damage and physical harm.

The entrance to the Clearstream Finance & Banking, LTD building was severely damaged and as a result was closed off for obvious reasons. There were many electrical wires, leaking pipes and conduits hanging everywhere. Many windows were shattered and blown out. The old and familiar massive leaded double entry front doors were blown off their hinges, making them inoperative and out of order. As a result, everyone had to use the side entrance.

He finally got to his office on the 20th floor and sat down for minute to reflect. Had he left on schedule this morning, chances are that bomb may have caused him a problem or possibly worse, some physical harm. He couldn't help but think he was the target and hoped that wasn't the case. He needed to find out who was responsible without making it too obvious.

Style decided to pay a friendly visit to Ulrich Melmer. When he arrived at Ulrich's office, there were a number of people standing around talking. Ulrich was nowhere to be found. Style thought this was rather unusual for this time in the morning for Melmer to be late. At the last minute, he asked one of Ulrich's staff members if they knew where Melmer happened to be. A quick reply came from his administrative assistant, Ana. "Mr. Melmer had arrived a little earlier today, just prior to the bombing. Suddenly within minutes after the blast, he left the building out the back door without any explanation. He called to let me know he was all right. However, as you can see everyone is concerned because under most ordinary circumstances he would be here to try to settle everyone's nerves when something of this magnitude happens. He usually is around to offer his assistance and provide leadership."

Style asked, if he could help in any manner.

Ana, replied, "No, not at this time but thank you for asking, Mr. Style."

He then excused himself. Frankly, he couldn't make heads or tails out Melmer's sudden departure. A few minutes later, he arrived at his office and discovered his telephone was ringing. Style picked up the phone and answered. It was Hans Schroeder. He could tell in Schroeder's voice, that he was nervous and concerned. He asked John if he was OK.

"Absolutely fine and doing just great Hans." Style replied. "Is there a reason why I should not be, Hans?"

"Well, I just wanted to make sure this bombing didn't affect you," said Schroeder. Of course, we are concerned about all of our staff and, in particular, our visitors like you. Would you like to have lunch today?"

"Yes, that would be outstanding, Hans. Where would you like to have lunch?"

Hans suggested "La Rouge, a popular upscale fast-paced café just around the corner. The local business crowd goes there and they have great French food with a wonderful atmosphere."

"Sounds great to me, Hans. I will take a taxi and join you there."

Hans replied, "I will see you there at 12:30 pm."

"Confirmed," said Style.

Frankly, Style was a little confused. In previous meetings, Schroeder always appeared to be in control of just about everything in his life, and from the sound of his voice, he practically sounded desperate and distraught. Suddenly, and without reason, Style gets an invitation to join Hans for lunch. He certainly didn't know what to expect.

Style arrived at La Rouge right on time, then was escorted to a private section of the café and seated in a booth. Schroeder apparently hadn't arrived yet. Style started to relax and ordered a beer. Within minutes, Hans walked up and sat down. They both exchanged pleasantries. The first words out of Hans's mouth were, "I think that bomb today was meant for me."

Style was shocked and asked, "What makes you think that, Hans?"

"It is a long story. I can't give you my reasons but suffice it to say I feel confident I was fortunate today that I arrived earlier at the office than normal. Otherwise, I would be spread all over the side of the Clearstream building."

Style replied, "I'm entirely confused. Are you involved in some questionable business practices?"

"No, I'm not involved in any questionable business," replied Hans.

"Ok, what could be the problem Hans?"

"For now, I would prefer not to talk about the bombing."

"Well, why can't you share your concern and problem?"

"Under the circumstances, John, the only reason I feel comfortable in asking you out for lunch is because you are a relative stranger and I hoped you would not inquire or probe me. I couldn't invite anyone on my staff without them asking a thousand questions. Certainly, I can't tell them how I feel about the bombing or suggest that the bomb was meant for me. Moreover John, I'm trying my best to get over this horrible incident and I just needed to relax and find relief somewhere with a friend. Additionally, I haven't even contacted my wife about today's explosion."

"Why not, Hans? Don't you think you wife would be worried about you?"

"Of course I do, John."

"I would suggest you call her as soon as we leave, Hans."

"You are correct, John; I will give her a phone call when we get back to the office. In the meantime, I just need to take my mind off this completely awful incident."

Immediately, Style said, "I promise not to probe you or raise the subject again."

"Great, let's just have a couple of beers and enjoy lunch."

"That sounds just wonderful. I'm hungry because I didn't have breakfast today. I would like to thank you for trusting me, Hans."

"You were the first person I thought about minutes after the bomb went off. As I said, I arrived early, went directly to my office and was enjoying a cup of coffee and bam. Perhaps in the near future I will share some information with you. Until then...let us focus on business or something else. OK, John?"

"Well, certainly I will keep it light, especially for our lunch today. I promise I will keep our conversation on the carefree side. Tonight, I have a date with an undeniably beautiful lady."

"Where did you meet her, John?"

"One evening I went for a walk and met the Concierge at the Hotel Grand Hyatt of Zurich where I happen to be staying. The very attractive Concierge, who is married, mentioned to me she had a sister who is single and that her sister is one or two years older than she is. She arranged a date with her sister for tonight."

"So tell me, where are you going on your date John Style?"

"Appropriately, the Concierge arranged for two tickets to the opera and made dinner reservations."

"How can you be so cheap, John?"

"No, you don't understand Hans. The Hyatt made available two tickets for the opera and dinner at the Piccolomini's Zurich for the guest who chose to stay in a suite instead of a regular room."

"OK, OK I believe you Style, I think."

"Why would I fabricate such a story?"

"I'm giving you a hard time, John."

"Good enough, I accept your bullshit in giving me a hard time, Hans."

"We have a Swiss expression, 'Wunderbar zeit nacht' — So, have a wonderful time tonight, John Style."

"In addition, make it a sagenhaft unheimlich gut ...fucking good night."

"Wow, you sure tell it like it is. I think you had one too many glasses of 'bier' Hans. However, I'm pleased that you are relaxed and having a good time."

"You are damn right, I'm feeling no pain young Mr. John Style."

"Would you like a ride home, Hans?"

"Absolutely not, I'm totally in control of all my faculties my young friend."

"Are you sure, Hans?"

"Yes, of course. I'm relaxed and I will be just fine Style."

8

To be prepared for war is one of the most effectual
means of preserving peace. A free people ought
not only to be armed, but disciplined to be
ready to defend freedom.
President of the United States
George Washington

When Style arrived back at the hotel, he started to think about Hans Schroeder's extremely strange behavior. *Why did he call me of all people? Does Schroeder suspect something? Could he possibly know what is going on?* Style needed to get a background check on his history to determine whether he could possibly trust him and would Schroeder be trustworthy enough to be recruited as an informer or possibly an agent. Style immediately sent an e-mail to DiSciascio requesting a background check on Hans Schroeder, with a wish to have a response no later than tomorrow afternoon.

The top-secret encrypted e-mail request asked for a thumbnail sketch providing a background check about Hans Schroeder. In the meantime, Style had other things on his mind, like his date for the evening. He arranged to have a formal black tuxedo delivered to his room before six.

Without realizing it, the tuxedo was already delivered to this room and was hanging in the closet. Style discovered the tuxedo by accident, just as he finished taking a quick shower. He started to get dressed and as he finished putting on his bow tie, he discovered a note was lying on the floor, just inside the door. It wasn't there earlier so it must have arrived while he was in the shower. He opened up the note without delay and naturally was somewhat concerned. The note was from Hans Schroeder and it was brief and laconic. Schroeder wrote the following:

John–

I would like to meet with you Sunday afternoon at 3 p.m. in the lobby bar Onyx, Park Hyatt Hotel. It is extremely important we meet. I'm concerned for my life and my family. I'm prepared in having a detailed discussion about the bombing and to provide my speculation on the reasons why I feel my life is in imminent danger. My wife and I discussed this bold move before I took the initiative in contacting you. Please be on time. Call tomorrow and leave a message to confirm +41 43 882 6234.

Thanks,

Hans Schroeder

The only thing Style could think about was that Schroeder remained safe until Sunday afternoon and with any luck the information he requested from DiSciascio on Hans Schroeder arrived before Sunday. He finished dressing and departed. Instinctively, Style was now beginning to feel a little apprehensive and some pressure. Every time he turned around, he felt as though someone was following or watching him. His reaction was only normal, considering the enormous amount of difficulties beginning to surface. Finally, the elevator arrived at the lobby. He walked over to the front desk and patiently waited alongside the reception desk. The time was just before seven p.m. He started to think it has been a long time since he had a date——at least two or three months. Wow! That is a long stretch of time without a female companion.

Within minutes Zosa appeared. She was ravishing and stunningly beautiful. Zosa was more exquisite and much taller in high heels than he could have imagined. She wore a gorgeously long tight black dress covered at the shoulders with a fur jacket. Style couldn't take his eyes off her. Her fragrance was intoxicating. At first, he felt like a young schoolboy on his first date in high school. Momentarily he was transfixed. She broke the silence and said, "Good evening, John Style. Is there something wrong because you are staring?"

"Yes, I am and for good reason. Hopefully your name is Zosa?"

"My sister Maria described you perfectly, John."

"Please excuse me for staring Zosa because you are so beautiful."

"John, you probably say that to all the women you date, don't you?"

"Of course not and I'm telling you the truth Zosa, really."

"I believe you John, for now. We had better leave for the opera. Curtain time is in just fifteen minutes."

"Zosa, what opera are we going to see?"

"The Italian opera, La Traviata by Verdi, it is a very well-known and entertaining."

"Zosa I have to confess, I have never been to an opera or even listened to one on the radio."

"I believe you will enjoy this opera. It is a dramatic account about a very tragic and passionate love story that is very popular with romantics. Some opera fans consider La Traviata to be one of the greatest theatrical operas and the most engaging performances with wonderful music."

Throughout most of the opera, John was beside himself; he would hastily take momentary glimpses of Zosa. She on the other hand couldn't ignore his obvious momentary flirting glances.

When the opera ended, they departed for dinner at Piccolomini's Zurich Italian Restaurant. Piccolomini's was within a very short walking distance. The evening was getting chilly and snow was falling lightly. John suggested taking a taxi. Zosa said, "No." She continued, "Let's enjoy the short walk on such a wonderful and beautiful evening."

They walked holding hands to the restaurant and arrived within minutes. Upon entering, they were greeted warmly by the owner of Piccolomini's. Hello and welcome to my family restaurant. I'm Alfredo.

He then introduced the Maître De to John and Zosa. John asked the Maître De, if they could they be seated overlooking Lake Zurich. He replied, "Yes, of course. We do have a table waiting for you both, in the most center of the restaurant, overlooking Lake Zurich. It is the perfect place to dine, savor fine wine and enjoy the beautiful landscape of Lake Zurich, especially with a beautiful woman."

At dinner, Zosa asked John what kind of work he was involved in that allowed him to travel so extensively. Of course, he couldn't tell her the truth and replied, "I'm a business and financial consultant to American industries hoping to expand operations in Europe, Africa, Far East and the Middle East."

"How fascinating and such a wonderful career. You must be smart, John."

"My Mom and Dad invested a lot of time and money in my education and I thank them for the privilege of being somewhat successful."

"John, you are being modest."

"The reason I'm in Zurich is to help negotiate and facilitate a very large contract with one of Zurich's largest financial institution. An American company is looking to expand its manufacturing operations into three European countries, including Switzerland. Because of the complexity and the size of the business loan, I anticipate being in Zurich for at least two months or longer. However, I will also be traveling in and out of Switzerland weekly because I have other business to conduct throughout Europe and the Middle East, at least for now."

"Your occupation sends challenging. Do you enjoy it?"

"Yes, in fact I truly enjoy my profession. It keeps me on my toes."

"What do you do for exercise, John?"

"Sometimes, when I can, I try to play tennis, workout in the gym, run or swim."

"Really, I would like to play tennis with you some day."

"You will probably blow me off the tennis court, Zosa."

"OK, John, I take that as a challenge."

"You name the place and time; I will be there to take you on, Zosa."

The dinner was excellent and so was the wine. They finished off one bottle of Italian cabernet and were half way through the second when they decided no more wine. Zosa turned to John and said, "It's getting late and although I don't have to be at work until noon tomorrow, we need to go."

"May I take you home?"

Zosa hesitated for a brief second and replied, "That would be nice, John. Although I live relatively close, I would suggest we take a taxi because of all the wine we drank tonight."

"I couldn't agree more."

They soon arrived at her townhome. John successfully managed to get a kiss and was about to leave when Zosa turned and asked John, please come in for a nightcap and listen to some music. John was beside himself. He started to get excited, just at the thought of holding her close. The more he inhaled her fragrance, the more romanticized and excited he became. Each was enjoying another glass of wine while listening to some soft jazz. They were dancing close to the fireplace, when they moved on to the warm comfortable couch. They were in a passionate embrace when she suggested they go to her bedroom. All evening John was undressing her with his eyes even before they arrived at her townhome. Once in the bedroom, John couldn't take his hands off Zosa.

Delicately, he removed her dress and carried her over to the bed. She was wearing a very petite black sexy bikini, almost transparent. Her matching black bra looked like it was painted on her beautiful body. He adroitly removed her bra and her breast seemed to ask to be caressed and held. He rolled her nipples in his hand and kissed each breast tenderly with love, as he deftly moved his other hand down over her taut flat lovely stomach. Ably, he removed her panties. Her fragrance was much to be desired. He managed to get his mouth close to her lips and started probing her with his tongue. Her vagina was covered with a very light amount of soft short down, almost too perfect but so exotic to behold. He would not stop caressing her with his tongue. She reacted with sighs and was passionately aroused by his wet, moist kisses. She reached down between his legs to caress him. She whispered in his ear and they seemed almost bonded together as one. Undulating and thrusting almost to the rhythm of the soft jazz music. He didn't want the evening to end and nor did she. Zosa suddenly erupted in to a passionate plea of ecstasy. Gradually they both collapsed in one another's arms. Both fell asleep at once, each holding on in a lingering embrace, not wanting the night to come to an end. At some point very early in the morning, John Style reflected on the beautiful evening he shared with Zosa. He soon realized how unpretentious a relationship could be when thoughtfulness of mutual love and passion is considered first and foremost. This is what a relationship is about, without any reservation thought John.

9

*We have to face the fact that either all of us are going to
die together or we are going to learn to live together and if we
are to live together we have to talk.*
Eleanor Roosevelt

orning came abruptly. John was awake early just lying there
enjoying her warm body. He was taking in her beauty and on
occasion would reach out his hand to softly and lovingly rub
her smooth silky skin. Soon, Zosa rolled over to get closer to John. She
whispered something in his ear. He started to laugh.

"OK, I'm game if you are."

Zosa replied, "I think we should have breakfast first. You should have
a good breakfast to get your day started in the right direction."

"No thank you," said Style. "I will just have a cup of coffee and watch
you get dressed." Zosa went in to the kitchen to prepare coffee. She
returned shortly with the coffee and a croissant. They both enjoyed sip-
ping the freshly brewed coffee and at the same time relished the peace
and tranquility of a cold winter Saturday morning. He embraced her
for it seemed like hours. Shortly, she got out of bed. She was naked and
breathtakingly delightful to look at. As she walked across the room her

breast were supple and almost perfect orbs, with large dark areoles and long nipples. She was tall, slender with long well defined muscular toned legs. He couldn't take his eyes off her. At this moment, he was transfixed. Her neat trim vulva is all he could think about and wanted to taste her once again. Finally, she said, "I need to get dressed and get ready for work."

"May I ask you Zosa, what type of work are you involved in that requires you to go to work on a Saturday afternoon?"

"I'm a professional dancer and I also instruct ballroom dance and ballet. Today, I have a rehearsal for a dance musical."

"Would it be possible for me to go to one of your rehearsals or perhaps attend one of your performances?"

"Of course, you may John. Just tell me when and I will get tickets for you."

"Has the play already opened, Zosa?"

"Yes, it opened just two weeks ago."

"Can you possibly arrange for tickets in the next two or three weeks, Zosa?"

"John, I will arrange for several tickets. Just let me know what weekend performance you would prefer. Once I reserve the tickets, I will contact my sister and let her know. She'll then arrange to have the tickets delivered to her desk at the Park Hyatt hotel."

"That is absolutely splendid, Zosa."

As she finished getting dressed, John sprang out of bed and jumped into the shower. He was finished quickly and started to dress. After he finished dressing, he called for a taxi. Before he departed, he confirmed he wanted to see her again within two or three weeks and told her he had a wonderful time and thanked her.

Zosa said, "I look forward to seeing you again, John."

It was mid-morning when he arrived back at the hotel. Immediately, John turned on his computer and started up his e-mail. There were several very important messages. The first one had to do with an escalated alert for all consulates and embassies around the world because of Islamic terrorist's threats and the continued violent demonstration in Cairo and Lebanon. Apparently, to avoid another Ben Gasi, most embassies based in Africa and the Middle East were closed down temporarily. This was only a momentary move by the State Department. The second message was by far the most important message and the one John Style was waiting for. He hoped that it contained the information he needed for his meeting tomorrow afternoon with Han Schroeder.

The message was sent from James DiSciascio:

Style–

The information you provided was more than enough to allow a surface background investigation on Hans Schroeder. His record is perfectly clean with no arrests, not even a parking ticket in the last ten years. He had a brilliant academic career while attending the London University School of Economics. Through hard work and doing an excellent job while performing several responsibilities, he advanced rapidly in the banking industry. He's a dedicated employee, who can be trusted. There is no record of his political beliefs or any political affiliations. He climbed his way up the corporate ladder from accounts payable to the Executive Vice President of Finance for Clearstream Finance & Banking. Hans has worked with Clearstream for twenty-five years. Schroeder is married with two children, ages 14 and 16, both girls. Finally, his mortgage is paid in full and so are both of his cars. He doesn't live beyond his means, pays cash whenever possible and has outstanding credit. His home is located on the east side of Lake Zurich, approximately ten miles from Clearstream.

In addition, we received a detailed description of the bombing that took place this past week. We have determined that the group directly responsible is National Democratic Organization (NDO). Interpol and British Intelligence Service (SIS) MI6 conducted the investigation. We just received the report at Langley within the last few hours. There is also a substantial amount of activity being picked up by our surveillance tracking telecommunications satellites confirming NDO is very active and on the move throughout Europe. Finally, there is alarming news coming in to Langley, at the Global Response Center (GRC). There is aggressive posturing by several Islamic terrorist's groups throughout Europe and the Middle East. As a result, we have optioned to place all of our locations in Europe and the Middle East on high alert. The U.S. military in Afghanistan and Iraq are on standby status. Most all other bases around the world have been escalated to high alert. I will keep you posted if something breaks. Once more, excellent reporting and be safe.

Continued success,

DiSciascio.

This is exactly what Style was anticipating. He picked up the room telephone and called the number Schroeder had left in the message from last evening. Style's voice message was to the point and clear.

Hans,

I'm confirming our scheduled appointment for tomorrow, Sunday afternoon at 3 p.m. I look forward to our meeting and discussions. In the meantime, please remain safe. Any questions or concerns, please call.

Thanks, John

Late Saturday afternoon Style decided to take the Porsche 911 Carrera for a spin, perhaps another ride around the lake and go touring. No sooner had Style climbed into the Porsche that he discovered there was definitely someone following him - the same person he saw milling around the hotel lobby. He chose to drive the east side of the lake because it was more mountainous and had many more sharp curves. As Style pulled out of the hotel parking lot, he immediately realized the same person who followed him through the hotel, was directly behind him. At once he accelerated the Porsche, rapidly building up speed. As he negotiated the motorway, it started to snow lightly. He continued driving faster until he was hitting triple digits. Once he achieved 115 mph, the car that was following was no longer in his rear view mirror. He didn't have any problems with stability or control of the Porsche, despite the snow coming down faster and beginning to build up on the road. As Style approached a cutoff in the motorway, he suddenly made a severe sharp left turn. The Porsche fish tailed briefly, but Style managed to get the Carrera under control. He swiftly maneuvered the Porsche to the right and up a dirt road. Style pulled in behind what appeared to be a vacant building or warehouse. He waited for approximately five minutes and then took off. Abruptly, he pulled out onto the motorway, accelerating faster and faster. This time he really was testing the Porsche. Finally, after driving at least an hour, he pulled into a roadside café. After enjoying a late afternoon cup of coffee and a French pastry, he decided to return to the Park Hyatt hotel. Cautiously, he pulled into the parking facility, climbed out of the

Porsche and walked into the lobby. The lobby was virtually empty and very quiet, almost eerie.

Before he entered the elevator, he decided to check the lobby bar Onyx. It too was empty of customers. Finally, he arrived at his room. He was beginning to wonder if his mind was playing tricks. Cautiously, he inserted the passkey and entered slowly. At first, everything appeared to be normal except when he entered the bedroom. His suitcase and clothing were emptied out and all thrown around the room. Both sets of dresser draws were on the floor and the box spring mattress was lying on top of the table. The bathroom was in total disarray. From the looks of things, they were definitely searching for something special. Earlier, before he left, he checked his laptop, IDs and passports into the hotel safe.

As always, he still had his weapons on him. There was nothing of value taken; as a result, he decided not to call hotel security but to keep the intrusion quiet. Instead, he called Marie, the Concierge on the house phone and asked if she noticed anything unusual that happened at the hotel in the last three or four hours.

She replied, "Absolutely nothing," and then asked, "is there a reason, Mr. Style?"

Style responded by saying, "When he arrived back at the hotel from his drive around the lake, the hotel appeared empty and he thought that was unusual."

Marie further explained, "Saturday is one of the least busy days of the week except in the evening when guest arrive for dinner."

"That makes perfect sense," said Style. "I look forward to seeing your sister Zosa when I get back from my trip to Slovenia and Austria."

Cleverly, the only reason he said something to Marie about the lobby being empty was to avoid any discussions having to do with his room. At the last minute he realized whoever stalked him downstairs into the lobby and then pursued him driving on the roadway had baited him from the beginning.

The obvious reason was to avoid a confrontation with Style and to break into his room and search for money, jewels or drugs. Certainly, it could have been something else, but what? Of course, this concerned

Style. His imagination was running wild. He hoped that he hadn't revealed anything through his actions or that he may have been over-heard in a mobile telephone call. He later reaffirmed his convictions and realized it had to be something directly related to Hans Schroeder and the bombing Friday morning. Style felt very uncomfortable and uneasy. As they say at the Farm: *Experience is a comb which nature gives us when we are bald or the trouble with using experience as a guide is that the final exam often comes first and then the lesson.* How appropriate, Style thought to himself; he learned several great lessons today. He would not make the same mistake twice.

10

I do not believe that the men who served in uniform in
Vietnam have been given the credit they deserve.
It was a difficult war against an unorthodox enemy.
General William Westmoreland

I t was early Sunday afternoon. Style was unsure of how much he should reveal to Hans Schroeder when they sat down in a couple of hours. After giving it a lot of thought, he decided the best approach was to take a very conservative position and allow Schroeder to open up and reveal as much as possible.

Just minutes before 3pm, Style put on his jacket and caught the elevator down to the lobby. Surprisingly, there were a number of people in the bar. Most were watching a soccer match on the large screen. Style selected a quiet booth back in the corner away from all the noise. He sat down and ordered a beer. At about the same time the beer arrived, so did Schroeder. He looked frazzled and out of sorts. Perhaps tense and nervous would be a much better description. He immediately sat down and said good afternoon to Style. They exchanged several more pleasantries, and then Style took the lead when he asked Schroeder what was going on? At first, Schroeder was unsure what to say in response.

Suddenly, Schroeder blurted out that he and his wife discussed the recent bombing and decided they needed to confide in someone whom they could trust. It was quite apparent they had no confidence or enough trust in the local police or felt too insecure to discuss the incident with somebody from his office. At first, Style was going to probe Schroeder on why he was selected as the confidant, but at the last minute, he decided to just listen. With absolute conviction, Schroeder said, "The bombing on Friday morning was definitely meant for him."

"Why do you feel that way, Hans?"

Schroeder explains, "It's very complicated but let me start by going back almost twenty years. At the time, I was a junior accountant working in the controversial tax sheltering accounts division of Clearstream."

"Do you know most of the history of Clearstream, Hans?"

"Yes, I believe I do. Originally, Clearstream was formed sometime in the late 1940s or early 1950s under a different name of Swiss Banking Services (SBS). They specialized in delivery and settlement of Eurobonds, large commercial real estate transactions and tax shelters. Soon thereafter, they started to merge with competitors."

"Do you know why the sudden outbreak of bank mergers, Hans?"

"This is purely speculation on my part, but I believe the United States banking industry was beginning to consider expansion in to several key financial centers in Europe. As a result, the consortium of small to mid-size banks started to merge, beginning with banks in London, Paris, West Berlin, Rome, Lisbon, Madrid and Zurich. When the mergers started, most of the bankers decided they no longer wanted individual accounts but to focus on large commercial enterprises, other large banks and financial institutions.

Eventually Clearstream developed into a bank of all banks by being a clearinghouse. Primarily, that is what we do today."

"What you are telling me Hans, is that the money I'm here to borrow doesn't necessarily come directly from the Clearstream vaults but from the consortium."

"You are partially correct John. Legally its Clearstream' s responsibility to make certain that all the contracts, terms and conditions are absolutely accurate and acceptable. They are ones taking the greatest risk.

Naturally, when the mergers started, all of the old records were moved in to the Clearstream corporate facilities."

"Hans, do you recall if there was ever a major fire at Clearstream?"

"During my tenure, there have been no fires at Clearstream and I don't believe there was ever a fire going back to the origin of the company. Consequently, there are many extremely old records in the Clearstream buildings including many file records going back to the early 1930s."

"What an amazing story Hans, I'm simply surprised by your outstanding knowledge and appreciation of Clearstream history."

"I'm not quite finished, John."

"As I said earlier, most of the accounting and finance business was with very large corporations, many were internationally based. The tax sheltering division promptly developed a very aggressive reputation and was notorious for playing a major role in the underground economy. Today, we have dirty terms for the underground economy and that is called, "money laundering" and "tax evasion." The deception has been going on since the start of World War II and possibly even earlier to the beginning of the 20th Century when the Swiss financial and banking business started to grow and prosper.

Today, Clearstream remains one of the largest of all the banks in the world directly involved in the underground economy but there are others providing similar services."

"Would this mean that Clearstream transacts finance and banking throughout most of Europe?"

"Yes absolutely and more than just Europe. They literally have thousands upon thousands of confidential accounts moving money across all of Europe, North America, South America, Africa and the Middle East to protect large security trades. They are the owners of many banks in the Caribbean and Bahamas. The amount of money involved is astronomical. Clearstream embraces a dominant position for providing cross-border clearing and settlement services to intermediaries situated in other member states. There was some speculation many years ago, most, if not all these banks, wanted to remove themselves from involvement in cross-border tax evasion but they simply couldn't because they were too deeply involved and they would lose everything."

"My God Hans, this is a most remarkable story."

"Today, most economists and accountants on the inside call it the moving parts of the 21st Century competitive world economics. Nevertheless, these banks have managed to hide their vast amount of underground business beneath a veneer cover of disguise and absolute deception."

"How do they accomplish the cover-up, Hans?"

"They have developed a very simple process or almost genius method. On the surface the smaller financial business transactions, are government funding and financing third world capitalization and United Nations collateral building for world causes. Naturally, all of these activities get the headlines every day, year-in and year-out. However, the reality is that third world capitalization is just a tiny fraction of the real activity. This publicity shrouds the real down and dirty part of the European banking business. The material financial banking transactions are the vast amounts of money laundering and tax evasion.

"So, what you are saying is that the largest deposits of business transactions are primarily questionable to say the least."

"Let me finish. Now this is the difficult part and why I firmly believe I'm being singled out to be assassinated."

"Is there something in particular that happened to make you feel this way, Hans?"

"Yes absolutely. More than a few years ago, I forget exactly when but somewhere around the turn of the millennium, I uncovered by mistake thousands and thousands of these so-called protected and hidden accounts. I thought all these records were destroyed or purged. In fact, in the late 1940s, there was an unsubstantiated story that Clearstream had a historic fire."

"Hans, wait a minute; I'm confused. Earlier you said there was never a fire at Clearstream."

"Yes, I did say that. Remember now Clearstream didn't officially exist until sometime around the early 1950s. I'm actually referring to the period of the mid-1940s prior to the incorporation of Clearstream and all the mergers."

"Now that makes more sense. Thank you for clarifying the apparent contradiction, Hans."

"Supposedly, the fire destroyed all traces of files and records that belonged to the persecuted Jews. Literally, most if not all these accounts were opened days before the Jews were sent to the concentration camps. I was able to estimate there were at least five million new accounts opened between 1938 and early 1944. I believe the amount of money involved by today's standard would be at least 75 billion dollars or more. Please understand, the numbers haven't been verified or audited. However, I feel reasonably confident with these approximate numbers. Jews didn't only own these accounts but there were also Russian, Catholic, Communist and Gypsy accounts. Furthermore, this also included most any country that Nazi Germany conquered. The banks were also accused of collaborating in hiding the treasured arts taken from Poland, Italy, France, Russia, Czechoslovakia, Belgium and the list goes on.

"Certainly, the treasured arts would add hundreds of millions of dollars to the already stolen money and gold taken from the Jews, Hans."

"Yes, absolutely without question, John. I need to continue my story. Coincidently, just prior to your arrival several months ago, I was invited to attend a classified meeting with Ulrich Melmer in his office. When I arrived, I didn't recognize anyone but Melmer. I wasn't introduced to anyone. I believe that was intentional. As a result, I couldn't tell you any of their names. At first, I thought this was going to be just another everyday closed-door audit. Therefore, I didn't think much of it. Frankly, I was absolutely convinced it was just that, another audit. However, as the questioning continued, I soon discovered they were not interested in the day-to-day financial matters. Swiftly, the discussions moved onto offshore banking, tax evasion and the underground economy. Then, I knew this was going to be a serious problem for me."

Style interrupted and asked, "How did they find out about you?"

"Frankly, I don't know. Someone apparently had seen me opening these classified files, which I wasn't aware were confidential. Obviously, I should not have been looking in this particular file cabinet."

"OK Hans, why where you looking in these files in the first place?"

"One evening when I stayed real late and I was trying to catch up on my paperwork, I discovered the file cabinet by accident while looking for a misplaced customer file."

"Did you make any copies or take any photographs?" asked Style.

"Are you serious John? Absolutely not. Why would I? I didn't realize at the time there was a problem or any issues."

"I guess that makes sense, Hans. Do you think the records are still in the same office and file cabinet?"

"I believe they are in the same office on the 20th floor, but they moved the cabinets into a secure room located in the corner behind all of the older files cabinets."

Style further questioned, "I don't understand why they don't destroy all of these records. This could be compelling, self-incriminating evidence. Certainly, these records could be used as substantiating facts and whoever is responsible would be prosecuted to the fullest extent of the law."

"I'm willing to speculate that there is a substantial amount of money still hidden and involved, but the records are needed for verification and identification," observes Schroeder.

"I will buy that, but the risk is enormous," said Style.

"I've learned over the years, people will do anything for money, even risk their lives over and over again," added Hans.

"Have you finished with the story, Hans?"

"I'm just about finished, John. There are just a few more points and I think the most important ones."

"What are they, Hans?"

"Without doubt and definitely the most intense questions were directly related to the problems on the old files that were supposedly destroyed in the late 1940s. I'm referring to the missing Nazi gold, the Jewish accounts, their misplaced money and the treasured art taken from the occupied countries."

"Did you actually see any evidence of these files, Hans?"

"Yes, absolutely, John. I'm telling you that I had them in my hands, read a few files and in fact, I remember a small number of details from the account files."

"Could you give me an example, Hans?"

"John, when I first started to scan through the files, I was in disbelief and astonished. At first, I was convinced I was in a dream. There was one particular file I thought was extremely interesting and most intriguing. The file name was David Molaski. The family was from Radom, Poland. There were over 20 names listed on the file, just from this one family. Unfortunately, as the report indicated, they were herded together in early 1942, and all were shipped to the Dachau concentration camp located outside of Munich, Germany. As you probably know, Dachau was the very first concentration camp established by the Nazis, sometime around 1933."

"Is that all, Hans?"

"No. Prior to the beginning of the war, the Molaski families were owners of one of the largest coal mining businesses in the world. Once the Nazis overran Poland, David Molaski apparently feared for his family's safety and fortunes and elected in late 1940 to open a Swiss bank account. Within months, he wired a transfer of over thirty million dollars into the new account, thinking it was totally secure. At the time I discovered the account, I immediately estimated what the thirty million dollars would be worth today: an astonishing eight hundred million to one billion U.S. dollars. This is perhaps one of the reasons I so vividly remember this individual account. One last thing on this particular account, all twenty family members were sent to the gas chamber. No living survivors were noted on the file. Additionally, there are other more similar accounts that I remember and I will provide you with a detailed written description."

"Hans, I need to ask you, who was asking most of the questions?"

"John, in the beginning it was Ulrich Melmer. As the discussions evolved, the unknown visitors started to ask more and more questions. They were very cautious how they asked the questions. In retrospect, I now understand why they didn't want to arouse any suspicion. If anything, they were extra cautious of how they asked questions. Often Melmer would interject or try to clarify a question."

"When they asked you direct questions that involved the Nazi gold and the intentionally misplaced or lost Jewish accounts, what exactly did you say Hans?"

"At that point John, I was able to put the story together and immediately realized I needed to be extra cautious. Therefore, I simply replied I didn't remember seeing any accounts that were that old or went back that far."

"This is an important question Hans - can you remember the exact question and how it was phrased?"

"Yes, I can John."

"This is exactly how the question was expressed: When you were looking through some of the old files, did you happen to see any records prior to the 1950s and could you describe some details?"

"Are you sure those are the exact words used in their question?

"John, I'm absolutely confident, without any reservation, that indeed was the question."

"Well, that is the story John. You probably think I'm either a dreamer, lying or emotionally off track."

Style was amazed. He sat there for a few minutes before he responded.

Finally, he turned to Schroeder and said, "I believe you, Hans, completely. I need to ask you one very important question."

"Yes, what is it?"

"Why did it take so long for Ulrich Melmer to begin these queries?"

"My response would be purely speculative. However, I think Clearstream has been feeling a lot of pressure because of the state of economy throughout Europe and the instability of the Euro. As you know, there has been growing pressure by the United States Government to open up the protected accounts owned by American citizens. These accounts reportedly haven't paid a substantial amount of taxable income. That is all I can provide, John."

"Certainly that is good enough for me, Hans."

"The only question remaining is what do we do next? Obviously, by telling me your story, I'm now thrust into the middle of this remarkable sequence of events. As a result, we need to work together and be extremely vigilant. My first concern is for your welfare and your family's safety. So, let us start with your family."

"John, you sound like you know what you are talking about today."

"Yes, to a certain degree Hans. My very best recommendation at this point is for your family to take a long vacation. I realize this is going to create problems for your teen-age daughters. However, it's the safest and best thing to do for now. Do you have any relatives living somewhere else in a distant rural community in Switzerland, Germany or France?"

"Yes, we certainly do," replied Schroeder.

"How far and where are they located, Hans?"

"My wife's mother lives by herself in the very southwestern corner of Switzerland, near France. My children will not be happy going there because it is a farm."

"Hans, the only other option would be for them to stay with some friends of mine in the United States. I don't think your daughters would like that option."

"You are probably right. At least I have some options."

"The sooner you prepare them the better off they will be, Hans. Now, tonight when you leave to go home, remember to do the following:

First, before you get into your car, open the hood to check to see if anything has been tampered with or altered. Second, if when starting your car there is a strange sound, get out of your car as fast as possible and don't remove the key. Third, don't take the same route home you ordinarily take. Fourth, tonight when you arrive home, turn off all the lights as soon as possible in the house and turn on all outside lights. Fifth, sleep on the floor away from the windows. Sixth, I assume you have no type of firearms is that correct, Hans?"

"Yes, that is correct, John."

"OK, then make sure you have a knife or hatchet and the same goes for your wife and daughters. Seventh, tomorrow morning make sure they are packed up and depart before dawn. Eighth, don't call your family on the family phone or company telephone. That also includes your mobile phone. Only use a secure phone like a public telephone or a hotel phone.

Ninth, this week, every day drive a different route to and from the office, even if it takes much longer. Preferably, if there is public transportation available, please take it. Tenth, if you have to drive, be aware of what is around you while driving. Constantly check your review mirror for anything suspicious. Eleventh, at this moment I would like for you to look around the bar to see if you see anyone who may look shady or questionable. If you do, don't react abruptly or call attention to yourself. Here is some paper, just indicate on it the general direction of where they are seated and provide a description of how they are dressed, including the color of their shirt or jacket or both."

"John, I don't see anyone questionable."

"Good. Twelfth and the final recommendation Hans, during the course of the week, don't call me on company phones unless it is expressly company business. Only use public phones. In addition, we need to meet several times a week and it must be outside of the Clearstream building and not here at the hotel. Hans, there is one last thing. I assume you don't know how to fire a weapon, am I correct?"

"That isn't completely correct John. I do know how to fire a rifle and shotgun."

"Great, Hans. Have you ever fired a handgun?"

"No."

"Is there a gun club or firing range we can visit or join in Zurich?"

"Yes, it's approximately 10km out of Zurich, on the west side."

"Tomorrow after work, I will join you there."

"That is confirmed, John."

"Wonderful; is there anything else I should know Hans?"

"At this point John, nothing at all. If I remember something important, I will certainly write it down and contact you as soon as possible. I can't thank you enough for listening and being a friend."

"One last thing; how about having coffee together first thing tomorrow morning at the International Café, located around the corner from the Clearstream offices on Lowen Place?"

"What time, John?"

"How about 7 a.m.? The the café should not be too busy then."

"I will be there at seven, John."

11

What is our aim? Victory, victory at all costs, victory in spite of all terror;
Victory however long and hard the road may be.
Sir Winston Churchill

As soon as Style arrived back in his room, he started to compose an e-mail to DiSciascio. The e-mail was to the point:

DiSciascio:

Today I had an extremely important meeting with Hans Schroeder. He revealed and shared much valuable information. He substantiated with detailed facts, evidence of the existence of the Nazi gold and the missing Jewish accounts. He claims that there was never an actual fire in the late 1940s that supposedly destroyed all or most of the Swiss bank records containing many secret numbered accounts. Schroeder insists that most of the stolen money taken from the persecuted Jews is still on deposit.

He successfully managed to provide enough specific details on some individual accounts from memory and categorically recalled essential factors including their names and the number of family members sent to a particular concentration camp. In one instance, he remembered the exact amount that was transferred and then wired electronically into newly established Swiss bank accounts. He also was able to recall the exact dates of these particular transactions.

However, there is one thing he couldn't accomplish and that was to make copies or take photographs of any of the files. The reason is because at the time he discovered the missing accounts, he was actually looking for some other misplaced files and accidently discovered the missing Jewish records.

We unquestionably have an ally in Schroeder. He can definitely assist us on the inside. I haven't revealed my cover but I think he suspects something. When the occasion occurs, I will recruit him and explain my role. However, that probably will not happen for at least several more weeks.

Now that most all of the evidence is in, it appears there is no doubt that Hans Schroeder was the target of the car bombing. He's certainly aware of that fact and so am I.

As a precaution, I encouraged him to move his family out of Zurich to be with other family members in a more rural and much safer part of Switzerland. He agreed completely. Before dawn tomorrow morning, his wife and children are packing up and moving in with his wife's mother on the Swiss French border.

Tomorrow, Schroeder and I will start developing an operations contingency plan and develop a day-to-day tactical strategy.

At this point, I don't believe Ulrich Melmer suspects anything of me. Tomorrow morning I have another progress meeting with Melmer.

Please let me know as soon as possible about my idea of recruiting Schroeder.

Be safe,

Style

As soon as Style finished sending his report to DiSciascio, he decided it was time for dinner. This time instead of driving the Porsche, he elected to go for a walk. He walked out the front door of the hotel and across the street to the metro subway. He started to walk down the stairs when he suddenly glanced to his left and noticed that once more someone was following him. This time he decided to play dumb. He continued walking giving the impression he didn't care and remained focused, casually taking in the sights. He stopped to purchase a newspaper and a magazine at a newsstand. Then he pretended as if he was reading the newspaper and occasionally would take a quick look to confirm the man was still following him.

As he approached the tollbooth, at the last minute he chose not to board the tram but instead decided to return to the street level and take photographs of the Opera House and Congress Hall. The person following him was still at a distance but quite evident. When Style finally arrived at the Opera House, he took out of his pocket a small compact 35mm camera and started taking photographs of the Opera House and the Congress Hall.

Both buildings were splendid architectural wonders. Since it was starting to get late, the sun was fading. The long dark shadows provided an excellent contrasting background for the absolute white quarry marbled buildings of both the Opera House and Congress Hall.

Style wanted to give the impression that he knew something about photography. Carefully he would take photographs from different angles.

As he was snapping photographs, Style stopped a stranger and asked would she take a photograph of him with the Opera House in the background. She politely obliged. He thanked her and continued walking towards Lake Zurich. The purpose for all of the pretention and disguise was to try to maneuver into a position to take a photo of the person following him without creating a confrontation.

Finally, as he got closer to the water, he took both of his hands, held them up as if to frame a picture and started simulating taking photos. At the last minute, he took out his camera and begun taking several pictures in the direction of the person following him. Style checked to see the results and pretended as though nothing had happened.

He finished up with several more photographs of the lake, than decided, it was time to leave and get something to eat. He headed back toward the hotel and at the last minute chose to stop at a nearby café for a quick bite. In the meantime, the person following Style apparently decided he had had enough and was nowhere to be seen. When Style finished his lite meal, he returned to the hotel.

Anxiously, he started looking closely at the photos he had taken. There were several very clear photographs of the man who was following him. At this point, Style felt extremely confident that he hadn't aroused any suspicion or created a potential compromise. Immediately, he elected to upload the photographs onto his laptop and e-mail them to DiSciascio.

He explained in the body of the e-mail the circumstances as to why the photos were taken and the need to get a reasonably fast turn-around from the Counter Terrorism Center (CTC). He realized it was a stab in the dark but that these photos were the only material evidence of others involved, other than Ulrich Melmer. Included in his request to the lab at headquarters, was for the technicians to include as much detailed information on the person in the photographs. He requested a reply by morning, if possible. At last, he could call it a day. Once more, he reviewed his notes to make sure he was prepared for his early meeting with Hans Schroeder.

Before Style's retired, he prepared an outline using his detailed notes as a guide to make certain he didn't miss anything for tomorrow.

Morning came swiftly. It was very early, just before six a.m. but Style was

out of bed right away. The first thing he did was start up his computer. There was a response from DiSciascio:

Style,

Once more, great job.

The lab researches successfully managed to match the person in your photographs with a known notorious figure from Germany. There was no mistaking his identity. Since the mid-1980s, he has been involved with several radical organizations in Germany, Austria, Switzerland, and Netherlands with occasion to visit South Africa and Southeast Asia to initiate radical extremism. He does a convincing job when he gives speeches to large audiences. The rap sheet on him is extensive and disconcerting. His name is Karl Uber. Today, elements of the radical Right can be found throughout Western Europe with National Front organizations in nations such as England, Switzerland, France and Austria, to name just a few.

However, the recent rise of right-wing activity in Germany, as seen in the Republikaner Party within the system and the ever present–Nazi and skinhead groups on the fringes of legality, poses a unique set of questions given Germany's past.

There are very important questions for Germans to begin asking themselves. Is the right-wing activity in Germany at all reminiscent of the kind of fascist extremism that plagued that country over sixty years ago?

The Second World War didn't eliminate Nazism; it simply eliminated it as a mass-based organization working within the German political structure and turned it into a sub-cultural movement. In considering the historical evolution of post-war right-wing activity, one can more easily assess the current concern regarding the recent rise of the Right in Germany. During the years immediately following the war, the Allies set forth on a road of re-education and de-Nazification in Germany.

However, when they realized that they were ill equipped for re-education and that the country couldn't function properly if every member of the Nazi party was excluded from German society, these programs began to lose steam. As early as 1950 those who played an important role in 1945 politics were returned to their former duties, excluding high ranking Nazi officials, of course.

For the most part, these former Nazis were loyal to the new regime and didn't try to undermine it internally. On the other hand, a number of former Nazis found it impossible to reconcile themselves to German defeat and held steadfast to the concepts and goals of Nazism.

In the 1950s and early 1960s, those who felt sympathy for the Nazi cause began

meeting in unobtrusive places and producing internal newsletters. They rallied around the ideas of "law and order," release of political prisoners, and the protection of traditional German values, as well as expounding discontent with so called collaborationists such as Konrad Adenauer.

Within the system, views resembling those employed by the Nazis were heard from the leaders of legal parties such as the BHE, the German party, and occasionally from the far right conservatives in the CDU. However, the stigma of Nazism carried by most post-war Germans allowed these extremist elements little or no success. Eventually, the inability to reach a consensus regarding the direction and policies of these organizations caused further fragmentation, and the membership in these organizations declined.

In the late 1960s and early 1970s, a new set of situations emerged in Germany, as well as in Western Europe, making the formation of the so-called "New Right" possible. The increasing number of foreign immigrants, as well as the worldwide economic crisis of this period, sparked a renewed interest in right-wing activity. However, by the early 1970s those who had been youths in Hitler's Germany were growing older and became cautious, as well as disillusioned.

Furthermore, with the membership in neo-Nazi youth groups growing smaller, it appeared as if the extreme right was dying out with the generation of the Third Reich. Nevertheless, the influence of the "Nouvelle Droite" in France and the resurrection of the idea of the need for a "third road between capitalism and communism" paved the way for the rise of the New Right in Germany.

The leaders of this movement belonged almost exclusively to the postwar generation and had studied with the same teachers who had influenced their left-wing contemporaries. Common to almost all elements of the New Right was a European orientation and a concern for the natural environment.

Outwardly, they rejected the crude theories of racial superiority of the German people, though they still held on to racist beliefs by disguising them in a more socially acceptable manner. Furthermore, the New Right chose to loosen its ties to Germany's Nazi past and tried to manifest its ideas within the realm of mainstream conservatism.

That isn't to say that radicalism was ended, and this is seen in the fact that the 1970s and 1980s saw incidents of right-wing terrorism and violence including, for example, the murder of foreign workers in Nuremberg and the attacks against U.S. soldiers in Frankfurt in 1982.

In essence, since the 1970s the right-wing movement in Germany has been polarized, resulting in basically four categories of right-wing activity. To begin with, the moderate, conformist, disciplined right-wing works within the German political system and is composed of small parties such as the NPD, the Republicans, and the Deutsche Allianz. They consider themselves to be part of the nationalist conservative bourgeoisie, and remain loyal to Germany's democratic constitution.

This conformist sector of the right stands for law and order, anti-liberalism, and anti-socialism. Furthermore, it considers reunification as only being partial concerning what it considers to be unrecovered German territories east of the Oder-Neisse line. Increasingly, the moderates are coming to be seen as a melting pot for those who want to translate feelings of racism and fear into political action.

Thus, if they are to have any success, a complete break with Nazi symbols and rhetoric is imperative. The theoretical circle of the new right emerged in the1970s out of the right's attempt to develop a modern theoretical orientation out of the intellectual quarry of Weimar's conservative revolution.

It stands for a Third Way between capitalism and communism, and the belief that genetic and cultural factors must serve to prove national identity, racial segregation, and autonomy of the peoples. This is the intellectual arm of the right and it isn't cohesive. Instead, competing theory-circles have emerged. Ultimately, the theoretical circle aims at aligning with the moderate right and seeks to appeal to these conservatives, as well as to the unsatisfied and politically undecided.

The final two categories of right-wing groups, the neo-Nazis, and the National Democratic Organization (NDO) protest scene, differ from the first two groups in their blatant use of racially motivated violence combined with Nazi symbolism. For the most part, the neo-Nazis

are led by men of yesteryear, and are supported by relatively uneducated young adults hailing
from the lower echelon of society. They aren't able to provide a concrete political agenda and
prey on the willingness of their young recruits to use violence. Furthermore, they can be classified
as anti-bourgeois and they adhere to rigid Nazi fundamentalism.

The above report was assembled and furnished by our intelligence research group located at Langley. The following information is an intelligence report that I compiled and wanted you to be updated on all the necessary relative activity of the "Gang of Thieves."

In conclusion, the final sect of the German right wing organization is the current group,
National Democratic Organization (NDO). This group is by far the most radical, violent and
least predictable of the known consortium.

As you already know, within this group, there exists an inner closed circle group called "The
Gang of Thieves." They are extremely violent and literally willing to put their lives on the line for
their principles. Their type of activism appeals to intellectuals, skinheads, old school right wing
and involves the provocative use of Nazi symbolism. "The Gang of Thieves," are very capable of
attracting very young college radicals who openly express idealism and are easily persuaded by
men such as Ulrich Melmer and Karl Uber.

Through its use of technology (especially computer games), and its emphasis on reaching
children in schools or in youth groups, it often upsets local communities. Thus, it is primarily
through these factions, the neo-Nazis and the organized right wing protest scene, that the Right
threatens the majority culture.

As far as an actual threat from the Right is concerned, these groups are regarded as very
aggressive politically and have successfully managed to attract a lot of financial support and
notoriety. The post-reunification surge of nationalistic neo-Nazi activity can be interpreted as
manifestation of a cultural crisis attributed to the very liberalization of immigration policy and
tolerance by most European countries such as Germany, France and Great Britain, especially
toward the Middle East and Africa. The question remains:

Will Germany ever return to the days of late 1930s and the early 1940s of Nazi Fascism
and the Third Reich? Although some scholars contend that the Third Reich isn't just a skeleton
in the closet of German history. Without doubt, the rise of right-wing activity poses a true and
serious threat to German Democracy. The vast majority of scholars agree that the conditions
in Germany between 1918 and 1933 comprise a particular social, political, and psychological
phenomenon which will most likely not be repeated in the modern world.

Thus, in order to form a rational and relevant conclusion on the degree of threat posed by the right-wing movement in the 21st Century, it is helpful in comparison to assess the conditions surrounding Hitler's rise to power in the 1930s. We believe it isn't possible.

However, in the meantime, Karl Uber and Ulrich Melmer are very dangerous men and should be treated as such. Without any doubt, so is the "Gang of Thieves," of which Melmer and Uber are members. I think you realize by now, we are definitely dealing with a group of very ambitious extremists. They not only have extreme political views but also are dangerous and unpredictable in their actions. If anything, the group is looking for some more publicity and world attention.

Each day moving forward, I urge you to be extra cautious and vigilant. Never take anything for granted and be especially aware of most everything around you. In other words, be constantly looking over your shoulder.

Good luck with your meeting tomorrow morning with Hans Schroeder. Please continue with the excellent work.

Success...Be safe,

DiSciascio

12

I must study politics and war that my sons may have liberty to study mathematics and philoso-
phy. My sons ought to study mathematics and philosophy, geography,
natural history, naval architecture, navigation, commerce, and agriculture,
in order to give their children a right to study painting, poetry,
music, architecture, statuary, tapestry, and porcelain.
John Adams

Style was up, shaved and showered and out the door within minutes. Before leaving his room, he checked to make sure nothing was left behind. John arrived at the International Café well before 7 a.m. and ordered a cup of freshly brewed coffee and started reading the *London Financial Times* he had picked up previously in the lobby of the hotel. At the moment, Style was the only customer in the café. As always, he checked for any last minute messages in the sports section. He noticed right away, there was a disguised message in a soccer story, indicating that Al Qaeda and the National Democratic Organization (NDO) had been having discussions. No other details were reported. Obviously, the message was intended for the agents throughout Europe but more specifically, directed at the CIA field agents and MI6 agents in Germany and Switzerland. Within minutes, Hans Schroeder showed up.

Schroeder asked Style, "How did you sleep here last night?"

Style sarcastically replied, "Of course I slept extremely well Hans. I want to make sure I always have the very first cup of coffee. You should know me by now. Hans did your family manage to get packed and leave for your mother-in-law's farm early today?"

"Yes, they were packed and on their way before five o'clock."

"What kind of resistance did your wife and daughters create for you, when you explained what they had to do?"

"John, actually they were more understanding than I expected and very mature about the whole situation. I give them lots of credit. To reassure them, I further explained that I would join them shortly."

"That is outstanding Hans, now we can focus on your safety going forward. Now, we both need to pretend that we know nothing at all. You are totally ignorant of anything having to do with Nazi gold and the missing Jewish accounts. Do you understood, Hans?"

"Yes I do John, absolutely."

"I suspect that you, Hans, certainly more than me, will be followed every time you leave the Clearstream building. Remember what I said last night about being extra vigilant, cautious and aware of everything going on around you."

"Yes, I certainly will John."

"Also, please remember not to call me from your office phone for any reason, unless it's directly related to work. Certainly, if there is an emergency, call me Hans. Do you have anything to add or perhaps you have some questions?"

"No, not yet but I know I will John. I can tell you I'm nervous and definitely concerned for my life."

"Hans, that is totally understandable. Please keep in mind, we are a team."

"I realize that now John."

"Tonight, remember we will meet at the Zurich firing range at 7:30 p.m.

Also, don't drive your car. Take public transportation or option for a taxi."

"Yes, I will meet you there at 7:30pm John."

"Before I forget Hans, I have a status contract meeting with Ulrich Melmer as soon as I get into the office this morning. Will you be attending Hans?"

"Yes, I know, I will be there John."

"Excellent. See you shortly Hans."

They both went their separate ways. As soon as Style arrived at the Clearstream office, he went directly to the office of Ulrich Melmer. Ulrich was seated in his large executive chair, when Style knocked on the door.

"Come in please," replied Melmer.

As soon as John Style entered, Hans Schroeder appeared within a few seconds. They both sat down and greeted each other. Melmer acknowledged both Style and Schroeder with standard pleasantries.

Melmer started the meeting off directly by apologizing for leaving the office Friday morning when the bomb went off. He further explained that he was extremely frightened and he panicked. After he arrived home, he realized the mistake he had made and it was simply too late to return to the Clearstream offices. His wife convinced him the best thing to do was to stay home and focus on trying to relax. She also encouraged Melmer to enjoy the weekend and to go skiing in the mountains and be refreshed to return to the office Monday morning.

Both Hans Schroeder and John Style reacted positively and simply said, not a problem. Transiently the conversation moved on to the DeSoto Industries financial contracts. The meeting lasted for several hours, and Melmer had lunch delivered. Later in the afternoon, they decided to take a break for the day and each left going in different directions.

Style returned to his office, as did Schroeder. It was quite apparent to Style, that Melmer wasn't focused on negotiating the financial agreements and business matters because he continued making the same mistakes and often repeated himself. This behavior of Melmer's was without doubt unique and very unusual.

John Style began to review his notes and at the same time, questioned himself about Melmer's state of mind. He started to re-think; perhaps Melmer wasn't responsible for the bombing and could be totally innocent and not involved. Melmer's behavior was both baffling and difficult to explain. On the other hand, Melmer could be just an actor giving a masterful performance. Style decided the best thing to do was to provide a detailed analysis and his personal observations to allow a psychological profiler to correctly determine whether Melmer was acting or telling the truth. Obviously, the remote analysis could be entirely incorrect. However, for now this was the only option available. Style decided he would send his complete observations and analysis later in the evening, when he compiled his evening report to DiSciascio.

━ ━

It was late, just before ten, Style and Schroeder spent over two hours at the shooting range. They both practiced and tried different caliber weapons, from .38 Specials, 9mm to .45 ACP. Surprisingly Schroeder did a wonderful job learning to shoot. This was his first time at a handgun range. He consistently was on target, shot with total steadiness and confidence. At one point Style turned to Schroeder to remark, "You know Hans you would be an ideal candidate to join my small arms shooting team back home."

In a confident and humorous manner, Schroeder replies, "I'm ready for Wyatt Earp———or John Wayne."

Style adds, "You can become a member any time you please, Hans."

"Well John, you didn't shoot too bad either, almost perfect scores and it didn't matter what weapon you fired."

"Hans, I give my dad all the credit, from all the years we practiced together in Montana. It all started when I was about eight years of age, my dad would take us out to Bozeman, Montana. There was a very large outdoor shooting range. After shooting on the range, we would literally go out into the deepest part of the forest looking for remote locations. We would search until we found an abandoned site and then set up targets. Then we would shoot our rifles and handguns until our fingers and shoulders had blisters. As a result, sometimes we managed to get black & blue on shoulders from all of the practice. Once we were finished shooting, we would go to one of the beautiful streams or rivers and go fly fishing to relax. My dad was terrific to my sister and me. One day, I will introduce you to my family Hans. They are tremendous parents."

"You know John, this sounds great to me. It is getting late. I will order two taxis. When I was a kid, I used to watch all those American cowboy movies and thought what a wonderful and wild way to live. It is easy now to understand how and why you are such a good marksman."

"Thank you Hans, I'll take that as a compliment. Yes, my mom and dad were the very best to my sister and I. There was nothing more important to them than the family."

Later, back at the hotel and just after opening his e-mail he discovered a

top-secret message had arrived from Langley.

It read:

TOP SECRET AND URGENT

As most of you are aware we received reliable information from an informed source, that the German radical right wing group, National Democratic Organization (NDO) and Al Qaeda are about to form an alliance. The purpose is obvious and as a result, all CIA field agents throughout the world are being notified. Despite the ideological differences between the two groups, there are several reasons for the sudden shift:

First and most paramount, by joining forces they now have an exceptional large number of radical terrorist, which can be more strategically positioned around the western world to create more terrorists activity, havoc and destruction.

Second, recently a major U.S. Defense Department sub-contractor was held-up and robbed of new electronic warfare (EW) technology. Electronic war technology (EW) is relatively new and has evolved from traditional forms like RF communications and radar jamming, but also the relatively new discipline of cyber warfare is designed to protect U.S. and allied computers and attack and disable enemy computers along with their cloud based data networks. Furthermore, a new term is cropping up———spectrum warfare, which includes traditional EW, but adds optical warfare, navigation warfare, and cyber warfare. The intent is to not only use RF transmitters to jam enemy radar and communications, but also insert viruses and other destructive computer code into enemy systems to spoof or disable them. At this point, we feel confident, the thieves aren't familiar enough with Electronic Warfare (EW) technology to understand completely what they now possess. As a result, we are convinced and highly assured the thieves don't technically appreciate the importance of what they have and couldn't possibly employ or utilize any aspect of the weapons in their hands.

Third, our informant provided enough material evidence to show the perpetrators of the U.S. Defense Department sub-contractor break-in and theft were committed by several people associated with the National Democratic Organization (NDO).

Fourth, Al Qaeda has successfully evolved into a franchise organization under the overall leadership of Ayman al-Zawahiri, making the terrorist organization even more dangerous and more difficult to track. Since 9/11, Al Qaeda is becoming more decentralized its hierarchical cell structure and improved financing methods, attack approaches and communication techniques to counter new intelligence efforts.

The group is responsible for four times as many terrorist attacks today as it was before the Sept. 11, 2001, attacks. Al Qaeda is still aiming to establish an Islamic caliphate, and is establishing training camps around the world toward that end.

Fifth, Al Qaeda funding remains a phenomenal mystery. The formal alliance between National Democratic Organization (NDO) and Al Qaeda will certainly enhance the financial picture for both radical organizations.

Respectfully submitted

CIA Headquarters Langley

Immediately after reading his messages, Style submitted his report on his meeting with Ulrich Melmer and Hans Schroeder.

13

If you will not fight for the right when you can easily win without bloodshed;
if you will not fight when your victory will be sure and not too costly;
you may come to the moment when you will have to fight with all
the odds against you and only a precarious chance of survival.
There may even be a worse case. You may have to fight when there is no
hope of victory, because it is better to perish than to live as slaves.
Winston Churchill

DUBAI, UNITED ARAB EMIRATES

As part of an agreement that John Style managed to obtain with Bryan Nogaki, Assistant Director of Global Operation, Style would continue competing on the ATP professional tennis tournament circuit for at least the next 12 to 24 months. Before he left for field ops training at the Farm, he had confirmed his commitment to play at the Dubai Duty Free Tennis Championships, United Arab Emirates. Most of the top players in the world were scheduled to compete in the 32 man draw, including the top seeds, Roger Federer (Switzerland), Novak Djokovic (Serbia), Raphael Nadal (Spain), Andy Murray (Great Britain), Jaka Bombac (Slovenia), Tomas Berdych (Czech Republic), and Juan Martin Del Portro (Argentina). John Style managed to secure a number eight seed, primarily because of the success he had at the recent Australian Open. Total prize money for the tournament is just under three million dollars and approximately $600,000 going to the singles winner, plus 500 World Tour ATP points. While Style was in Zurich, just about every day he would go to the gym to stay in shape and he also managed to play tennis at least five days a week at a private indoor tennis club in the northern part of Zurich. The recent time off from tournament play allowed his shoulder and knee to improve dramatically.

Before leaving Zurich, Style told Ulrich Melmer and Hans Schroeder that he had to travel to the Middle East very unexpectedly to resolve some management consulting issues.

Ulrich seemed almost relieved and expressed to Style to have a prosperous trip as he looked forward to getting together sometime early next week.

At the same time, he also apologized to Zosa that he might be late getting back into Zurich on Friday evening. However, he would do everything possible to attend her play, hopefully on time. Zosa said she understood, but told John to please come no matter what day or time he arrived back in Zurich. At this point, Style was well aware of his need to continue with his cover and to do well at the ATP tennis tournaments.

Prior to leaving Zurich, Style received a tip from another field agent in Germany that an Islamic informant, wanted to meet to discuss extremely valuable information. Coincidently, he specifically mentioned he was going to be in Dubai the same day Duty Free Tennis Championships started. Since Style had a bye the first day, he arranged to meet with the informant that evening at the Dubai International Airport Hotel. He needed backup and notified DiSciascio as soon as possible. Within 30 minutes, he was notified that backup would be available. Arrangements were made to meet with the backup in the men's room of the lobby of the Dubai International Hotel at 7:30 p.m. The scheduled meeting with the unknown informant was for 8 p.m. in the Safar cocktail lounge, of the airport hotel. Just prior to leaving his hotel room at the Duty Free Tennis Tournament, located approximately 20 miles from the Dubai International Airport Hotel, Style received an urgent follow-up message from DiSciascio.

Style:

We managed to get the identity of the now known informant. His name is Aahil Al Hazmi, extremely dangerous and borderline chronic liar. Once before he attempted to be an informant for us in Cairo, Egypt but changed his mind at the last minute and bailed out, leaving us in very awkward position. Preliminary information seems to suggest he knows of some valuable intelligence.

Apparently, he mentioned to one of our contacts in Munich, he knew the whereabouts of planned meetings between National Democratic Organization (NDO) and Al Qaeda. Plus, he was aware of the European cities targeted to be bombed and the exact location of where the bombs will be placed. Last thing, he contends the report contains pertinent details on how Al Qaeda is getting funded.

He expects to receive something around ninety thousand to hundred twenty-five thousand dollars cash in exchange for the information he possesses. Style, you can pick up the cash at the nearby U.S. Embassy, in Dubai. Incidentally, the U.S. Embassy is located on Al Twar Road, not too far from the Dubai International Hotel.

Before considering any payment, obtain from Aahil Al Hazmi what is called teaser intelligence information that can be verified as to its legitimacy. He'll anticipate and should understand your excusing yourself to make a phone call. Do this immediately while you are in discussions.

After you obtain confirmation that the document is valid and the information appears acceptable, you must feel satisfied the intelligence is reliable, pay Al Hazmi. However, don't give Hazmi more than one hundred thousand dollars and then leave right away. After you depart the hotel, call Base Ops instantly.

Base Ops will be able to establish whether the remaining information Al Hazmi

provided is accurate and trustworthy. Finally, Al Hazmi contends he has met the NDO leader Ulrich Melmer. Your backup's name is Dave Robie, Chief Middle Eastern field agent. He'll meet you on time at seven thirty. Everything confirmed. Be extremely careful.

Success

DiSciascio

Style had two hours before he was to meet with his backup, Dave Robie, Senior Case Officer, Middle East. He was beginning to feel uptight and started to sweat. This lonely anxious feeling, reminded him of waiting to walk into a large crowded tennis stadium to play an important tennis match. His stomach turned into knots, he could hardly swallow, his throat would be parched dry and his knees weak and he would begin to question himself. The obvious difference however, was that this was life and death. He kept on reminding himself, he was prepared. In addition, he would repeat to himself the CIA field agent motto, I'm a member of the greatest team, I depend on the team, I concede, etc., etc., etc., etc., etc., over and over again. Style picked-up the cash he needed at the U.S. Embassy and headed directly to the Dubai International Airport Hotel. Once he arrived, he casually walked around the beautiful lobby. At 7:30 p.m., Style headed straight to the lobby men's room. He entered cautiously. There was only one other person that Style could see. The man was dressed in a business suite washing his hands standing at the sink. The stranger turned slowly around and in a low voice he introduced himself, "John Style, I'm Dave Robie." His accent was undeniable from New York. After exchanging a few fine points, they swiftly worked out the logistics.

Right away, Style left and walked into the Safar cocktail lounge, took a seat not too far from the bar and ordered a drink. There were at least seven Arabic men in the bar at the time all dressed in their traditional tharwb or long white robe. There were no women whatsoever. Suddenly it occurred to Style women were not welcome in the bars in Dubai. Style learned passingly that the tharwb is the standard Arabic word for robe and is customary Arabian clothing for men.

Since he was the only person in the cocktail bar dressed in a Western business suit, he was obvious and could be approached without difficulty. Within minutes, a middle-aged man with very dark skin sat down alongside Style. He also was wearing a white tharwb.

"Mr. Style, my name is Aahil Al Hazmi and I believe you have something for me?" Style turned to the informant and asked, "Are you alone Mr. Al Hazmi?"

"Yes, absolutely I'm alone."

"Mr. Al Hazmi, as you know I would like to see some evidence of the information you are willing to sell to us."

"Of course, here are just ten pages of my valuable information. I will provide the remainder as soon as you verified the accuracy and reliability of the document."

"Mr. Al Hazmi, please excuse me. I will return at once"

"Take your time Mr. Style."

No sooner had Style got to the small alcove just outside the cocktail lounge to make a phone call that all hell broke loose. Immediately, Style dropped to the floor to take cover behind a large studio couch. Everyone in the lobby of the hotel started running in panic. Three Arabic men dressed in tharwbs, walked in to the bar, each carrying an AK-47, and opened fire. Style and Robie each returned fire from their 9mm Sig Sauer's. Both of their weapons were no match against the firepower of the AK-47. However, individually Style and Robie got off a full clip (15 rounds) and managed to down two of the assassins. One assassin was dead. The other managed to get back on his feet and tried to continue shooting. Within seconds, he was hit several more times, finally he collapsed dead. The third hit man escaped out the front door of the hotel to a waiting van. Before escaping, he successfully picked-up the brief case containing the files of information belonging to the informant Al Hazmi. All the men who were in the cocktail lounge were slaughtered by the sheer power of the 7.62X39mm size rounds. It seems every wine and liquor bottle was shattered along with hundreds of glasses. Glass, splinters of wood, fragmented granite and aluminum furniture was embedded in all the walls, along with blood splatter everywhere. All the tables and chairs were destroyed and lying in pieces. The stench of fresh human blood and flesh was over-whelming. There were bodies everywhere. Both Robie and Style attempted to provide aid, but it was too late for all of the victims. In the distance, they could hear the sound of ambulances and sirens. Instantly, both realized that had to leave fast, especially before the Dubai police showed up and to avoid an international incident. Style started to realize as they were fleeing from the scene, eleven people were just shot dead in an instant, including the bartender. He also suddenly comprehended how fortunate he and Robie were. No injuries or wounds and in one piece.

Robie turned to Style and said, "We are luckiest damn bastards in the world."

"Yes, we are without doubt," replied Style.

Directly, Robie dropped off Style at the Dubai International Tennis Tournament Hotel. At this juncture, food was the last thing on Style's mind. He was emotionally exhausted and physically drained. Since his match wasn't until late in the morning, he decided he would wake up early and have a good breakfast. However, he needed to prepare a complete report and send it off to DiSciascio tonight without delay. Once more, he understood how fortunate he and Robie were tonight.

Style removed the ten-page document from his brief case that was given to him by the murdered informant. There were ten pages randomly removed from the original file. The pages were not in any particular order. After carefully reviewing all of the pages, Style concluded that some of the information would not help at all. However, there were several pages with yesterday's date on them that indicates that the National Democratic Organization (NDO) and Al Qaeda both depend substantially on receiving their financial support from the Swiss bank accounts at Clearstream. This is the first solid lead that clearly links all of the terrorist groups directly with receiving financial assistance from the Swiss banks. There was one paragraph that specifically states who is receiving what funds and how often they receive money. There is no denying that the wealth and money taken from the poor Jews on their way to the concentration camps is indeed this blood money. He assembled all of the facts and wrote an exhausting account of tonight's terrorist attack at the Dubai International Airport. Immediately, he e-mailed the top-secret message to DiSciascio.

He decided to call it a night and finally retired at around eleven.

14

The patriot volunteer, fighting for country and his rights,
makes the most reliable soldier on earth.
Thomas J. Jackson

DUBAI, UNITED ARAB EMIRATES
Duty Free Tennis Championships
Style's first round match was scheduled Tuesday morning at eleven, against one of the upcoming new young talented players from Croatia. Style successfully managed to win the match in straight sets, 6-2 and 7-5. He also won the second round match on Wednesday in three sets, but lost today in the quarterfinals to the eventual winner Roger Federer.

Despite the fact that Style had his hands full playing in the tournament, he managed to meet again with agent Robie to discuss the recent events, review all of the sudden activity and the obvious chatter between National Democratic Organization (NDO) and Al Qaeda.

According to Robie, security has been tightened throughout Dubai, Middle East and North Africa because of all the apparent chatter on the web. Obviously, these unsettling reports have created distractions for the tennis players competing in Dubai. Robie further amplified that major cities in Yemen have been put on high alert. As a direct result of

Yemeni-gathered intelligence that Al Qaeda in the Arab Peninsula was planning major attacks and disruption any day. Robie and Style were able to discuss in detail the current terror alerts which have prompted the closure of several United States embassies due to intercepted conversations between Ayman al-Zawahri and several of his field Lieutenants.

Style shared his information with Robie regarding the random ten pages given to him by the slain informant. Robie's first response was, "Do you think Style you were to be included in the terrorists attacks last night?"

"Absolutely, I was just damn fortunate to have walked out of the bar ten seconds earlier. Otherwise, I would be chopped meat. Robie, I want to thank you for being there and helping. You did a great job and I want you to know I told DiSciascio that fact in my report last night."

"Yes, I know Style; DiSciascio has already congratulated both of us in an e-mail I received about an hour ago. You probably have the same message waiting for you when you return to your room."

"Hopefully I can catch the last flight to Zurich tonight."

"Why are you so anxious to leave Dubai, Style...have a heavy date in Zurich?"

"Someday Robie, I'll share that story with you."

"Style, the next time we get together, I will expect you to explain your story in detail."

"What about all of the chatter that I hear has been going on and is this at all related to what happened last night?"

"I don't think so, Style. The majority of the chatter has been primarily focused on establishing which major European cities have been selected as targets to plant car bombs.

"Are you positive, Robie?"

"Yes, absolutely, Robie further explained to Style, initially the chatter was electronically picked up over a week ago ordering the leader of Al Qaeda's affiliate in Yemen to carry out an unspecified attack and to coordinate their strikes simultaneously with the National Democratic Organization in major European cities. Their intent is quite obvious - to create havoc and panic throughout all Europe and the Middle East."

Style asked Robie, "Do you know what European cities are being targeted?"

"At this time, I don't know. I could only speculate on where," said Robie. "My best guess would be an easy target like London, Paris or Brussels. These cities are laidback and easy targets because they are very open, and essentially terrorists can move quite freely. To add credibility to the conjecture, the head of Britain's MI5 Security Service said recently there remained a serious risk of a lethal attack taking place in London and Paris."

Style adds, "It is just too damn bad we couldn't get the rest of that report last night. Supposedly, it listed several of the major cities in Europe targeted for bombing by Al Qaeda and the National Democratic Organization (NDO). In fact, the lists contained the exact physical locations of where the bombs were to be placed."

"My God, Style, our timing was all screwed up."

"Are you kidding me you SOB, Robie? My timing was near perfect."

"I know, I know, I'm just giving you a hard time, Style."

"Before I forget, let me finish what I was saying earlier about targets, Style."

"OK, continue."

Robie at once adds, "The Eiffel Tower and the surrounding Champ de Mars Park were briefly evacuated this week because of a bomb alert, the fourth such alert in the Paris region in as many weeks, but a search turned up nothing. Most European cities are getting paranoid and it seems people are constantly looking over their shoulder and are distrusting of everyone. Their fear is justified."

"I have straightforward knowledge," said Style, "that the French Interior Minister, a short time ago, warned France that it faced a real terrorism threat due to a backlash from Al Qaeda militants in North Africa, with fears growing of an attack from home-grown cells within French borders. As a direct result of heightened concern, the American government is making available pre-cautionary measures for Americans to consider while vacationing in Europe. Is that correct Robie?"

"Yes, Style. Just yesterday as a follow-up, the U.S. State Department made available some guidelines and advice. Currently, information suggests that Al Qaeda and affiliated organizations continue to plan terrorist attacks, targeting American tourist. U.S. citizens are reminded of the potential for terrorists to attack public transportation systems and other tourist infrastructure. Terrorists have targeted and attacked subway and rail systems, as well as aviation and maritime services. U.S. citizens should take every precaution to be aware of their surroundings and to adopt appropriate safety measures to protect themselves when traveling in Europe and the Middle East."

Style observed, "We need to remind ourselves over and over again that over 3000 people died that fateful day, September 11, 2001, when the World Trade Center and the Pentagon were targeted by Al Qaeda. There is a high probability that it will happen again. Perhaps not on the same scale, but nevertheless, we remain straightforward easy targets for terrorism. Such is the nature of revenge that this religious war will never be won, but instead will be fought for as long as there are people with revenge in their hearts and they simply can't accept other religious beliefs, especially on the same level."

Robie further amplified, "there has been a wider travel warning for Americans and the State Department has ordered non-emergency U.S. government staff to leave Yemen and other Arab states."

"It appears the Middle East and all of North Africa is about to explode", said Style.

Robie suddenly interjected, "absolutely! "Look what is happening with our closest ally Egypt. The entire country is upside down. Christians are being murdered by the Moslem Brotherhood all over Cairo and in the outlining cities, churches are being rampaged, looted and burned to the ground. The quicker we can put an arm around National Democratic Organization, the better off we will be. As far as the Middle East is concerned, that is going to be an entirely different problem."

"The State Department has no answers at this point," said Robie.

Style adds, "Who do you trust? We send a billion dollars in aid to both Egypt and Pakistan and we are no better off."

"Style, I understand you are in the process of unearthing material proof how radical terrorism is getting their funding. Is that a fair observation and question?"

"Yes, that is correct, Robie. We are definitely headed in the right direction and hopefully when I return to Zurich tonight, we can finish putting the puzzle together."

"When do you expect to return to Zurich, Style?"

"Definitely tonight as I said earlier; I hope as soon as I pick up my check for getting to the quarter finals."

"How much is the check worth, Style?"

"I believe the check should be around one hundred twenty-five thousand dollars."

"Wow." responds Robie. "By the way, I watched your match today against Federer. You played extremely well and pushed him to a third set."

"Yes, I almost beat him; well, not exactly. I was exhausted and tired and that was reflected in the final third set score, 6-2. That sounds like I'm making excuses. Frankly, I know I couldn't beat him. Federer is a great champion and I personally feel he's the best tennis player ever to walk on to a tennis court. I have the greatest respect for him. He's truly a wonderful ambassador for the tennis profession."

"Are you serious, John?"

"Yes, absolutely; I say that without any reservations."

"Well, Style, I enjoyed meeting with you and having our brief discussion. Be careful and I look forward to seeing you shortly."

"Thanks again, Robie, for your great backup and support. Success and remain safe."

As soon as Style picked-up his ATP tournament check from the treasurer of the professional tour, one of the last things he needed to do was confirm his upcoming schedule with the ATP operations center. He promptly acknowledged he was scheduled to play the Grand Prix Hassan II, in Casablanca, Morocco in approximately a month's time, followed by the Monte Carlo Rolex Masters held in Monte Carlo, Monaco, then the Barcelona Open Banc Sabadell located in Barcelona, Spain, leading up to the French Open held at Roland Garros, Paris, France. He realized his tennis schedule was going to get extremely busy the next few months.

He booked the last flight on Emirates Air Lines out of Dubai International Airport, United Arab Emirates, to Zürich-Kloten Airport, Zurich, Switzerland. Flight time should be approximately seven hours, allowing Style plenty of time to rest and make his planned date with Zosa.

15

Good things come to those who work their asses
off and never give up Imagine there's no countries it isn't
hard to do, nothing to kill or die for and no religion too,
imagine all the people live life in peace
John Lennon

TALIAN ALPS

In the meantime, Ulrich Melmer organized an important meeting with the faction group Al-Zawa Europe, representing World Al Qaeda. The major get-together was set for late evening, at a remote location in the southern part of Switzerland, near the Italian Alps. Most of the National Democratic Organization (NDO) committee members, representing all of the European countries would be in attendance.

Much earlier in the day, Melmer and Karl Uber met to develop a preliminary outline strategy for their portion of the presentations. Their goals for this very important summit were to introduce some philosophical and strategic rethinking on how to expand operations into more countries around the world, and also to dramatically improve how they could recruit more terrorists, possibly jointly. The primary focus emphasized recruiting engineering talent.

Both NDO and Al Qaeda have recognized that they had to change the manor of their aggressiveness when they have successfully infiltrated a country. Al Qaeda in particular realized its fatal mistakes in Iraq during the war. They alienated the Iraqi people, who turned against the group that had killed so many civilians and imposed severe Islamist rule.

Also on the agenda to discuss were the recent successes in Syria. There were more Al Qaeda-allied factions groups pushing into different regions of Syria creating havoc and turmoil. They successfully managed to have most of the world question the Bashar al-Assad regime on their use of chemical weapons. It was quite apparent from the beginning of the civil war in Syria that Al Qaeda would make it appear that al-Assad was entirely responsible for initiating the use of chemical weapons against his own people, when in fact it was Al Qaeda. This new and very successful type of strategy would be presented and discussed at the conference, along with the need for financing and establishing a softer, warm and fuzzy image, endearing more people in infiltrated countries and, most critical, the sharing of intelligence.

A major focus of the meeting was Al Qaeda and NDO's long term and overall theme for the conference, "Strategy to the Year 2020."
There were five major points emphasized:

1. Trigger and aggravate the United States and the West into attacking a Muslim country by staging a substantial or string of attacks on major United States cities that result in massive civilian casualties and substantial property damage, similar to the September 11, 2001 attack.

2. Provoke and inflame local resistance to occupying forces.

3. Expand the conflict to neighboring countries, and engage the United States and its allies in a long war of attrition.

4. Convert Al Qaeda into an exact philosophical ideology and set of operating standards that can be loosely franchised in most other countries without requiring direct command and control, and via these franchises incite attacks against the United States, Great Britain and countries allied with the United States and the United Kingdom, until they withdraw from the conflict, as

happened with the Madrid train bombings, but which didn't have the same effect with the London bombings.

5. The United States economic system will enviably falter or even collapse by the year 2020 under the tremendous strain of multiple engagements in too many countries around the world, making the worldwide economic system which is dependent on the United States also collapse leading to global political instability, which in turn leads to a global jihad led by al-Qaeda and a Wahhabi Caliphate will then be installed across the world following the collapse of the U.S. and the rest of the Western world countries.

The financing portion of the conference was held in a private meeting much later in the evening. In fact, there were just two people present, NDO leader Ulrich Melmer and Abu Alouni, major spokesperson and head of operations for Al Qaeda, Europe. The two men discussed the history of the financials of both organizations and what had to be done to expand further income to support terrorist's activities. Of course, both at once acknowledged some of the history in the initial financing for Al Qaeda and NDO going back to the 1990s. Some of the funding came directly from the personal wealth of Osama bin Laden. Soon thereafter, Clearstream Finance and Bank Limited, along with SFINMA, Switzerland's largest and most successful banking companies, stepped in and became the predominant source of funding by far and the largest source of revenue for worldwide terrorism. Although, there was some speculation that funding was originated in Kuwait and Saudi Arabia, eventually that was later proven completely wrong.

Furthermore, the heroin trade was a major source of revenue for world terrorism for a short period of time, lasting from 1998 to approximately 2001. Interestingly enough, a supposed WikiLeaks released memo that originated from the White House and the Secretary of State's office, proclaimed that the primary source of funding of Sunni terrorist groups worldwide was from a wealthy source in Saudi Arabia.

Abu Alouni turned to Ulrich Melmer and observed, "If only those idiots in Washington knew the true facts, they would be absolutely amazed and feel rather stupid."

Ulrich chuckled and added, "You are absolutely correct, Abu."

"How long will the existing funds last, Ulrich?"

"At the present run rate of expenditures, I would estimate another twenty years."

"By the way, how much money is in all of the Clearstream accounts that is to be used for our peaceful activities?"

"As of yesterday, when I left Zurich, there was approximately 85 billion U.S. dollars.

Now that makes me feel real comfortable and confident that we will easily achieve our 2020 year goals," said Alouni.

"Absolutely, without any question Abu. Once the United States economic system fails by 2020 and the rest of the world begins to tumble financially, we will be in an excellent position to start a global jihad and take advantage of the world chaos."

"Abu, I would like to complement you and all of Al Qaeda for doing such a masterful job in creating absolute turmoil in Syria. The Whitehouse in Washington, D.C., is totally confused and now the British won't provide any type of support, making the U.S. go it alone. You magnificently succeeded to convince most of the Western world that the Bashar al-Assad regime was exclusively responsible for the use of chemical weapons."

"Ulrich, I distinctly remember the United States televised debates from the United States Capital. How foolish they all looked."

"Yes, you are correct," added Ulrich. "How about President Obama, making all those stupid remarks about the Bashar al-Assad regime? Just how naïve is he? Then, denying he said anything about establishing a red-line. The man must be smoking something stronger than cigarettes, when he takes does brief walks outside in the garden. What an ego."

"The American press treats Obama like some type of god and continue to be his biggest promoter and they don't even realize or recognize it," said Alouni.

"You are absolutely right, Alouni. There is no doubt, we accomplished our mission in Syria."

Ulrich boasts, "I just wonder how foolish the United States' Central Intelligence Agency feels today. Supposedly the CIA is the most powerful spy agency and yet it has gone awry, looking absolutely stupid Abu."

"They are total ass holes. I will bet they are trying to cover their tracks today, Ulrich."

"Let's get back on track and finish, Abu. What do you think of my proposed idea of establishing a more moderate, softer, warm and fuzzy image, attracting more people once we infiltrate a country?"

"As you know, I don't have autonomous authority to make major decisions. However, I will tell you I support the proposal without any reservation. When I return to Pakistan tomorrow, I will recommend adopting your suggestions. Further, I anticipate all of Al Qaeda will agree in principle."

"Alouni, I have one more observation and this will be my last point. Both our organizations need to do a better job of intelligence communications on a worldwide basis."

"Once more, Ulrich, I also agree with your statement for creating a strategic plan of intelligence sharing. The more critical and timely intelligence information we can mutually share, the less likely we fail. Again, I will highly recommend all of your ideas. Although, we certainly come from radically different cultures, we both have identified who our enemies are."

"Yes, without any question Abu, it's the Jews and Christians in the West. They all are Infidels."

"But, we should not forget the greatest enemy, Ulrich: capitalism."

"We are definitely on the right path in destroying everything having to do with capitalism and democracy, Alouni. When I return to Zurich tomorrow morning, I will send you a complete copy of our presentation and copies of our financial discussions."

"Wonderful, Ulrich. I will also send you all of our ideas and plans, as well. In addition, may I suggest that we have a conference call every ten days or at least every two weeks?"

"That is a great idea my friend Abu. Let me first e-mail you a very secure telephone number at our corporate offices in Zurich. I can assure you it is totally protected and clean for absolute privacy."

"The one thing that you don't have to be concerned about or worried over is the Central Intelligence Agency's tapping your phone lines," Abu confirms.

"Abu, you are right. That is one thing we don't even think about."

"Well, I think we had a very successful meeting Ulrich. I look forward to our discussions in the coming weeks and months."

"Have a safe trip back to Pakistan my friend."

16

*If we desire to secure peace, one of the most
powerful instruments of our rising prosperity,
it must be known that we are at all times ready for war.*
George Washington

ZURICH, SWITZERLAND

When Style arrived back in Zurich, it was very early in the morning and the sun was just beginning to rise. He caught a taxi at the airport and immediately headed back to the Park Hyatt Hotel. The hotel managed to make available the same suite he had previously. At the last minute, he decided to take a warm relaxing bath. While he was bathing, he started to think about having to live a double life and how complicated it makes living day to day. He couldn't wait for the time to come when he could be honest with himself and others. He certainly was justified in having this conflict and had a tremendous fear of accidently revealing his true identity or, worse yet, perhaps someone else would uncover his true identity prematurely. Style thought of this problem every day.

In Style's daily report to DiSciascio, he specifically mentioned he would tell Hans Schroeder the whole story either next week or perhaps over the weekend. The sooner DiSciascio gave the green light to have open discussions with Schroeder, the better. Then it would be more beneficial to contact Schroeder as quickly as possible. By confiding in someone he could trust, at least then he would have an ally to facilitate the investigation to a higher level. Time was of the essence. So far, the investigation had gone extremely well and Style wanted it to remain that way.

As he put on a bathrobe, he realized he hadn't seen Zosa for a long time. There is no doubt he was getting anxious to see her again. Naturally, he would love to share his tennis success but he realized it would cause too many problems, especially for the team. Style reminded himself often of the CIA team motto's significance and its importance. *"I'm a member of the greatest team, I depend on the team, I concede to it and forego for it, because the team, not the individual, is the supreme winner."* It's a total team commitment.

Prior to leaving for the tennis tournament in Dubai, United Arab Emirates, Style had an important meeting with Ulrich Melmer and Hans Schroeder. The meeting was confounded by Melmer's inability to remain focused, talking in circles not making sense, often repeating and slurring his words. Melmer's behavior was unique and strange. DiSciascio submitted Style's concerns to a staff psychological profiler who concluded the following in a report:

Style:

First, let me congratulate you on a very successful trip to Dubai. Although, we didn't secure the entire document, we did, however, successfully manage to put together a comprehensive picture and extrapolate very revealing information. The ten pages that were given to you from Aahil Al Hazmi, allowed the lab to put pieces together. There were a number of substantial facts revealed in the ten pages alone. Just the paper and the ink furnished a trail of information. We also learned of the identity of the two terrorists killed in the shootout.

Second, as a direct result of this report, we managed to do additional follow-up and nabbed two potential bombers just outside the city of Brussels. Apparently, their target was the large Museum of Natural Sciences and the Museum of Fine Arts in downtown Brussels. The intent was for the bomb to go off Sunday afternoon when both museums are at their busiest. Fortunately, the terrorists were caught in the act of assembling a very powerful bomb, therefore one hundred lives were saved.

Third, I already extended to Dave Robie an excellent job well done and I would like to offer you, Style, my personal congratulations for an excellent job accomplished.

In response to a previous request, I would like to offer the following synopsis compiled by our team of professional staff psychological profilers:

One of your concerns was whether Ulrich Melmer was acting or telling the truth in your most recent meeting with him and Schroeder. Let me first give you some background informa-tion on how profiling works.

The process of psychological profiling began over a century ago, but was first directly used by the CIA as a reliable method in mid 1950s. Investigators discovered through research and intriguing patterns, similarities between criminal's behaviors. Some of the patterns uncovered reveal that criminals, having suffered from child abuse as youngsters, whether it was sexual or physical, developed abnormal behaviors later on. As children and teenagers, they started fires, were cruel to animals or children and then in the late teenage years to early twenties, were engaging in petty crime and defying authority.

Investigators putting together a profile use either inductive or deductive approaches. Style, this is only a brief outline of the entire report. You should receive the complete report at your hotel no later than tomorrow morning. The report is quite exhaustive and comprehensive, cov-ering over 75 pages. I think you will find the data extremely interesting and informative. You probably have nothing better to do over the weekend anyhow, so read this report.

Finally, based on the details you provided on Hans Schroeder, I concur with your assess-ment. Without delay, arrange a meeting and share your story on your true identity. At this point in your investigation, having an ally, especially someone you can trust and who works on the inside, would enhance the process to move the project more rapidly.

I would like to congratulate you on your great performance at the tennis tournament in Dubai.

Be careful & Success,
DiSciascio

Not only was this information extremely enlightening from the CIA staff profilers in Langley, Style recognized these were simple guidelines; he decided he would use them but with caution and be cognizant when-ever he was around Melmer. In fact, Style decided when time permitted he would read the complete 75 page report over the upcoming weekend.

Style concluded he needed to share this important information with Hans Schroeder within two or three days. The reasons were many. It would allow Style and Schroeder both to anticipate Melmer's strange behavior. Also, it would assist in taking the initiative with Ulrich Melmer. Style would be able to establish an aggressive position going forward, consequently being more effective in furthering discussions with Melmer.

Because Style was convinced that Schroeder's phones were being monitored, he decided it would be unwise to call Schroeder at his home.

So, to avoid any compromise and as a precaution, sometime over the weekend Style would drive out to Hans Schroeder's house to discuss what he had learned from the CIA staff psychologist who profiled Melmer. Also, it would be an excellent time for Style to reveal his true identity to Schroeder and to begin the recruiting process. Style is convinced that Schroeder would be trustworthy and dependable, without question. It's a risk that Style had to take at this junction.

Schroeder has all the necessary requisites to trust as an ally and work as an inside agent. He already has demonstrated his ability to work independently or to be part of an investigating team, work under pressure with short deadlines, interact effectively with short deadlines, and interact effectively with people who have different values, cultures, or backgrounds. There is no doubt he uses sound judgment and elicits information in difficult and sensitive situations, prioritizes multiple projects and tasks, and communicates clearly, concisely, and effectively with technical and non-technical personnel.

Schroeder has managed through the years to also acquire considerable negotiation skills, employing tact, discretion, and diplomacy. Furthermore, Schroeder has the skill to assemble and assimilate large quantities of data, distinguish key issues, and draw suitable conclusions.

Schroeder's primary focus would be exclusively inside of Clearstream and nothing more. Of course, he doesn't have to worry about clandestine operations. At this point, all Style needed was someone who could be trusted and is reliable. Additionally, Schroeder could more easily secure confidential files without compromise and circumvent being confronted. Once the investigation is complete, Schroeder could retire. Certainly, the CIA would reward him well.

Since it was midafternoon, Style called the desk of the Concierge to talk with Zosa's sister Marie, and asked if she had received the tickets for the play tonight.

Marie replied that she had and would have the tickets delivered to his room momentarily. In addition, she told him that her sister was anxious to see him tonight. "Showtime is eight o'clock; the play is wonderful and very entertaining. My sister will amaze you with her talent."

"I look forward to seeing her, I can assure you, Marie."

"Zosa sings two solo songs and is in most of all the dance numbers throughout the evening performance. Everyone in our family has seen the musical several times. I promise you will enjoy yourself, John. Also, I took the liberty of making dinner reservations for you and Zosa at Hummerbar's. The restaurant is a local favorite, especially for the late theatre crowd."

"What is the name of the musical, Marie?"

"The play is entitled 'Pajama Tops and Bottoms,' Mr. Style. The play is very European and engaging, with lots of singing and dancing - very entertaining."

"And where is Hummerbar's located, Marie?"

"Hummerbar's is conveniently located in the Hotel St. Gothard and specializes in Continental and Seafood cuisine."

"Is it formal, Marie? I was thinking of wearing a tuxedo."

"Yes, that would be outstanding, Mr. Style." Marie also related that the atmosphere is an elegant dining experience, the food preparation is exceptional with fresh lobster, oysters, and shellfish specialties. She suggested Style leave for the play at seven-thirty and take a taxi. "I know you will have a great time this evening."

"Marie, thank you for your assistance and I look forward to seeing your sister once again."

"My pleasure, Mr. Style."

"Marie, there is one last thing. I picked up a real nice gift for Zosa while I was on my business trip. Do you think it would be acceptable for me to give Zosa a gift?"

"Mr. Style, of course you may give her a gift. I know my sister well. She would appreciate anything you gave her. I have to admit Mr. Style, I'm curious, what kind of gift did you get Zosa?"

"I will tell you only if don't tell your sister. Promise?"

"I promise, Mr. Style. I would never tell my sister."

"All right, I trust you. I purchased a real nice set of natural-white body line pearls with a hint of rose sparkle."

"They sound beautiful, Mr. Style. My sister will simply love them"

"Thank you, Marie, for all of your help."

"Have a wonderful time, Mr. Style."

17

Even peace may be purchased at too high a price.
Benjamin Franklin

This evening, John wanted to make very special. He had such mixed feelings. He missed Zosa terribly. At the same time, he recognized the need to be somewhat distant and not become too emotionally attached. He was falling in love and at this juncture in his investigation it could and would cause potentially serious and deadly consequences. Emotional relationships are nothing short of complicated. An emotional attachment would certainly jeopardize everything he had accomplished. Somehow he needed to control his emotions, making it less awkward and compromising for himself and especially for the team. After all, Zosa wasn't aware of the truth and conceivably could suddenly end the relationship if and when she was told the truth. He had no option but to continue to mislead her. Any woman would feel deceived. Style created an impression of himself for her in order to protect his true identity and for her personal safety. Was that being honest with her? No. It was a lie and deceptive. Without doubt, he was playing a psychological game with himself and Zosa. He was now beginning to realize and understand the meaning of an honest relationship and the commitments involved. Style's physical attraction to Zosa would never last a lifetime unless there was an emotional attraction as well. Because he had deceived Zosa, the emotional relationship didn't exist. Now, he fully understood his situation. As a result, he rationalized in his mind that he would simply enjoy the relationship for what it was, just physical and nothing more.

He had a rented tuxedo delivered to his room and was just putting his bow tie on when he received a phone call. It was Hans Schroeder.

"Hello John, this is Hans Schroeder. I just left the office and decided at the last minute to give you a call."

"How are you doing Schroeder? Is everything OK?"

"Yes, everything at the office has been quiet, except I now think someone is following me night and day."

"Schroeder, are you positive?"

"Yes, absolutely, Style, and I'm not paranoid either. I'm extra cautious. In fact, I'm calling from a public telephone booth. I called you on a chance more or less."

"Great job, Schroeder. I would like to get together this Sunday afternoon. Where would suggest we meet?"

"Ordinarily, I would say come out to my home, but I'm afraid they have my home wired.

"I understand; so where do we meet, Hans?"

"There is a nice café approximately ten kilometers from your hotel on the east side of Lake Zurich by the name of Henri's. Is three in the afternoon a good time for you, Style?"

"Yes, that would work out just perfect, Schroeder. I will meet you at Henri's at three Sunday afternoon."

"That sounds great."

Seven-thirty was fast approaching. Style finished dressing and left his room. He realized that he still would not see Zosa for at least another three hours. There was a taxi waiting for him when he arrived at the front of the hotel. He instructed the driver to take him to the musical show "Pajama Tops and Bottoms."

The driver immediately replied, "yes sir, You will certainly enjoy the show. It is lively and entertaining."

The theatre was but fifteen minutes from the hotel. When Style arrived at the show, he hurriedly entered and was escorted to his seat almost on top of the stage. He sat down and started to read the evening's program. Of course, he was looking to see Zosa's name. Her name was listed as the co-star for "Pajama Tops and Bottoms." Soon, the musical started and there she was on stage in all her beauty. For the moment, Style was literally in heaven. The musical indeed was extremely entertaining and enjoyable to watch. Zosa's many dance numbers were exhilarating and sensational. When she completed the second of her two solo song numbers, Style was spellbound. Finally, the last act ended and Style went backstage to join Zosa. Within five minutes, she was out the door and in his arms. They hugged and kissed as if they had been separated for years. It seemed like a long time before anyone said something. They were still embraced when John finally said to Zosa, "Your performance was

breathtaking."

Zosa turned to Style and replied, "Thank you John; I performed extra hard tonight to show you that I was a very good dancer and entertainer."

"My God Zosa, you were spectacular and electrifying. You have so much talent."

"I would love for my parents to have shared in the enjoyment in watching you perform tonight Zosa. Now I understand when your sister Marie said that I would thoroughly enjoy watching you entertain and she was absolutely correct. Do you know you and your younger sister Marie could easily pass for twins? It is most remarkable how you both look identical."

"John, often when we were in our early teens, we would switch roles and most times we got away with it."

"Did your sister tell you when I first met her at the hotel, I asked her for a date."

"Yes, John, my sister told me the whole story. In fact, I was meaning to ask you to explain your version."

"Well, it goes like this."

"John, I'm just kidding with you."

"Yes, I know. How about having dinner? Your sister carefully chose Hummerbar's located in the Hotel St. Gothard. It specializes in Continental and Seafood cuisine according to your sister."

"That sounds absolutely wonderful. I need to go back to my dressing room and finish dressing. I should not be more than 15 minutes. Is that OK?"

"Of course, Zosa; please take your time. I will wait for you out here."

"Definitely not, John. Please come into my dressing room and wait for me there."

"Are you sure?"

"Yes, absolutely, John."

Once more Style couldn't keep his eyes off Zosa as she undressed. Within 15 minutes she was ready and looked stunning in an absolutely out of this world dress. The black and burgundy off the shoulder design, was breathtaking on Zosa and exquisitely accentuated by her beautiful body. The designer dress was made just for her.

They arrived at Hummerbar's on time at around ten o'clock. There was a piano bar with a jazz trio playing soft music, adding to the romantic evening. The restaurant's exquisite décor complemented both the music, as well as Style's beautiful date.

At dinner, Zosa started asking John more about his business and how he handled the constant travel. Her queries were sincere and not probing. Style recognized that Zosa's questions were genuine and heartfelt. She was definitely interested in Style's business affairs. As much as Style wanted to share the truth with Zosa, he knew he couldn't even provide a tiny hint of being a CIA field agent, especially at this time. For dinner, they both had lobster, the specialty of the house and one of the best wines available, Le Petit Lousteau 2010, a French Regional Bordeaux. Both agreed that the lobster was out of this world and the wine was outstanding. After dinner, they enjoyed listening to the soft listening contemporary jazz; they also danced several leisurely slow numbers, embraced as one. When they returned to the table, Style presented his gift to Zosa. When she opened the box, she gasped and instantly knew they were real pearls. She paused briefly and asked John to put them around her neck. "These are absolutely beautiful; thank you for such a wonderful surprise."

Style appeared a little uncomfortable but finally managed to get the band of pearls around Zosa's neck and secure the latch. The pearls looked stunning against Zosa's beautiful black and burgundy off shoulder dress.

They really delighted in each other's company and were a magnificent couple together, charming and beautiful. As soon as they finished their last after dinner petit liqueur, they realized it was getting late. It was time to leave and John had arranged for a taxi to be waiting.

Once in the taxi, Zosa turned to John and asked if he would spend the evening.

John was hoping for such an offer. "Absolutely Zosa."

Once they arrived at Zosa's townhome and stepped inside, both were undressed in seconds and in her bedroom embraced on the bed. Her intoxicating fragrance seemed to electrify Style.

He was so excited and anxious. Zosa on the other hand was deliberate, reserved and teasing Style to further excitement. She knew what she was doing and literally had control of the situation. He on the other hand couldn't rein in his masculine drive. Zosa on occasion would whisper something into Style's ear, creating more of an intensity and drive in Style. At one point, she suddenly rose up and casually got out of the bed and walked around completely naked.

She wanted Style to see her naked well-conditioned body in all of its exquisite pleasing beauty. Zosa didn't do it with any sense of arrogance, but simply to further excite Style. Her full pear shaped breasts with the large dark areoles were simply delightful to look at and touch. It was obvious Zosa didn't believe in the contemporary practice of shaving all of her pubic hair. Instead, she kept her pubic hair trimmed short and very neat, allowing her pouting lips to be slightly seen but at the same time her sex triangle was almost a secret hidden place. Zosa was captain of her ship and she knew how to navigate the erotic sea of love.

All night they engaged in many forms of lovemaking. Her sexual climaxes were erotic and exciting for Style to hear. She whimpered slightly and exhaled in exotic tones every time Style managed to bring her to climax. He couldn't get enough of her sexually, especially going down on her to perform oral sex. Finally, after it seemed many hours of lovemaking, they both collapsed, exhausted and holding on to one another.

"Good morning, John. Would you like some fresh coffee?"

"Yes, I would. What time is it? I can't believe it's morning already."

"Sleepy head, it's getting late; its seven thirty."

"Zosa, last night was terrific and wonderful."

"I agree; it was better than before. I guess practice makes perfect. Do you want to practice more, John?"

"Are you serious, Zosa?"

"Of course, just tell me when you want to start. I'm always willing and available."

"I'll have coffee first, then something to eat. Is that OK with you?"

"I'm ready when you are, John."

Zosa served John coffee and French pastries in bed. Again, she was utterly naked walking around, knowing how this excited Style. He couldn't take his eyes off her. She knew how to parade her naked beauty to maximize the erotic effect on Style. He was in heaven, lusting after her every move. She kept on asking John if he was ready yet. Finally, after finishing at least three cups of coffee, Style politely turned to Zosa and said, "I just can't continue sitting here and watch you walk around naked. It is simply too much to handle. You are exquisite and so exciting to look at."

"So, John, you noticed?"

"Have you always been such a tease?"

"I'm no tease. I just enjoy making love to you. You bring out the very best of my lust and provide me with total and utter satisfaction. Making love with you is pleasurable and fun. I do enjoy teasing you. I especially enjoy getting you so excited you nearly explode with pleasure, losing all of your self-control."

The remainder of the morning and early afternoon, they both took pleasure in making love. Their energy level was almost Olympian in physical endurance and stamina. Finally, at around four in the afternoon, they both succumbed to exhaustion. They rested for approximately an hour or so and abruptly Style was out of bed and in the shower. Zosa joined him shortly. Both Zosa and John where having a delightful time teasing and soaping each other down. It didn't appear that either of them would end the sexual encounter and it would go on forever.

At long last, Style turns to Zosa and asks, "How about a relaxed dinner tonight?"

"I'm surprised you didn't realize I never once mentioned work or having to practice my dance routines today."

"Zosa, I apologize for being so selfish. Yes, you are correct. How did you manage to get a Saturday evening off?"

"It wasn't easy but the director and producer both owed me a big favor. Now, let me get back to your question about dinner tonight. Yes. I'm now very hungry."

"Where do you suggest would be a nice place for a relaxed casual dinner, Zosa?"

"I have just the place, John."

"Great. Is it far?"

"Yes, it's approximately fifty kilometers north out of Zurich but worth the drive."

"Great, then we'll catch a taxi back to the hotel to pick up my Porsche."

"OK, sounds great to me John. Would you care to spend another evening with me?"

"Yes, I would enjoy that a thousand times over, Zosa."

18

In war there is no prize for the runner-up
General Omar Bradley

Style returned to the Park Hyatt Hotel very early in the morning after spending the last two evenings with Zosa. Both nights were simply spectacular, thought Style. He reflected while enjoying a cup of coffee in the hotel breakfast room. He found himself day- dreaming often about Zosa and their romantic and loving relationship.

She didn't demand or expect anything, other than the physical relationship, contrary to his guilt ridden Puritanical feelings. Style was convinced she would put pressure on him. Why? Not once did Zosa give him any serious indications that she was looking for marriage or even a commitment. Style was absolutely dead wrong about Zosa. She was the most independent, intelligent and loving woman he knew. However, Style carried guilt for whatever reason. As a result, he came to recognize his personal short-comings.

There is no doubt he had a tremendous amount of emotional need to be with Zosa. That was most obvious. That alone created serious problems for him. He simply couldn't divorce the physical from the emotional need. Fortunately, for now, there was no serious conflict. He just needed to accept things for what they were, a wonderful physical relationship with a very beautiful woman.

There was a knock on the door. His enormous breakfast arrived.

He started to think how sex has such a dramatic effect on your appetite. He couldn't believe he ordered four eggs, pancakes and at least ten strips of bacon, plus several pieces of toast. He couldn't recall how many glasses of orange juice he consumed either. He knew he had at least one whole pot of coffee. To justify all of the calories he just consumed, he decided before he left for his meeting with Hans Schroeder he was going to the gym to work out.

He was reading through the morning edition of the *London Financial Times* looking for any possible information or recent updates from contacts in both London and Paris. He was searching for recently filed information on Al Qaeda and National Democratic Organization. As always he searched through the soccer scores for updates. There was nothing. Everything seems to be quiet. This could be interpreted to be both good and bad. Today was going to be an important day as far as Style was concerned, knowing he would have to share everything with Schroeder. Just knowing this motivated Style.

Hopefully, this wasn't going to be a major blunder on his part. He felt extremely confident this was the correct decision. Not only was Style self-assured that this was the absolute right thing to do, but necessary at this point in the investigation.

Having someone as important as Schroeder working on the inside, almost guaranteed the investigation was going to lead him and the team to all of the necessary evidence and prove their original contention that Al Qaeda is getting the financial backing from the stolen money that belonged to the poor Jews persecuted by the Nazis in World War II.

Just prior to leaving for his planned meeting with Hans Schroeder, he finished reading the exhausting 75 page study on psychological profiling. Although the study was filled with psychological and psychiatric terms and explanations, Style was able to comprehend its importance and was convinced it would be extremely helpful in transacting business with Ulrich Melmer. He was definitely taking this report to share with Schroeder.

Certainly there would be many other benefits as well. He also recognized that Hans Schroeder would surely appreciate the importance of reading the report and further understand the complicated mind of Melmer. Just considering the many ways he and Schroeder can begin using some of the interpreted meaning in the reading of body language and reading of the eyes would be enormous help in furthering their investigation.

Just before one thirty, Style left for the gym. He anticipated working out for at least an hour then taking off immediately to join Schroeder at Henri's on the east side of Lake Zurich at three o'clock. Style finished his workout and immediately climbed into his Porsche. He drove the 911 as if he were in a road race, intense and fast. The drive time was exactly twenty-five minutes, so he was just a little early. Schroeder hadn't arrived yet, so he asked for a table for two. Within minutes, Hans Schroeder showed up right on schedule, just like an accountant.

"Good afternoon, John Style. It's great to see you once again."

"Thanks, Hans. How is your family getting along living with your mother-in-law?"

"Everyone seems to be settled down and accepting the situation."

"How was your business trip, John, and where did you go?"

"We have a lot to talk about, Hans, so I hope you can spend several hours with me."

"No problem whatsoever, John. I have until tomorrow morning."

"OK smart ass. I'm quite serious. I have a lot of very important and confidential information to share with you."

"Boy, you are serious. OK, I'm all ears Style. So begin."

"First, let me start from the very beginning, Hans. That way you will understand a lot easier."

"I'm waiting, John."

"How long ago where you informed that a consultant representing DeSoto Industries would be coming to Zurich to discuss financial arrangements for financing a major real estate development in multiple European cities?"

"I can't say for sure, but at least two months ago, I think. Why?"

"At first, this is going to be difficult to believe or understand. I'm not who I seem to be, Hans. I created an image for covering up my real identity."

"Well, get to the bottom line, John."

"Just like a finance guy, Schroeder. I work for the Central Intelligence Agency as a field agent. Let me start on how I was recruited and bring you up to date."

"So far, nothing makes sense, Style."

"Hopefully, when I provide all of the details you will slowly realize the why, who, how, where and whats." Style's presentation lasted at least an hour and half. He provided all of the details and goals of the CIA. Nothing was withheld. Schroeder appeared surprised and speechless. Then suddenly he blurted out an unexpected question.

"You mean to tell me Style, you are a professional tennis player on the tennis circuit?"

"Yes, that is accurate."

"Furthermore, you recently just returned from Dubai where you played in a major tennis tournament and lost to my hero, Roger Federer."

"Yes, Hans, that is correct."

"Approximately, a year ago, my family and I met Federer at a Clearstream promotion in Zurich. As a result, we had lunch several times whenever he visited our city. My family admires Roger Federer. He has been a wonderful ambassador for Switzerland, Europe and the World."

"Schroeder, I can understand why you feel the way you do about Federer. He happens to be one of my best friends. Despite all of his success, he remains unchanged from the first day I met him. He and his family are splendid people to be with, in spite of the phenomenal success and wealth he has acquired. But, let's get back on track."

"I would like to make an apology, John."

"It's OK, but we need to keep on track so you understand more of my role as an agent for the CIA. There is plenty more information for you to know. Perhaps we should order a snack and then I will continue."

They both ordered light sandwiches and more beer.

Throughout the discussion, Schroeder would ask pertinent questions and Style would provide the most truthful and honest answers.

"Style, I think I understand everything. I have to be honest with you when I called about being shadowed, you were so knowledgeable as if to suggest you had experience on dealing with such matters. At first, I couldn't understand how a financial consultant could be so thorough when it came to police type proceedings. You were so systematic and professional. But most important, it was your self-confidence in how you managed the process. There is no doubt you provided me, and especially my family, with the confidence and assurance that you knew what you were doing. That was very reassuring, John. At that moment, I knew I could trust you with my life. Truthfully, I'm glad we have become friends."

"Now that you have listened and asked questions that concerned you, there are several more things for me to discuss with you. At this point, you could probably guess what I'm about to ask you, Hans."

"John, before I get involved in speculation, I would rather you asked me directly."

"That is more than fair and I understand, Schroeder. As you probably are aware, this is a very complicated investigation. I definitely could use your assistance on the inside of Clearstream and the quicker you decide to join, the better. Certainly, you realize there is substantial and serious danger. Worse yet, there could be physical harm or possibly deadly consequences. Both terrorist groups we are focused on are determined and committed to their respective causes. Al Qaeda and NDO have demonstrated over and over again that life has no meaning, especially for people of the western cultures. Not a pretty picture, Hans. I can tell you from my personal experience, there is substantial danger."

"Foremost John, you and my family are the only people I would sacrifice my life for. I can say without any hesitation, I welcome the opportunity of working with you as an inside agent. These are bad guys and they need to be stopped without delay."

Style reached out to shake hands with Schroeder and further addressed some other issues of significance.

"Hans, there isn't much time to provide professional training. As a result, on a daily basis I will provide you with information and training. For example, here is a comprehensive report on physiological profiling. I personally found it to be extremely helpful in understanding the perplexing personality of Ulrich Melmer. There is no doubt he's a compulsive liar and actor. For any and all information I provide you, please find a safe hiding location and put it there until you have finished reading it. Don't make any copies for obvious reasons. Once you have completed reading the material, give it back to me. In addition, I was going to suggest making your home totally secure and install detection systems to sense hidden listening devices, but then I realized that would reveal your cover. As a result, we won't touch anything in your home. I'm going to provide you with a totally secure mobile phone that transmits what is called white communication interference, allowing you to make absolute secure calls. Also, I'm sure you remember several weeks ago when we went to the shooting range, there were obvious reasons for us going there."

"Yes, of course, the picture is becoming clearer now, John."

"Tomorrow after work we are going to return to the shooting range. At that time, I will provide you with your own weapon. In fact, there will be two handguns. If you prefer, today when we depart and are outside, I can furnish you with both weapons. The first weapon is the standard issue Sig Sauer P226, 9mm with a fifteen round magazine and Siglite night lights and for backup a Smith & Wesson Bodyguard,. 380, six-shot mag, polymer light frame that you carry on your ankle. Both will have holsters and several boxes of ammunition. I'm very familiar with Switzerland's weapon laws. In Switzerland, private possession of handguns (pistols and revolvers) is permitted under license, but you must prove just cause. The fact that you are in the banking business, and can also prove you are being followed, is substantial enough reason for just cause. I already circumnavigated the administrative process and had the U.S. State Department and the CIA complete the paper work. Here are your firearm licenses for both weapons. Tomorrow when we meet, I will begin training you. Initially, there will be simple things like using a small 35mm camera, picking locks, duplicating keys, removing your finger prints and securing a site. One day this week, most likely Wednesday, we will need to find a convenient and secure location to have meetings. We will begin constructing 3-D dimensional layouts of the Clearstream building, floor by floor. Also, by tomorrow evening, I will have completed building an electronic by-pass system to be installed on all security systems, including cameras, doors, locks vaults, cabinets and most executive offices. Then, I believe we can then install the by-pass system late Tuesday evening. This will allow us to move freely about without disturbing the Clearstream alarm system and avoid being discovered by any of the motion detection systems. Since the front entrance is under repair, we will use the back entrance all the time."

"Why are there restrictions, John?"

"I will explain later, Hans."

"OK."

"I can assure you, shortly we will be able to move around Clearstream offices blind folded if necessary. So far, I've done all of the talking Hans, do you have any questions?"

"Yes. Many, John."

"Fire away, Hans. Before you begin, here is our schedule for the upcoming week."

Style handed Schroeder a sheet of paper that outlined their meetings, initial location for getting together along with the days and times. "Hans make sure you keep this list hidden and out of sight. At the end of the week burn it. Understood?"

"Yes, John."

"Each week I will provide a new list of goals along with the respective information."

"I totally understand, John."

"OK, now for your questions."

"John, there is one very obvious question I need to ask."

"Go right ahead, I have nothing to hide."

"Why would a touring tennis professional who is making a lot of money decide to jeopardize his life to be an agent for the CIA?"

"When I first joined the CIA, I had some reservation. However, that has changed after I completed my formal training at 'the farm.' The farm is actually CIA headquarters located in Langley, Virginia. The primary reason I decided to join the team is because I love my country and I strongly believe in the U.S. Constitution and everything it represents. My dad is a U. S. Air Force Veteran, having served in Viet Nam as a fighter pilot and I remember all the years he sacrificed to defend our country. As a result, I had to remind myself I also had a responsibility to my country and by joining the CIA as a field agent, I think I have accomplished that goal."

"That makes sense, I think."

"Before I forget, there is a motto that all CIA Agents have to memorize. Let me share it with you, Hans. *'I'm a member of the greatest team, I depend on the team, I concede to it and forego for it, because the team, not the individual, is the supreme winner.'* Once I started repeating the saying, the more it made sense. Today, I firmly believe in every word and I guarantee you, Hans, I will always be there for you whenever you need me."

"John, that saying is very deep and I believe you. Before I get into asking some serious questions, how do you manage to be on the tennis circuit and do your job as an agent, and before I forget, how did you do at the Dubai tennis tournament? It was Dubai, correct?"

"I made it to the quarter finals and I believe I mentioned I lost to your Swiss buddy, Roger Federer. Also, I have an agreement with the head of the CIA to continue playing on the ATP tennis tournament circuit. Originally, when I was recruited, they insisted I remain on the circuit as a cover. So far, it seems to be working out. I don't know what I would do if I suddenly started winning more tennis tournaments. Obviously, my face would be printed on all of the sports pages and on television. For now, that isn't a problem. To be honest, I'm near the end of my professional tennis career."

"Alright John, you have been totally honest with me. Let me ask some tactical and logical questions for day to day strategic activity and strategy planning."

"Go, Hans."

19

Older men declare war. But it's the
youth who must fight and die.
Herbert Hoover
President of United States

Late Sunday evening when Style finally got back to the hotel, there was another high priority message waiting for him from James DiSciascio. Immediately Style opened up his confidential e-mail:

Style-

We have just learned from severable reliable sources, Al Qaeda is in the process of trying to upgrade and develop new technology to allow them to target and shoot down, jam, or possibly remotely take control of U.S. Air Force drones in a fanatical effort to put an end to the unmanned airstrikes that have overwhelmed the terrorist organizational structure.

Al Qaeda field commanders have commissioned a select association of engineers within the terrorist's organization to take advantage of the weaknesses of the U.S. Air Force drones that have successfully killed approximately just over fifty-five hundred targeted terrorists since 2002.

Many of the terrorists killed were high-level extremists. One of the most severe weaknesses of the drones is how they are managed remotely. The longer the distance to the selected target, the weaker the control signals become. Anything that exceeds the thousand mile range, the signal is reduced by as much as 50%. As a result, a more local and much stronger transmission can literally take over and acquire control of the drone and re-direct it.

It is totally conceivable that Al Qaeda could develop a sophisticated telecommunication white software transmission system that literally could redirect or destroy launched drones at the moment of launching. As of today, nothing can be done to prevent it from happening. Fortunately, Al Qaeda has had limited success demonstrating their ability to force down or disrupt drones from accomplishing their programmed mission. We and the FBI in our research and development laboratories, have run a substantial number of testing studies and have determined the weaknesses of the drones are directly related to how they are managed, operated and controlled remotely, thousands of miles away.

One of the major weaknesses is the global positioning system or GPS design system. If Al Qaeda can successfully jam GPS signals being transmitted to the drones, it is highly likely many of the drones won't reach their pre-determined targets. It is also abundantly clear; Al Qaeda could use a sizeable number of large aluminum radio controlled balloons, releasing them simultaneously confusing the incoming drones. Al Qaeda has effectively managed over the years to attract trained engineers, beginning with one of its top leaders and one of the masterminds behind the September 11, 2001 attacks, Khalid Sheik Mohammed, who is a very gifted mechanical-engineer.

We also discovered in 2012 that the terrorist group was making a great effort to recruit new engineers and technicians with knowledge in drone and missile technology. Al Qaeda is actively recruiting some of the top electrical, mechanical & software engineering talent at MIT, Georgia Tech, University of Chicago and at most top European engineering universities. This type of recruiting is very expensive. When they are successful in identifying a young, talented first or second year engineering student, Al Qaeda will offer a fully paid four and six year scholarship, including all their personal expenses and ten thousand dollars spending money per year of study.

Once they graduate, the student is offered a substantial signing bonus. Then the goal is to recruit them to become a terrorist. We have estimated the Al Qaeda recruitment and scholarships programs are costing them at least twenty-five to thirty-five million dollars a year. Sometimes the appeals by Al Qaeda for technically trained and skilled engineers have gone public and will appear in a display ad or run in the classified section of an American newspaper. For example, the Chicago Tribune posted a large six by six inch display want ad last fall looking for talented engineers, paid in full by Al Qaeda. In January, a plea for help was sent out online via the jihadist magazine Azan and Al Jazeera America. This is the exact ad that ran in several American newspapers:

"Any opinions, thoughts, ideas and practical implementations to defeat drone technology should and must be communicated to us as early as possible and we are prepared to pay substantial bonuses. Also, if you provide a lead to someone who could develop a method to overcome the drone technology, we will provide generous rewards."

Quite extraordinary that Al Qaeda is blatantly recruiting for talent in our own country and getting away with it. This is beyond bizarre; it is unquestionably crazy! Even though the most commonly used military drones, such as the Predators and Reapers, are difficult to even detect when flying at twenty to twenty-five thousand feet. We are aware that there is still a growing unease among the White House, Pentagon and the U.S. State Department about Al Qaeda's determination to find a way to defend against them. The intent of providing this most disconcerting information is to underscore more than ever, the extreme importance of your mission.

Please don't misconstrue the intent or the purpose of this message. We realize you are doing an excellent job and everything humanly possible, but time isn't on our side. I believe with the additional assistance from Hans Schroeder that your undertaking should be slightly less difficult.

Remain vigilant and safe.

Success,

DiSciascio

The moment that Style finished reading the report, the hair on the back of his neck stood straight up. He kept asking himself, how any American citizens could consider joining a radical terrorist organization such as Al Qaeda? Even the free press promotes these bad guys. Style believes completely in Free Speech and Freedom of the Press, but this is taking the First Amendment to the United States Constitution a little bit too far.

Style started to think about tomorrow and suddenly realized that it was going to be an extremely busy day.

Directly after an early morning breakfast, Style was off for the office. When he arrived at the Clearstream corporate offices, he suddenly realized the building construction to repair the bombed front entrance of the structure was well under way.

He went directly to meet with Ulrich Melmer and Hans Schroeder. When Style arrived at Melmer's office, Schroeder and Melmer were already seated at the conference table. Style yelled out, "good morning gentlemen. Did you both have a good weekend?"

Melmer was the first to reply, "absolutely."

Within moments, Schroeder also gave his two cents by saying he went to the mountains to ski and had a terrific time.

"Before we get into our meeting this morning," Melmer said, "how did your business trip go last week?"

For a moment Style thought perhaps Melmer was aware of something, but slowly realized that couldn't be possible.

Style turned to Melmer and replied in a relaxed voice that everything went extremely well, and in fact, went better than expectations.

Melmer remarked that was terrific. "Does anyone need coffee or anything else? If not, let me take out my notes and we will get started."

The meeting lasted approximately three hours. It was just after noon when Style turned to ask both Melmer and Schroeder if they would like to go have lunch. Melmer said he couldn't because he had a doctor's appointment.

Schroeder replied enthusiastically, "Yes indeed. Are you finally picking up the tab today, Style?"

"Hans, just for that remark, I will definitely treat you to a double decker peanut butter and jelly sandwich. How is that? Seriously, where would you like to go Hans?"

"I think today, Chinese-Thai cuisine would be ideal."

"Great idea Hans; where is there a good Asian restaurant?"

"We will need to take a taxi, but the food is wonderful at Ming's."

They arrived at Ming's within twenty minutes and ordered. As they were eating, Style turned to Schroeder and asked him what he thought of the reports that he gave to him yesterday.

"The first thing I must say, your CIA does a thorough and complete job. The information is so timely. The seventy-five page report on profiling was outstanding, and just this morning I was able to use most of the knowledge in watching Melmer. His eye movement and body language spoke volumes."

"Of course you didn't by chance use any of that knowledge on me, did you Hans?"

"John, I would never do anything like that?"

"For some reason Hans, I simply don't quite believe you. Have you finished reading all of the reports?"

"Yes, and here are all of the reports you gave me."

"Thanks, I have a new report that I just received last evening and I would like for you to read it now. It should not take more than five minutes."

Schroeder promptly finished reading the newest report from DiSciascio and turned to Style and remarked, "Now it is easy to understand why these bad guys have to be cornered and done away with as fast as possible."

"You are absolutely correct, Hans. First, we need to dry up their source of funding. I firmly believe we are headed in the right direction. Tonight, when we meet at the shooting range, I will bring with me a key making kit and a set of lock picks."

"John, this feels so out of the ordinary for me. I'm now going to be a cat burglar. I realize this is completely necessary to be an agent. You have to realize, all my life working as a certified professional accountant, there is a silent code of telling the truth and nothing less. Please don't get me wrong, I'm totally committed to assisting in doing the right thing. I understand completely why this is all necessary. It is just the idea of feeling like a common thief and especially having these tools and equipment."

"Schroeder, I can relate to your mixed emotions and conflicts. I went through the same experience."

"If I may say so, John, you have given me the motivation and confidence."

"That is exactly the attitude you must maintain, Hans. Now, let's discuss our schedule for this week. Yesterday, I mentioned late that Tuesday evening we will install the electronic by-pass system on all security systems, including all entrances, exits, cameras, doors, locks vaults, cabinets and most executive suites."

"John, won't they notice that the security system has been tampered with?"

"That is a damn good question. All of the by-pass components will be thoroughly hidden and not seen. Any chance or possibility of anything being discovered is extremely remote. Furthermore, some of the changes will be done via software and that will be definitely transparent to everyone, including everyone in the management information system department."

"How long do you anticipate the installation of the by-pass system will take, John?"

"Realistically, I believe somewhere around two to three hours at most. We should be finished and wrapped up by mid-night. Of course, if there are any conflicts or sudden interruptions, we could be delayed. Otherwise, I feel quite confident three hours and no longer. In addition, yesterday I mentioned we would construct a 3-D dimensional layout of the Clearstream building. After having a discussion with DiSciascio last night, he convinced me to allow the counter terrorism center (CTC) at Langley build the model and they will complete constructing it more rapidly and, more important, more accurately. Apparently, they have this new million dollar printer that can produce the results in a matter of several hours, layer by layer, using liquid materials like rubber and plastic. He promised they would then deliver it back to us no later than Thursday morning this week. It will be delivered to the U.S. State Department Embassy here in Zurich."

"That is extraordinary, John. How do they get the information and layout of the Clearstream buildings?"

"Tonight when we have finished practicing on the shooting range, I will return to Clearstream and begin taking photographs with this very special Nikon 35mm 3-D camera. With a bit of luck, I should finish taking photographs of all of the facilities within two or three hours. Later tonight, when I get back to my room, I will then download the file to CTC."

"You simply amaze me, John."

"To be honest with you Hans, some of the things I'm doing are for the very first time. However, I can assure you I'm very confident despite being a tender-foot. Fortunately, the training I received was the very best. You would not believe how thorough and professional the CIA trains its field agents. All agents must be capable of speaking at least three languages fluently. That is just a starter. All CIA agents must have graduated in the top ten per cent of their class."

"Style, I'm a little confused. How did you manage to pull the wool over their eyes?"

"Now, that is really hitting below the belt Schroeder."

"I'm just giving you a hard time, John."

"I realize that. Before I forget Schroeder, whenever you and I are alone or whenever we communicate on official business and that includes e-mail, mobile phone, etc., we need to discontinue using our first names. It is an official CIA policy to only use last names when addressing one another. It avoids confusion, especially when under duress and issuing instructions or orders. There are several more details for us to discuss, but going forward let us start adopting this important policy. However, when we are at the Clearstream offices, first names make more sense."

"I understand completely, Style."

"The last item for tonight: here is your Nokia mobile telephone that will provide total secure channels when placing and receiving phone calls. I can assure, you never have to be concerned about anyone ease dropping or tracking you on any of your conversations and that also includes texting and or sending e-mails. It is completely secure and encrypted on a special wireless spectrum."

"Great, I can tell you, Style, that today and yesterday was extremely educational. Now let's kick ass and make my day."

"Again you have a sensational attitude. Clint Eastwood would be proud of you. You and Eastwood have a lot in common, especially since you are approximately the same ages."

"Now wait one minute, Style; that is really bullshit. Let's get it straight right now; I'm not in my eighties, but just turning sixty. Do you understand?"

"Wow, did I hit a sensitive cord? You know for an old fart, you can be like a bull with a bee up his ass."

20

They wrote in the old days that it is sweet and fitting to die for one's country.
But in modern war, there is nothing sweet nor fitting in your dying.
You will die like a dog for no good reason.
Ernest Hemmingway

Finally, Style went back to the Clearstream facilities and managed to successfully take photographs of every room, hallway, rest room, executive office, closet, storage space, basement, old boiler rooms, and on all of the floors throughout the Clearstream office buildings. He arrived back at the hotel just after mid-night. He checked the photographs before uploading them to Counter Terrorism Center, to make certain that all of the photos were well defined and sharp. Immediately, he e-mailed them to CTC with copies to DiSciascio. Once he finished submitting his daily reports, he started to outline the schedule for tomorrow. He recognized that tomorrow was going to be a turning point and extremely busy. The next morning after breakfast, Style called Schroeder.

"Good morning, I trust you slept well last evening."

"Yes, especially since I discovered that no one followed me home last night or into the office today."

"I wonder why the sudden change for not following you, Schroeder."

"That is a good question. I have been followed just about every day for the last two weeks."

"Hopefully, that is good news Schroeder. In the meantime, here is our schedule for today."

After listening to the details of the planned schedule, Schroeder clarified some issues and then said, "I will see you in the office when you arrive, Style."

"Great."

Just before Style left for the office, he received a telephone call from DiSciascio.

"Style, the rising tension in the Middle East is getting more serious by the day. As you know Egypt, Libya, Iran, Yemen, Lebanon, Afghanistan & Pakistan are in turmoil. It is extremely difficult to tell the good guys from the bad. Al Qaeda seems to be playing both sides of the fence, making it very difficult to put our boots on the right side of the bed. The reason for this emergency call is that we just learned early today that Al Qaeda is planning a major offensive."

"OK, DiSciascio, what would you like me to do?"

"At this time, nothing. However, let me fill you in on some of the details. The rise of Al Qaeda's affiliate in Syria, Al Nusra Front, which we have designated as a terrorist organization months ago, could marshal in a long and deadly confrontation with the West, and ultimately bring Israel into the conflict."

Style suddenly observed, "You bet your ass it could."

DiSciascio continued, "Today inside Syria, the group Al Nusra Front is exploiting a widening sectarian rift to recruit Sunnis who saw themselves as disenfranchised by Assad's Alawite minority, an offshoot of Shite Islam that dominates Syria's power and security structures.

Al Nusra appears to have gained popularity in a country that has turned more religious as the uprising, mainly among Sunni Muslims, has been met with increasing force by authorities. Al Nusra has claimed responsibility for spectacular and deadly bombings in Damascus and Aleppo, and its fighters have joined other rebel brigades in attacks on Assad's forces. According to the National Security Center, (NSC) the U.S. Intelligence group, Nusra claimed responsibility in one day alone last month for forty-five attacks in Damascus, Deraa, Hama and Homs provinces that reportedly killed dozens, including sixty in a single suicide bombing."

Style continued with his explanations and further enlightened, "Because of the obvious confusion, the State Department, White House and both Houses of Congress are very bewildered. Moreover, I understand the President of the United States has presented his case to the Congress and the reaction has been mixed from both sides of the political aisle."

"Style, I'm sure you are already aware that we can't get involved in a political debate or takes sides, but we must do our job and follow orders. Nothing less and nothing more and that will keep our ass out of hot water."

"DiSciascio, I'm very cognizant of the political rules of engagement and it makes perfect sense to me. I understand completely."

"Unfortunately, Style, this entire subject is deadly serious. The whole thing is an absolute mess and getting worse by the moment. Every day, when I wake up, I ask myself, what the hell is the Middle East coming to? It is a powder keg just waiting to explode. Consider, just a few years ago when a Middle Eastern country had an internal political problem, it was much easier to resolve. Today, the moment an issue develops in one Middle Eastern country like Egypt, Yemen or Syria, the entire region is dangerously imperiled."

"DiSciascio, it appears that the Syrian civil war could broaden to include Turkey; Iran, Palestine and Israel."

"Unfortunately, Style, it is far worse than that. As you probably know, Russia has supported Syria for the past twenty-five years. Conceivably, they could get involved, along with China. This means several potential and very serious immediate problems. We could find ourselves back in the cold war."

"I couldn't agree more. I think I know where you are headed with this,

DiSciascio. Possibly another 1973 oil embargo developing into a major world crisis followed by an oil shortage and all hell breaks loose."

"Yes, you are absolutely right, Style, another embargo, but on a substantially larger scale. Let me get back on target and get immediately into the real purpose of my phone call. I would like for you to keep focused and on-track with your extremely important assignment."

"No problem, DiSciascio. I'm completely focused and have a tactical plan in practice day-to-day."

"That is outstanding. There is one last thing, Style."

"Yes, what is it?"

"Schroeder will probably query you on our role in the Middle East. Do your best to avoid any confrontation or debate, but don't ignore the subject. Try to handle it the best way possible. I know you will. The last thing we need now is for one of our major inside informers on this tough assignment to suddenly get cold feet and quit."

"Believe me, I do understand and thank you for the update."

"Be safe. Keep up the great work Style; you make my job so much easier."

"Thanks again, Sir."

As Style was driving to the office, he started to reflect on his conversation with DiSciascio. The world is mad. Playing professional tennis is so simple. You go to practice, work hard to improve, and then days later you play a tournament as hard as you can to keep the little yellow ball inside the white lines and not worry about an artificially created redline. Perhaps the President and his adversaries should engage in a tennis match to solve the world problems. Certainly, there will be a winner, but no one suffers the loss of his or her life.

Once Style was in his office at the Clearstream facilities, he immediately started to plan for the evening's proceedings. He already coordinated a meeting with Schroeder at approximately seven o'clock. Style intentionally contrived a number of problems with the Clearstream Finance and Banking contract, as an excuse to get together later in the evening to resolve serious issues with some of the details. He knew that Ulrich Melmer would not be interested in attending this last minute meeting and he was absolutely right. Immediately, Melmer called Schroeder and asked would he attend the meeting Style requested and resolve any outstanding contract issues or difficulties. Immediately, Schroeder responded and said he would attend the meeting.

"What time is the meeting, Ulrich?"

"Seven o'clock in Style's office."

"I understand, Ulrich; I will definitely be there at seven."

"Thank you, Hans, for your help."

Finally, at around seven, as soon as Schroeder arrived at Style's office, they immediately started on the Clearstream contract. Obviously, both recognized full well what the real intent was for the contrived meeting. Both Style and Schroeder realized it was highly probable they were going to be monitored or listened to for a short period. Therefore, they performed a brilliant acting job for the first two or three hours. By ten o'clock, most all of the Clearstream employees had departed and immediately Style and Schroeder set in motion their next moves.

First, all of the security alarm systems, burglar alarms, wireless security, surveillance cameras security systems cameras and monitors needed to be mapped out to allow Style to prepare building an electronic by-pass system for installation late tomorrow evening.

Second, if necessary during this most difficult and demanding task, they would create a diversionary backup in the event someone from security or anyone for that matter, questions what they are doing in the building so late, or worse yet, they get caught while in the act of mapping out the security systems.

Third, and the final task for the evening, they are to do a run through, floor by floor, beginning with the top floor and working their way down to the basement and boiler rooms. Style wanted to make certain when they started the installation of the by-pass system tomorrow evening, everything would go just like clockwork. Nothing was going to be left for chance.

Style explained to Schroeder, "I anticipate that the run through should probably last at least two hours."

Style, "What do you want me to do while you are taking photographs and assessing each of the different security systems?"

"Most important Schroeder, you need to monitor the halls while I'm in the different offices."

"I understand completely, Style."

"Thanks Schroeder, I'm very familiar with the movement and frequency of when security walks through each floor of the building. Here is a copy of their activity. Notice Schroeder, I detailed all of their habits and where I anticipate they will be at any given moment."

"Not bad details for a tennis bum, Style."

"Excuse me, you mean tennis professional. You just will not let up Schroeder, will you?"

"Of course, not, why should I? I enjoy giving you a hard time, especially after you called me an old fart."

"Just to let you know, I watched and monitored all of their activities for over a week. Not once did they change or alter their routine schedule."

"I hope that routine continues tonight for our sake."

As planned, everything was finished just after mid-night. Style turned to Schroeder and said, "I think we did an outstanding job. I believe we have every security device mapped out."

"How do you know you managed to find all of the security devices?"

"I have a special electronic meter that traces any type of an electronic pulse or signal, to determine whether it's analog or digital signal and its signal strength, Schroeder."

"So far, no one has any idea what we are doing," declared Schroeder.

"I trust and hope you are correct, because we can't afford any screwups, period. In addition, we were fortunate; we didn't have to employ any diversionary tactics. I hope that we don't have any problems tomorrow evening. Now, let me show you and demonstrate how you remove your fingerprints or anything that would suggest we were in places we should not be."

Style, took out his fingerprint removal kit and a special cloth. He immediately proceeded to show how the fingerprint kit works. At first, it was awkward for Schroeder to remove evidence as fast as Style, but eventually he became proficient and started to develop a lot of confidence in himself.

"It is getting late Schroeder, let's get a drink and call it a night."

"That sounds like a great idea to me."

"There is a small café just down street. I believe it will be still open. Let us go, Style."

They both arrived at the same time and each ordered a drink.

Schroeder turned to Style and commented that he thought he would make an excellent CIA field agent. "What do you think, Style?"

"Are you sure you want me to give a reply, Schroeder?"

"Yes, I would."

"Well, I will say you did an outstanding job, my friend, and I say that in all honesty. In fact, I will go one-step further and admit if I were given a choice for an assigned partner, there is no doubt I would request you."

"Wow! That is outstanding for you to say, Style."

"Seriously, I mean it. Unfortunately, when you are deployed as a clandestine field agent in either the Counter Terrorism or Global Response teams, you work alone. The reasons are many, but very understandable."

"Is that the reason when you hear the expression 'lone wolf,' they are referring to clandestine field agents?"

"No. The expression, 'Lone Wolf,' refers to an individual terrorist who has proven he is capable of committing a wide range of violent attacks. These have included mass shootings, bombings, assassinations, anthrax attacks, and a variety of other incidents. Reasons are many and often include political purposes, but the lone wolf will also commit violent acts for money. For a long time, it was believed that for an act of violence to be considered "terrorism" it had to be a group or a cell that committed the attack. That view is beginning to change as the world has witnessed some horrific attacks by lone wolves. An excellent example would be when Maj. Nidal Maljik Hasan, who shot and killed thirteen fellow soldiers and injured scores of others at Fort Hood, Texas, in protest to the wars in Iraq and Afghanistan. Perhaps one of the most well-known acts of lone wolf terrorism was Timothy McVeigh (with some help from Terry Nichols) when they blew up the Federal Building in Oklahoma City, Oklahoma, killing 169 people in the worst act of homegrown terrorism in U.S. history. With a bit of luck, Schroeder, I trust that clears up what a lone wolf does?"

"It is still vague but I'm beginning to understand. Certainly I will never understand why someone like McVeigh, would do such a horrible thing against people he didn't know. However, the more information you share with me, the easier the subject becomes for me to understand."

"I can appreciate where you are coming from, Schroeder."

"As a Swiss citizen, we live a life made easy because of our neutrality. As you probably already know, Switzerland has remained a neutral country since the 19th Century. In fact, it wasn't until 2007 or 2008, that Switzerland became a member of the United Nations. As a result, lone wolf can mean something different to various people, Style."

"Yes, in a manner of speaking Schroeder. I don't wish to confuse you, but on the other hand, Al Qaeda chief Ayman Al Zawahri has called on Muslims to continue attacking Americans on their own soil in order to bleed the United States economy. He's desperately hoping this will resonant and if it doesn't his next step will be to encourage and promote so-called lone wolf attacks. However, he prefers more terrorist attacks similar to the intensity and severity of the September 11, 2001 attack, which he called a punishment for America's continuous war on Islam and Muslims.

"Style, how do you know all of this shit?"

"We are constantly getting intelligence information, memos and briefings."

"It's hard to imagine how many daily events take place around the world that must be monitored and evaluated to determine how it will impact the rest of the world."

"That is a wonderful observation, Schroeder. Please let me continue.

Ultimately, it's Al Zawahri's goal to have America's Department of Homeland Security to continue appropriating the enormous expenditures for homeland security. Obviously, the expenditures are designed to protect American citizens at airports, public events, and Federal and State facilities throughout the United States. Zawahri's has a vision, both short and long-term expectations, to hemorrhage America's economy through security and military spending. Long range, Al Zawahri seems to think, this type of constant spending will bankrupt America financially. Short term, it creates frustration, long lines, and inconveniences and is very expensive to maintain."

"Several years ago, I took a business trip from Zurich to New York, and I couldn't believe how long it took to get through the security checkpoint at Kennedy International Airport, in New York City. Yes, very inconvenient and frustrating Style, but safe."

"Al Zawahri would like to keep the Unites States on a constant state of alert, never knowing where and when the next strike will occur. He accepts, as factual knowledge, keeping America on its constant guard only requires scattered strikes here and there. At the same time, Al Zawahri has called on Muslims to kidnap westerners to trade for Muslim prisoners detained in the west. Despite the relative small size of the Boston Marathon bombing, Al Zawahri sees long-term benefits and a very profound negative effect on the psyche of people living in Boston and throughout America. Western counter-terrorist professionals have warned that radicalized lone wolves, who might have had no direct contact with Al Qaeda, posed as great a risk as those who carried out complex plots like the 911 attacks."

"Is that a valid fact or some contrived imaginative story, Style?"

"Yes, absolutely that is the truth. As I said earlier, Zawahiri is convinced that the U.S. economy would be bled dry by provoking it to continue in its massive expenditure on its security. There is no doubt that the weakest link in the American armor is the economy. The American debt is over twenty trillion dollars and growing. However, the United States is quite a remarkable country despite a crippled economy. Today, it appears as though the United States has finally managed to recover from the financial banking disasters of recent years."

"Are you sure that is correct?"

"Yes, I'm certain. However, Zawahiri misleads all of his followers by telling them America is falling apart. This is an example of one of his many methods in motivating his fighters. He uses every imaginable propaganda method available. He also uses an old communist ploy by suggesting if they keep America in such a state of tension and anticipation, it would only require a few disparate attacks here and there to bring America to its knees."

"Are you positive that is what he means, Style?"

"Yes, this rhetoric is more of Zawahiri's philosophical bullshit. He claims time and again, Al Qaeda defeated the West in the gang warfare in Somalia, Yemen, Iraq and Afghanistan, and so they should follow it with war on its own land in the United States of America."

"You seem to have a very clear understanding of their philosophy and what makes them tick."

"You are damn right. I have been studying Al Qaeda, the Middle East viewpoint, and their way of life long before I became a member of the Central Intelligence Agency."

"So, does that make you an authority and specialist on Middle Eastern affairs?"

"Not quite, but I do understand how they manifest their radical Islamic terrorist attitude toward the west. Let me finish my previous thought process. Al Zawahiri is convinced that one brother or a few of the brothers can do disparate strikes. At the same time, Muslims should seize any opportunity to land a large strike on the United States, even if this took years of planning."

"How do you think they feel today about the manner in which they tactically operate globally, Style?"

"I personally feel that they would admit without hesitation that Al Qaeda doesn't sense it is in the best position organizationally to accomplish what it used to do easily, which is to organize and launch attacks as necessary, and sometimes at the last moment. This was easily accomplished when under the leadership of Bin Laden. Today, the fact remains Al Zawahri lacks the charisma of Bin Laden, consequently fund- raising has been more difficult and now more than ever depends on income from the hidden Swiss bank accounts managed by Ulrich Melmer and the National Democratic Organization (NDO).

"Do you envision a possible rift in their partnership at any time?"

"Yes, indeed that is an inevitable fact. It is near impossible for two organizations with so different a philosophical view to sustain a long-term relationship. In my opinion, I believe that Al Zawahri resents the relationship with NDO and when something dramatic happens with the funding, Al Qaeda will suddenly strike back hard and create hell for Ulrich Melmer and the National Democratic Organization. Nevertheless, I'm convinced beyond a shadow of doubt that once we succeed in turning off the spigot of free flowing funding, Al Qaeda will have an extremely tough time remaining in the terrorism business and remain partners with NDO."

"Style, once again, your knowledge is outstanding. You provide me with an enormous amount of confidence working together as a team."

"I would like to get back to the original observation you had, Schroeder. When we are assigned in the field as a non-official cover (NOC), a term that applies to an agent sent to spy on a foreign country or organization and might pose as a journalist or a businessperson like me. The bottom line is we don't have partners and we work totally alone when in the field on clandestine assignments."

"Well, I really didn't expect anything different. I think you realize I wasn't serious when I said, I think I would make an excellent CIA field agent, Style."

"I realize that, Schroeder. Is there anything else we need to discuss before I do a wrap-up for the night?"

"I don't think so."

"Remind me tomorrow to provide you with infrared cameras and heat detecting surveillance cameras that you can install inside and outside of your house. I will instruct you on how to install them. It is relatively easy. This should provide you with a measure of protection and some prevention. You can monitor the entire system on both your PC and your new Nokia mobile phone. When you are at the office, you can visually track and record any activity. The moment that the heat-detecting camera is activated, you will be notified instantly on your mobile phone."

"That sounds too easy. Does it matter where I am to be notified? For example, would I be warned in the basement of the Clearstream offices or skiing in the Alps?"

"I'm confident you would be notified in the basement of a building, but I'm not positive about a remote mountainous location. Also, before I forget, tomorrow I will give you very small listening device called bugs. Technically, they are called bug drops. In fact, they even look like an insect. I would like you to place several bugs in Melmer's office."

"Where would be the best location to drop them?"

"Select inconspicuous locations like in the corners where they can't be seen. Put another one on the underside of his topcoat lapel and when possible, drop one on the back floor of his Mercedes, preferably under the front seats."

"How do they function, Style?"

"They perform a dual purpose, to listen and to track. Several of the bugs will turn translucent and appear almost invisible."

"Quite amazing devices and I will take care of planting the bugs. You make being a spy so easy. So far, everything sounds great and thanks for your help with everything and for giving me the confidence, Style."

"How about getting together first thing tomorrow morning for breakfast, Mr. Schroeder?"

"Now we are getting formal. Where would you like to meet?"

"I believe there is a wonderful café not too far from the hotel, just two streets northwest toward the lake."

"What time Style?"

"How about seven sharp? I will get there a little earlier and call you with the name of the café and directions."

"Great, see you first thing in the am."

21

He who did well in war just earns the right to begin doing well in peace.
Robert Browning

The top of the morning to you, Style.

"Yes, I slept great last night my friend."

"I'm in the mood for a big breakfast, Schroeder."

"So am I."

"Last night when I arrived back at the hotel and reviewed my notes, something occurred to me that I need to address as soon as possible."

"What is that, Style?"

"We need to arrange to begin looking closely at the general ledger and all of the accounting books going back as far as the mid-1930s. I realize that securing the books will be extremely difficult but I know of an alternative option. All I need is to have access to the back office accounting IBM AS400 systems. I understand it happens to be an Oracle based accounting package running the back office."

"Yes, that is correct, Style. Now, don't tell me you can make yourself invisible and you simply just walk in the Clearstream accounting office and take seat at a computer station."

"That is exactly what I was thinking. Just like the character in the old movie, 'Topper,' where Cary Grant walks into a bank and disappears. Seriously, I will address that subject in one minute. Let me begin by asking some basic questions.

Do you think most, if not all, of the financial records have been input into the computer systems?"

"Yes, I believe everything has been converted. Several years ago when Clearstream upgraded their financial software, they converted all of their files, including all the old files and certainly all of the new data including reports, personnel records, operations, administration, e-mails, minutes from staff meetings and all financial data."

"Schroeder, are you certain all the financial archives going back to the 30s were included in the conversion process?"

"Certainly, I can't guarantee that everything was converted but I feel confident enough to say, I would be willing to bet my life. Is that good enough, Style? Furthermore, at the time the conversion project started, I was the executive responsible for managing the changeover process. You can rest assured during the entire conversion process I had every department throughout Clearstream involved in the changeover process. I also made certain that included all the old archives records going as far back as 1929. If any files or records are missing, they were intentionally by-passed but not by me or the team working on the conversion process."

"That is good enough for me Schroeder. Just to clear up some points of concern, I don't need to be on premise to hack in to or break codes to gain access to the Clearstream management information systems. Initially, all I need is the daily security password."

"Surprisingly enough, Style, the password isn't changed every day. They are very slow in changing the password. Sometimes the password remains in effect for weeks."

"Nevertheless, Schroeder, I can then create a bogus sign-on name and by-pass the Clearstream firewall. Once I accomplish that, I can begin writing code to allow both of us to have complete access to the Oracle accounting software and the entire database of all financial information. I will design a software code that will be completely textbook perfect, comprehensive, undetectable and to some degree, transparent.

By accomplishing this, we will not leave any audit trails, and MIS or IT operations will not know that we extracted and copied files."

"You are telling me there will not be any trace whatsoever, Style."

"I'm absolutely confident about not leaving any evidence as you are about betting your life on the history conversion process."

"That is perfect, Style. I don't mean to sound cynical, but I just can't believe you can accomplish total entry into the Clearstream system without being discovered or detected."

"Schroeder, you are definitely challenging me. I understand your doubt. For now, you will simply have to accept what I say on faith. Perhaps, if I explain some details, you will begin to change your mind and understand. Would that help?"

"Possibly, please don't get too technical. I'm not good with computers. Although I use my computer every day, the only thing I really understand is finance. On the other hand, I believe I'm very capable of learning swiftly."

"Before I continue and move ahead, let me ask several basic questions."

"You said it correctly Style, 'basic.' What questions do you have Style?"

"I don't remember being introduced to anyone on the executive staff with a title of Chief Security Officer (CSO). Is there anyone that carries that title or similar position?"

"No, not even close."

"Is there someone in security that is considered to be on the executive staff level?"

"Are you kidding? Clearstream security is entirely independent and the security staff is retained as subcontractors. Why?"

"That tells me a great deal about the relationship between the management information systems (MIS) or IT and security. The fact that they are totally segregated and separate also means that their respective systems don't communicate with one another and aren't capable of doing so. For example, when we turn off one of the cameras for a very brief moment, the IT or MIS department will not be notified. Instead, when security is notified, it will be completely localized and a very high probability that nothing will be done. They will assume it was a minor glitch and the situation ends."

"Style, what is the difference?"

"If the systems were totally integrated, chances are once the IT department was notified and alerted, it would set off an alarm throughout the entire Clearstream facility."

"The picture is becoming more clear Style. Despite all of the money that we continue to spend on renewing and upgrading IT products and services, Clearstream remains behind the technological curve in not using the latest state-of-the-art software and hardware systems. Is that what you are trying to say, Style?"

"Perhaps when this whole adventure is over you can suggest to the executive staff that today the world is full of great risk and peril, and the value of being prepared with the best security systems available can't be measured by its price tag, but by what it stops."

"That is an excellent observation Style, but I think when we are finished with the investigation, I'm going to be officially retired."

"Now, are you sure you want to retired? Don't be so defensive Schroeder. The fact remains, we benefit from Clearstream's MIS operations department not being ahead of the curve and not having adopted a more efficient manner of integrating all of their discrete systems, especially security. In fact, I'm delighted and thrilled. It makes our job as gatecrashers much easier and less complex."

"Do you have to use the term gatecrashers, Style?"

"Does the term 'gatecrasher' bother you, Schroeder? Because if it does, how about the word 'spying' or better yet, 'hackers' and 'pirates' of the highest level? So don't give me a hard time."

"Now aren't we getting a little bit too sensitive, Style? I realize it is getting late and I really don't care what name you use for our spying."

"Great, let us get back on track, so we can finish and leave. At this point, let me introduce another related subject: firewalls and software security."

"You mean some type of protection from someone on the outside world attempting to get in to the Clearstream systems through the internet, is that correct, Style?"

"Go to the head of the class because you are absolutely right on the button, Schroeder."

"I do know a few things about the World Wide Web, Style, but just enough to cause the IT department headaches and problems."

"That is very typical of financial people. I'm kidding you again, Schroeder, but at least you understand just enough to have an intelligent conversation on the subject."

"That is fair enough, Style."

"Let me begin with the firewalls. Firewalls tend to allow outgoing traffic but block incoming traffic unless there is a pre-existing session. For Transmission Control Protocol (TCP), this is easy, once the connection is established, the firewall will allow connection in both directions. What do you think, Schroeder?"

"Well, every time you make observations or say something entirely new like hacking into the Clearstream software, I'm not surprised anymore by anything you say or do."

"Is that your question?"

"Certainly not. Frankly, I don't know enough about software applications to ask a sensible question. What I know is financial applications and accounting."

"Fair enough, Schroeder."

"OK, let me finish what I started. I can immediately write a software line of code or patch by using a User Datagram Protocol (UDP); this is a bit trickier since there is no concept of a session. Protocols as UDP based Domain Name System (DNS), are requesting response protocols so once the client sends a request, a response is expected from the server. The firewall will register the request on a given port and allow a response to come back a short time later. So one trick is that if one is expecting UDP traffic, is to send a small amount of garbage or trash data. This will be ignored by the server, but positively will open the firewall to allow us in to the system on the front side and be admitted as incoming traffic. This work-around will be very transparent to everyone, especially the accounting department and MIS operations. I can assure you, Schroeder; this will work and no one will discover a trace of us being inside the system. From inside the back office of the operational side, it will appear as though someone in the Clearstream facility has requested information and they are now getting a response from the outside world. I think that covers everything for now."

"Style, I need to ask you a very simple question, not related whatsoever to the immediate subject. Have you ever been drunk or intoxicated?"

"Why would you ask that question at this time, Schroeder?"

"I asked the question because it seems your brain is constantly analyzing and thinking on a very high level and is never relaxed."

"That is the Sherlock Holmes in me I guess. As for getting intoxicated. Let me answer your most profound question. Yes, I have absolutely gotten tanked, in fact, on several occasions, Schroeder. Believe me, I can have a good time when the occasion arises. When we finish this project, we will have a great time and celebrate. I will guarantee that I will have a couple of bourbons. How is that?"

"All right, I will believe it when I see it. Sounds absolutely out of this world and I look forward to the occasion of seeing you having more than a few, Style."

"Good, let's finish breakfast and get to the office."

"What time should we meet tonight, Style?"

"How about ten and come to my office. Once again, it is going to be a very busy evening installing the by-pass system. I anticipate everything should go smoothly without any glitches or hiccups. In our preparations so far, we have left nothing for chance and managed to be extra cautious every step of the way."

Later that evening, Schroeder arrived at Style's office on time at ten.

"Are you ready, Schroeder?"

"Damn ready, sir."

"OK, OK, Schroeder."

Style suggested they start down in the basement and work their way up to the top. They left without delay and made it appear they were simply going for a walk to get some exercise. The time was just after ten o'clock. Style anticipated it would probably take three or four hours to install all of the devices. About two hours into the installation, one of the security guards happened to change his walk-through routine by a few minutes but not enough to effect continuing with the installations. It appeared at first that Style would have to change the schedule slightly, but Schroeder managed to corner the guard and start a conversation, delaying him from entering the office where Style was hidden in the drop down ceiling.

"That was close, Style."

"You are dead right, Schroeder. I waited as long as I could and decided I needed to continue. When I heard him coming, I was just climbing into the ceiling at the moment you stopped him. Just before he walked in, I managed to pull up the rope ladder and close the ceiling off. I remained utterly motionless as he walked directly under the portion of the ceiling where I had just secured myself. All I can say is 'whew'. That was close. Great job, Schroeder. By the way, what did you say to him?"

"Fortunately, I just read in the Clearstream company newsletter that his wife had a baby and I asked him how his son was doing. He quickly corrected me and said 'daughter.' That is all he said and then left hurriedly."

"Thank heavens, Schroeder; those few seconds enabled me to scramble and recover all of the tools & electronic equipment. As I said several times before, you are slowly becoming a real professional sleuth, fast on your feet and quick thinking."

"Hopefully you are telling the truth and not kidding with me, Style."

"Now would I do that to you? I'm serious. You know that sometimes you can't take a compliment without giving me a hard time. We are just about finished, Schroeder, with just one more office to go."

"I will be glad when this is over and complete, Style. I'm getting a little edgy and nervous and I don't know why either."

"Just keep up the great work, Schroeder, and we will be finished in approximately fifteen minutes and no longer. There now, we are finally finished. That wasn't so bad. How do you feel now?"

"Style, as I said earlier, I'm now relieved and the edge has been removed."

"I understand how you feel, Schroeder. So far, you have been magnificent and simply terrific."

"Are you serious, Style?"

"Yes."

"When I get back to my hotel room, Schroeder, I will complete the installation of the software, allowing me to connect all of the devices and then allowing me to have full remote access to monitor the security system throughout all of the Clearstream facilities."

"When do you sleep, Style?"

"I can assure you, Schroeder, I will sleep peacefully tonight."

"Before I forget, we can also use our mobile phones to view all the activity and movement on the Clearstream security network. Let me have your mobile phone, Schroeder, so I can program it for you to have total communications with the security network and MIS operations. Again, thanks for your assistance."

"It is always a pleasure to work with you, Style."

"One last thing with this phone; you can either use a pin or your fingerprint to use the phone. So make sure you create a secure pin number to prevent someone from getting into the phone and seeing the top-secret applications and viewing your phone history. Once you read your e-mails, make sure you are erasing all of them. We don't want the bad guys to have any remote possibilities of getting access to any information whatsoever."

"Yes, I will do that right away. You know something, Style; you are one devious son-of-a-bitch, but someone who deserves a lot of respect and I would trust you with my life."

"That is a great thing to say, Schroeder. I hope that that is something we both can avoid.

"Early tomorrow morning, the 3-D dimensional layout built by the counter terrorism center (CTC) of the Clearstream building should be delivered to the American Embassy. First thing in the morning, I will go to the Embassy and pick up the model, then return to the Park Hyatt Hotel and secure it in the hotel safe. When we are together tomorrow night, we can then do a rehearsal walkthrough just using the model. It is extremely important we time everything down to the second, because there is so much to accomplish when we actually do it live under extremely stress-ful circumstances. The more practiced and familiar we become with the layout, the quicker we complete each task with less problems. Eventually, we should be able to do it blind-folded."

"Of course, Style, you aren't serious."

"On the contrary, Schroeder, I'm dead serious."

"There are hundreds of tasks that I sequenced beginning in the base-ment and working our way to top floor. I'm thinking of moving ahead with plans of doing the live search of all of the files Friday evening. By then, everything will be in place and we will have memorized every step on every floor and office of the Clearstream buildings. When we start, we will have to know by memory, every window, exit, closet, doorway, office, file cabinet, heating and air conditioning duct, number of steps up to the next floor and the exact time security is expected at any given location. Schroeder, I realize you are extremely familiar with everything in all of the buildings, but this will provide an extra measure of precaution and added degree of security. If everything goes as planned and there are no hiccups, I expect the entire process to take just about all Friday night."

"My God, Style, we will definitely be prepared."

"You are damn right, Mr. Schroeder, damn right. Before I forget, I neglected to ask earlier today, do you think anyone followed you home last night?"

"No. I am certain because when I left the office, I circled around several streets and doubled back before I headed out to the main motorway number three. Perhaps they have decided I'm no longer a problem and dismissed any concerns about me."

"Schroeder, please do me a favor and remember, nothing is what it seems. Especially now that everything appears just about complete and getting closer to the finish line. Don't let your guard down, no matter the circumstances. You must promise me you will keep on your toes every day, especially when you are home alone. Perhaps something to consider this weekend is for me to come out to your home and spend the weekend."

"Why don't you just invite yourself, Style?"

"Are you serious, Schroeder?"

"Style, don't take me so literal all the time."

"Your sense of humor, Schroeder, is quite remarkable and sometimes untimely."

"I don't think your girlfriend will particularly like you spending the weekend away from her, Style."

"Don't worry about that. I have that covered."

"Tonight, Style, I would simply like to go home and relax."

"That is a wonderful idea."

22

Diplomats are just as essential in starting a
war as soldiers are in finishing it.
Will Rogers

hat a great day, Schroeder."

"Yes, this is one fantastic day. The weather is sensational, air clear, cold and crisp. Snow is in the air for sure. You know what that means, Style?"

"No, but I know you will tell me, right?"

"Actually, I will. Great skiing is ahead for the weekend."

"Now you have become a weather forecaster?"

"You know what I mean, Style; don't give me a hard time, especially first thing in the morning before I have a cup of coffee."

"Sorry, Schroeder. I forgot you were very sensitive. Earlier this morning, I stopped by the American Embassy to pick-up the 3-D dimensional layout of the Clearstream building. Those folks at the Counter Terrorism Center (CTC) sure know what they are doing and are damn quick at doing it. The 3-D scale model is perfect in every detail. As soon as I picked up the scale model, I returned to the Park Hyatt Hotel and secured it in the hotel safe. Later tonight when we get together, we will use the 3-D scale model to begin our tactical reconnaissance planning in preparation for our eventual spy mission. How does that sound, Schroeder?"

"As always, Style, you are incessantly on top of everything. You are the best."

"Do I detect a little sarcasm, Schroeder?"

"Absolutely not."

"Getting back on track, while I was at the Embassy, I was updated with the very latest information on Al Qaeda."

"Well, what the hell is going on, Style?"

"Originally, for today, I planned to tell you I thought the end was just around the corner. However, that has changed. The news provided from the Global Response Center (GRC) and the National Security Center (NSC) is somewhat disconcerting and could throw a monkey wrench in our overall plans."

"How do you mean? I'm not familiar with those terms. What is 'around the corner' and 'monkey wrench?'"

"Hans, it more or less means, you can see the light at the end of the tunnel or we are getting close to finishing the project and monkey wrench means more potential problems."

"OK, Style; what is the monkey wrench news?"

"Apparently, within recent weeks, Al Qaeda and the National Democratic Organization (NDO) had a major conference in the southern part of Switzerland, more precisely in the Italian Alps. The essence of the meeting was to discuss joining forces and becoming allies. The 'get-together' was initiated by your boss Ulrich Melmer and Al Qaeda, headed by Abu Alouni and Al Zawa Europe, representing World Al Qaeda. The report indicated that NDO members came from most of the European countries, approximately ten in all. Apparently, the CIA agents and MI6 team assigned to do the surveillance did an outstanding job of ascertaining and gathering vital information. They successfully managed to get a complete list of all the attendees."

"That is quite remarkable. I assume they were never detected or discovered in accomplishing their mission, Style?"

"You are correct and all the information they obtained, helps us in our mission tonight. Now guess who else attended?"

"I have no idea, Style. Who?"

"You know our friend from the recent past, Karl Uber."

"That could explain why I haven't been followed in the last several days and weeks."

"That could be, Schroeder. The primary reasons for the meeting were to introduce philosophical and strategic rethinking on how to expand terrorist operations into more countries around the world. In addition, there was some discussion of tempering their aggressiveness, especially after they successfully infiltrated a country. According to the report, Al Qaeda has realized it has made some fatal mistakes, most notably in Iraq during the war when they estranged the Iraqi people. Apparently Al Qaeda killed many civilians for no ostensible reasons accept that they insisted on imposing severe Islamic rule. Also, Al Qaeda discussed most of their successes in Syria, Yemen and Libya. Additionally, there was serious mention of trying to create a more refined and warmer image of both Al Qaeda and NDO. But perhaps the most important part of discussions had to do with financing. I have a copy of both presentations (Al Qaeda and NDO) for you Schroeder. Here, please read this thoroughly and let me know tomorrow what you think."

"Certainly, I will read it completely, Style."

"How did the CIA know of the meeting and how did they get copies of these exceptionally obvious confidential materials?"

"Schroeder, as you know we have been tracking most of the terrorist around the world for years. These guys (Al Qaeda and NDO) sometimes leave tracks so obvious, there is no mistaking who they are, where they are and where they are going. I don't wish to make it appear so simple and cavalier, but the CIA and MI6 have been on their trail every waking moment, night and day. The overall theme of their conference was, Strategy to the Year 2020."

"If you ask me, Style, that is protracted planning and are very optimistic for both your short and especially long term goals."

"Absolutely right, Schroeder; just like finance guys too."

"All right, I get the picture."

"Just a little a humor tossed in to the melee, Schroeder. When you read the extensive report, they specifically emphasized and outlined ten major points."

"Style, it appears that they are becoming more sophisticated and are certainly more aware of image building and public relations."

"Yes, indeed they are Schroeder. What is perhaps the most eye opening of all the information we gathered from the meeting was the financial picture of both organizations. The financial meeting was completely private, attended only by Ulrich Melmer and Abu Alouni. The two men debated their respective financials of both their organizations and what they needed to accomplish in order to substantially increase income to support terrorist activities. They both revealed some rather thought-provoking information. Abu Alouni acknowledged that some of the initial funding came directly from the personal wealth of Osama bin Laden. Then Ulrich Melmer openly elaborated that Clearstream Finance and Bank Limited, along with SFINMA, became the predominant source of funding and the largest source of revenue for worldwide terrorism. I have to ask you Schroeder, how is it possible that Melmer has gotten away with this criminal behavior for so long?"

"I'm absolutely stunned, Style. I worked with the man for over twenty years and I had no idea he was involved in embezzlement, murder, assassination, cover-up and stealing on a grand scale. I am extremely outraged. I just wonder if his wife or anyone in his family is aware of his outrageous behavior."

"I think he has managed to hide all of his corrupt activity from his family. There is another interesting fact that was disclosed at their conference. The heroin trade was another major source of revenue for world terrorism for a very brief period of time, lasting from mid-1998 to early 2000. Fascinating enough, there was an additional revelation released supposedly through WikiLeaks. The released memo that originated from the White House and the Secretary of State's office sent in early 2011 proclaimed that the primary source of funding of Sunni terrorist groups worldwide was from a wealthy source in Saudi Arabia. However, at this private meeting, Abu Alouni turned to Ulrich Melmer and observed, "if only those damn jerks in Washington only new all of the true facts, they would be downright astonished and realize how uninformed they are." At one point Abu Alouni asked Ulrich how long would the existing funds last? Ulrich replied perhaps another fifteen to twenty years and amplified that there was at least eighty-five billion U.S. dollars on deposit at Clearstream.

"Now, Style, I personally find that to be astonishing. I have no idea how Melmer could possibly have hidden that much money without someone from the executive team uncovering any irregularities. I'm totally baffled and shocked."

"Let me continue, Schroeder, with more details. Apparently, Al Qaeda and NDO feel so confident that the United States will experience a major economic crisis by the year 2020, that the entire world financial market will tumble; it will then give these two fanatical terrorist groups an excellent opportunity to start a global jihad because of the world chaos and turmoil."

"They are absolute assholes beyond belief, Style. I just don't understand why someone like Melmer would get involved in something so bazaar and out of characte, especially when you consider, he has a very expensive and outstanding mansion located directly on Zurich Lake, beautiful grown children with grandchildren, a lovely wife and all the money in the world. It doesn't make any sense whatsoever. I'm shocked. What possesses someone to compromise their whole value system for an absurd radical ideology and fanatical terrorism?"

"Frankly, that is a great question, Schroeder."

"Melmer has everything a person could possible need or want in life, Style."

"Now get this, Schroeder. Evidently, they were both discussing how stupid and foolish the CIA functions and operates. They inferred that we were thoroughly clueless and not aware of any of their activities whatsoever."

"Do you know, Style, I would do anything in the world to see their twisted faces when both of those fucking assholes are caught, or better yet, shot dead. What arrogance and audaciousness."

"Schroeder, that day will come shortly."

"Do you have any more information, Style?"

"Just a couple more points. They have plans of having conference calls either every ten days or at least every two weeks. Of course, we will eavesdrop on all of these conferences calls, much to their surprise. Apparently, they are so overly confident we are unaware, they feel self-assured no one will create any problems or be able to listen to their secure telephone and cellular conversations."

"I simply can't believe what is happening to my company, Style. When this news breaks, it will literally destroy Clearstream Banking and thousands of people will lose their jobs. The entire city of Zurich will be dramatically impacted by the news. On the other hand, I understand our moral and principle obligations are to our country and the free world. I can assure you I haven't wavered whatsoever on seeing this problem resolved to the very end. If anything, I'm more resolved than ever to catch and prosecute these maniacal assholes."

"Thank you for your continued support, Schroeder."

"Personally, I couldn't conceive of any other way of dealing with these terrorist bastards, other than being merciless in our treatment of them for the scum they are. Unfortunately, Switzerland banned capital punishment and adopted the new law to ban capital punishment in the Swiss Federal Constitution. It was abolished from federal criminal law in 1942. However, there is Swiss military law that provides for the death penalty when treason is committed. Perhaps when all of these bastards are finally apprehended and brought to justice, the Swiss constitution can be amended to allow capital punishment just for these terrible, animalistic people."

"Well said, Schroeder. Well said."

"There is another somewhat related item I need to discuss with you this morning."

"Yes, and what may that be my young partner?"

"That is a great sense of humor, Schroeder. As always, I'm just giving you a hard time. I started to think earlier this morning when I was shaving and realized we have been in a reactionary mode in respect to Ulrich Melmer. We both have been concerned about you being followed. Isn't that correct?"

"Yes, but what is your point?"

"Why don't we reverse the tables and take the initiative by following Ulrich Melmer and perhaps his associate, Karl Uber? I realize that locating Karl Uber will not be easy to accomplish, but I believe when we begin keeping close tabs on Melmer, he'll lead us to Uber. By the way, did you plant the bugs I gave you?"

"Yes, absolutely, Style. I did exactly as you instructed."

"Great work, Hans. Here is a listening headset and a single earpiece that will allow you to listen to all of Ulrich Melmer's conversations when he's in his office or in his car. The respective bugs will generate a unique transmission that can be picked-up and tracked as far as a one-mile radius. In addition, you can listen to phone calls no matter where Uber is, as long as he's wearing the coat with the bug under the lapel and within range. Obviously, that means we can listen to all of his phone calls when we are in the Clearstream offices. Furthermore, whenever he's driving his Mercedes, we can also listen to all of his mobile phone conversations. What do you think, Schroeder?"

"Great stuff, Style."

"OK, after we finish our meeting this morning, I will get on the telephone with base operations at Langley, and request that they turn on all of the transmission and receiving devices we recently installed at Clearstream, allowing us to tune in to the bugs you planted. Once the system is on with all green lights, we can begin to eavesdrop on Ulrich Melmer's conversations and track his whereabouts."

"Style, I need to ask a really stupid question."

"I'm ready, Schroeder, and remember there is never a stupid question."

"How does the Counter Terrorism Center in Langley know which systems at Clearstream belong to us?"

"Actually, Schroeder, that wasn't a stupid question at all. In fact, I would say it was an excellent observation and a very intelligent question."

"Well, how does the system know, Style?"

"I was about to explain. All of the devices we are working with have microchips, which are intelligent enough to transmit an exceptionally unique and easily identifiable signal. Once the systems in the war room are turned on, a very large world map will display every intelligent device along with their respective nomenclature, serial number, and location which will also provide the quality of the transmission signal."

"That must be a very busy map, Style."

"Let me clarify a point. This particular topographical map is limited, concentrated and only focused on the devices we installed and bug drops you scattered about recently. Most likely, it will appear on a large video screen intended for Clearstream in Zurich."

"Now, that makes more sense."

"Furthermore, Schroeder, the mapping system will evaluate and determine the strength of the amplification, regardless of whether it is either a digital or an analog signal. In the event there is ever a device that doesn't provide a return signal, we can assume it is either malfunctioning or has been removed without our knowledge. All of the devices we installed, including the bug drops are designed to keep functioning continuously for at least thirty-six months. As a result, we have nothing to worry about for a while."

"Frankly, Style, I knew all of that crap even before you started to explain it. I was just testing your knowledge."

"Makes sense to me and I would not doubt you for one minute, Schroeder. We need to make arrangements to meet tonight to begin some of the final steps of our eaves-dropping and gathering information. However, before we start the grunt work, we need to examine closely and memorize everything in the 3-D dimensional layout of the Clearstream building."

"Why such detail, Style?"

"In the event we are discovered, or worse yet cornered, I have contingency plans in place that will create substantial diversions."

"Like what?"

"First, I have a remote control device that will turn off all of the lights in all of the buildings. As a result, the only thing that will function will be flashlights. By the time security is able to recover and get back on their feet, we will have escaped. That is where memorizing the 3-D layout, showing us every nook and cranny of the Clearstream building, will dramatically provide an advantage and help us in our escape. Also, at the same time, every fire, police and ambulance department will be notified and show up, creating more distractions and diversions."

"As I said days ago, you have an evil and devious mind, Style."

"Since the 3-D scale model is back at the Park Hyatt Hotel, we should meet tonight at my hotel room at around six-thirty. I can order room service, and then we begin memorizing and testing ourselves. That whole process should take approximately two hours and no longer. Once we are finished, then we can return to Clearstream. What time would work best for you at that point, Schroeder?"

"Now, that is a first, Style."

"After all, I do have a lot of respect for you, Schroeder. OK, let me restate the question. How about getting back to my office or perhaps in the lunch room at ten?"

"Style, I believe your office is better and I think there will be too many people still cleaning the floors in the lunchroom."

"OK, it will be ten tonight, Schroeder, so we can do the grunt work.

Remember, there is something I brought up yesterday that needs attention as soon as possible."

"Oh, you mean getting the daily password, allowing access into the general ledger and all of the accounting books."

"Yes, that is correct Schroeder. It would be ideal to have total access to all of the old accounting books, but since we can't remove them, the next best thing is to have remote access. Then, I can rapidly retrieve all the accounting information I need from the IBM AS400 systems and the Oracle financials accounting software engine that also includes extensive validations data with all the repositories and centralized control. This will be done simultaneously with the retrieval of the detailed audit trails that accommodate access to transformational diverse corporate management information along with the accounting rules. However, Schroeder, first you must take care of getting the daily password."

"That sounds too confusing to me Style but if you say so, I believe you. Consider getting the daily password accomplished, Style. I will have the password information tonight."

"Great work, Schroeder. That was one fulfilling breakfast."

"I totally agree."

"I'm ready to go, Style; just show me the way. Frankly, I'm so damn motivated and excited to kick ass."

"You are one mean son-of-a-bitch, Schroeder."

"You can say that again."

Style arrived back at the hotel, and arranged for the 3-D scale model of the Clearstream building to be delivered to his room. Of course, it was in a very large covered box, to protect the contents. When Style finally entered the room, he immediately put the scale model on display on top of the credenza alongside the television. The model was at least four feet high and approximately three feet by three feet with a detachable roof and removable floors within. It was a perfect replica down to the large double entry front doors. Every window, elevator shaft, stairway, office and storage space were accounted for. Nothing was missing. At seventhirty, Schroeder showed up and they immediately started to rehearse the walk-through process. Each took turns memorizing steps to the exit stairs and elevator. Room service interrupted the study long enough to allow the food to be setup and drinks poured. Once the waiter finished, Style signed the tab and he left. Without delay, they continued the systematic memorizing process. By nine-thirty, they were satisfied and finished a few last details. Soon thereafter, they proceeded back to Clearstream offices to finish their difficult assignment.

23

We must all hang together, or assuredly we shall all hang separately.
Benjamin Franklin

The task ahead was daunting and demanded total concentration for both Style and Schroeder. It was going to take considerable time and patience to complete most, if not all, of the tasks that Style originally outlined and planned. Their goal was to obtain and secure as much evidence and information that could be used in a court of law. In the final analysis and without saying, Style wasn't as concerned about what criminal prosecution system would prevail, as long as justice was carried out.

When Style and Schroeder arrived back at the Clearstream offices, they discovered there were still a number of people in the buildings. To avoid any possible problems or speculation, they decided to go have coffee at a nearby café for at least an hour or so. To pass time, they started to speculate what justice system would best be suitable and responsible for the prosecution of the criminals accountable for the theft and embezzlement of billions of dollars.

Style suggested that there was certainly substantial incentive for the United States justice system to prevail and be the primary final legal word in carrying out justice for those millions of innocent victims from World War II, and especially those victimized by the theft of all their worldly possessions, money and specifically those who lost their lives as victims at concentration camps.

Immediately following Style's observations, Schroeder provided a unique and interesting response, suggesting on the other hand that The International Court of Justice (ICJ), which has its seat in The Hague, Netherlands, is the principal judicial organ of the United Nations. The ICJ could exert a substantial amount of pressure on both the United States and the European Union. Most important, they would provide the fairest and best climate for the criminal proceedings.

Style contemplated what Schroeder said suggesting that doesn't justify why they should prevail as the legal authority. What could be there justification for wanting to try the case?

"Just recently," Schroeder explained, "the ICJ has acquired substantial courtroom experience on the subject of bank conspiracy, embezzlement, computer fraud, bank fraud and aggravated identity theft when it instituted a new level of justice for the European Union's new anti-money laundering banking directive and is extremely familiar with all the current legal processes, especially in Europe. Inevitably, as a result, they will insist on being the primary court for the proceedings. Furthermore, in recent years, The Hague has been extremely focused and successful in prosecuting bank embezzlement crime in both Switzerland and Germany, using the now very familiar WEED Act (World Economy, Ecology and Development). Contrary to popular perception, Switzerland and Germany are a popular destination for money laundering and embezzlement activities. Being a liquid market with high cash flow makes the country attractive, while also complicating the monitoring of financial flows. Its central location between Eastern and Western Europe makes Switzerland and Germany an ideal trading center. Regulatory weaknesses amplify the problem. As a result, they have a thorough knowledge of what is necessary to provide the best judicial environment in order to have a successful prosecution, while offering the most fair defense and unbiased courtroom atmosphere."

"From a pragmatic standpoint, there is one large consideration that needs to be addressed to satisfy the legal perspective, Schroeder. And that is both Al Qaeda and the National Democratic Organization remain political factions without borders. Certainly, that would absolutely create some serious legal problems for the International Court of Justice in The Hague. I can tell you, there is no doubt the Department of State, White House and the American justice system will do everything possible to have the trial moved to the United States."

"That makes sense, Style. Are you suggesting, the very controversial United States military detention camp located in Guantanamo Bay Naval Base, Cuba, be that unbiased environment?"

"Most assuredly, Schroeder."

"Style, that doesn't make much sense whatsoever, especially after all the public criticisms and disagreements your President has created these last couple of years over the unscrupulous treatment of Islamic terrorist prisoners in Guantanamo Bay. In fact, he insists on not calling them terrorist at all. I believe he also has ordered everyone in his administration not to use the word 'terrorist' when referring to the Islamic bad guys. Isn't that correct?"

"Yes, that is correct and I will not deny it either."

"Have I hit a nerve, Style?"

"Schroeder, you know damn well how I feel about not calling these known bastard extremists, assassins and cowardly bombers terrorists. It is the most absurd and stupid argument in the world to try to suggest known terrorists should be treated with tenderness and sensitivity. They are terrorists, pure and simple."

"Wow! I did wind you up."

"Yes you did, Schroeder. However, because the President of the United States doesn't acknowledge the word terrorism, doesn't suggest or imply the rest of the United States should not be honest and express the truth in how they feel. Unfortunately, most of the free press in the United States, including the New York Times, Washington Post, and Associated Press Wire Service and all the major television networks like ABC, CBS, NBC and CNN, have adopted the President's soft shoe routine and are treating terrorists like they are long lost ancestors and friends. They make it appear that we are engaged in some insignificant family feud or small petty argument. They all should call a spade a spade, especially the President of the United States. His progressive thinking will get this country into serious trouble. Mark my word."

"I understand, Style."

"Schroeder, when all is said and done, the absolute bottom line is that it is imperative we do the best and most professional job achievable. Absolutely nothing less. In the final analysis all of the data, evidence and information we secure, must be as complete and as thorough as possible."

"I totally agree. Have you finished your coffee, Style?"

"Yes. I'm ready to go. That discussion consumed at least an hour and that afforded us an excellent opportunity to debate, Schroeder. A discussion like that is healthy and keeps you on your toes."

"Yes, it does."

It was just after ten o'clock and the Clearstream buildings appeared absent of people. At this point, neither Style nor Schroeder needed any tools or a tool bag, just a small device to pick locks. What was needed more than anything else was for both Style and Schroeder to become stealth and remain as invisible as possible. Both were dressed in black from their athletic shoes to the mask and cap on their head. In addition, both had their respective Nokia mobile phones that now provided a window of access into the Clearstream security system. They couldn't only see, but could also listen and hear movement or conversation well in advance if someone was coming close or in proximity to any of the offices they were searching. Style optioned to start with the finance department because it was the most secure office, with the greatest risk. Immediately when they entered, they started in the very back of the room at the last file cabinet. Style started to search one file drawer at a time. On average, it took at least five to ten minutes per file cabinet. Each file was photographed along with a digital video recording. Once finished with a file, Style was extremely careful when he returned the file to its original location. Some files contained more information than others, and because some of the files were very old, they were treated with extra delicate handling. As a result, Style and Schroeder wore latex gloves to avoid leaving any fingerprints or evidence. In some instances, a handful of files did cause some problems. However, most were very easy to deal with despite the age of the files. Many files dated back to the late 1920s. Approximately three hours into the project, they finally finished with the finance department. So far, there were no threatening problems with security or any unexpected visitors showing up. Next, they started in the personnel offices. It was apparent after Style and Schroeder had worked for about two hours, both concluded the files in the personnel department were in worse shape, which didn't make sense whatsoever. There were files in the wrong place, and some files were totally misplaced or simply thrown together for no apparent reason other than just laziness and sloppy administration. However, there were very few files missing. As a result, Style had to be extra careful that every file was replaced exactly to its original position. Nevertheless, it never really affected their progress, because by now, both were very efficient in accomplishing their

respective jobs. By five in the morning, they were ready to wrap it up. In approximately seven hours, they achieved their mission and that included photographing and video recording all of the records throughout all of the buildings. Surprisingly, that also incorporated all the executives' offices, including Melmer's office and all of his personal files. Prior to departing each of the different departments, they also managed to plant listening and GPS bugs in most of the file cabinets. This was done as a precautionary move in the event Melmer and his crew decided to move all the file cabinets to an unknown destination, and just in case something happened to all of Style's evidence.

"I just remembered something extremely important, Schroeder."

"Yes, what is it Style?"

"Do you have the daily password code to allow me total access to all of the Oracle financial accounting systems?"

"Actually, Style, I was waiting for you to ask that very question."

"Well, do you have it Schroeder?"

"Be patient. Yes I do. Here is the password for today and tomorrow. From what I understand, they haven't changed the code in over a week."

"That is fantastic news, Schroeder."

"When will you begin retrieving all the accounting information from the IBM AS400 and Oracle financials accounting systems?"

"Probably when I return to my hotel room this morning, Schroeder."

"Do you think you will need anything from me when you start the download process, Style?"

"No, but if I do, I will give you a call."

"Sounds great, Style"

At this point, Style and Schroeder were both enthusiastic about their success. Once they departed the Clearstream buildings, they separated each going in a different direction. Just prior, Style told Schroeder, "I may call you later in the afternoon after both of us had some rest. Is three o'clock or so ok with you?"

Schroeder replied, "I look forward to your call."

The moment Style got back to his hotel room; he prepared his report for DiSciascio.

After a very long night, Schroeder and I finally finished taking photographs and digital motion pictures of all of the files at Clearstream. At the bottom of my report, please find attached the digital files. We also accomplished the installation of security and motion detection cameras and installed GPS tracking devices in all of the file cabinets, attached GPS chips on individual files in the event someone decided to remove files. Finally, Schroeder also placed bug drops in Ulrich Melmer's office, car and attached several to some of Melmer's top coats and jackets.

I would like to thank the Counter Terrorism Center for their wonderful designs of the construction and building of the 3-D model of the Clearstream facilities. As a result of receiving the 3-D model earlier than originally planned, we were able to complete the task one day sooner. It was built to perfect scale and was extremely useful for Schroeder and me in our preparation and training. Sometime today, after I take a rest, I expect to begin writing software application programs to allow me to hack in to the Clearstream financial accounting systems and retrieve all the accounting information I need from IBM AS400 systems, and the back office application software of the Oracle financials.

Once I complete writing the program interface, I will than begin extracting all of the vital accounting documents, including most of the old archives going as far back as the late 1920s. More than likely, it will probably take me at least four to six hours of writing lines of program code to functionally allow work-arounds. I will not bore you with the details.

Finally, I should be able to complete and then transmit all of the information to you and the Counter Terrorism Center at Langley within two days.

Be safe,

Style

As soon as Style rested, he was at his computer and prepared to begin outlining the necessary steps for writing the software programs allowing him access to the Clearstream accounting system. As he originally anticipated, he was able to finish writing the complex application software in just over six hours. He did some testing and, fortunately, was successful in his initial entry into the IBM AS400 systems and the back office Oracle Clearstream accounting financials. Initially, the system was slow and seemed to grind to a snail's pace. He soon was able to isolate the problem to either the telephone lines, at the local telephone company's digital subscriber lines (DSL) or the Park Hyatt Hotel. Fortunately, there was no problem at the Clearstream location. Shortly, Style abruptly discovered part of the difficulty was the trunk lines at the hotel and some issue with the telephone company. The phone company corrected their problem fast. A short time later, the Park Hyatt Hotel fixed their trunk lines. In fact, Style decided to ask the hotel manager to arrange for a private trunk line. Of course, the general manager said it was going to be expensive.

Style responded by stating he needed a dedicated line to facilitate the transmission of a substantial number of digital photographs and digital recordings. Naturally, this was only the partial truth. He requested that all of the additional telephone charges be added to his hotel bill and he would satisfy the entire balance first thing in the morning. In the meantime, he decided to give Schroeder a break by not calling him as planned.

Literally, by early evening, the extraction of all the financial materials was complete. Immediately, Style, began to transmit all of the Clearstream records, including the digital photographs and video recordings of the accounting, financial and personnel records to the Counter Terrorism Center at Langley. He also transmitted copies to DiSciascio in London.

Once he finished, he realized he hadn't eaten all day and decided it was about time to take a break and have dinner. At the same time, he could pause, take a short break and celebrate, just slightly.

24

The political object is the goal, war is the means of reaching it, and the
means can never be considered in isolation from their purposes.
Karl von Clausewitz

*L*ater in the evening at around eight, Style decided to call Zosa to
ask if she would be interested in having either breakfast or lunch
tomorrow. He had talked with her several days ago and explained
to her he couldn't break away until he was finished with this aspect of the
financial project.

It was obvious both wanted to see one another, but circumstances were
dictating all of their decisions. Zosa was extremely busy with her play and
there was some speculation that once the play ended in approximately
eight weeks or possibly less, they would take the musical play on the road
to other cities in Switzerland, and then open engagements in Austria and
Germany. Of course, that could change if there was a favorable response
by the theatre crowd to the new dance routines and the additional songs.
Initial reviews have been terrific; at least that is what Zosa's sister, Marie,
indicated. The only other option available to Zosa at this time would be
to begin auditioning for another musical play set to open in Zurich, possibly mid-Spring. In all the years Zosa had been singing and dancing in

musical plays and cabarets, she hadn't been required to travel at all. This certainly would be her first time.

When Style telephoned Zosa, he realized there would be an excellent chance she would not be at home because of the time in the evening. As expected, when he called there wasn't an answer, so Style decided she was probably performing at the theater and left a voice message, indicating to please call regardless of the time it was when she picked up the telephone message. In his message, he specifically suggested they either have brunch or lunch tomorrow, preferably in a nice quiet and romantic setting.

Sometime after midnight, around 2 a.m., Style's mobile phone rings. It took him four or five rings before he was able to answer the phone.

"Hello, John, this is Zosa. Sorry, I woke you up."

"Please don't apologize. Thank you for returning my call, Zosa. You are right. I'm still asleep. What time is it?"

"It is very early in the morning and I'm just getting home from the theatre, John. Good morning, sleepy head. As I just mentioned, I'm now just getting home from the play. I realize you have been keeping strange, very long and demanding hours, John."

"You are certainly correct, Zosa. These last weeks have been rough."

"How do you mean, John?"

"My schedule has been extremely demanding, both day and night. Please understand, I'm not complaining, because I truly enjoy my work. Some nights, I'm not finished with work until early morning."

"I don't know how you can maintain such an exhausting grind, John. I trust you are compensated well for all of your hard work."

"Yes I am, Zosa. The good thing is we are finally getting to the end of the project and I can begin to see the light through the forest."

"Certainly that is good, right John?"

"Yes, it is Zosa."

"Let me get to your message immediately before you fall asleep on me, John. Tomorrow for lunch sounds fantastic. How about if I come to the hotel at twelve, then we can go for a drive and search for a nice café on the east side of Zurich Lake?"

"Thank you. That is just a wonderful idea, Zosa."

"John, there is only one caveat."

Yes, what is the problem?"

"Nothing major, but I need to return home no later than five-thirty, allowing us enough time to have an enjoyable afternoon together. I must return to the studio for a late afternoon rehearsal. Beginning tonight, the producers are introducing several new dance routines. We have been practicing these new dance routines all week, and everything is working just fine. So far, reviews have been very good."

"I understand completely. Certainly, there is no issue whatsoever with five-thirty."

"Thank you for being so understanding and willing to listen, John. Now you go back to sleep and I will see you at noon tomorrow."

As soon as Zosa hung up, Style was fast asleep. When morning arrived, it was as if he just put his head on the pillow. It was early, just past six. Style slept deeply and was fully rested. He looked at the bed where he slept and thought, "I don't think I moved an inch the entire night." Finally, he rolled out of bed, and then ordered room service. Immediately, he started up his laptop and checked his mobile phone just in case someone tried to call. The very first thing in Style's Outlook e-mail message box was a top-secret encrypted message from DiSciascio.

Style

We received all of the documentation, including the digital photographs and digital film. In addition, Counter Terrorism Center (CTC), at Langley received their copies as well. Since it is too premature to provide any professional observations, I can personally tell you, we are extremely satisfied with the results so far. Once the Counter Terrorism Center finishes their assessment, they will notify me. I should receive some indication within three days at the latest. Remember, there was a hell of a lot of information. All of the work you submitted was outstanding. Additional copies of your files will also be sent to Global Response Center (GRC) and the National Security Center (NSC). We congratulate both you and Schroeder for a great job. I think tonight you deserve to go out and have a good time. In fact, hoist a few for me as well. Before I forget, please thank Schroeder for me and tell him "outstanding work." Will talk with you shortly

Be safe

DiSciascio

As soon as Style finished reading his reports, he started to clean up. He decided to go down to the hotel gym and workout. When he finished his tough two-hour workout in the gym, on his way back to his room he decided to see if Marie was at the Concierge desk.

"Good morning, Mr. Style."

"That is a great welcome, Marie, and a good morning to you. Do you know every time I see you, I swear it is Zosa and I want to hug you. I just wanted to let you know that your sister and I are going for a ride this afternoon, and we plan to have lunch on the Eastside of Zurich Lake. Do you have any suggestions for a romantic setting with great food?"

"Yes, I have an excellent recommendation, Mr. Style."

"I hope that it isn't too far, because your sister has a rehearsal later in the afternoon."

"The café is called, Cheeky, approximately fifty kilometers or less than one-hour drive time, taking the A3 Motorway south along the East perimeter. It's a beautiful day to enjoy the spectacular Swiss Mountain range."

"Thank you, Marie"

"Mr. Style, tonight my husband and I will be attending my sister's musical play again. Would you be interested in joining us? I realize that you have seen the play, just as we have, but they have added changes with more dance numbers. You know what that means, Mr. Style. Certainly, you will be very pleased, because my sister will be on stage more often."

"That sounds fantastic; yes, I would like very much to join you and your husband tonight."

"I will arrange to have a ticket sent to your room no later than five this afternoon. Is that all right with you? I have the afternoon off to do some shopping."

"Marie, will we be seated together?"

"Of course, Mr. Style. The ticket will be on your hotel room desk, next to the telephone."

"That will work just fine, Marie."

"Wonderful. We will see you tonight at the theater."

"I look forward to meeting with you and your husband tonight, Marie."

"Drive carefully, Mr. Style."

"I will and thank you, Marie."

"I just remembered something Mr. Style; we expect snow beginning around noontime. The snow is expected to be especially heavy around the lake. So please be extra careful."

"I understand and I will be extra vigilant, especially with your sister Zosa in the car."

"Please tell my sister, I will stop by her townhome later in the afternoon to pick-up a couple of items. She will know what I'm talking about as soon as you tell her."

Since I will be with your sister this afternoon, I won't tell her that I'm going to her play again tonight. It will be a big surprise."

"Obviously, Mr. Style, I won't say anything either."

Immediately after leaving Marie, Style returned to his hotel room to clean-up, shave and take a shower. Once he was dressed, room service had already delivered his light breakfast of just coffee, a glass of orange juice and croissant, along with the morning London Times. He finished reading the London Times rather hastily. There was nothing of note throughout the newspaper. He decided to take it easy with another cup of coffee and admire the landscape of beautiful Zurich Lake and the breathtaking Swiss Alps. There was a very light amount of snow beginning to fall. The snow was clinging to the branches on the trees, along with the streets and roadways. Zurich Lake looked just like a winter nirvana, glistening and shimmering with a partial sun peeking from behind the large cottony clouds, reflecting off the ice covered surface of the lake. This happened to be one of those rare moments that allowed Style to relax and reflect while at the same time be thankful for everything God gave him. Soon, Style fell into a deep sleep while reading a Hemingway novel, "Farewell to Arms," when suddenly his mobile phone rang, and he was in a third stage of non-rapid eye movement sleep. Finally, when he answered his phone, he could hardly speak. On the other end, Zosa was being polite and trying not to shout, but she had no choice but to begin yelling: "Hello, hello, hello, is this John Style?"

Style, finally realized who was calling and said, "I apologize, Zosa; I fell asleep at the last minute."

"Please John, don't worry about such a small thing; you were simply too tired and needed more rest."

"That is very nice of you to be so empathetic and understanding. Now I know why I enjoy your companionship so much."

"You are most welcome. Are you sure, John, that is the real reason?"

"Yes, Zosa, now you are teasing me again."

"Well, it is now noontime sleepy head. The reason for the phone call was too simply remind you that I'm down in the lobby waiting for you."

"I will be down right away."

Style made it down to the lobby in record time.

"Zosa, you look absolutely beautiful and radiant."

"Thank you, John. That is a very kind thing to say."

They embraced and kissed passionately. As matter of fact, the young clerk at the front desk was getting a little embarrassed by their open romantic display of affection.

"Are you ready to roll, Zosa?"

"Bring it on, John. See, I'm beginning to talk like you."

"I talked with your sister earlier and she recommended a café by the name of Cheeky on the Eastside of the Zurich Lake, not too far, approximately thirty minutes away."

"Guess what, John? I already talked with my sister and she did tell me that she recommended Cheeky."

"Well, what do you think?"

"My sister gave a great recommendation because Cheeky is one of the best restaurants on the lake, with an out of this world luncheon menu in a splendid setting. In addition, my sister told me that she would stop by my townhome later in the afternoon. Message delivered."

"Out of curiosity Zosa, did you sister happen to mention that she managed again to get me an extra ticket for your musical play tonight?"

"Certainly I'm thrilled you would take the time to see my play again. Yes, my sister tells me everything. Naturally, my sister and I share all things important. There are no secrets between us."

"I kind of suspected that would be the case."

"Why is that, John?"

"No particular reason. It's nothing important, Zosa."

Because there was at least two or three inches of snow already on the roadway, Style realized he couldn't be foolhardy driving the Porsche, especially since he didn't have very much experience driving in the snow. Before they departed the hotel parking lot however, they managed one more passionate embrace. As they held one another, John ran his hand slowly down Zosa's back, taking pleasure in her sensuality. Gently, he kissed her on the cheek and said, "I truly enjoy being with you and holding your hand."

Zosa realized that John was getting excited with passion and simply said, "We had better leave before there is too much snow on the road."

John understood and momentarily they were ready to leave. Zosa appeared comfortably seated. Style patiently and deliberately negotiated the Porsche 911 on to the A3 Motorway. Within thirty- minutes or less, they arrived at the café despite the hazardous driving conditions. He parked the Porsche and slowly they walked into the café and were seated next to one of the bay windows overlooking the snowed covered lake and mountains. Style ordered a bottle of one of the best French Bordeaux's on the wine menu. At once, Zosa had to remind Style She could only have one glass of wine because of rehearsal.

Style told her he understood completely——if he had to play in a tennis tournament, he would do same thing. Immediately, Zosa replied, "Now you are a tennis professional, John."

Suddenly he realized what he said and hastily clarified, "That was just a figure of speech."

"I understand, John. However, I still challenge you to a tennis match…soon I hope."

"Zosa, just name the time and location, and I will be there, no matter where you want to play a tennis match, beautiful lady dancer."

"Now, that is indeed a serious challenge to take on, my serious, sleepy American business financial consultant. However, the most important description would be kind and loving man."

"Wow! I'm sure on the spot now. Despite the overwhelming odds, I will take on your competitive spirit and accept your challenge my beautiful, tall, talented Swiss entertaining snow princess."

"Next week John, I will call you to set a tennis date. Then we shall see."

"I'm ready, Zosa."

They spent close to three hours enjoying themselves talking, kissing, and holding hands. Despite the freezing cold temperature, they walked on the deck overlooking the beautiful lake. At about the time they were ready to leave, the sun suddenly peered through the heavy overcast clouds and, at the same time, it stopped snowing.

Style navigated the Porsche carefully through the now melting snow, as though he spent many years driving in hazardous and dangerous snowy conditions. He was extra cautious. Within a short period of time, they arrived at the theatre where Zosa was performing. Zosa hurriedly said, "Thank you, John" and asked if he would like to join her later after the final curtain?"

John replied right away, "Absolutely I can't wait to hold you in my arms again."

They kissed and she departed.

Style drove back to the Park Hyatt Hotel and parked the Porsche. When he entered the hotel lobby, at the last minute he decided to go for a brief walk around to the back of the hotel to enjoy once more the breathtaking beauty of Zurich Lake. Because of the cold, there was no one to be seen. Everywhere he looked it appeared very empty as though people were told to abandon the lake because of the great flood coming. However, it was peaceful and welcoming from the everyday noise of urban city life.

Finally, Style chose to return to his room and read. Before picking up his book, he checked his watch and realized it was early enough to call Schroeder on the mobile phone to see how he was getting along. There was no answer after five or six rings, so Style left a voice message asking Schroeder to return his call early tomorrow morning. Then Style remembered, Schroeder mentioned something about going skiing in the mountains over the weekend. For no apparent reason, Style turned on his laptop to check for messages. As soon as he opened his Outlook e-mail file, there was a flash message from Global Response Center.

Field Agents:

Reliable sources are indicating that both Al Qaeda and the National Democratic Organization are on the move. These sources also indicate that both organizations are in the process of either committing an assassination or setting off a large explosive device or possibly both. Collaborative informers are saying the information is highly reliable and have confirmed that the attack and/or bombing appear to be imminent and impending. The threatening act will most likely take place in a major European city sometime today. We will certainly keep you updated.

Thank you,

GRC

It was now just past six o'clock and Style started to the shower when suddenly he receives a mobile phone call.

"Hello Style, this is DiSciascio with a major update from GRC and CTC. Please listen carefully. CTC has just received absolute confirmation that Brussels or Zurich or both are the targeted cities. From all intelligence available, there is no evidence of any major world dignitary in either city."

"I think I understand, DiSciascio. I definitely will be on total alert and very careful."

"Style, before I hang-up, I need to ask you, have you been followed at all recently?"

"Not since, I returned from Dubai."

"Do you know if Schroeder has been tailed?"

"No. That was one of the last things we discussed when we finished our project together."

"Where is Schroeder now,?"

"That is a good question, DiSciascio. I haven't been able to reach him. In fact, I attempted calling him about an hour ago. I did leave a message to call me ASAP. However, earlier in the week he mentioned he would go skiing in the mountains if it snowed and it has snowed plenty."

"Style, if you hear from him, contact me immediately."

"Yes sir."

"In the meantime, be extra vigilant."

"Yes sir, I will."

"Be safe and goodbye Style."

"Goodbye DiSciascio."

As soon as Style finished his discussion with DiSciascio, he took a quick shower and dressed. After he finished putting his coat on, he checked both weapons to make sure they were loaded. He also made certain he carried an extra supply of shells. At this point, he had no idea what to expect. Style was uncomfortable and it showed. There was no doubt, he felt uneasy. He kept on telling himself, "these miserable cowards, what bastards they are." He called down to the front desk and asked that a taxi be available in five minutes in the front of the hotel. He explained he would be down right away.

Within a few minutes, Style was boarding the taxi and on his way to meet with Marie and her husband at the theater. Approximately a half mile away from the Park Hyatt Hotel, there was a tremendous explosion that shook the taxi, breaking windows and causing the driver to lose control of the cab. Fortunately, at the time of the explosion, he was driving moderately slow in order to negotiate a turn at a corner, not too far from the theater. The cab hit a parked car and flipped on to its side. The taxi driver appeared to have serious injuries only, but not life threatening. Style was somewhat startled and appeared to be in a daze. He was bleeding slightly from the top of his head. He thought he was fine, at least for now. Immediately, he assisted the taxi driver out of the cab.

Within a few minutes, the driver was conscious and doing just fine. He appeared to have minor injuries, but was very emotional. Style called for assistance. Within minutes, a number of Zurich police patrol cars, fire trucks and an ambulance showed up. Style immediately informed the first response unit that he was OK, but thought the taxi driver needed assistance and was going into shock and needed to be checked-out. In a short time, more response units arrived. Style was listening intently to all the radio communication chatter and was able to put together in pieces that the explosion occurred within a very short distance from the theatre district and close to where the taxi crashed.

He asked one of the patrol officers what happened?

"First, I need to ask you what happened to you, sir?"

"I'm just fine. There is nothing wrong with me officer."

"It doesn't look that way, sir. You are bleeding very badly."

"Officer you were about to say something about the bomb location?"

"Yes, you are correct." Immediately, the cop said he thought the exact location of the explosion was at the theatre where the musical 'Pajama

Tops and Bottoms' were performing. Without hesitation, Style took off in the direction of the theater. All Style could think about was Zosa. Within minutes, he arrived on foot in front of the theater.

He couldn't believe his eyes. The entire front section of the theater had collapsed and was now on fire. The blaze started to spread rapidly to nearby buildings. There were many people hurt. Soon, they started carrying out dead bodies from inside the theater. There were at least twenty or more dead bodies strewn about in the front of the theater, all uncovered. Many had died in a horrible manner. There was blood, body parts, shattered glass, splintered wood, metal, broken bricks and every imaginable piece of material from the theatre scattered everywhere. Most, if not all the adjacent buildings, windows were shattered and broken. People who survived the bomb blast were walking around in a daze, either looking for help or searching for loved ones. Style did his best in providing first aid to some of the victims. Soon, he too looked like he was a victim covered in blood. Despite everything, Style continued looking and hoping nothing had happened to Zosa. From the corner of his eye, as he was kneeling down to assist a young woman, he recognized a dress not too far away. The dress looked identical to the dress Zosa wore the last time they went out to dinner after her performance at the 'Pajama Tops and Bottoms' show.

He ran over immediately and dropped to his knees to take a much closer look and without doubt, it was Zosa. There was no mistaking the black and burgundy off the shoulder design of the dress either. She was dead. Around her neck was the pearl necklace he recently gave her. Obviously, she bled to death because of all the serious head and body wounds with some of the most horrific injuries to her torso and legs. Zosa's beautiful face was now ripped apart. Literally, she was crushed to death. Now, Style was in total shock. He couldn't accept that Zosa was dead. He managed to get to his feet, carrying Zosa's lifeless body. He was clutching her body in his arms, as if he were at a religious ritual. He simply couldn't help himself. John Style thought he might as well be dead. The emotional pain was so excruciating and totally without any sense of comprehension. At this moment in time, nothing made sense. Cautiously, someone came up to Style and asked could they help?

He mumbled something very incoherently. Style was trying his best to understand, but simply couldn't. Finally, a nurse convinced Style to sit down and let her get assistance to take Zosa's body to the waiting ambulance. Reluctantly, Style let the emergency ambulance driver take Zosa away.

Style sat on the cold snowy ground oblivious to everything going on around him. Because the emotional pain was so deep, he wept openly, loudly and completely. For one of the very first times in his adult life, Style couldn't function, both physically and emotionally. He stood up and started to yell to the heavens, "why God, why?" Soon, Style collapsed.

In the meantime, the fire continued to rage and spread to adjacent buildings. All hell seemed to break loose at the same time. Making matters worse for the fire response and medical care units, were the old narrow streets. Everywhere you looked there was congestion with cars, people, on-lookers and emergency units trying to get to their destination. It was getting cold and it started to snow heavily. Unfortunately, most of the surviving victims were not even conscious of the cold or snow. Because of the chaos and madness, many victims who were not yet provided any type of first aid treatment, walked around in a trance. John Style was indeed one of those victims.

25

Chiefs who no more in bloody fights engage, But wise through time,
and narrative with age, In summer–days like grasshoppers rejoice,
A bloodless race, that sends a feeble voice.
Alexander Pope

UNIVERSITY HOSPITAL ZURICH, SWITZERLAND
The following morning, Style learned rather unexpectedly that he was lying in a hospital bed. At first, he thought he was dreaming and having a nightmare. In addition, he discovered he had bandages around his head; his leg was elevated and was in a cast. He never realized the extent of his personal injuries sustained in the taxicab crash. Style had suffered lacerations to the back of his head and face along with multiple wounds to his torso and leg. Fortunately, it was nothing serious no broken bones or torn ligaments. He simply couldn't comprehend that he was now in one of the best hospitals in Switzerland, the University Hospital Zurich. He looked far worse than he actually was. His head was swathed in bandages and his right leg was heavily dressed in a temporary binding and raised up in the air via a pulley system.

One of the nurses came in to his room and introduced herself. "Mr. Style, I'm Susan Beucler, your personal nurse during the daytime shift."

"Hello, Miss Beucler."

She asked if he was interested in seeing guests today. Although groggy and under heavy pain medication, Style said he would see visitors and asked if she had any idea who they may be.

"Not exactly sure, Mr. Style. I was just trying to make sure you felt well enough for visitors today. If anyone shows up, would you like me to first screen them first?"

"That isn't necessary, Miss Beucler. Thank you for asking. I just feel like I'm having a bad nightmare."

"You are very fortunate, Mr. Style."

"Why is that?"

"Well, first you lost lots of blood from the explosion and the accident. When you arrived last night, you were in shock and lost consciousness the moment you were placed in this room. Since you are just beginning to comprehend the circumstances of what happened last evening, most everything will seem surreal and like a dream."

"I'm already having nightmares, Miss Beucler. Do you have any idea how long I will remain here in the hospital?"

"No. On the other hand, I'm sure it will be for at least a week or longer. Your doctor should be here in approximately two hours and you can ask him all the questions."

"All right, thank you again, Miss Beucler."

As soon as the nurse left his room, Style went in to a deep sleep. Approximately three hours later, Style started to hear strange voices and slowly woke up.

"Good morning, I'm Dr. Hiunger, your physician and orthopedic specialists. How do you feel, Mr. Style?"

"I can honestly say, not one hundred percent doctor."

"Fair enough, let me give you an assessment and then I will tell you both the good and bad news. How is that?"

"That sounds fine, doctor."

"First, you were very fortunate, considering the overwhelming damage and destruction the massive bomb created last night. Many people were killed and there were literally over a hundred people severely hurt. Many of those survivors are now patients here at University Hospital

Zurich. You suffered a contusion and concussion, but not critical. In addition, the lacerations on the back of your head and down your cheek should heal with no problems. The stitches in your head and face will remain for approximately a week. You will definitely have a scar on your face but over time, it will begin to become less noticeable. The wounds and bruising to your torso were slightly more serious but not critical; however, they will cause you some discomfort for a while. The intravenous in your arm is for pain. If you experience discomfort or pain, just press the red button that is attached to the side of the bed. It will provide instant relief. Now, for the most critical injury - your leg. As I said previously, you were extremely fortunate, Mr. Style. Although you didn't suffer any fractured bones or torn muscles or ligaments, as a precaution, I highly recommend we keep you in traction for at least four to seven days. By the fourth or fifth day, I will then examine you closely again. Do you have any questions so far, Mr. Style?"

"Yes, actually I do doctor. Will I be capable of running and playing tennis again?"

"Initially my response is you should not have any problem recovering and getting back to a normal life."

"What exactly does that mean doctor?"

"That will depend entirely on you, Mr. Style. First, in order to have a reasonable and normal recovery period, you need to be patient and disciplined enough to follow my medical instructions. Second, it also means you must attend physical therapy as required, listen to your nurses and take your medications as prescribed. That simple, just follow my directive and everything else will fall into place."

"So, there will be no complications or serious problems, doctor?"

"As I said, you should have a normal recovery and do well, Mr. Style."

"That is good news, doctor. I have another question. If I do everything you recommend, can I begin playing serious tennis in two or three weeks?"

"I can't guarantee you anything. However, in my professional opinion, yes, you will be capable of playing competitive tennis, but more likely in a month or two."

"Great, doctor. I realize that I'm most fortunate to have suffered so little. Thank you for treating me so well and being candid with me."

"You are welcome, Mr. Style, and I will see you tomorrow at about the same time."

"I have one last question, doctor."

"Yes?."

"Are you familiar with the family name, Dena?"

"No, Mr. Style, I don't recognize the name."

"Doctor, perhaps you may recognize the names Zosa and Marie Dena."

"No, I don't recognize either name. Is there is a special reason you ask about them?"

"They are sisters and I was supposed to meet them at the musical 'Pajama Tops and Bottoms.'"

"Sorry, I can't help you. However, I will ask the staff and post a notice with their names and at the bottom of the posting, I will add your name and room number. How is that?"

"That would help immensely and thank you. Good-bye doctor, I will see you tomorrow."

Later in day, as Style was lying in bed, he started to look closely at his room. Obviously, it was private. Nevertheless, there is something unexciting about hospital rooms; they all look identical, no matter what country you are visiting. Typical of all hospitals, all night long Style's sleep was disturbed and interrupted. It started first with a blood pressure check, temperature measurement, medications, replacing the bedpan, intravenous changes, and more needles and on and on, it never seemed to stop. There is no doubt he was beginning again to feel the effects of the pain medication. Style was getting tired and it showed. He asked the nurse to turn down the light in his room. Shortly, he was in a deep sleep. Finally, at about four in the morning and for about two straight hours, Style could rest and sleep.

When Style woke up at around six, he was hungry. Thirty minutes later, breakfast finally arrived and it wasn't what Style expected. There was no coffee, one poached egg, small apple juice and toast, no butter. He finished his breakfast right away and asked for more. Of course, they said no because he was on a special diet prescribed by the doctor, with a reduced number of calories.

Just before nine, Style received his first visitor.

"Good morning Mr. Style, I'm Dana Fox, the United States Ambassador, here in Switzerland."

Because of the severe nature of the tragedy two days ago, we were just notified early today that you were a patient here at University Hospital Zurich. As you can imagine, most everything is in a state of confusion throughout Zurich. You were the only American citizen to survive. There was an American married couple in line at the theatre; unfortunately, they both were killed instantly when the explosion occurred. As of early today, there is no indication or evidence to show who is responsible for the explosion. Immediately, when we were notified at the Embassy that you were a patient, we contacted the CIA in Washington D.C. It is my understanding your case officer and handler, James DiSciascio, will be arriving in Zurich sometime this afternoon.

"I look forward to his arrival, Madam Ambassador."

"In the meantime, is there anything we can do to help you at this time Mr. Style?"

"No, I don't think so, nothing at this time, Madam Ambassador."

"I understand that Zurich Hospital is one of the best hospitals in Switzerland and throughout Europe."

"The treatment so far has been wonderful, Madam Ambassador."

"Now, is there someone in your family I could contact to provide the good news about your physical condition?"

"At this time, I don't think that would be a good idea, Madam Ambassador."

"I think I understand your circumstances, Mr. Style."

"Here is my business card. On the back, I listed my personal mobile and home phone numbers in the event you need any assistance."

"Thank you for taking time to come visit, Madam Ambassador."

"You are most welcome. We would like to wish you a speedy and safe recovery. Please visit with me at the Embassy when you are discharged from the hospital if you have the time. I understand you visited the Embassy just recently."

"Yes, I did. I picked up an important package."

"How recent was your visit?"

"Within the last week and I stayed for just a minute."

"Well, get your rest and listen to your doctor."

"Thank you Madame Ambassador and be safe."

Between visits from different medical specialists and the late afternoon visit from Doctor Hiunger, orthopedic specialists, Style managed to sleep. Just before dinnertime, at around five-thirty, James DiSciascio walked in to Style's room. At the time, he wasn't quite a sleep, but in a different world because of the pain medication slowly dripping its way through Style's blood stream intravenously.

"Hello, Style, do you recognize me?"

"Of course I do, James DiSciascio, my boss."

"How do you feel?"

"Like shit, both physically and emotionally."

"Don't hold back, Style. Your attitude is normal but I understand you are in reasonably good shape physically. I also have been told you are giving the nurses a difficult time."

"I would love the opportunity to give the nurses a hard time."

"I understand you will be in the hospital for at least a week and a few days - total recovery time to be approximately three weeks. Has your doctor provided you with that information?"

"Why? Do you miss me that much and want me back to work?"

"Frankly Style, I think your ass should be working right now and no excuses."

"You know DiSciascio, you are one mean son-of-a-bitch. Let me get back to your question about recovery. I anticipate no more than 14 days or so to full recovery, more or less."

"Now Style, you are splitting hairs."

"I understand tomorrow or the next day, I will begin physical therapy. DiSciascio, do you have any detailed information yet on who is responsible for the bombing or did someone claim responsibility?"

"Yes and no. I realize that is a hollow answer. We think we know and I expect we will have conclusive facts sometime tomorrow or the next day, after the Counter Terrorism Center in Langley completes their analysis of the evidence. As you know, we are cooperating and teaming with British Intelligence Service MI6 and Interpol. All three intelligence agencies are working feverishly on lab test to determine who is responsible for the bombing. We all have our own theories, as I do personally. However, no one has stepped forward and claimed responsibility for the bomb blast. That is very unusual and we think we know why. Do you recall the last phone call I made to you?"

"Yes, the one containing the major update from GRC and CTC confirming their reliable sources indicating that Belgium and Zurich would be bombed."

"Obviously, they were right, Style, and I only wish we knew where the bomb was to be planted in Zurich."

"I need to ask you, DiSciascio, did Zosa, the woman I was dating survive or did she die in the explosion? I need to know as soon as possible."

"I understand, Style."

"My reason is very simple. The sooner I do know all the facts, the better for me to begin accepting the reality and moving on. I want to catch these fucking assholes responsible for the bombing and kill all of them myself."

"I understand how you feel. Yes, Zosa is dead. That is all I can say at this time. From the preliminary information I managed to ascertain at a meeting approximately three hours ago, she is one of the casualties. I wish I had more facts and details, but that is it. Tomorrow afternoon when I return, I will have more specifics. As a precaution, we are in the process of posting security guards to your room and throughout the hospital."

"I don't understand. Why is that necessary, DiSciascio?"

"When I return tomorrow, I will be able to share additional facts with you. That is all I can say on this matter at this time. How do you feel emotionally? I realize that is a difficult question, Style. However, I need to understand your state of mind, as much as possible."

"DiSciascio, I will be honest, I'm depressed a little and this is an extremely difficult time. I can't recall a time in my life that one event has affected me so much. I think and dream of Zosa frequently. Thank heaven for the heavy pain medication. It least allows me to rest and sleep and to stop thinking of her."

"I understand, Style. That is the reason I asked you such a tough question. Tomorrow, I will also bring with me a staff counselor. She will listen to your story and I can assure you, from my personal experience, she will be exceptionally helpful. Is that all right with you, Style?"

"Yes absolutely, I look forward to speaking with her."

"Great. That makes my job much easier."

"No problem, boss."

"Until then, is there anything else you need or want?"

"Yes, my mobile phone is missing and so is my Sig Sauer P226. In addition, somehow I lost my back-up weapon, the Smith & Wesson Bodyguard. You remember, that is the gift the team gave me.

"Yes, very familiar, Style."

"The Smith & Wesson sure helped me out in Dubai. In fact, I believe the Bodyguard helped take down one of the bad guys. The P226 was outstanding. I managed to get off two clips and no misfires."

"Are you sure that is all, Style?"

"Since you are being so nice, DiSciascio, I also need at least four boxes of shells, two for each weapon."

"Don't push your luck. I have you covered. When I return to tomorrow, I will have all of your gifts. Now, are you positive you don't need anything else? Perhaps you would like a new suit or maybe an expensive pair of Italian shoes?"

"As of matter of fact, seeing that you are in such a generous mood, I would also like to have several new dress shirts and a couple of ties."

"Now you are pushing your luck. I think I'm going to see about getting you checked out of the hospital tomorrow."

"Great, that is fine with me."

"All right, Style, I will see you tomorrow. Please get some rest and don't be so irritable when I return. And leave the nurses alone"

"Good night, sir."

As soon as DiSciascio left the room, Style tried his best to analyze and consider why the need for security guards. Because of the heavy sedation and some discomfort, he recognized that his brain was a little fuzzy, but he was rational and some things were starting to become slightly clearer as each minute passed. However, the medications were beginning to take their prescribed affect, allowing Style to once more relax and slowly fall in to a deep sleep.

The night passed fleetingly. It was mid-morning; Style awakened abruptly from a deep sleep by the voices of several visitors. Immediately he recognized one voice belonging to James DiSciascio but the other voice belonged to a women.

"I trust you are feeling a little better today and not so irritable, Style."

"DiSciascio, I do feel much better. Despite the bad rap, oxycodone does work and allows you to relax and sleep."

"Do you remember our conversation yesterday, Style?"

"I think I do. Are you referring to the staff counselor recommendation you suggested?"

"That is correct. I have with me today, Dr. Glenda Holmes, our professionally trained clinical staff psychologist."

"Good morning, Mr. Style. I realize you are having a difficult time, but I'm confident I will be able to assist in working out some of your conflicts. Does that sound reasonable and acceptable with you?"

"Most certainly it does."

"Doctor, may I interrupt you briefly?" inquired DiSciascio.

"Of course, you may, Mr. DiSciascio."

"Style, here are all of your gifts, excluding the suit and shirt. However, I did get you a new tie, along with both weapons: Sig Sauer P226, Smith & Wesson Bodyguard. In addition, four boxes of shells and the Nokia mobile telephone. For security reasons, I need to place the weapons and ammunition in your personal vault, located in your locker. You probably aren't even aware that your locker is in the closet, alongside the bathroom."

"As you can see, DiSciascio, I haven't been out of this damn bed yet."

"I do understand Style. I will return in approximately one hour. Doctor, do you need more time than an hour."

"No, that will be just fine for our initial discussion."

"I will see you later, Style."

"Thanks for everything, especially the tie, DiSciascio."

"Mr. DiSciascio, please close the door when you leave."

"Of course, doctor."

"All right let us get started, Mr. Style. Obviously, James DiSciascio shared most of what happened last Saturday evening. Before I begin asking you questions, I would like you to provide as much information as possible of how everything transpired leading up to and including the bombing, followed by the car accident. Is that a reasonably fair question to ask to start our session, Mr. Style?"

"Yes, indeed very fair, Dr. Holmes."

"To help you feel more relaxed and comfortable, let me share some information with you first. Some symptoms of depression can be a natural reaction to a sudden stressful event———such as a sudden death of a close loved one———and changes in one's ability to do prior work or leisure activities. Symptoms of depression are common after the sudden loss of a close loved one, relative or family member. Nearly ten to fifteen percent of family survivors will develop depression in the first few months after the sudden loss. It is very healthy for you to have allowed my visit so soon after the tragedy. Does this make sense to you Mr. Style?"

"For the most part, yes it does."

"Wonderful, let me continue. Researchers suggest several reasons for the increased risk of depression after experiencing the sudden death of a loved one. The risk of depression can be caused by the sudden brain chemical imbalance and differences in gene makeup. Your personal situation and the number of serious injuries are compounded because of the serious contusion to the lower back portion of your head. The body trauma definitely is an added factor. You may experience some mood changes in the next couple of months, Mr. Style. Now that you are aware of these possible mood changes, please be cognizant and be patient with yourself. These mood changes are very normal and nothing for you to worry about."

"Doctor, that is excellent advice and helps me understand more of my situation."

"Unexpected sudden death throws all of us a hard curve; even the most well-grounded person falls into a near state of hysteria at times. This holds especially true when we lose someone that we love dearly. When someone dies in a tragedy, such as the one Zosa perished in, it happens so suddenly that we experience both shock and surprise. We don't know who to turn to or trust. There is no chance to say goodbye, no chance to make wrongs right again. All you can do is reflect and feel somewhat guilty. Often, you wish you could change things around, but unfortunately you can't. It is completely and utterly devastating and it takes very special handling to help people deal with the death of a loved one when it happens. We often don't know what hit us or how we should deal with it. And the loss of a loved one to a sudden tragedy is one of the hardest single events that we have to face in life.

"You are absolutely correct about that, doctor."

"Now please share with me in your words, the events leading up to the Saturday evening bombing the best way you can recall. If you don't mind Mr. Style, I would like to video tape our discussions. Is this all right with you?"

"I have no problem whatsoever with video tapping."

"All right, let's begin."

Almost an hour and half later, Dr. Holmes turns to Style to suggest, "I believe that will be enough for today. I will return later in the week for additional discussions."

"That is fine, doctor. Is there anything unusual or possibly wrong with me, Dr. Holmes?"

"Of course not, Mr. Style, and please understand the purpose of our discussion is to determine how soon you may return to your assignment. Remember, you have experienced a very serious traumatic event. I understand you are aggressive and anxious to get back to work but first you need time to recover."

"I think I understand, doctor."

"Here comes DiSciascio. Now, I must leave and will return at the end of the week for more discussions."

"Thank you for your help and good-bye, Dr. Holmes."

26

What a cruel thing is war: to separate and destroy families and friends,
and mar the purest joys and happiness God has granted us in this world;
to fill our hearts with hatred instead of love for our neighbors,
and to devastate the fair face of this beautiful world.
Robert E. Lee, letter to his wife, 1864

D r. Holmes finished her first session with John Style just about two hours after James DiSciascio departed Style's room. Before Dr. Holmes left, she scheduled five subsequent appointments with Style, spaced out over the next couple of weeks.

Style was reflecting on his discussion with Dr. Holmes, when DiSciascio appeared once more. "How was your discussion with Dr. Holmes?"

"I thought the discussion was very helpful and allowed me to express my mourning without guilt or self-approach. I will see her again the latter part of this week and several more times in the next couple of weeks. I told her I looked forward to her visits."

"That is very healthy indeed, Style. Now, let us discuss the reasons for the sudden introduction of additional security."

"Perhaps the President of the United States or the Pope is coming to stay at the hospital because of its world reputation," suggested Style.

"Good try, Style. We need to be serious for a while. You do recall, yesterday I mentioned that I decided to post additional guards from the U.S. Embassy around the Zurich Hospital. The management here at the Zurich Hospital has been kind enough to understand the circumstances, especially since you can't be moved for at least another week or more. The guards are United States Marines attached to the U.S. Embassy here in Zurich and from Berne, Switzerland."

"Why didn't we just select a private security company?"

"Under the circumstance, we didn't want to compromise. The U.S. Marines are simply the best in the world, Style."

"What does all of this entire security guard posting mean?"

"It means the bombing that occurred this past Saturday evening was without a doubt intended for you Style. I can't make it any clearer. I realize that is harsh, but the facts support my position."

"Do you know what you are suggesting, DiSciascio?"

"At this point, all I can do is go along with the facts."

"Then, indirectly I'm responsible for Zosa's death and all the other innocent victims of the terrorists bombing Saturday evening."

"Style, I understand how you feel. You aren't responsible for anyone's death. I certainly realize the enormous complexity of the circumstances. The fact remains, your girlfriend Zosa was without doubt at the wrong place at the wrong time and you are very fortunate to have survived."

"DiSciascio, if it were not for the fact I was running late, the traffic was congested, and it was snowing heavily, I also would be the victim of the terrorists."

"If that is the case, indeed you are extremely fortunate, Style. Now, that doesn't make your circumstance any better."

"At this moment, I feel much worse and more depressed."

"I do identify with you, Style. I didn't want to share this with you. However, I must. I lost my entire family under similar circumstances when my family joined me on an assignment in Eastern Africa. I'm not trying to deflect or diminish your situation. Please believe me, I do relate to your loss and to the overbearing guilt of surviving such a horrible nightmare."

"Thank you for sharing your tragic experience with me, DiSciascio. I never realized for one moment. That was terribly selfish of me."

"Tomorrow morning when I return and you are feeling slightly better, I will bring with me a representative from MI 6, British Intelligence Service (SIS), Section 6 and several technicians from Counter Terrorism Center laboratories. These technicians have been working feverishly night and day on the evidence from the bombing at the theatre. The purpose will be to present all the evidence we have and to discuss the facts. Once we finish our discussions, we will then determine the best course of action after reviewing all the available options. There is no doubt we will have a healthy discussion. Are you up for a considerable discussion tomorrow, Style?"

"Yes, especially now more than ever before, DiSciascio."

"All right, I will see you tomorrow. Goodnight. More than likely when I do return in the morning, we will probably change your hospital room in to a war room. Is that all right with you, Style?"

"Are you kidding, DiSciascio? I look forward to digging my heels in again."

"I expect to arrive at around ten in the morning. I believe by then, you will have had your breakfast and hopefully, your bedpan changed."

"You never stop being a comedian, DiSciascio. In addition, it's your sarcastic and cynical New York background now coming to the surface."

"Style, do you realize if it were not for the fact you were in bed and your leg hoisted to the ceiling, I would deck you."

"Just try it boss."

"Good night, almost tennis professional."

"Oh my God, I will get you, DiSciascio."

"See you in the morning Style."

The next day, just after ten in the morning, DiSciascio shows up with an entourage.

"Style, let me introduce Charles Hawkins, Supervisor for MI6 Central Europe, British Intelligence Service (SIS), Section 6 and Glenn Herd, CIA laboratory munitions and bomb technician and Evelynn Yamashita, CIA Terrorist Strategist and technical tactician forensic scientist. I have already discussed with the head nurse that we will be having a business meeting. She explained the only thing we need to be aware of is making too much noise. On occasion, a nurse will knock on the door to make certain you are doing all right. The reason why I decided to include you in our meeting was very simple. There is no doubt to date you have done an outstanding job on the Clearstream project. Despite your injuries being severe, I wanted you to observe and contribute your intelligent and unique insight on the next steps in dealing with Al Qaeda and National Democratic Organization (NDO). First, I would like you to listen to the initial findings on the technical forensic scientific ballistic analyses of last Saturday evening's tragic event. Now, during the presentation process you are most welcome to interact and ask pertinent questions. Do you feel up to that?"

"Yes, of course I do, DiSciascio."

"Great. Let me get started by making a few observations on investigating a crime scene. The investigator of a scene where a bombing has taken place must be schooled in both basic physics and chemistry, and also forensic science, or the application of scientific techniques for the purpose of solving crimes. One of the first matters of interest to the investigator, obviously, is the nature of the explosion itself. At the low end of the spectrum are unsophisticated devices such as pipe bombs, which are usually little more than a metal pipe containing black powder from shotgun shells.

Much more complex is explosives using nitroglycerin or TNT. Nitroglycerin is found in dynamite, which combines sodium nitrate, nitroglycerin, and inert compounds. One notorious variety of explosive is ammonium nitrate, used in the 1993 World Trade Center bombing."

"This sounds like a chemistry class," observed Style.

DiSciascio continued with more of his observations. "All, or most major bomb investigations, are an elaborate high-tech piece of choreography conducted by different groups of organizations, sometimes as a team and other times individually. However, most occasions require that city, state and federal agencies work in partnership in their investigations. Furthermore, often we also work closely with International governments. In all cases, we have two goals: preserving evidence so the perpetrators are brought to justice and then helping investigators figure out who built and planted the explosive device or devices. Because we are invited guest in Switzerland, we defer much of the decision making to the Swiss authorities and Interpol. However, because we have substantially more experience, the Swiss government decided to delegate the United States management control and leadership, teaming with British Intelligence MI6. Just as fires and explosions are closely related phenomena in physical and chemical terms, bomb-damage assessment is an aspect of forensic science closely related to arson investigation. In both cases, authorities analyze a crime scene for telltale signs of the nature of the materials that facilitated the conflagration. First, I would like for Charles Hawkins, MI6, to provide his findings and British Intelligence's recommendations for the next stage."

"Good morning to everyone and as James DiSciascio mentioned, my name is Charles Hawkins. My experience in the field of terrorism is extensive and long. First, I have been a member of British Intelligence MI6 for over 15 years. I was the lead investigator in the July 2005 London bombings in which four Islamist home-grown terrorists detonated four bombs, three in quick succession aboard the London underground trains across the city, and later, a fourth on a double-decker bus in Tavistock Square. Apart from the four bombers, fifty-two civilians were killed and over seven hundred more were injured in the United Kingdom's first suicide attacks. Homemade organic peroxide based devices packed into rucksacks caused the explosions. The bombings were followed two weeks later by a series of attempted attacks, which failed to cause injury or damage. Although the press has reported the terrorists were independent homegrown extremist, later facts substantiated they were actually active and current members of Al Qaeda. Ladies and gentlemen, this is the first time that I've participated in an intelligence meeting conducted in a hospital room. It certainly is a chilling reminder of the nature of how dangerous our business happens to be."

Hawkins' presentation was meticulous and thorough. He didn't pull any punches in providing MI6's analysis and conclusion. Clearly, in MI6's judgment, there is no doubt that Al Qaeda is unquestionably the terrorist organization responsible for the bombing. In addition, MI6 was able to lift a clear fingerprint from one of the mangled timers. MI6 and Interpol both ran the fingerprint through their respective databases and the fingerprint was identified belonging to Karl Uber, a member of National Democratic Organization (NDO). "This evidence is crucial because it is the very first time we have been able to directly link anyone associated with NDO to a terrorist bombing. I can add that Karl Uber is an experienced chemist and bomb maker. The CIA's Counter Terrorism Center also has identified other unique sets of fingerprints."

All of the evidence Hawkins presented, lead to a conclusive determination of the type of bomb used. In addition, MI6 identified other material evidence including the type of detonators and other components such as tapes, wires, timers, switches, chemical residue and batteries that were all traceable to previous Al Qaeda bombings, including the 2005 London bombings. Hawkins elected to defer his recommendation until he had an opportunity to see and hear all of the other facts from the CIAs CTC and Global Response Center (GRC).

"Mr. Hawkins, I need to clarify something you said about chemical residue," said Style.

"Yes, what precisely is your question, Mr. Style?"

"What type of test do you use in the field, especially when weather conditions are harsh and cold, to conduct a reliable chemical residue test?"

"Excellent question, Mr. Style. We use a portable explosives residue test kit. It is specifically designed for work in the field under the harshest conditions, including extreme cold, snow, heat and rain. This kit provides rapid screening for explosive residue to verify the presence of nitrates. Due to improvements in testing technique, the process is extremely sensitive and ideal for field or lab use, even in harsh weather conditions. Amazingly, tests can be performed with debris the size of a grain of salt. While not conclusive for the presence of explosives, it is an effective screening tool for pinpointing 'hot' locations."

Next, to present their evidence and conclusions were Glenn Herd, CIA's Counter Terrorism Center (CTC), lead technician for the laboratory munitions bomb analysis group, and Evelynn Yamashita, CIA's Global Response Center (GRC) terrorist strategist and technical forensic scientist.

Evelynn Yamashita was spokesperson for both teams.

"Glenn Herd and I, both agree with findings of British Intelligence. There is no doubt Al Qaeda is the responsible organization for detonating the massive bomb that killed over 40 innocent people and injured more than 200 victims at a popular Zurich playhouse this past weekend. The overwhelming amount of chemical evidence in the aftermath, ranging from the acrid, acidic smell of the air to specific types of molecular residue is easily linked to previous Al Qaeda bombings. There was also substantial physical evidence that identified the perpetrators' van as the vehicle used to carry and house the bomb. We managed to find a piece of metal that contained an automobile identification serial number that matched a stolen van from the city of Geneva, Switzerland. Furthermore, at the time the van was stolen, a hidden security video camera in the parking facility managed to tape the two men involved in the theft of the van. Both men have been identified as Al Qaeda operatives. At the exact location of the blast crater, there are additional substances that contributed to 'feathering,' meaning the process of being stretched by the blast or, 'bluing,' exposure to welding-torch-like heat, and 'dimpling,' whereby the metal close to the blast liquefied and shot out, colliding with nearby objects and leaving tiny craters on their surfaces."

Evelynn Yamashita paused for a minute and asked the group if there were any questions or observations.

Instantly, Style jumped in and asked, "Earlier there was mention of other unique prints found on several pieces of evidence and on some shrapnel. Have any of those prints been determined yet?"

Dana Fox replied, "Yes. One set of the prints belongs to Ulrich Melmer, a Swiss citizen. The other two sets of fingerprints, unfortunately, haven't been identified with anyone listed on databases at Interpol or British Intelligence's MI6 or CIA's database in Langley, Virginia."

To finish the meeting, DiSciascio provided the summary and wrap-up. "Just as fires and explosions are closely related phenomena in physical and chemical terms, bomb-damage assessment is an aspect of forensic science closely related to arson investigation. In both cases, we carefully analyzed this crime scene despite the harsh weather conditions for telltale signs of the nature of the materials that facilitated the conflagration. Some of the evidence included clothing, body parts and the skin from many of the dead victims. Again, the evidence overwhelmingly supported our analysis that the persons responsible for setting off the bomb were Al Qaeda. What's more, and in my opinion, there is substantial evidence to bring to justice and prosecute, National Democratic Organization (NDO) headed by Ulrich Melmer and Karl Uber."

"DiSciascio, has Melmer and Uber been picked up yet and booked?"

"Style, I will get to that a little later."

"OK, I understand. I'm just anxious to get going."

"In wrapping things up, I anticipate within the next seventy-two hours, the Swiss government will be executing legal proceedings and search warrants against Clearstream Finance & Bank LTD, and Swiss Financial Market Supervisory Authority (SFINMA). In conclusion, I would like to thank everyone for taking the time to come to the University Hospital Zurich for this top-level security meeting. I do agree with MI6 Charles Hawkins' observation when he said, ladies and gentlemen, this is the first time that I've participated in an intelligence meeting conducted in a hospital room. It certainly is a chilling reminder of the nature of how dangerous our business happens to be. I couldn't agree more. Moreover, we are the fortunate ones, because not only do we have one of our own in John Style lying in a bed as a survivor, but there are at least eighty other survivors from last Saturday's tragic event as patients in this very hospital. Some of the survivors are in very serious and critical condition. Many have lost limbs and some are blind for the rest of their lives as a direct result of this barbaric and gruesome tragedy. Again, thank you my trusted friends and fellow police officers of the world. You all have done an outstanding job."

DiSciascio decided to stay and spend more time with Style.

" Well, what do you think at this point, Style?"

"I'm not surprised by the recommendations or conclusions whatsoever DiSciascio. In the meantime, I need to address a minor issue. As you know, I have a verbal agreement with our boss, Bryan Nogaki, regarding my legal contract with the Associated Tennis Professionals (ATP). My signed contract with ATP is clear; I'm committed and obligated to attend and participate in the selected professional tennis tournaments that I selected at the end of last year. Because of my current circumstances, obviously I can't attend the next two upcoming professional touring events. The next tennis event is the BNP Paribas Open, Indian Wells, California and the other, Sony Open Tennis Tournament, Miami, Florida. Both of these events are an ATP 1000 tournament, each offering five million dollars in winnings. Originally, when I submitted my intent letter to the ATP Tournament sanction committee, I included both Indian Wells and Miami in my selection process for the new calendar year tournament schedule. Even though I can't play now, I feel very fortunate to have survived, and certainly, the ATP will not have any issue with me not playing in either event because of my condition, especially when they receive my medical report from this hospital and Orthopedic surgeon, Dr. Hiunger. However, I would like to participate in the Grand Prix Hassan II, Casablanca, Morocco and the next event Monte-Carlo Rolex Masters, Monte-Carlo, Monaco. The Casablanca tournament begins in six weeks and Monte-Carlo, the following week. I know I can be prepared to play. There is one minor issue and that is the medical report that will be submitted to the ATP."

"Style, don't worry about that report. We have everything covered. The report will only show that you were involved in a taxi accident and nothing more."

"I knew you were my boss for a reason, DiSciascio."

"Frankly I believe getting back into competing at the ATP tennis tournaments in Casablanca and Monte-Carlo will be the exact challenge you need to help you recover quicker and get back on your feet. Additionally, just to let you know, I did receive a phone call from our boss, Bryan Nogaki, yesterday. He wanted to express his concern for you and asked if you needed anything. Nogaki also shared the agency's grief for your loss."

"Would you please convey my thanks to all of our teammates and partners within Global Response Center, Counter Terrorism Center and finally everyone in field Counter Terrorism?"

"Of course I will, Style. Nogaki also suggested it was an excellent idea for you to participate in the next professional tennis tournaments, however, only when you have recovered well enough to compete."

"That is outstanding, DiSciascio. That makes my decision to play in Casablanca and Monte-Carlo that much easier."

"Furthermore, I need you out of my hair for a while, Style."

"Thanks, DiSciascio; I needed a good swift kick in the ass. But seriously, thank you for your support and understanding. By getting back into a demanding workout routine every day, I can set reasonable goals each day and get back in shape. Perhaps the most helpful aspect of getting back into drills and daily tennis workouts, the competitive refocusing, will do my head good. I think you know that I'm referring to the everyday depression I must face and the guilt I have."

"I do understand, Style."

"Especially now that I know for certain, the bombing was targeted specifically at me, though it wasn't immediately clear to me in the beginning. The whole picture is certainly becoming more transparent. If indeed I was the specific target for the bombing at the theater and the one earlier at the Clearstream corporate offices, I feel guiltier than ever. I constantly think about all those innocent men, women and children. On a personal level and especially now, I feel completely responsible for Zosa, and her sister Marie's, death."

"Style, you can't continue treating yourself this way. It is too harmful and unhealthy. Do you recall my mentioning when I lost my entire family when they came to visit with me for just two weeks on an assignment in Eastern Africa?"

"I do remember and I think of it sometimes, but I just can't help myself, DiSciascio. It is tough."

"Honestly, I'm glad we had this open and very candid conversation, Style."

"To help with the emotional pain, I was planning on visiting with Zosa's mom and dad, but now I'm simply not prepared to explain the truth. However, someday I will have enough courage and I will either call or visit and tell them the entire story. Of course, I will not discuss everything, just our relationship and how we met."

"That sounds reasonable, Style. We need to discuss several other important developments, all directly related to Clearstream and Ulrich Melmer, but we can wait until tomorrow."

"The first thing in the morning I start therapy. Frankly, I can't wait to get started. Later this afternoon, the orthopedic surgeon will visit and will do an evaluation and some testing. I hope that he gets this damn contraption off my leg soon. Lying in bed with one's leg raised in the air on your back all day is a test of one's patience. In fact, I think Al Qaeda has encouraged the hospital to set this rig up. Seriously, look at me. I can't piss unless someone helps me."

"Style, now wait just one minute. I hope you aren't suggesting I help you take a piss. That is pushing me a little too far."

"No absolutely. I wasn't suggesting anything of the kind." "I'm glad I cleared that up before you left, DiSciascio."

"Let me get back to you tomorrow, Style. I will call you first thing tomorrow morning to get your scheduling for the day so that I don't interfere with any medical arrangements. Does that sound reasonable my young tennis professional?"

"That is perfect. I will say it again, thank you for your continued support."

"Oh, I neglected to ask you, Style. Have you heard from Hans Schroeder?"

"No, and I'm not surprised either."

"Why is that?"

He left to go skiing over the weekend and he did mention something about extending his stay for at least a week or more. At the time we had the discussion, I really wasn't paying much attention. However, I understand there is unquestionably no mobile cellular service where his cabin is located. On several previous occasions, Schroeder specifically mentioned there was no telephone or cell service in the remote area where his cabin is located in the Swiss Alps."

"Style, I need to ask you a difficult question. Is there any chance Schroeder is a double agent?"

"DiSciascio, I stake my life that Schroeder couldn't be a double agent."

"You certainly sound convinced."

"I repeat. Impossible."

"Please remember Style, things don't always appear as they are."

"Good enough, DiSciascio."

27

In the councils of government, we must guard against the
acquisition of unwarranted influence, whether sought or unsought,
by the military–industrial complex. The potential for the
disastrous rise of misplaced power exists and will persist. Dwight D. Eisenhower
President of United States

The following day, Dr. Hiunger had requested Style's leg be removed from traction. Immediately following the traction removal, Style started his physical therapy session. The physical therapy was much more intense and difficult than he thought it would be. However, he was thankful to be free from of the pulley and ropes. In addition, for the first time in nearly a week, he could go to the bathroom without a bedpan. Now that he was out of bed, he could freely walk in the hallway getting some exercise, stretching and flirting with the nurses.

Earlier, Style arranged to meet with DiSciascio at around one o'clock. As soon as DiSciascio arrived, he started to give Style a hard time.

"My God, Style, are you trying to escape? Who gave you permission to take off your collar? You know that is exactly what I need at the office to manage you guys. Did you throw away the traction and cords?"

"Yes, actually, I did."

"I hope that you realize I'm giving you a hard time, Style."

"No, I didn't realize. All along, I thought you were dead serious."

"Do you remember yesterday when I mentioned we need to discuss several extremely important developments?"

"Yes."

"When we started the investigation from the outset of the bombing, we have been working closely with Interpol. You probably are also aware that Interpol is the world's largest international police organization, with 190 member countries. Their role is to enable police around the globe to work together to make the free world a much more difficult place for terrorist and criminals to operate. The reason I'm sharing this mundane and basic information with you is that Interpol has uncovered some important information and evidence within the past seventy-two hours."

"What did Interpol discover?"

"It seems our friend Ulrich Melmer and his close friend Karl Uber have decided to leave Switzerland. Coincidently, they left approximately two or three hours after the bomb blast at the theatre. On the surface, their departure would not be an issue but according to sources at Clearstream, Melmer withdraw over thirty million dollars from Clearstream Banking Finance & Bank LTD. He justified the withdrawal, claiming it was part of a loan for the company you were retained as a professional consultant and financial adviser for."

"Do you mean the DeSoto Industries loan, DiSciascio?"

"Yes, exactly Style. Furthermore, he told one of the bank examiners he was going to meet up with F. William MacFarland, the CEO of DeSoto Industries at a hotel in Dusseldorf, Germany sometime Sunday afternoon. To complete the transaction, the only thing Melmer needed to do was have MacFarland sign the release form and the business deal is satisfied."

"My God, how gullible can they be, DiSciascio?"

"From most all indications and sources, he definitely headed in the direction of Germany soon after the bombing occurred. Ordinarily, it would have been easy to stop Melmer at the Swiss German border but because of the Schengen Agreement, which came into effect in March 1995, it substantially relaxed border controls between member countries of the European Union. Consequently, there is no official record of Melmer crossing the border from Switzerland into Germany. However, much later that evening, Melmer stopped to fill-up at a service station in Stuttgart, Germany, headed on the north side of the autobahn. Interpol confirmed there is a record of a credit card purchase at that same service station with Ulrich Melmer's credit card number and signature. Furthermore, the attendant at that service location also mentioned there was a passenger with Melmer, fitting the description of Karl Uber. There were no other passengers in the car."

"You mean to tell me, Melmer left his wife and family behind?"

"Right now, that's what it looks like to us. We find it extremely strange that Melmer left Zurich without his wife. Evidently, Interpol is in the process of interviewing Melmer's wife to determine if she was aware of any of his terrorist activities. His very expensive Mercedes S500 Pullman was pulled over for excessive speeding on the autobahn, north of Frankfurt, on route B44. Melmer was only issued a warning ticket. According to Interpol, since late Monday, both Ulrich Melmer and Karl Uber haven't been spotted or seen, and it appears they have vanished. However, sometime Monday, Melmer managed to cash the $30 million dollar cashier's check at an exceptionally reputable regional bank in Frankfurt, Germany. Apparently, Melmer had a long business relationship and history with this international bank and as a result, the bank officer didn't see any conflicts or issues in cashing the check."

"So where does that leave us today, DiSciascio?"

"One of our first priorities is to locate and follow Melmer and Uber. As you probably know, Style, the thirty million dollars will not last that long to support both Al Qaeda and National Democratic Organization (NDO) terrorist activities around the world. The two terrorist groups would run through the thirty million dollars in less than three years at most or perhaps less. Both organizations have limited options. Initially, they can use some of the thirty million to go on a crime spree to rob banks and hold up casinos or start kidnapping very high profile celebrities, athletes, royalty and/or politicians."

"What about the possibility of Al Qaeda and NDO returning to the drug trade?"

"The risk is too great and it would take too much time. My personal point of view is, they will go for the more conservative and less risky route and plan to develop a kidnapping ring and target high profile people. Moreover, I believe this completely elaborate scenario was all part of their original plan."

"Are you suggesting, DiSciascio, they were willing to take a calculated gamble and put eighty billion dollars or so at risk?"

"Yes, exactly Style. Although the bombing was something they would have preferred waiting to do, inevitably, this was going to happen whether you were the target or not. You simply hastened their options and that included the time and location. On the surface, you made things easier for them."

"Are you saying this to make me feel better, DiSciascio?"

"Definitely not Style."

"Think about all the recent terror threats and dangers that Al Qaeda has caused throughout most of central Europe. Every warning until the bombing at the playhouse in Zurich has been nothing but threats. Both terrorists' organizations couldn't back off this time and had to follow through with the execution. It was principle and nothing less. Remember they aren't conventional people or thinkers. When we think politics, we believe in a democracy where everyone has the right to vote peacefully and equally. Terrorist political belief system is based on anarchy, confusion, disruption and unconditional control. They thrive on this absurd reasoning and logic."

"I recognize and am very aware of their radical thought process, DiSciascio. Nevertheless, I just can't grasp why Ulrich Melmer's has a need to be a radical terrorist leader. As far I was able to learn and see about Melmer's personal life, he had everything going for himself, including wealth, power, status, family and career. He gave all of that success away simply to be an animal on the lowest order. What a fucking asshole. I can't wait until I get my hands on that miserable son-of-bitch and bastard cave sucking parasite."

"That brings me to the next subject, Style."

"What do you mean boss, the next subject?"

"Once you are released from the hospital and recovered well enough to start earning your keep, I mean to keep you busy doing your job."

"What exactly do you mean, DiSciascio?"

"For one thing, Style, you accomplished your mission with Clearstream. Recently, Interpol has issued a restraining order on all bank transactions at Clearstream Banking Finance & Bank LTD. and the Swiss Financial Market Supervisory Authority (SFINMA). Unfortunately, the banking industry in Zurich is going to be substantially impacted."

"How do you mean. I don't quite understand."

"I anticipate the banking business in Switzerland will be turned upside down and inside out. Yes, unfortunately there will be innocent victims and some collateral damage. In the final analysis, it will make the banking business in Switzerland, particularly Zurich stronger and more vibrant in the end. All of the evidence that you and Schroeder managed to secure has subsequently been presented to several different international courts of justice for prosecution. The courts of law consist of several different international jurisdictions including, The International Court of Justice (ICJ), which has its seat in The Hague, Netherlands and United States Federal Court, Washington, D.C. Without beating around the bush, I don't care which court of justice does the prosecution, as long it happens and without delay."

"Here, here, well said, DiSciascio. I couldn't say it any better myself."

"Both you and Schroeder did a thorough and professional job."

"This sounds like a soft shoe routine. Are you trying to tell me that I'm no longer needed on this case or for that matter, any case, at all for a while?"

"Style that would be the last thing in the world we would do, especially with your investigative talent, thoroughness of seeing the bigger picture, professionalism to the craft and commitment to your country."

"Wow, what a build-up. OK, how much do I owe you, DiSciascio?"

"Seriously, we need to discuss both short and long-term strategies. As you already know, we understand your professional tennis commitments and obligations. We have agreed completely to those commitments on several different levels."

"You know DiSciascio; I'm really enjoying this conversation."

"I can see that Style. Based on the scheduled date of your first upcoming

ATP tennis tournament beginning the first weeks of April, in Casablanca, Morocco, you have seven weeks until then. Is that correct, Style?"

"Yes, that is correct and I'm glad you know what a calendar looks like."

"Therefore, we have plenty of time. Once you have completed your therapy, both physically and psychologically, we anticipate you will be ready to go."

"Where will I go?"

"I'm talking about you getting back on the job."

"I understand and you are correct, DiSciascio. I would like to incorporate time to train, workout and get back in shape on the tennis court as well."

"Again, we are in total agreement. In fact, we would like to suggest having available someone from the professional tennis circuit who has retired to help get you back into condition. Moreover, we think it would be a good idea to share your true identity with that person."

"But why DiSciascio, that could possibly compromise everything. I personally don't think that is a good idea, at least not now."

"Obviously, this will be your choice, Style. Certainly, we can discuss this in more detail at some future date. We think it would provide you more freedom and independence, definitely allowing you to be more effective. Naturally, the person you choose would have to agree not to disclose your identity and to be discreet. Whomever you select, I would highly recommend they would be an American citizen. Again, I will explain later how I think we can manage that process. At Langley, the debates about risk and reward persist. These circumstances are one of those times where the risk is worth the reward."

"DiSciascio, I would imagine the same thought process went into recruiting some smug professional tennis player and making him into a field agent."

"You are dead right, Style."

"That tennis professional has become an asset to our whole organization."

"Thank you, DiSciascio."

"Style, there is another important subject we need to address before I depart today."

"Yes, please continue. Are you going to give me more kudos, boss?"

"Do you remember that late night in Atlanta, Georgia, when agent Kent McIntosh recruited you?

"I think I do but refresh my memory."

"He specifically said if you were successful in accomplishing your assignment you would be substantially rewarded.

"I vaguely remember, but I was exhausted and tired that night."

"Let me refresh your memory."

"OK, I'm all ears, DiSciascio."

I believe McIntosh said, "You will earn over two million dollars the balance of this year and double that amount next year. Now do you recall Style?"

"Somewhat, but I didn't think he was very serious and perhaps he was just over stating."

"Well, here is your check for two million dollars, less federal taxes."

"How can the agency get away with doing this, DiSciascio? Is it legal?"

"Too many questions, Style. Of course, it is legal. Someday when we have a lot of free time and we are fly-fishing on one of the beautiful rivers in your adopted state of Montana or perhaps on one of the beautiful rivers in the Blue Ridge Mountains of Georgia, then I will give you a good answer. I hope that will satisfy your sense of integrity."

"Yes, sir that will."

"Now, take the damn check before I give it away. This will be last time I see you for a while. First thing tomorrow morning, I return to England and merry ole London. Later this afternoon, I have a scheduled meeting at the American Embassy here in Zurich. You should receive your orders no later than the day after tomorrow. As we already discussed, in addition to your upcoming professional tennis tournaments there is an additional change coming."

"DiSciascio, don't do this to me. You are sending me to Afghanistan or to Moscow, correct?"

"No, but you will see in two days. You will be pleasantly surprised. Before I forget, with the new orders you will be given an option on the choice of two cities to set up your operation. I can't provide any more details or information."

"Why is there all this damn secrecy?"

"Because, Style, you are a pain in the ass. I will be talking with you in two days. Goodbye and for God's sake, be safe."

Style just realized that physical therapy started in a few minutes and he needed to get prepared for the workout. It is essential to do his best in order to be let go in a few days. His orthopedic doctor, Dr. Hiunger, mentioned earlier today if he did well enough with physical therapy today and tomorrow, he would be prepared to sign his release papers from the hospital. Looking back on this whole sequence of events, especially the loss of Zosa, it has been difficult and trying. At this point, he needed a change of scenery. Style was now excited about the prospect of a new city.

The following day, Style was motivated. He was like a kid. All he thought about was in less than twenty-four hours he was leaving the hospital with perhaps a change of scenery. Later in the evening, he received an unexpected phone call.

"Hello John, this is dad."

"Dad, how did you find me?"

"A gentleman by the name of James DiSciascio called us early today and filled us in on everything John. Of course, your Mom and I were surprised when he told us about your new role."

"Dad, thanks for taking the time to call at this difficult time. This has been a long uphill battle."

"We wish we could be there at your side son. How are you doing? I understand you were injured in a car accident and the young lady you were dating was killed soon after by a bomb blast."

"First, I'm doing great and expect to be released from the hospital tomorrow morning. Yes, it's true Dad; the woman I dated was killed, actually I call it murdered. She was a beautiful, very smart and an understanding woman, just like Mom. I truly enjoyed her company and I miss her Dad."

"I understand son. Is there anything that we can do for you now, John?"

"No, but it was extremely difficult in the first days after I was informed of her tragic murder. How are Mom and Sis doing?"

"Both of them are doing just great John. They send their love and wish you well. After I received the phone call from Mr. DiSciascio, I sat down with your mom and sister to share the news. Of course, both became emotional."

"Are they there with you, Dad?"

"No, John. Your mom and sister are out together shopping. Your mom was very upset when I told her of your accident. However, I didn't mention anything about your new additional occupation."

"I understand. Please tell them I miss and love them."

"I will do that, John. When do you think you will come home for a visit? We need to arrange a trip to go fly-fishing out in Montana and do some hunting."

"That is exactly what I should be doing, dad. Once again, I sure would like to go fly-fishing and backpacking in our favorite places in Montana. When I return home, I would like to go fly fishing in the area around Glacier National Park."

"John, consider it done and on the calendar."

"Dad, I think about that often. However, I will not be able to go fly-fishing for at least five or six months."

"I understand John. I will make arrangements for next summer."

"In the meantime, however, I do have two tennis tournaments coming up."

"I'm confused John. How do you manage to work for the CIA and play professional tennis?"

"It is a very long story, Dad. I will explain everything when we get together."

"I understand, I think. Where will you be playing your tennis tournaments?"

"The first tournament is in Casablanca, Morocco, and the next event is Monte-Carlo, Monaco. I will not be able to play Indian Wells, California or Miami because of an injury to my leg.

"How serious a leg injury did you suffer?"

"No breaks or tears, just twisted."

"Both Indian Wells and Miami tennis tournaments are just around the corner. In addition, I will not be in condition to play Davis Cup, currently slated the week in between Indian Wells and Miami. I have already notified the Davis Cup Captain that I couldn't play because of a serious car accident. He said the team wished me well in my recovery. However, I definitely will be ready to start tournament play in Casablanca. Morocco."

"John, I will not ask you anything about your decision to join the Central Intelligence Agency. I will wait until you come home."

"Thanks, Dad."

"However, I can say the man who called me, James DiSciascio, is definitely interested in your welfare. When he called to let us know about your accident, he provided an explanation and some details. Apparently, he's extremely pleased with your performance."

"Yes, Mr. DiSciascio is an excellent boss."

"Now remember, John, please call us on occasion, if possible." "I will Dad. Please tell mom and sis I love them and my love to everyone at home. Good-bye."

The following day, Style was up early and pacing his hospital room. The nurse had already informed him as soon as his doctor completed his final examination with him he would be discharged and could leave the hospital. Breakfast arrived, and at the same time, so did a phone call from DiSciascio."

"Style, how do you feel?"

"Just great and anxious to leave here. I would like to thank you for calling my family, DiSciascio."

"You are most welcome and I understand, Style. Now, for the information and news I mentioned two days ago. You will be receiving an envelope within the hour or less with your confidential assignment. Let me clarify the latest assignment and not mince words. We would like you to take on the responsibility of tracking down Ulrich Melmer and Karl Uber."

"Where will I set up operations?"

"I realize that you are anxious but you are jumping ahead Style. There is just one slight hitch in the overall strategy. I would like you to listen intently to my outline."

"I'm all ears and taking notes."

"As a direct result of all the recent events in Zurich and the latest information that Melmer and Uber are on the run, Counter Terrorism Center is confident both men are working more closely with Al Qaeda leader, Asif Zardari, the known radical Islamic terrorist. Recent evidence has shown he's directly responsible for initiating the Zurich bombing. Although Melmer financed the entire process, Zardari is the guy with the manpower and the grit. Officially, his title is Al Qaeda's Director of Middle Europe Recruiting and Political Instability."

"He has quite a title, DiSciascio."

"In reality, the designation is just about perfect for him. He's one mean son-of-a-bitch. He doesn't care about life, just his cause. He'll do anything, and I mean anything, to serve Al Qaeda's cause."

"Where is the hitch?"

"We are going to locate you to the city where we believe Zardari has set up his operations, Frankfurt, Germany. Do you remember Ulrich Melmer's personal history?"

"Yes, actually I do remember."

"Where was he born and raised as a teenager?"

"Frankfurt, Germany."

"You are absolutely correct, Style. In addition, the National Democratic Organization (NDO) has its largest base of operations, support and membership in Frankfurt. It seems Frankfurt, Germany, is the focal point and major attraction for most radical terrorist organizations in Europe."

"What a small world, DiSciascio. I believe this will keep me busy and attentive."

"Definitely, your hands will be full. You should receive your formal orders shortly. After you read your orders, give me a call. We have much to discuss and review."

"Yes, DiSciascio, I will definitely call you the moment I receive the orders."

Finally, Style seemed relieved, now that he knew where he was being assigned and had some understanding of the mission. It seemed everything was happening at once. As soon as Style finished his phone conversation with DiSciascio, Dr. Hiunger walked into his room.

"Well, young man. You have done a remarkable job in your recovery. If only all my patients were disciplined to understand the importance of rehab. I have already signed all of your release papers and as soon as the nurse returns with the different hospital forms for you to sign, you can then leave. How is that?"

"That sounds wonderful doctor. Once again, thank you for your exceptional care."

The nurse walked in minutes after the doctor departed and handed several forms to Style. Without delay, he signed all the necessary paperwork. A courier from the American Embassy arrived just as Style was getting into a wheelchair so he could be rolled out of his room and down to waiting transportation.

"Sir, is your name John Style?"

"Yes it is."

"I have these orders for you, sir."

28

The world has achieved brilliance without wisdom, power without conscience.
Ours is a world of nuclear giants and ethical infants. We know more about war that we know
about peace, more about killing that we know about living.
Omar Bradley

he moment Style got into the taxi, he opened the parcel containing his orders. The official orders were exactly as James
DiSciascio described. Style wasn't at all surprised or astonished
by the instructions and orders. It read:

John Style–

*The Central Intelligence Agency is proud to announce the promotion of John Style to
Assistant Case Officer, Eastern, Central and Western Europe and the Middle East. You are
now responsible for the capture and arrest of: Ulrich Melmer, former CEO Clearstream, and
now Director of National Democratic Organization (NDO); Karl Uber, Assistant Director of
NDO; Abu Alouni, Al Qaeda Head of Operations, Europe; Asif Zardari, Al Qaeda Assistant
Head of Operations, Middle Europe (reports to Alouni).*

*As Assistant Case officer, you are charged with the added responsibility to pursue the
apprehension and conviction of the above listed terrorists. You will use whatever force and
means necessary in the performance of your assignment. Furthermore, you are now assigned the
additional responsibility of managing the following team of field agents:*

Fred Capella, Serbia; Dave Clapp, Croatia; Thomas Colli, East Africa; Marilyn DeFeo, Egypt; Lynda Enequist, Poland; Susan Gross, Portugal; Robert Handwerker, Russia; Kenneth Harvey, Turkey; Dave Robie, Great Britain; Joseph Piccolo, Romania; George Probert, Austria; Richard Weiner, Thailand.

Their responsibility and yours, is to pursue the aforementioned radical terrorist groups and anyone associated with either of these organizations.

Furthermore, to avoid any possible issue of safety, it is the recommendation of both Global Response Center (GRC) and Counter Terrorism Center (CTC) to setup CIA operations at the Hyatt Regency Hotel, Cologne, Germany, located on the Rhine River. This location is approximately one hundred ninety kilometers from Frankfurt, or just over one-hundred miles. The reason is obvious, and that is to prevent the risk of putting any of our agents directly in harm's way. You will continue to report to Mr. James DiSciascio, Senior Case Officer, located in London England.

This is a new era of direct infusion of advanced U.S. military technology in tactical and limited engagements. In addition, other consequences have pushed the CIA, along with many of its clients and allies, closer to the gray fields of assassination and political disruption. You have total and absolute authority under the rules of the Geneva Convention, to use whatever military means necessary, including the targeting of specific individuals for assassination. As a result, we will make available any and all of the newest proven technology for your use, including:

- *Embedded computing-cryptography experts and software engineers who are qualified to re-engineer or re-tool in the field and on the job any host of changes in re-programming or modifying application programs. They will assist in translation issues, whether in German or Arabic.*

In addition, the following technology will be available as needed:

- *Manpackable killer drones able to seek out and destroy targets. A two-man team can carry these mobile units. The backpackable system weighs six pounds. It is like a smart mortar system, yet instead of launching up and then down on a sharp ballistic arc, it lofts into the air, helps the operator search for targets, and attacks targets when found. We have given the Manpackable drones the nickname "Switchblade." The "Switchblade" flies swiftly and quietly, and strikes with precision to keep collateral damage to a minimum. The operator can call off a strike, if necessary, even after the munitions are armed. Your team will receive four Manpackable killer drone and munitions.*

- *Unmanned aerial vehicle (UAV), Laser Truck Mounted Weapon Systems- a 60-kilowatt fiber laser module for a truck-mounted laser weapon system intended to shoot down enemy unmanned aerial vehicles (UAVs), rockets, artillery rounds, and mortar. Your team will receive two UAVs and two three-ton trucks, fully loaded with back-up weapons, ammunition, munitions and back-up parts inventory.*

The reasons for supplying your team with this extra proven technology is to make certain you have all the necessary weaponry at your disposal in the shortest time period. When needed, we expect these proven weapons to be used to their fullest potential.

Finally, we have rented a vacated one hundred thousand square foot warehouse on the Rhine River, not too far from the Hyatt Regency Hotel, Cologne, Germany. The purpose of the warehouse is to provide more than enough necessary space for all of your conventional weapons and new technological weapons, such as UAVs. In addition, the warehouse is more than adequate to hold periodic training and meetings for your staff. The German government has already been briefed and they have given their approval. In addition, Interpol and British Intelligence MI6 have also been informed and signed on for backup and support. Both Interpol and MI6 will have available teams of tactical units specializing in intelligence for your discretionary use. Included in this envelope, under a separate cover letter, is the warehouse rental contract and a map providing the exact location of the warehouse.

In closing, if you have any questions or issues, please convey them without delay and as fast as possible to Senior Case Officer James DiSciascio or the Counter Terrorism Center, Langley.

Signed,

Bryan Nogaki
Assistant Director of Global Operations
Central Intelligence Agency,
Washington D.C.

It was obvious all decisions were definite and determined well in advance on the location. Now, all Style needed to do was go back to the Park Hyatt Zurich, make arrangements to check-out tomorrow morning and then make flight reservations to Cologne, Germany. Perhaps a better option would be to consider driving to Cologne. It is approximately a six-hour drive, Zurich to Cologne. He decided to wait until later in the evening to make a decision. Style arrived back at the Park Hyatt Zurich Hotel quickly. As he stepped out of the cab, memories started to flash before his eyes. He was sad and it was obvious. He tried everything possible to take his mind off Zosa and Marie. Immediately upon entering the hotel, several people working at the front desk recognized him.

"Good morning, Mr. Style, and how are you feeling?"

"Thank you for asking everyone, I'm feeling just great and glad to be out of the University Hospital Zurich. University Hospital is a great hospital with wonderful doctors, nurses and offering wonderful care. The citizens of Zurich are very fortunate."

Immediately the general manager of the hotel came out of his office to visit with Style. The discussion lasted but a few moments.

"Mr. Style, I personally will make all the necessary arrangements and reservations at the Hyatt Regency Hotel, Cologne, Germany."

"Thank you for your assistance. My stay here at the Park Hyatt Zurich for the last number of weeks, has been outstanding and without equal. Thank you for your wonderful and professional treatment and gracious service."

"It has been our pleasure to serve you, Mr. Style."

Style retired to his room and ordered room service. The first thing he wanted was an old-fashioned hamburger with french-fries. Shortly, there was a knock on the door.

"Hello sir, this is a gift from the staff here at the hotel and a note from the general manager."

Style paused for a minute and turned to the young man and said, "Please tell everyone thank you. This is very kind."

Included in the note was the confirmation for fourteen rooms at the Hyatt Regency Hotel, Cologne, Germany, starting tomorrow evening.

Later in the afternoon, Style received a call from DiSciascio.

"Style, I expect you already received the envelope containing the orders."

"Yes, I did."

"Do you have any questions on any aspect of the instructions?"

"No, DiSciascio, everything was quite clear."

"Are you sure?"

"Well, there is one minor question and perhaps a concern."

"What is the problem, Style?"

"Now don't get pissed when I ask this question."

"Don't tell me, Style, that you want a harem to entertain you guys. Better yet, you would like to have college girls provide tutoring in German."

"How did you know DiSciascio? The reality is that I just completed learning to speak and write German. Do you know if there is a reasonably good indoor tennis facility in Cologne?"

"That happens to be a somewhat reasonable question. However, I don't know anything about tennis facilities in Cologne or for that matter here in London."

"All right, I will handle this problem myself. I do have a question on the field agents."

"Yes, Style."

"The file didn't contain information on the agents' backgrounds or histories. I would like to know each of their experiences, profiles and language skills."

"I will get that information to you before you checkout of the hotel tomorrow morning. Would you also like to have their respective tennis ratings, Style? You know I'm giving you a hard time. Before I forget, how do you feel?"

"Thanks for asking. I'm doing great. Later, I will go down to the gym here in the hotel, get some exercise and work on my leg."

"How are the wounds on your face, chest and the back of your head?"

"Just before I left the hospital, the nurse removed all the stitches from the side of my face and the back of my head. They say that the stitches in my chest and side have to remain for a few more days. My face looks like I was in a fight with Mike Tyson. However, the scar on the cheek makes me look like a bad guy. So, don't mess with me, DiSciascio."

"It sounds like you have everything under control, Style."

"I'm getting there, very slowly. Before I forget, I would like to thank you for calling my family and providing an update on my condition and situation. I bet my Dad was confused at first when you mentioned that I was now working for the CIA."

"When I first mentioned who I was, he certainly was a little puzzled. However, he soon became more comfortable and said, 'That is definitely my son.' Your dad reminds me of my grandfather Style, very concerned and caring. Is there anything else?"

"Yes, my last question, DiSciascio. Will the rest of my team arrive in Cologne by tomorrow evening?"

"Definitely, everyone should be on location in Cologne no later than eight tomorrow evening, Style."

"Auf VEE-dair-zayn. That is good-bye in German, DiSciascio."

"Is that the extent of your German tutoring? I would seriously suggest you get your money back, immediately. Auf VEE-dair-zayn to you too, Style."

Style stood gazing out the window and realized it was getting late into the evening. The sky was a steel gray and quickly getting overcast and it looked like it was going to either snow or sleet. Despite the weather, at the last minute Style decided to get some fresh air and go for a walk along the lake for the last time. As he was walking, he started to reflect on many of the good times he had in Zurich. Snow started to fall lightly, similar to the first night he went out on a date with Zosa. As he was walking, he also passed Piccolomini's Italian restaurant. Momentarily, it brought back more fond reminders of Zosa. Despite the cold, Style continued his walk down to the theater where the bombing took place almost two weeks ago. When he finally arrived at the theatre, everything was empty and abandoned. The theatre was simply a shallow empty cavity. The streets and sidewalks were cleaned up and all the debris removed. It seemed as though nothing happened. It looked like a ghost town. There was nothingness. All traces of the bombing had vanished and no evidence remained to suggest a horrific bombing took place a short time ago.

On his way back to the hotel, Style received a phone call. "Hello Style, this is Schroeder."

"What the hell happened to you Hans Schroeder?"

"I just arrived back home after a week of great skiing in the mountains."

"Many things have happened since you were gone Schroeder. Unfortunately, most were tragedies and nightmares."

"What do you mean tragedies and nightmares?

"The day after you left to go skiing, there was another bombing. However, this time the massive bomb killed over 40 innocent men, women and children and injured more than 200 people at the Zurich playhouse where Zosa had her musical play."

"I can't believe it, Style."

"Now, the worst news is that Zosa and her sister Marie were both murdered by these cowards and scum of the earth."

"Oh, my God Style. I'm so sorry."

"Apparently, Interpol, CIA and British Intelligence MI6 all agreed I was the target. According to all of the evidence, our friends Ulrich Melmer and Karl Uber are the perpetrators. In addition, Al Qaeda is responsible for providing all the manpower. Furthermore, Melmer and Uber are now on the run and suspected of being in Frankfurt, Germany. When the bomb blast occurred, I was in a taxi on my way to the playhouse to join Zosa and then have dinner after the show. The taxi crashed. At the time of the accident, I thought I was fine but somehow I managed to walk to the playhouse. I don't know how I made it, but I did. I actually found Zosa and held her in my arms. Schroeder, Zosa was literally crushed and blown apart. Her beautiful face was ripped into shreds. Apparently, I collapsed and then was taken to University Hospital Zurich by ambulance. I had no idea that I had sustained any serious injuries. Today is my first day out of the hospital after close to two weeks. The stress and depression have been overwhelming. The whole sequence of events has been surreal and difficult to comprehend."

"What can I do, Style? I realize I'm too late, but there is no cellular signal where I have my cabin in the mountains."

"I understand, Schroeder. There is a lot for us to discuss. Is there any way you can meet with me first thing tomorrow morning for breakfast at the Park Hyatt Zurich."

"What time, Style?"

"Can you make it at seven?"

"I will see you then."

Style decided it was time to return to the Park Hyatt and get some rest. It was bad enough he had to hobble along, but now his leg was beginning to cause some discomfort.

Within a matter of thirty minutes or so, Style was back at the hotel and anxious to get into bed and rest. He elevated his leg after bathing it in the tub. He felt much better now and decided it was time to go to sleep. He knew tomorrow was going to be a tough long day.

The next morning, Style was up early and feeling rested and ready to go. He packed up his personal clothing, tennis gear and piled everything together in one pile in the corner near the door. Hurriedly, he left his room to join Schroeder at breakfast. He was anxious to see Schroeder again. When he arrived at the café, he could smell the great aroma of the Swiss coffee and the buffet breakfast. He sat down and ordered his breakfast. Minutes later, Schroeder walked up to Style and reached out to shake his hand.

"I don't know what to say, Style, except I'm terribly sorry for not being here with you."

"Schroeder, as said last night, I completely understand your circumstances."

"Your face is badly cut along the cheek and down the jaw line."

"Fortunately, I feel much better than I look. I had the stitches removed yesterday from my face and the back of my head, but I remain with stitches in my chest and on the side near my ribs. Despite everything, I actually feel reasonably well. My leg was the real problem. I was in a contraption to elevate my leg for at least three or four days. What a relief to get out of bed on my own to shower and clean up. How is your family Schroeder?"

"They are just wonderful and enjoying their visit on the farm. My concern is you, Style."

"I'm doing just much better now. I had professional counseling at least five times by a CIA staff clinical psychologist. There is no doubt; the counseling helped me, especially having to contend with reality of Zosa's death. It has been hard, especially in the very beginning. Physically, I will recover and get on with my life. In fact, I start training this week for a professional tennis tournament scheduled in six weeks in Casablanca, Morocco."

"Now, that sounds like the Style I know."

"Schroeder, there is a lot to discuss and I have only so much time to do it."

"What is the rush, Style?"

"That will be part of our discussion this morning."

"Are you quitting, Style?"

"Schroeder, unconditionally no and that is definite. I have a mission to complete and I'm more determined than ever to complete my assignment. Where do I begin? First, let me tell you what has happened to your company, Clearstream. Sometime last week, Interpol and the Swiss authorities temporarily closed the doors to Clearstream. Apparently, at this time, there are a number of different world agencies auditing the Clearstream financial books. Once they complete the audit, Clearstream will be able to open and continue their banking business."

"Style, in your professional opinion, how do you think Clearstream will fair once the investigation is done?"

"Frankly, I think they will have a hard time in the short haul. However, because the Clearstream Finance & Bank LTD organization has such a professional team of committed staff and loyal employees working for them, in the final analysis they will recover and become more successful. All of the information you and I managed to retrieve will be used as evidence in the eventual prosecution and conviction of Ulrich Melmer and Karl Uber. First, they need to be apprehended. Also involved in the criminal indictment is the National Democratic Organization and Al Qaeda."

"Well, I speculated this would happen, Style, and sure enough it happened. You know it is about time for me to call it quits and take it easy."

"Now here is something for you to ponder. Interpol, British Intelligence and Central Intelligence Agency, have all highly recommended you, Schroeder, for the position of Chairman and Chief Executive Officer of the new Clearstream Finance & Bank Ltd. Company."

"There is no doubt I will need to give it some serious consideration, Style."

"At this point, I can't imagine there is a rush for your decision. I have something for you from the company store."

"What company store are you talking about Style?"

"I'm referring to the CIA. Without your assistance, we couldn't have accomplished our mission and successfully managed to get to the truth about all that stolen money and wealth. Now the courts must prove the Swiss Banks, in particular Clearstream, collaborated with the Third Reich in first, stealing it, then hiding the gold, cash, and jewelry stolen from the Jews. It is so hard to believe it has taken over seventy years to find the answers and to get to the truth. Unfortunately, many of the victims and their families will never be located or found to be compensated the way they should be. On the other hand, in the final analysis justice did prevail. I thank you Hans Schroeder. There is no doubt what you did was exceptional and you made some considerable personal sacrifices. As a thank you from the American government and the American people, Schroeder, here is a check for one million dollars from the Central Intelligence Agency and United States government. The check is made out to Hans Schroeder, dated today."

"But why, I don't understand, Style."

"Please believe me, there are many reasons, but most of all, without your assistance I don't believe I could have accomplished my mission as safely and as thoroughly. Furthermore, we completed the assignment within a much shorter period than originally planned."

"Of course, you aren't serious, Style, about the million dollars."

"Here, take the check Schroeder and see for yourself. I would suggest that once we finish our business today, you deposit this check."

"Wait until I share this news with my wife and children. I still can't believe it. Thank you Style and please thank the entire team for their support and help. Style, do you have any idea how much of the original eighty billion dollars is now secure?"

"I don't have the exact amount, but I will speculate something close to fifty billion dollars. We can't account for approximately thirty-five billion dollars at this time. However, I feel confident we will locate the missing funds. Now Schroeder, the fact remains we have only solved half of the assignment."

"I don't understand, Style."

"You certainly are justified in being somewhat confused. Schroeder, I now must get down to some serious discussions. After I present our current situation and all of the facts, you may decide this isn't for you. I will understand and you can go home to be with your family and enjoy the new retirement bonus. Frankly, that makes sense to me".

"This must be extremely serious based on the tone of your voice, Style".

"It is."

"Style, before we continue, I need to ask you, how are you doing?"

"Thanks for asking Schroeder. Each day, I feel much better. However, I would be lying if I didn't admit I really do miss Zosa's company. Let's get started so we can finish up. Do you recall earlier that I remarked that first they need to be apprehended?"

"Yes I do Style."

"Of course, I was referring to Ulrich Melmer and Karl Uber and anyone associated with their organization NDO and Al Qaeda. In addition, I'm now charged with the added responsibility to pursue the apprehension and conviction of Melmer and Uber. I have been appointed the authority to use whatever force and means necessary in the performance of my assigned mission. Furthermore, I was also given the additional responsibility of managing a team of twelve field agents and you in pursuit of my assignment, Schroeder."

"When do these field agents report, Style?"

"Sometime tonight, at the latest, I move all operations to Cologne, Germany."

"Cologne is one of the most beautiful cities in Europe, Style."

"I've been informed many times today how beautiful Cologne is."

"Why did the agency select Cologne for operations?"

"Both Global Response Center (GRC) and Counter Terrorism Center (CTC) highly recommended Cologne because of its proximity to Frankfurt. All intelligence reports indicate that Melmer and Uber are now hiding somewhere in Frankfurt with the two Al Qaeda leaders, Abu Alouni, Al Qaeda Head of Operations, Europe and Asif Zardari, Al Qaeda Assistant Head of Operations, Middle Europe (reports to Alouni). Apparently, NDO and Al Qaeda have a substantial number of members based in Frankfurt. The thinking that went into the selection of Cologne does make sense. I will have much more freedom to move about and setup tactics without compromising my position. Most important, at the outset, I don't put any agents directly in harm's way."

"The CIA knows their shit, Style. It appears to be more like a military deployment than a civil action."

"In a manner of speaking you are correct, Schroeder. Early this morning when I received your check by courier along with some other confidential information, I was instructed to also be anticipating in Cologne, a deployment of a team of MI6 agents and number of Interpol police agents."

"Style, I need to ask a stupid question."

"Yes, go right ahead."

"Earlier, you mentioned something about a professional tennis tournament in Casablanca."

"Yes, as a matter I fact I did."

"Do you really think you will be prepared to play and compete in six weeks or so?"

"I feel very confident; I will be ready on many different levels. Now, here is an extremely difficult question for you, Schroeder."

"Style, I think I know the question. Like you Style, I'm committed to getting these assholes. What role will I play?"

"Technically, there is no role yet. However, I will develop one without delay. I would like you to discuss this assignment with your wife first. I just caution you not to share any details or reveal where we are going."

"That sounds very reasonable and fair, Style."

"I expect you will also tell her there is considerable risk and danger. In addition, you will not be able to communicate with her until we have completed our assignment. Is that perfectly clear, Schroeder?"

"Would I hold back telling my wife the whole truth, Style, especially after you have given me a heavy lecture on the subject?"

"Are you patronizing me, Schroeder?"

"Sir, I would never do something like that to you."

"Now, if she expresses any serious doubts and says no, I expect you to be up front and honest with me. Is that clear enough, Schroeder? I hope that you do."

Yes, I think that is perfectly clear, Style.

"All right, we are now a team again."

"That is outstanding, Style. I will need to go home and pick up a bag of clothing and some personal items along with my weapons. Where should we meet and at what time?"

"I will drive to your house and pick you up at two this afternoon. Originally, I was seriously thinking of flying but now driving makes more sense. I believe the drive from Zurich to Cologne is approximately six hours. With the Porsche 911, it should take us less than four hours."

"That is exactly what I'm concerned about, Style."

"Before you leave, please call your wife, then go to the bank and deposit your check."

29

Here in America we are descended in blood and in spirit from
revolutionists and rebels – men and women who dare to dissent from
accepted doctrine. As their heirs, may we never confuse honest
dissent with disloyal subversion. Dwight D. Eisenhower
President of United States

Style managed to pick-up Schroder at exactly two as scheduled. "Tell me Schroeder, did you call your wife and inform her of everything, including the risk and danger factors?"

"Yes, I did, Style."

"I trust you did Schroeder and you aren't telling me a white lie."

"What are you going to do me, if you discoverer I didn't tell her, send me to the back of the class? Nevertheless, I absolutely told her everything."

"That is good enough for me, Schroeder. How did she react to the bonus check of one million dollars?"

"She and my daughters are probably out this minute having a real good time and probably taking the neighbors out as well."

Schroeder promptly packed his suitcase and bags into the trunk of the Porsche. Style was on Schroeder right away when he remarked, "My God, you have enough clothing for a year or more."

"I have only three bags. Your tennis equipment takes up more space than ten women going to a fashion show in Paris."

"All right, you win. Let's go."

Style and Schroeder both climbed in to the Porsche and headed north to Cologne, Germany.

"Schroeder, have you ever been to Cologne before?"

"Yes, many times, Style. It is a beautiful city with wonderful museums."

"Can you share any more information or possibly provide some insight perhaps as to what makes Cologne unique and special?"

"I would be delighted. As you already know, Cologne sits directly on the Rhine River and I believe it is one of the top five largest cities and is the oldest city in Germany. The most impressive attraction is the number of old cathedrals in Cologne. It is actually known as the city of churches. In the early nineteenth century, the Cologne Cathedral was promoted as the tallest structure in the world with something over five hundred steps to the top, offering a magnificent view of the city. The reason I personally find Cologne so attractive and beautiful is the many outstanding museums and galleries. Is that enough culture for you?"

"That is an excellent insight and most interesting. Are there any more things you can share about Cologne? The reason I ask so many questions about Cologne is because I understand that Cologne was almost completely devastated from all the carpet and incendiary bombing by the Allies in World War II. Somehow, it managed to survive and become a vibrant and beautiful city, with a strong economy. I admire the people of Cologne for their courage and fortitude."

"Yes, that is as it should be, Style. On the much lighter side and without doubt the best thing about Cologne and especially for you and me, it has its own beer. The beer is known as Kolsch and in point of fact is protected by the German law so that only beers brewed in and around the Koln region (Cologne) can bear the name. The beer has a sensational tangy taste. When it is warm outside, this beer has the most refreshing savory flavor. It has a little sweeter taste than other German beers."

"Now, I can say without any reservation that was the most interesting thing you've said, Schroeder, in a very long time and it was most informative."

"That is one of the things I enjoy and admire about you, Style. You have a true appreciation of other cultures, especially for someone who hasn't yet reached the age of thirty-five."

"When I first started to travel on the professional tennis circuit, I discovered by taking the time and learning something about the city where the tournament is played, I had less of a problem with being lonely and being homesick in a strange city. More importantly, I enjoy learning."

"That makes a lot of sense and I agree with your attitude."

"Now, Schroeder, I need to brief you on how this operation is to be organized and successfully implemented. After I explain my strategy, I would like to hear your reaction and input. From a recent intelligent report I received just after we left the hotel, most all of the field agents, whom we will met later tonight, recently have received intensified guerrilla warfare training in explosives and sabotage techniques. At least half the members of the team are also trained snipers. We are entering a new phase of engagement with NDO and Al Qaeda, and terrorism in general. The rules have been radically altered. The American legal system has dramatically changed its position on assassinating terrorist. In the last decade alone the playing field has been leveled in the fight against terrorism and has been radically transformed so terrorist are now on notice that they are no longer the hunters, but the hunted. Today, the U.S. intelligence community has more flexibility and options, including assassination."

"What has changed in the last ten years, Style?"

"Today, all of our partners in this operation, including Interpol and British Intelligence, are in agreement, we will use whatever means it will take to eliminate terrorism. We all signed a statement indicating we will employ all the force necessary to apprehend and prosecute the enemy. Although in 1976 the then President of the United States, Gerald Ford, altered the playing field by signing an executive order banning assassination as a direct result of exposure of CIA plots in Central America and Southeast Asia in the 1950s, 1960s and early 1970s. In recent years, that ban has been lifted. Witness what happened to Bin Laden just a few years ago."

"Is that considered an assassination or military engagement?"

"What do you think, when you send in two Blackhawk helicopters in the middle of the night on a tactical mission filled with a highly trained platoon of Navy Seals, most accomplished in sniper warfare. That certainly wasn't a tea party as I saw it. Most assuredly, it was an assassination team."

"Was the determination to target a political figure, terrorist organizer or head of state the real issue, or was it the means employed to assassinate him, Style?"

"That is an excellent question, Schroeder, and that is one of the reasons I wanted you to be part of this team. You think fast on your feet and see through the bullshit right away. In response to your question, I would say you could accept it as being all of the factors, but in the final analysis, the ends justified the means. The decision was both strategic and pragmatic. You could also rationalize a justification."

"You mean morally defensible, Style'"

"Exactly, and it would be based on the very principle of self-defense."

"How can you say it would be self-defense?"

"The reason is simple, Schroeder, because of what these bastard terrorists have been getting away for over three decades or longer. They have realized all this time, not being associated with a particular country or nationality and not restricted by geographical borders has been a great advantage and benefit. This advantage in turn allows them more freedom to function and operate with impunity, retreat to anywhere that is both a convenience and a safe haven. For one moment, think about most of the radical terrorist organizations since the 1970s up to the current time, beginning with the following: IRA, FARC, Hamas, Taliban, Hezbollah, Al Qaeda, ELN and the list goes on. The common denominator is that none of these bastards had to worry about borders. If they were ever threatened at one specific geographical location, they rapidly managed to relocate to another site. A good example would be Al Qaeda or the Taliban. Both terrorist organizations were first located in Afghanistan. When it became much too heated, they immediately moved across the border into Western Pakistan. Pakistan did absolutely nothing. Sometimes they setup shop in Syria, Iran, Iraq or Lebanon. We are now taking the battle and the war to their fucking camp for a change.

We will prevail. Not only will we capture or kill Ulrich Melmer and Karl Uber, but we will also be decisive in apprehending these Al Qaeda leaders and their followers."

"As you know, Style, this intellectual gymnastics will continue until the end of time. Ideally, in our lifetime, when there are no more international conflicts, wars, terrorist activities, religious differences or political disagreements, there will be peace, but that will never happen. Personally and idealistically, I would like all wars and conflicts to disappear and never exist again."

"Unfortunately, Schroeder many people in the world for too long a period had the same idealistic belief system. Don't defend yourself. Somehow, through hope and prayer, hostile behavior will discontinue and conflict will suddenly end. That is the personifications of giving up and living in a fantasy world. Of course, that type of thinking is too perilous and naïve, especially in today's world. Now let me get back to an earlier point regarding the question of moral dilemma. I think you know me well enough that if I ever have a moral dilemma in the heat of battle, I would stop and ask myself, 'is this the ethical thing to do?' You positively would have the right to question me, because I would not care ever to be accused of arrogance of certainty."

"I will definitely remember and if necessary, I will remind you, Style."

"Look at the sign, Schroeder. We aren't too far from Stuttgart. It is hard to believe we have already traveled over two hundred kilometers."

"I can assure you I know where we are. I have been watching the speedometer ever since we left my home. You are averaging 145 kmh to 150 kmh and that is much faster than I would actually prefer. I realize that on this stretch of the autobahn there are no speed limits, however, please drive cautiously."

"Are you nervous with my driving, Schroeder?"

"No, I'm not nervous, just cautious, and I'm eager to arrive in one piece."

"Perhaps, you would like to drive, Schroeder?"

"No, I will just sit here and enjoy the spectacular autobahn and the beautiful German scenery."

"What do you think about stopping for something to eat when get to Frankfurt in approximately another hour or so?"

"That sounds extremely good to me. I'm hungry and I have to take a piss unless you want this expensive black Porsche to be yellow when we arrive in Cologne."

As they approached Frankfurt, Style turned to Schroeder and said, "I have some real good trivia for you."

"All right, what is this trivia, Style?"

"Did you know the animal lounge at the Frankfurt International Airport is the world's largest animal airport facility, handling tropical fish to elephants to, yes, snakes on planes?"

"Now that is something I really didn't know."

"Schroeder, not only will I stop in Frankfurt for something to eat, I will also pick up the tab. As a matter of fact, I encourage you to order several beers, so you can relax the remainder of the trip."

"When we get to Frankfurt, hopefully in one piece, I will order a few beers, guaranteed."

As they continued their drive, Style couldn't help but think to himself about a question DiSciascio posed to him several days before regarding Schroeder. "Are you sure that Hans Schroeder can be trusted?" It was a troubling question, considering all of what Schroeder has managed to accomplish in helping with the Clearstream investigation, almost from the very beginning. The inference is quite clear from the way DiSciascio posed the question. At first, when DiSciascio asked if Schroeder was completely honest and up front, Style never hesitated and responded, "I would trust Schroeder with my life." Without his cooperation and assistance, we would still be searching the old file cabinets.

In Style's mind, he couldn't escape the observations and concerns expressed by DiSciascio: do we have a brilliant double agent willing to risk everything in his life? Just after the first bombing in Zurich, at the headquarters of Clearstream, Style clearly remembers receiving a background check from DiSciascio and the CTC on Schroeder that was spotless. His dossier was almost clinically clean with no criminal arrests, not even a speeding or parking ticket. His employment record is outstanding and he steadily rose up the corporate ladder through hard work and dedication. Even when he was a student attending the London University School of Economics, he wasn't involved in any political or campus activities. Furthermore, even today, there are no radical affiliations or political ambitions whatsoever to raise a red flag. Finally, Schroeder had a stable family home environment and he appeared to be happy and content. If Schroeder is a double agent, he's without doubt one of the very best. Style is always reminded of the story told to him by Bryan Nogaki, Assistant Director of Global Operations, CIA, of Eddie Chapman (Agent Zigzag). Chapman was the most successful double agent of World War II because of his deceit and his ability to withhold emotions and to act as if in a Shakespearean play for over a thousand times. The Nazi's never once suspected he was a British agent. In addition, he remembered what DiSciascio said to him when they first met in London — "Style, always remember, nothing is what it seems." Style decided the best course of action was to remain cognizant and be alert to the unexpected. Certainly keeping an open mind is always the best defense, because in the spy game, anything is possible and plausible, no matter how absurd.

Just prior to arriving in the city of Frankfurt, Style's injured leg started to cause him some discomfort. He elected to pull off to the side of the autobahn and got out to stretch his legs. He also discovered he was having issue with his torso where he remained stitched up. It wasn't serious, but just uncomfortable. Fortunately, he only would have to drive another ten miles or less.

Schroeder asked, "Is there anything I can do to help."

Typical of Style, "No thanks, Schroeder; everything seemed to hit me at once. I'll be just fine in a few minutes."

They both were resting against the side of the Porsche and Style decided to ask several questions about Schroeder's family. At first, he only asked because it was cold and something to do to keep busy. Style soon realized there appeared to be some inconsistencies from previous versions, but not enough to justify raising a red flag. The sun was now low on the horizon; it was windy, cold, and cloudy and had all the makings of a snowstorm brewing. Soon, they both jumped back into the Porsche, leaving a rubber slick twenty feet long. The German autobahn has taken on an almost legendary mystique. The reality is a little different from the legend. The myth of no speed limits is countered by the fact that "tem-polimits" are an unpleasant fact on most of Germany's highways, and traffic jams are common. Signs suggesting a recommended speed limit of 130 km/h are posted along most autobahns, while urban sections and a few dangerous stretches are less. However, for now the traffic was light, so Style pushed the Porsche 911 Turbo engine to the max. Within min-utes, they found a roadside restaurant, Apfelwein Wagner. The restau-rant served hearty German dishes of wurst and schnitzel, slow-cooked steak with horseradish sauce, grilled sausages and, of course, home brewed German beer. They both ordered just about everything on the menu and a beer each. Soon, it became apparent, neither was fit to finish the drive to Cologne. It was obvious they had too much to eat. To be fair, Style decided to flip a coin to see who would finish the drive. Style won and chose to continue driving. Schroeder was more uncomfortable than ever. Approximately an hour and a half later, just as the snow started to fall with more intensity, they pulled up to the front of the Hyatt Regency Hotel, Cologne. It was obvious Schroeder was relieved and could now exhale. Immediately they went in to the hotel to register. The general manager came out of his office to greet Style and Schroeder. "Welcome to the Hyatt Regency Hotel, Cologne, Mr. Style and Mr. Schroeder; we look forward to serving you both. How do you feel Mr. Style?"

"Thank you for asking, Mr. Brunne. Today, I feel very good. Can you tell me if any of the following people have checked in to your hotel?" Style provided a list containing all of the names of the agents expected by eight to eight thirty tonight.

"No one has checked in yet, Mr. Style. Would you like to have a list of their pre-registered rooms?"

"Yes, I would, Mr. Brunne; that would be helpful. Thank you for the list. In addition, could you leave a message for all them to call my room the minute they each check in?"

"Yes, Mr. Style, I would be delighted. Finally, here are you room keys. Each of your rooms has premier views of the Rhine River, Rhine Cathedral and downtown. Thanks to its central location in Cologne City, the hotel is only five hundred meters away from the city center. Our luxurious suites feature a king-size bed, cabin shower and soaking tub. Sir, if you ever need anything, please phone me anytime. Here is my business card. The bellhop will show you to your suites on the top floor."

"Schroeder, how about meeting in the lobby bar, Glashaus, at eight o'clock."

"That sounds too good to be true. Finally, I can celebrate that we arrived in one piece. I don't think you realize how fast you drive Style and especially in the snow."

"I'm thrilled you feel safe, Schroeder. The rest of the team should be here and checked in no later than eight-thirty."

As soon as Style checked into his room, he noticed the room did have a spectacular view of the Rhine River and the Rhine Cathedral, just as the general manager described. The room furniture and décor was contemporary and nicely arranged with a separate bedroom. Once he unpacked his clothing and shaving gear, he immediately set-up his laptop and went to work. There was a brief e-mail from Global Response Center, indicating that all of the field agents should arrive at the Cologne Hyatt Hotel as expected, no later than the scheduled time of 8:30 p.m. Style decided to send an information request to James DiSciascio and to Counter Terrorism Center.

DiSciascio,

Since yesterday, I started to reflect on your question in regards to Hans Schroeder. As a result, I would feel much better if the CTC can revisit the background check of Schroeder and do a more thorough and comprehensive investigation. I want to make certain that there are no possible issues with him being a double agent, especially at this late stage in our investigation. It would be ideal if I could receive the information by tomorrow morning at the latest. Has any additional information on the Zurich bombing become available?

Be Safe

Style

Style changed into blue jeans and headed down to the "Glashaus" lobby bar to meet with Schroeder. Immediately upon entering the lobby bar, Style realized, after looking around, that Schroeder hadn't arrived yet. He settled down into a corner booth and ordered a beer. Within minutes, Schroeder walked in and settled down alongside Style.

"Well, what do you think now, Schroeder?"

"I need a good, strong German locally brewed beer to start my night on the right foot."

"Why, do you want to go for a drive, Schroeder?"

"Are you kidding, Style?"

As Style and Schroeder bantered on, the rest of field agents walked into the bar and found their way to where Style had a booth.

"John Style. Hi, I'm Richard Weiner, and I would like to introduce field agents Fred Capella, Dave Clapp, Thomas Colli, Marilyn DeFeo, Lynda Enequist, Susan Gross, Robert Handwerker, Kenneth Harvey, Dave Robie, Joseph Piccolo and George Probert."

"Welcome team, I'm John Style, and allow me to introduce Hans Schroeder. Schroeder was extremely instrumental in accomplishing the first half of our assignment recently in Zurich at Clearstream Finance & Bank LTD. In fact, Schroeder was the Executive Vice President and worked there for over 20 years. He did an excellent job in assisting us to extract and upload very critical information on the misappropriations (theft) of billions of dollars that belonged to the Jews who were sent to concentration camps in World War II. First, let's get to the important things - ordering drinks. May I suggest we have a beer or two before dinner? Then we can adjourn to the adjacent Glashaus room for dinner. Since no one seems to object, let me make reservations for fourteen at nine."

Most everyone were strangers and hadn't worked together at any time. This was exactly the right setting and opportunity for everyone to get acquainted and develop camaraderie. Thomas Colli recently was stationed in East Africa, Marilyn DeFeo came in from Egypt, Kenneth Harvey arrived from the Turkey and Richard Weiner came in from Thailand, Lynda Enequist was based in Poland, Susan Gross departed Portugal yesterday, Fred Capella, left Serbia this morning, Dave Clapp, came in last evening from Croatia, Robert Handwerker arrived here early today from Russia, Dave Robie came in today from Great Britain, Joseph Piccolo was based in Romania and finally George Probert, formerly based in Austria.

All of the agents were veterans of different campaigns and engagements. This is very typical of field agents who are brought together to form a unit and work as a team. Because of the nature of the spy game, there isn't sufficient time to bond; however, they are required, by necessity, to swiftly form professional relationships of trust and teamwork. After all, each agent depends on having their back covered under duress and in hostile circumstances. It didn't take long before everyone was comfortable and relaxed. Each of them was sharing their own personal war stories from previous assignments. Style couldn't have asked for a better environment to get his group oriented and working together as a team. Colli and DeFeo simultaneously asked Style for more details on the status of Clearstream banking.

Style instantly responded, "Obviously, the reason we are here tonight is the recent success we had in Zurich and the sudden departure of Ulrich Melmer, former CEO of Clearstream Finance & Bank LTD and one of the leaders of NDO, Karl Uber. Both of them and several Al Qaeda leaders departed to Frankfurt, Germany, after they set off a massive bomb that killed over forty men, women and children and injured more than two hundred innocent victims at a musical theater in Zurich. Incidentally, a woman I was dating who starred in the musical 'Pajama Tops and Bottoms' and her sister were both murdered waiting in line."

"What exactly does the bank of Clearstream Finance have to do with World War II, Nazi gold, Al Qaeda and NDO?" asked DeFeo.

Style turned and said, "Without making too complicated a story, let me provide a short version. We were able to prove the financing of Al Qaeda and NDO terrorism originated from the illegal confiscation of money, gold, bank accounts, jewelry and paintings by Nazi Germany from the Jews at the beginning of the World War II in 1939 through 1944. There was an estimated nine-hundred eighty-million dollars of central bank gold, around one hundred billion dollars in today's values, along with indeterminate amounts of stolen treasured arts and other assets during World War II, which was kept under wraps by the Swiss Banks for over seventy-five years. Approximately fifty-billion dollars of the original eighty-five billion dollars has been accounted for once we were able to examine and audit all of the old and current Clearstream bank accounting records."

"If my math is correct, where is the other $35 billion dollars?" asked Clapp

"As you can imagine, determining and accounting for every penny hasn't been easy. The accountants and CPAs continue every day to audit the books and try to put all of the pieces together. We realize a big chunk of money is missing, but I feel confident most if not all of it will be accounted for in the final analysis."

"Hi, I'm Susan Gross and I would like to ask, ultimately, who will get the greatest share of the money once all of it is located and found?"

"Another good question, Gross, and that has yet to be determined. I could speculate but that would not provide an adequate enough answer, and certainly would be unfair for me to do so under the circumstances. If it were not for Hans Schroeder's direct assistance and direction I'm convinced I would still be buried inside an old World War II file cabinet looking for evidence. Today, Interpol has issued a restraining order on all bank transactions at Clearstream Banking Finance & Bank LTD, and anything having to do with the Swiss Financial Market Supervisory Authority (SFINMA). As I described earlier to Schroeder, the banking industry in Zurich is going to be substantially impacted and turned upside down. There will be several innocent victims and some local businesses affected by the bank closure. However, in the end, it will most likely strengthen the entire banking business in Switzerland, particularly in Zurich. Most all of the evidence that we managed to secure, has successively been handed over to several different international courts of justice for prosecution. Some of the courts of law consist of various international jurisdictions including The International Court of Justice (ICJ), in The Hague, Netherlands and United States Federal Court, Washington, D.C."

Style continued, "I personally would like to see justice accomplished without delay. Now, that brings us to the present time. Are there are more questions before we leave for dinner?"

Weiner raised his hand and asked, "Why are we setting base operations in Cologne and not Frankfurt?"

"There are several good reasons, Weiner. At first, I asked the same question. Let me begin by saying this decision was made jointly by both GRC and CTC. They both decidedly favored Cologne because of its proximity to Frankfurt. Most all intelligence data indicates Melmer and Uber are now in hiding some place in Frankfurt with two Al Qaeda leaders, Abu Alouni, Al Qaeda Head of Operations, Europe and Asif Zardari, Al Qaeda Assistant Head of Operations, Middle Europe (reports to Alouni). Ostensibly, NDO and Al Qaeda have a considerable number of members based in Frankfurt. The rationale behind the thinking that went into the selection of Cologne as a base of operations does make perfect sense. Cologne will allow us much more freedom to move about and setup tactics without compromising any strategic advantages. Critical to our success and safety is that we don't put any agents directly in harm's way."

Kenneth Harvey suddenly asked, "Before we leave for dinner, may I ask one more question - what type of support, back-up and commitment?"

"Great question and I'm thrilled someone asked it. Harvey, would you mind restating your question and just speak a little louder so everyone hears you?"

"What type of support and backup can we anticipate in the event we encounter a major force of radical terrorists?"

"All right, fair enough question. Paramount, we have been designated with the authority to use whatever force and means necessary in the performance of our assigned mission. We are teaming with British Intelligence MI6 and Interpol. As most of you probably already know, Interpol is the world's largest international police organization, with one-hundred ninety member countries. Today, I don't have available the exact number of forces committed, but I feel confident to say at least forty to fifty reinforcements will be made available when needed. Finally, tomorrow I will show you some of the new weapons made available to us for this assignment and I think you will find them to be very impressive indeed. If there are no more questions, let us adjourn to dinner. The general manager here at the Hyatt Cologne has set the stage for a wonderful dining experience for all of us. We are eating in the Rheinsaal room. At the same time, we may continue with our informal meetings and discussions."

As everyone was walking slowly into the beautiful large dinning facility, you couldn't help but notice the floor-to-ceiling windows offering a spectacular view of the Rhine River, the Cologne Cathedral and the Old Town of Cologne nestled on the horizon of the old magnificent river. To provide warmth and coziness, the room had dark mahogany paneling with a very large open-hearth fireplace. The size of the hearth was big enough for ten men to stand abreast and still have enough room on the sides to walk. It was as tall as the room, at least twenty feet. The room was warm and toasty, creating an atmosphere of luxury and comfort.

Momentarily, Style interrupted everyone's brief period of relaxation and said, "I hope that you all enjoy dinner and please have a good time tonight. This is just a reminder; we will meet early tomorrow morning at eight in the lobby of the hotel. Initially, the Hyatt will provide us transportation to the vacant warehouse, one mile south on the Rhine River."

30

If we do not end war – war will end us. Everybody said that,
millions of people believe it, and nobody does anything. ——*H.G. Wells,*
Things to Come (the "film story"), Part III, adapted from his 1933 novel The Shape of
Things to Come, spoken by the character
John Cabal

On a cold, gray, blustery morning, everyone piled into a large van and departed south on a bumpy dirt road running parallel to the main highway alongside the Rhine River. It didn't take long to arrive at the old World War II abandoned warehouse. Once Style opened up the old heavy wooden doors, the stench and smell that suddenly rushed out all at once was overwhelming and utterly disgusting. The smell reminded everyone of animal cages inside a timeworn antiquated zoo. Since the warehouse was at least a minimum of seventy-five years old and perhaps even much older, everything appeared ready to collapse at any moment. Eventually, everyone started to become acclimated to the unpleasant environment. The warehouse was a striking contrast to the stunningly exceptional and beautiful architecture of the Cologne Hyatt Hotel with the capped peaks and sloping bays that elaborately displayed the marble and glass interior of the large voluminous lobby. Style suddenly interrupted everyone's train of thought and observed, "Unfortunately, this will be our base operations center for the foreseeable future. If you have a complaint, please register your sentimentalities with the general manager of the Cologne Hyatt Hotel. Joking, of course."

Harvey jumped in real quick and said, "It actually grows on you. Just pretend you are lost in the jungle and suddenly you have become an animal trainer."

"All right, everyone let me bring to your attention a few items for your business pleasure. The first two objects are just to your right."

There stood two three-ton trucks, fully loaded with back-up weapons and a reserve parts inventory. Inside each truck, there was an unmanned aerial vehicle (UAV), laser truck- mounted weapon systems, a 60-kilowatt fiber laser module for the truck-mounted laser weapon system intended to shoot down enemy unmanned aerial vehicles (UAVs), rockets, artillery rounds, and mortar. In addition, each truck was designed with the intent of transporting a platoon of soldiers or marines. However, for their purposes, initially they would only carry just six or seven people each, supplies, weapons, munitions and hardware. In the event they needed to get into somewhere uninvited or blow something, they had C-4 explosive blocks. There were approximately ten pounds of C-4 with detonators. They had a refresher class on handling C-4 and where it could best be employed such as pressing into gaps, cracks, holes, bridges, equipment or machinery.

Colli quips, "God damn it, I'm back in the U.S. Marine Corp. The only thing missing is the chow hall, spit shines and roll call."

"Great observation," yells Robie.

Style interrupts adding, "Let me provide a quick description of the other remaining military hardware. The following items are brand new technologies and made available to the CIA through several U.S. Government contractors, however, certainly not gratis. Initially, they were purchased by the good graces of the U.S. Marine Corp. The U.S. Marines first field-tested and then approved all of these weapons for combat use. CTC and GRC soon thereafter requested ten units for field agents.

Naturally, a former Green Beret officer of the U.S. Army, Handwerker adds his two cents, "I'm not sure I feel secure enough with the U.S. Marines doing the testing. Of course, I'm not serious, but I needed to ride Colli a little."

"These Manpackable killer drones are capable of seeking out and destroying targets up to a distance of ten thousand feet or two miles. All of us will be divided into three man teams to carry each of these mobile units. The backpackable system is lightweight at approximately six pounds. It is like a smart mortar system, yet instead of launching up and then down on a sharp ballistic arc, it lofts into the air, assists the operator searching for tactical targets, and attacks targets when established. The U.S. Marines have given the Manpackable drones the nickname 'Switchblade.' The 'Switchblade' flies fast and quietly, and strikes with precision to keep collateral damage to a minimum. This is one of the primary reasons the CIA decided it would be a good weapon of choice for urban hand-to-hand fighting. Are there any questions?"

"Yes, I would like to make an observation," Gross says.

"What is your observation," replied Style.

"I happen to notice, that Hans Schroeder is taking fastidious notes, but hasn't asked any questions yet. I find that strange."

"What do you think Schroeder?" questioned Style.

"Obviously you put me on the defensive, Gross. To be perfectly honest with you, I'm an accountant and not very familiar with military hardware or the language of combat. I prefer to learn slowly and when I feel comfortable enough with my knowledge, then I will ask questions."

"That is good enough for me." Gross yells out.

"We have a lot to cover today, so let me finish. The operator can call off a strike at the last minute, if necessary, even after the munitions are armed. CTC has assigned us four Manpackable killer drones to be used at our discretion. We have one additional unit for backup. Also, included is a dummy 'Switchblade' to be used for training purposes. Later this afternoon, we will meet to begin training on the Manpackable killer dummy drone. Everyone will have an opportunity to field test and put the killer drones through its paces and become efficient in the use of these new field weapons."

Piccolo interjects and makes a brilliant observation, "You would think Langley is expecting a U. S. Marine regiment or squad of Navy

Seals, to be on the ground alongside us when we arrive in Frankfurt with all these weapons and particularly the type of amphibious truck transportation."

DeFeo decides to add her two-cents, "Not a bad idea; I go for the U.S. Marines and Navy Seals to assist and backup."

Style interrupts, "Sometime later this afternoon I should receive a courier package from the U.S. Embassy in Berlin, containing the latest logistical maps on Frankfurt with the surrounding terrain and the most current state-of-the-art navigational GPS systems. These logistical maps and GPS systems will be used to assist us in the pursuit and apprehension of Ulrich Melmer, Karl Uber, Abu Alouni, Asif Zardari and all of their members, directly or indirectly, associated with NDO and Al Qaeda. Are there any questions so far?"

Colli raises his hand to ask, "How many members of Al Qaeda and NDO are there in Frankfurt?"

"At this point the number we have is just an estimate. It looks like there are at least seventy-five to one hundred active members of both terrorists' organizations based in Frankfurt. I expect to receive a more accurate number by tomorrow morning."

Weiner asked a follow-up question. "When do you think we will be prepared to leave for Frankfurt and when will British Intelligence MI6 and Interpol be available to assist us in Frankfurt?"

Style reacted by saying, "I expect we will be ready to move out no later than two or three. British Intelligence MI6 and Interpol are both ready and waiting for us to notify them. They are going through similar drills approximately twenty miles outside of Frankfurt"

Capella raises his hand abruptly and asks, "What about a safe house, just in case?"

"That is without doubt an excellent observation. There is a provision for two safe houses in Frankfurt. Presently, I don't have any details but I expect to receive over a dozen or more wrist based GPS systems that will have the safe house addresses already programmed into the critical address locator and their respective coordinates. In the event any of you have an emergency situation, open the address directory listing and highlight both safe houses and the GPS will take you to the nearest safe house location. I have been informed each location has a control room with a complete array of computer systems. Tomorrow when you receive the GPS watches, you will also receive passcodes. There are three levels of entry. The first passcode is to be utilized to get in to the safe house. The second code is your individual eye print (iris) allowing access to the control room and the last entry code is your respective fingerprints to make use of the computer systems."

Robie suddenly interrupts to make an extremely important point by saying, "I trust this safe house is truly that and indeed a safe house. I speak from experience when I had to use a safe house in Viet Nam. The damn fucking safe house was anything but safe. It appeared our enemies knew more about our covert activities and our secret safe house then we did."

"Obviously, I have no idea what to expect. I trust GRC completely, when

they tell me the safe house is secure, reliable and totally trustworthy."

The remainder of the morning and afternoon, the group of agents practiced using the new dummy Switchblade and Manpackable killer drones. As soon as they finished and became proficient in the use of the drones, they moved on to personal weapon target practice. It was obvious by the end of the day that everyone was anxious to get started on the assignment. The warehouse was getting colder as the sun started to go down. Just before five o'clock, Style indicated it was time to stop for the day. Once the old heavy creaky doors were finally opened, and despite the cold blustery wind coming in off the river, everyone stepped outside to welcome the fresh air.

This time of year the sky seemed to be a constant gray and became steel gray as the night fast approached. Snow was beginning to lightly fall. Hurriedly everyone jumped into the van provided by the hotel and immediately transported them back to the Cologne Hyatt Hotel. Once they arrived back at the hotel lobby and stepped inside to get warm, Style proposed going to the bar for a nightcap; however, no one seemed interested. Since no one was interested, Style turned to ask, "Are there any questions on any aspect of the orientation and training today?"

Weiner, observed, "I think I can speak for everyone and say the training was outstanding. However, right now, all of us are exhausted, damn cold and tired. I think most everyone would like to go to their rooms to rest and get a second breath. In fact, I will personally order room service tonight."

Style replied, "That sounds like a good plan and I couldn't agree more. All right everyone we will meet at eight in the morning in front of the hotel."

It was easy to understand why everyone was tired and exhausted; the damn warehouse wasn't heated, and it was damp and cold all day. I need to arrange for several large space heaters to provide sufficient warmth to allow training to be more comfortable for the next two days. Everyone was justified in feeling miserable because the temperature had dropped dramatically to twenty-five degrees Fahrenheit around mid-day. In fact, it started to feel like a meat locker at the butcher shop. As soon as Style arrived back in his room, he checked his messages. No sooner had he sat down, his mobile phone rang.

"Hello Style, this is DiSciascio."

"Yes, I have been thinking of you today. I was freezing my ass off in the beautiful warehouse you rented. Thanks."

"All right, I screwed up Style, but you needed a warehouse that was convenient and available. I need to discuss several urgent matters with you. Is there anyone with you now?"

"No, I'm in my room alone, DiSciascio. This sounds extremely important."

"Style, hold on to your hat. CTC at Langley ran another background check on Hans Schroeder as you requested."

"Obviously, then you received a response, DiSciascio."

"Yes indeed, I did. Some of the information is surprising, Style."

"Don't hold back. Tell me the results."

"After exhausting every available source of information, CTC did uncover some questionable behaviors and/or dead time."

"What the hell is dead time, DiSciascio?"

"There is a period of time, two-years to be exact, in his work history going back to the early 2005 and 2006. Those two years are entirely unaccounted for in Schroeder's life history. There is simply no explanation. The other issue we are concerned about is his marital status and his two children. The children's birth certificates don't list Hans Schroeder as the father."

"Hmmmm, that could be an administrative mistake or possibly he's the adopted father."

"That was our first consideration. After further checking, we discovered Schroeder hasn't attempted to legally be their father and according to legal documents from the city of Zurich, Schroeder even has refused financial responsibility for them. This is causing us a lot of concern."

"Now, that would be just cause for me to be concerned after he has told me on a number of occasions how much he has enjoyed being a father and taking care of them."

"Style, we are doing our best to uncover more facts on Hans Schroeder and his circumstances. More than anything the two-year gap is a genuine concern. There is however, another real severe problem, Style. This isn't directed at Schroeder, at least not now."

"OK, what other good news can you share? This is getting to be one hell of a conversation."

"Just recently, the Switzerland government hired a team of certified public accountants to audit the Clearstream Finance & Bank LTD bookkeeping records and they uncovered some major discrepancies, other than the recent thirty million dollars taken by Ulrich Melmer."

"You mean to tell me, there are more funds missing."

"I was going to ask you if perhaps you made a large withdrawal from Clearstream Finance & Bank LTD, when you were doing all the downloads, Style?"

"I know you are kidding, DiSciascio."

"Absolutely, I'm not serious, Style. This problem could be a real catastrophic disaster. There is approximately thirty-five billion dollars unaccounted for from the original eighty-five billion dollars confiscated by the Nazis from the Jews and hidden by Melmer. It seems this money will never be totally accounted for to the last penny."

"Oh my God, DiSciascio; how can that be?"

"There is speculation that Melmer used the thirty million dollars to mislead everyone and throw us off by covering-up the theft of the thirty-five billion dollars. Once he manipulated the process, he somehow managed to electronically transmit the thirty-five billion dollars on the day of the bombing in Zurich."

"How did he pull it off, DiSciascio?"

"That is the great mystery, Style. CTC, MI6 and Interpol are working closely with the Swiss and German government to solve the disappearance of all the money. Preliminary reports indicate the monies were transferred to a bank in Frankfurt. The bank they identified is ReiseUMB German National Bank."

"I'm sure the bank officers will cooperate with the investigation."

"As of today, from all indications, the bank officers and directors aren't cooperating with the investigation whatsoever."

"Obviously, they are part of the conspiracy, don't you think, DiSciascio?"

"Now, this gets real interesting, Style. They specifically told German police and Interpol investigators to first obtain a warrant and a court order for them to open up the bank's accounting books. Naturally, this has delayed and hampered the investigation. The speculation now is whether the bank officers are directly involved in the conspiracy to commit bank theft and fraud."

"This is becoming mad and absurd, DiSciascio."

"As a direct result, five arrest warrants for the bank executives were issued. Immediately, German police and Interpol followed-up with a raid at the Frankfurt, ReiseUMB National Bank, in which more than twenty police cars surrounded the building. According to the prosecution, twenty-five ReiseUMB Bank employees in addition to the bank executives have been accused of bank fraud, bank theft, serious tax evasion, money laundering and attempted obstruction of justice, including their Chief Executive Officer and Chief Financial Officer."

"Has the European Union been informed yet?"

"Style, the moment Reuters' news service released the story, the EU reacted swiftly and was outraged over the entire fiasco. Immediately they contacted Interpol and almost demanded the problem be resolved in a hurry. Unfortunately, everyone who is a member of the EU is beginning to understand both the short and long-term repercussions of this potential economic disaster.

Here is the difficult part of the story. If indeed the thirty-five billion dollars isn't found soon, the EU economy would be dramatically de-stabilized in the first half of the upcoming year and in to the near future. How far in to the future is purely speculative but I would guess it would take another five to seven years to recover for everyone, including Germany. This is an economic catastrophe beyond comprehension Style. Furthermore it will have a dramatic effect on the American economy, both short and long term."

"I do understand their position, DiSciascio. I do remember the EU GDP growth is projected to turn positive gradually in the second half of the year before gaining some traction into next year. As domestic demand is still constrained by a number of impediments that are typical of the aftermath of deep financial crises that Europe has witnessed this past decade. Germany has taken on the burden of being the stabilizing economy since it bailed out Greece, Ireland, Portugal and Italy."

"You are completely correct, Style. In addition, Germany has loaned substantial funds to Spain to help them with their economic crisis. We are being pressed to the wall for answers and at this junction, we need to do something fast. I recognize you are extremely busy, but if you could possibly think about the thirty-five billion dollar theft and discuss this problem with your team, perhaps they could brainstorm some type of explanation. I can assure you that Langley, GRC, CTC and everyone in the field is looking for an answer. Pressure is getting rough from all corners, including the State Department and the White House. Something needs to be done quickly to avoid a world economic collapse. First, we need to find where the thirty-five billion dollars has gone. Second, determine how it occurred. Third, who is responsible other than Ulrich Melmer and Asif Zardari, head of Middle Europe Al Qaeda. Finally, I'm making available the following agents for immediate backup. All of these field agents are experienced and excellent team players and highly dependable.

Do you have a pen and paper to write down their names? I will also e-mail their complete files. They are in no special order. Are you ready?"

"Yes, go right ahead."

DiSciascio gave the following names:

Janet Wilbur, Sweden; MaryAnn McLaughlin, Belgium; Joseph Hackett, Norway;

Thomas O'Brien, Saudi Arabia; Henry Cotteli, Denmark; Sam Toy, China, Jennifer Christine, France; John Quinn, Iraq; Jim Archer, Japan; Elaine Kelly, India.

After Style managed to write down all the names, he asked DiSciascio, "Could these agents match the professionalism and effectiveness to the team of agents who arrived last night?"

"Yes, absolutely, I would bet my life on each of them."

"That is good enough for me, DiSciascio."

"When and if you need these named field agents, immediately contact the Global Response Center and they will arrange to have the necessary agents on duty with you within 24 hours. In the meantime, we will continue working on Han Schroeder's two missing years and marital status. Keep up the great work. How is your leg doing?"

"Today, because of the cold, it has caused some problems, but overall I feel much better.

"How are you doing emotionally?"

"I would be lying, if I said perfect. I think of Zosa often, but fortunately, because I'm kept so busy day in and day out, it allows me to escape from thinking of her all the time."

"Have you been able to practice tennis, Style?"

"No, but I plan on practicing tomorrow evening or the next day. In fact, the tennis director at a nearby indoor tennis club made arrangements for me to practice with two of his teaching pros."

"Are you suggesting Style, you are that good, that you can play two opponents at the same time?

"Since you don't know anything about tennis, DiSciascio, just me let explain briefly; to get in shape and improve my timing, the practice time will involve two on one drills and not competitive match play. I now hope that you understand."

"I do, Style, and that is the best news I have heard all day. I will probably be talking with you sometime tomorrow. Good night and be safe."

"Good night, boss."

The moment Style hung up the phone, he realized he had to confirm the tentative schedule for tennis practice with the local tennis club. Also, early tomorrow morning he had a doctor's appointment at the local hospital to have the stitches removed from his torso. Style then called the front desk of the Hyatt to speak to the general manager about arranging the rental of large commercial size space heaters. The general manager immediately replied, "not to worry, Mr. Style, I will make certain that six to eight large commercial size gas space heaters are delivered to the hotel first thing in the morning."

Style promptly suggested whoever was going to provide the heaters, please wait until he arrived in the lobby of the hotel to meet with them, so they could follow him to the location where the space heaters would be installed. "If for some reason I can't get back to the hotel in time, I will delegate someone to sign the paperwork and provide directions to the location where the space heaters will be installed."

"Yes, Mr. Style, is there anything else you need?"

"Not at this time and thank you for your help, Sir."

As usual Style was out of bed early. He had a very busy schedule today. First, he needed to call Hans Schroeder and arrange to meet for an early breakfast.

"Good morning, Schroeder. I have been very busy and, as a result, I have been neglecting our daily conversations."

"Believe me, I do understand, Style, so don't worry about it"

"How about having a buffet breakfast in fifteen minutes downstairs in the lobby club room?"

"I will see you in fifteen minutes, Style."

"Good morning, Schroeder. How is your wife and daughters? I'm sure you've had an opportunity to call them since we arrived."

"Yes, as a matter of fact, I spoke with everyone just before I came down to breakfast. Everyone is doing well. Thanks to the U.S. Government and the CIA, they have had a lavish time spending money on clothing and teen-age things."

"Schroeder, this is a very difficult question and I don't have an option but to ask."

"What is the problem, Style?"

"In order to move your status ahead as a recruited field agent, Langley headquarters had to do a thorough background search on your personal history and credentials, including your family history. Before I ask you these important questions, I need to ask you are you doing all right, Schroeder? Are you sure your family is doing well living with your mother-in-law on the farm near France? The reason I ask, it seems since you got back from your week's ski trip, you haven't been yourself."

"My family is doing OK. Let me address the other question about my attitude. Exactly, how do you mean 'not yourself?' What the hell do you expect?"

"Well, for example, on the drive from Zurich to Cologne, you appeared irritated and jumpy. Everything I said, you questioned as if you no longer trusted me. I just want to make certain Schroeder that you feel part of our team and I would like for you to know that if you ever need someone to trust, that is me."

"I'm not holding anything back, Style."

"Well you haven't convinced me. However, I don't have any other option at this point but to accept your word. Let me get on to the real reason for our discussion this morning, Schroeder."

"This sounds quite serious, Style."

"That all depends on your response and answers to several questions, Schroeder. Case in point, can you provide a suitable explanation for a two-year gap in your employment with Clearstream Finance & Bank LTD, starting in 2005 and ending in early 2007?"

"That is very easy to explain, Style. Around February 2005, I somehow contracted both spinal meningitis and pneumonia. I was extremely ill, and for a short period, I was even put in quarantine at the hospital. Once I was removed from the very critical list at the hospital and out of danger, Clearstream and Melmer suggested I needed a long rest and as a result, I was transferred from Switzerland to a warmer and dryer climate."

"Where were you moved, Schroeder?"

"I was transferred to a hospital in New Zealand. I stayed in that hospital for at least six months. Then, once I recovered and gained enough strength, I was relocated to an apartment in the city of Christ Church, New Zealand. I remained in New Zealand until approximately January or February 2007, and then I returned to Zurich, Switzerland once I recovered."

"Why didn't the Swiss Federal Office of Public Health (FOPH) have any record of your illness? As you know all public health records in Switzerland are fastidiously maintained as part of the Swiss national health policy act. They had no registered records in any hospital in all of Zurich or for that matter in all of Switzerland. Furthermore, there was no listing of a patient by the name of Hans Schroeder for the period of 2005 through 2007, in hospitals in Austria, Germany, France or Italy. Can you clarify or give an explanation, Schroeder?"

"No. I can't give you a rational explanation, but I can assure you that I was sick with spinal meningitis and pneumonia."

"Is it possible that you were drugged by Ulrich Melmer and were led to believe you had meningitis and pneumonia?"

"That is the most absurd question, Style. I had all of the symptoms of meningitis."

"All right, can you at least tell me the name of the doctor who treated you initially?"

"No, all I can remember is that I was removed from Clearstream on a stretcher and taken by ambulance to a hospital. This is totally insane the way I'm being treated with these ridiculous questions."

"Please understand, Schroeder; these aren't stupid or ridiculous questions. They are absolutely necessary."

"You make it sound like I can't be trusted, Style."

"OK, how about your family? Did your wife and children go with you to New Zealand?"

"No. I decided it would be best to go alone allowing me to recover more rapidly without having distractions or added pressure worrying about my family."

"Who originally made that decision?"

"Ulrich Melmer is the one who suggested it to me when I was diagnosed with meningitis. He thought it would be a precautionary move so the children would not be exposed to the illnesses."

"You realize all this information will need to be verified and substantiated. Can you provide any documentation, including receipts of travel, passport information, apartment rental lease and the release papers from the hospital in New Zealand?"

"Style, are you kidding? Who would keep all those records for this length of time and especially going back several years ago?"

"You must understand, whenever a long time period, especially as long as two years is missing from someone's personal past or work history, the CIA will justifiably raise a red flag and the agency will definitely be concerned. Let me get to the next question, Schroeder. This one is more personal, but it also raised some concerns at Langley."

"Yes. What is the other problem?"

"There is a question of your marital status and why you aren't listed as the father of your two daughters on the children's birth certificates. When I was asked, Schroeder, about your children, I thought possibly that could be an administrative mistake or that you are the adoptive father. However, after further investigation and analysis, we discovered you didn't attempt to officially adopt them. Furthermore, according to legal documents, you also refused to be financially responsible for them."

"Now, that really pisses me off. What can I say at this point, Style? Let me clarify several important issues. Yes, I'm not the girl's birth father, but I'm their legal guardian under Swiss law. After my second daughter was born, I filed a petition under the Swiss Civil Code for adoption. At the time, I was in my early thirties."

"I don't understand, Schroeder; how does that affect the adoption process?"

"The Swiss Civil Code explains that individuals have to be married for five years or be over the age of thirty-five. My wife and I were married less than twelve months and I was just thirty-three years old. Consequently, we never corrected the problem, and I can assure you, I never once neglected the children emotionally or financially."

"At this point, Schroeder, your explanation is credible enough and explains partially some of the issues. I would like to make it clear that all I can offer you is the satisfaction that I will at least continue to maintain all my confidence in you."

"Style, I understand why there is a requirement to be painfully thorough, but my marriage and children, that is pushing the security background investigation much too far."

"Schroeder, what you don't consider or perhaps realize is that everyone who elects to join the Central Intelligence Agency must go through the same background investigation. I had to go through the same scrutiny and background check as you are now experiencing. There are absolutely no exceptions. The litmus test is when the final report is filed. As you may know, the litmus test determines whether a potential candidate has the necessary clearance for high office or in this case, someone applying to work in a confidential top-secret field such as the CIA, NSA, FBI or Secret Service. All of your answers determine whether you proceed or not. As soon as the clearance results are finalized, you are notified of the outcome. If you pass, you begin the next phase and that is the academic testing and physical assessment. Once you pass these tests you are notified to start in on the formal training process. Hopefully, you should now understand why it is essential of me to ask these extremely tough and probing questions, Schroeder."

"There is one thing in this discussion that is being ignored, Style."

"Yes, what is that Schroeder?"

"You guys recruited me. I had no interest in becoming an agent for the CIA until you bridged the subject going back to just after the first bombing at Clearstream headquarters."

"That is unquestionably correct, Schroeder. However, that doesn't diminish the fact you remained interested and wanted to pursue becoming an agent for the CIA. In addition, it doesn't mean that the agency is willing to compromise its very high standards. If I remember correctly, you continued to ask me questions every day as to when you would be allowed to join the CIA. Is that correct, Schroeder?"

"Yes, I agree I was anxious to join and become a member."

"Do you also recall when I presented you with the reward check for the one million dollars and I specifically mentioned that I would understand if you wanted to go home to be with your family and enjoy the new retirement bonus. Frankly, that made sense to me. And you replied, that like me, you were committed to getting these assholes, and wanted to know what role you would play? Furthermore, I suggested that you discuss this assignment with your wife first. I just cautioned you not to share any details or reveal where we were going."

"Yes, I do recall having said that, Style."

"One of the last things you said to me on this matter was that sounds extremely fair. You don't forget a damn thing. Finally, the last point I made was that I expect you will also tell her there is considerable risk and danger. In addition, you will not be able to communicate with her until we have completed our assignment. Is that clear, Schroeder?"

"I do remember the entire conversation, Style and I admit I said all of these things."

"Now that we have that cleared up, perhaps I had better ask you this especially appropriate question, Schroeder. Would you like to give notice and to call it a day?"

"Do you mean quit and walk away, Style?"

"Yes, that is exactly what I'm asking you, Schroeder."

"Definitely not Style, I'm not a quitter. I do understand and as you know from the very beginning, I have nothing but the highest respect and regard for your professionalism."

"Schroeder, let's eat because I'm hungry. Today, we have an extremely busy day ahead."

Style wasn't completely satisfied with his conversation with Schroeder at breakfast. Immediately after breakfast, he submitted a report to DiSciascio, outlining all of his concerns and recommendations. As soon as Style and Schroeder finished breakfast, Style explained that he had to go to the hospital to have the stitches removed from his torso.

Style turned to Schroeder and mentioned to him "The rest of the team should be in the lobby of the hotel at eight."

"I will be there at eight to meet with them, Style."

"Thanks, that will help me out today, Schroeder."

Style further detailed the schedule for the day, but was reluctant to share the latest intelligence briefing he received from CTC. He did mention to Schroeder, however, that there should be someone waiting for him from a company that rents large commercial size gas space heaters. "Schroeder instruct the rental company to follow you to the warehouse so he can setup the gas space heaters throughout the warehouse."

"I will do that, Style; is there anything else?"

"Yes, there is one additional thing and that is the invoice for the space heaters. The general manager at the hotel has arranged to add the rental charges of the space heaters to my room bill. As a result, all you need to do is make certain they complete the setup and installation of the heaters, then simply initial the acceptance and get a copy of the receipt. Finally, please tell the rest of the team I will be at the warehouse as soon as I finish my checkup at the hospital and the stitches are removed. In addition, this morning I complete my last physical therapy on my leg."

"Yes Style, I understand and I will take care of everything."

31

War will exist until that distant day when the conscientious objector enjoys
the same reputation and prestige that the warrior
John F. Kennedy
President of United States

ater in the afternoon, after an intensive day of training, Style decided to allow everyone to leave early at around three. He reviewed his notes to make sure everyone had an opportunity to work with all of the systems. Upon arrival back at the hotel, Style explained to everyone he had arranged to practice tennis at a local indoor tennis club. He didn't think he would be finished practicing and working out for at least three hours. Therefore, he suggested everyone not to wait for him but to have dinner and he would join them later for a nightcap in the lobby bar. Style flagged a taxi and within minutes arrived at the Cologne Indoor Tennis Club. The director of tennis greeted him the moment he checked in at the front desk. The director introduced Style to two of the staff-teaching professionals who would be working with him for the evening. He explained his circumstances and injury to his leg but insisted they put him through a rigorous workout and practice session for the next two or more hours. Strangely, the club had ten clay indoor courts. All of the courts were perfectly manicured and professionally maintained. The Cologne Tennis Club was first class with a total workout facility, offering a steam room, sauna, twenty-five meter indoor pool and an exercise gym with weight training. In addition, the club also offered racquetball and volleyball. After Style completed his three-hour tennis workout, he returned to the Hyatt Hotel. Upon entering the lobby bar, there was only one person from the team seated in the corner. It was Richard Weiner.

"Hello Weiner." yelled Style.

"Did you have a good workout, Style?"

"Yes, I did and it was exactly what I needed. It was tough, thorough and I managed to get in some great workouts practicing volleys, groundstrokes, serves, overheads, return of serve and two-on-one drills. It was exactly what the doctor ordered. Enough with the tennis, tell me what you think so far, Weiner?"

"Up to now, I give the two days of training an A minus."

"That is a pretty good grade, why just an A minus?"

"Because it is still fucking cold in that fowl smelling old World War II warehouse, that's why."

"Fair enough, Weiner. You seem to be more of the leader of these guys and they look up to you. Would you agree with my assessment?"

"Indirectly I would, and that is because I have more time with the company. Also, I have a tendency to wrap myself in the flag and I think I'm a more outspoken than the rest, except for Harvey and a few others."

"Yes, I noticed that right off. This is a great opportunity to have a confidential discussion with you, Weiner."

"Why is that, Style?"

"We have a serious potential problem developing and I will need a sounding board to help solve it. But more than that, I need an immediate backup and support."

"I'm all ears. What is the problem?"

"Before I begin, I already had a discussion with DiSciascio and he was the one who suggested I talk with you."

Style explained in detail the history of the relationship with Schroeder. He didn't leave out anything. In addition, he was very upfront when DiSciascio, GRC and CTC all expressed their reluctance and concern for continuing with the masquerade.

"My God, Style, if this decision were up to me, I would cut Schroeder loose without any reservation. Why would you want to risk twelve agents' lives for this apparent double agent?"

"OK, I think I know why you feel the way you do, Weiner. However, just listen to my logic for a minute. For argument's sake, let us assume you are completely correct and Schroeder is a double agent. Don't you think it would be far better to know where your enemy is camped than to not know and take unnecessary risk all the time? By having him in your sight of vision, you have more control and can technically react much better. I can always manage to provide misleading information to keep him busy and throw him off guard on occasion."

"Style, that is all well and good, but how do you reconcile that in the meantime he's feeding these Nazis and Al Qaeda bastards vital information on what we are doing."

"That is correct; however, I will make certain the information he receives is filtered, edited by me and misleading. If anything, the information he gathers will hinder and create problems once he starts to report it and then they use it. In fact, I have already started providing him misinformation regarding the new military weapons. In addition, I provided him with specific dates of when we anticipate on making our first moves. You have seen what he's like. He doesn't socialize and most everyone else is cautious and keeps their distance. Furthermore, in this particular case, if anything, I need to make Schroeder continue to feel wanted and a necessary member of the team. This, in turn, will make him feel safe, secure, and hopefully more likely to unconsciously divulge important information when he lets down his guard. Personally, I need to understand and uncover more of Schroeder's personal vision and motivation."

"What kinds of results do you expect you will receive from gaining his confidence and trust?"

"To be perfectly honest with you, Weiner, at this point I'm not sure. However, this is no different than recruiting a double agent."

"How is that, Style?"

"Since I became aware of the possibility that Schroeder could already be a double agent, I anticipated that some of the information I learn from him may never be perfect or good enough. Nevertheless, I think as long as we can survive, grow and expand, I will get exactly the intelligence we need to satisfy us moving forward. On the other hand, it is conceivable that he'll render and reveal some confidential details of NDO specific locations or places of where Melmer and Huber are hiding out. There is a possibility I could also learn of the manpower of Al Qaeda in Frankfurt. I certainly realize that much of what I just said is speculative and pure conjecture on my part. At this moment, we simply don't have any inside intelligence."

"Why don't we just arrest him and send him away to jail and begin interrogation?"

"Because then, Al Qaeda, Ulrich Melmer and the National Democratic Organization may close up shop and flee. If that happens, for all intents and purposes, we are back to square one."

"Indirectly, that is exactly what we are trying to achieve."

"There is one major problem with them fleeing."

"What is that, Style?"

"There is thirty-five billion dollars still missing. If they escaped with that money, they would simply set-up operations in another country. Just as important, the thirty-five billion dollars alone would cause economic chaos and panic throughout all of Europe. Certainly, it would have a dramatic effect on the United States economy as well. No, the smart thing is to allow him to remain part of our team and let him think what he pleases and we will spoon-feed him information. Also, I will keep a close eye on him. We will provide him with just the right information at the right time."

"Just suppose someone else from our team discovers the truth about Schroeder?"

"Obviously, I will have to deal with that issue when it occurs."

"Style, Schroeder appears to be a very intelligent guy. Am I correct?"

Yes, absolutely Weiner, without question he's very smart. Where are you headed with this observation?"

"Well, it occurred to me that he must be aware of what is going on, especially with your knowledge of him being a double agent."

"There is no doubt he understands the circumstances because I have already had a lengthy upfront discussion with him. I explained in detail there were several major problems that needed to get resolved and that I personally couldn't do anything about the investigation or get directly involved. At this point, everything is out of my hands and control. Schroeder's reaction was total disappointment and resentment."

"Why?"

"Because he feels that he demonstrated his loyalty and commitment when he directly assisted me in breaking in to the Clearstream financial banking system and also made copies of all the files belonging to the persecuted Jews and their stolen wealth. Since this whole controversy is now front and center, I'm trying to understand why he cooperated so easily. Furthermore, Schroeder's professional assistance was quite remarkable and thorough."

"Style, perhaps all he wants to do is just throw you off and gain your confidence."

"No, if that were the case, we would still be going over the microfiche records and it would take approximately an additional two or three years to get where we are today. When he and I started this project, he was convinced it was the correct thing to do."

"Then what the hell happened?"

"I believe in the very beginning when I first arrived at Clearstream, he was an NDO operative. However, when we met and developed a friendship of trust, I believe I unconsciously influenced his thinking. Most recently, going back to the bombing at the theatre in Zurich, he seemed different and changed dramatically."

"How do you mean, Style?"

"After he returned from his cabin, following a long week skiing in the Swiss Alps, he became more difficult to reason with, distant, sometimes even belligerent. Prior to his ski trip, we often had friendly conversations that were open and upfront but that has changed considerably. He started to doubt me more often and questioned everything I did. Now that I'm able to reflect more on the circumstances and the problems, I'm able to see things differently. Certainly, there is the real possibility that NDO and Al Qaeda are holding his family hostage and he has no option but to acquiesce to their demands. Mind you, I'm just guessing at this point. As you know being in the spy business and married causes much pain, separation and sometimes compromise."

"Do you really think, Style, that Schroeder's family is being held hostage and he had no other options but to follow their instructions."

"Yes, I'm beginning to think in that direction."

"For those very reasons, Style, I'm not married, because of the separation and distrust, especially when you take your family with you on an international assignment and expose them to potential danger."

"I would guess, knowing Schroeder's personality, that being a spy isn't exactly something he wants or needs and is being forced in to this situation."

"I think I'm beginning to understand a little more, Style. What would you

like for me to do to make your job a little easier?"

"Beginning today, whenever you are around Schroeder, make mental notes on his activity and general behavior. If you discover that his behavior is questionable or strange, please contact me as soon as possible. Also, try to get close to him and gain his confidence without making it too obvious. Currently, I'm the only person on the team he trusts. If indeed he were a double agent, I would prefer that we are successful in gathering as much information on NDO and Al Qaeda through Schroeder's naiveté and direct or indirect involvement contributing valuable information."

"I believe this is a big risk, Style, but I'm team player all the way."

"Great, Weiner. That is all I need to know. Thanks for listening. This was an extremely helpful discussion in more ways than one."

"There are just one or two other things that I would like for us to do and we need to accomplish them before we retire for the night.

"What is that, Style?"

"I would like to get hold of Schroeder's mobile phone without his knowledge and place a bug inside the unit."

"Does he have a standard issued CIA GPS phone?"

"Yes, he was issued the mobile phone just a couple of weeks ago."

"I will handle that for you Style. Give me the bug. I know exactly where to place it inside the phone. This is the reason they call me the magician. Believe me, it will be done by breakfast time."

"Are you sure you can pull it off, Weiner?"

"Style, its money in the bank and Schroeder will never know that his phone was temporarily out of his possession."

"Thanks. That will help me tremendously. Now, I need to discuss our plans for our last training session and to review the strategies that I just received from Counter Terrorism Center (CTC) for initial preparation and engagement with NDO and Al Qaeda. I would like to get your feedback and reaction, Weiner. Before I forget, did you receive this report today from Langley regarding the terrorist bomb makers?"

"Which report is that, Style?"

"The report that came in this afternoon that includes information that these same bomb makers are also believed to have targeted American troops in Afghanistan, may have mistakenly been allowed to move to the United States as war refugees, according to FBI agents investigating the remnants of roadside bombs recovered from Iraq and Afghanistan."

"No, I didn't receive that report yet. Please finish what the report said."

"There was a discovery of two Al Qaeda Iraq terrorists living as refugees in Bowling Green, Kentucky, who later admitted in court that they did attack U.S. soldiers in Iraq. This prompted the FBI to assign hundreds of specialists to an around-the-clock effort aimed at checking its archive of one-hundred thousand improvised explosive devices (IEDs) collected in the war zones for other suspected terrorists fingerprints. The point I'm trying to make is here we are on the terrorist's front door step trying our best to eliminate them and our own government is legalizing their citizenship so they can settle down in the mid-west to cause more 9/11s. What the hell is wrong with this picture?"

"Style, I would not be surprised if there were many more than what the report indicates. These types of terrorists are the real bad ones because they are the trained bomb makers. What makes this so difficult is these asshole terrorists are watching football games on Saturday afternoon assembling the bombs in middle America like Cleveland, Detroit and Bowling Green and our government is screwing up all the time trying to be politically correct and then releasing them. It is an endless cycle. We capture them, they are sent to Guantanamo Bay, in Cuba, repatriated, then released and we start all over. That is called job security. You know damn well, most, if not all, of the terrorist who get released, will be firing a gun or rifle at us on some night in a dark deserted alley."

"I will bet when we confront these fucking assholes in Frankfurt, at least a quarter of them have been in an American prison somewhere. Homeland Security must be going crazy, Weiner. The whole process is like a revolving turnstile. We capture a few terrorists, send them to prison after being prosecuted and then they are freed by the justice department after spending little time in the slammer. The story never seems to change, especially under this administration."

"Style, you're definitely correct. Can you imagine what it is like having to secure the nearly unguarded northern border of the United States?"

"No thanks, Weiner. My job is tough enough."

"I remember a test question when I returned to the 'Farm' for additional training. How long are the United States-Canada borders and how many land points of entry are there?"

"Are we now playing Trivia, Weiner? Well, what are the answers?"

"The U.S.-Canada border extends for five thousand five hundred miles, with just over one hundred twenty land points of entry. That is why we have such a problem with illegal immigration and drug trafficking. In addition, these many entry points also facilitate illegal entrances of terrorists and those that would do this country harm. As I said earlier, that is pretty damn good job security. That is enough of my flag waving for today."

"How about one more drink before you retire, Style?"

"OK, it has to be small because we have a lot to do for our last training day, Weiner."

"I realize, Style, you are relatively young, but have you ever given any thought about the day you must retire?"

"Well, that is how I got involved in this situation when I was recruited in Atlanta."

"No, I don't mean professional tennis. I'm referring to the spy game."

"Well, to be honest with you, Weiner, I haven't given it much thought."

"Here is something to think about. What do former spies do when they quit the spy game? Plan covert action campaigns against the landscape committee consisting of gray haired nasty old ladies in the Home Owners Association? Perhaps re-line the tennis courts with double and triple white lines at the local tennis club a day before the club championships for the fun of it? No, the majority of former CIA case or field officers work as consultants or contractors within the U.S. intelligence community. Seriously, this is something to think about, Style. I know what you are thinking. This guy Weiner has had too many. All right you are probably right. If you don't mind, Style, I would like to call it a night."

"You know, Weiner, this was a terrific conversation. Okay, at least most of it was. I'm not sure about the last portion; however, it was entertaining and informative. Good night."

32

Give me the money that has been spent in war and I will clothe every man,
woman, and child in an attire of which kings and queens will be proud.
I will build a schoolhouse in every valley over the whole earth.
I will crown every hillside with a place of worship consecrated to peace.
——*Charles Sumner,*
U.S. Statesman of the American Civil War
Period Dedicated to Human Equality

The next morning, Style was just getting out of bed when he received an unexpected phone call.

"I realize it is early, Style, but I just wanted you to know I successfully planted the bug in Schroeder's mobile telephone."

"What time is it, Weiner?"

"Six o'clock, Style; time to get up."

"Thanks for doing that. I know it was risky."

"Actually, because Schroeder isn't a professionally trained field agent, his personal security precautions leaves a lot to be desired. He was so sound asleep, I could have driven a motorcycle into his room with a marching band and he still would not know that I placed a listening device inside his mobile phone."

"Again, thanks for your help. All I need to do now is contact the Global Response Center (GRC), and notify them to activate that bug."

"Is there anything else you need at this time?"

"Yes, I would like to set aside some time later during the training session at the warehouse for us to discuss and review a few critical items."

"It must be important."

"Yes, it is extremely important and of great consequence, Weiner."

"I look forward to our day of training at the beach, boss."

A few minutes later Style receives a phone call from DiSciascio.

"Style, I have more information on Schroeder and it's not good at all."

"All right, let me have it."

"It seems Schroder never departed Switzerland for any length of time until 2008 and 2009. In 2008, he attended a financial conference in London, England for approximately four days and returned directly back to Zurich. The following year, he flew to the United States to participate in a global Chief Financial Officer's (CFO) bank industry specific three day seminar conducted at the Hilton Hotel in mid-town Manhattan. Once more, he returned non-stop to Zurich, Switzerland. You realize, Style, what all this means; Schroeder is either a terrible liar or he has been thoroughly brainwashed."

"There is a third option, DiSciascio, and that is he's one great double agent."

DiSciascio was quick to reply, "Personally, I think he has been systematically indoctrinated and programmed to believe he was sick with meningitis and then caught pneumonia. In addition, the hospital and resort he claims he was sent to weren't in Christ Church, New Zealand, but were somewhere in close proximity to Zurich, Switzerland. Furthermore, it wasn't a genuine hospital, but a facility made to look like a hospital in a tropical environment."

"DiSciascio, that is just pure speculation and conjecture and how do you know he didn't leave Zurich and wasn't treated at a facility near Zurich?"

"Style, believe me, I don't want to make this any more difficult than necessary. The most glaring evidence is his passport. There is nothing to corroborate that he traveled outside of Switzerland. Remember, during the period he suggested he was very sick. Switzerland was still transitioning into the European Union and as a result, whenever you crossed the border into the neighboring countries of Italy, Slovenia, Austria, Germany or France, you had to produce a passport. There is no record on Schroeder's passport of ever going across any of the neighboring countries beginning in the 2005 to early 2007 time period. Now, that includes driving, flying, traveling on a train or bus, and also travel by ship."

"DiSciascio, I think you are right. However, I think his family is being held hostage by these fuckin dirty, scumbag animals and he has no other choice but to cooperate with them becoming an informer and double agent."

"What do we do knowing we have a spy among us, Style? I understand the circumstances and that everything is very delicate. We can't reveal we know because these SOB cowards would fold up their tent and go home, literally. That would ruin our chances of getting to first base."

"I believe I have a very good idea, DiSciascio."

"All right, let's hear it."

"I've already planted a bug in Schroeder's issued mobile phone. Call me in thirty minutes. Create a big lie by saying to me we need to change our strategic overall operational plans to another date because we've added another three hundred more agents composed of the CIA, MI6 and Interpol forces, to move on to Frankfurt by the end of the week. When the call comes in, I will have only Schroeder with me at breakfast and I'll place the call on the mobile speaker phone so Schroeder hears everything. Now what do you anticipate will happen, Style?"

"If my Sherlock Holmes intuition is correct, as soon as our conversation is ended, knowing Schroeder, he'll most likely excuse himself and then he'll immediately call Ulrich Melmer."

"You seem very confident, Style."

"I will bet my life that is exactly what he'll do."

"I give it the green light. At this point, there is absolutely nothing to lose. Okay, Style, I'll call you at exactly seven. You need to call Schroeder and arrange to meet for breakfast."

"Consider it done, DiSciascio."

Immediately after his conversation with DiSciascio, Style called Schroeder and suggested they meet for breakfast at seven. A little while later, Schroeder joined Style for breakfast. Within a few minutes, Style received a phone call from DiSciascio. As planned, Style put the call on his cellular speakerphone. Fortunately the restaurant was empty at the time and they were seated in a corner booth by themselves. Just in case, Weiner had already notified the rest of the team to avoid sitting with Style and Schroeder. As Style was carefully taking notes from the discussion with DiSciascio, Schroeder was noticeably upset. As soon as Style replied in a defiant manner to DiSciascio that he didn't think it was a good idea to delay the overall strategic plan to the end of the week, Schroeder leaned over to Style and said, "Excuse me, I need to get something from my room. I'll be right back."

Style simply said, "Okay"

"Style got back on the mobile phone with DiSciascio and abruptly explained what had happened."

"It sounds as though your plan is working, Style. Call me later and let me know what transpires."

"I will do that as soon as possible, DiSciascio. In fact, call me back again in ten minutes and reinforce the decision to expand the operational team by the additional three hundred men and to delay our strategic operational plans to move on to Frankfurt by the end of the week."

"Why, Style?"

"Just in case the bug in Schroeder's phone wasn't turned on for the earlier call I assumed he made."

"Okay, done."

Schroeder returned to join Style a short time later to finish his breakfast.

Style asked, "Is everything all right?"

"No problems. Why do you ask, Style?"

"From the manner in which you jumped up and left the table, I thought there was a serious problem."

"I simply forgot to mention something important to my wife earlier and I knew we would be extremely busy training most of the day, so

I decided that happened to be an excellent time to do a follow-up call to her."

"The team will again meet in the lobby at eight a.m. I don't know whether you heard my phone conversation with DiSciascio earlier, but it seems almost certain our training will be changed slightly to accommodate some overall strategic plans before we can move on to Frankfurt by the end of this week. I will receive confirmation momentarily?"

"I only heard a very brief portion of the call and that was when you first answered your telephone."

Just as both Style and Schroeder were getting up to leave the restaurant, Style received another phone call from DiSciascio. Again, Style put the call on the speakerphone.

"Hello, Style here."

"This is DiSciascio again. I would like to confirm we decided to delay our move and add at least three hundred more men. That means you and your team won't be going in to Frankfurt until the end of the week. Please advise every one of your team members of these last minute changes and that they will be staying in Cologne for another five days, until at least Saturday. Shortly, you will be receiving a package by courier from the U.S. Embassy containing your specific instructions."

"Thanks DiSciascio, I understand."

As soon as Style finished his conversation with DiSciascio, he turned to Schroeder and said. "You heard the man, everything has changed. I need to get back to my room to notify everyone else on the team. I will see you in approximately thirty minutes, Schroeder."

It was quite apparent that Schroeder was also anxious to get back to his room. The moment Style hung up the mobile phone he headed back to his room to contact GRC to make certain they managed to record Schroeder's most recent telephone conversation. Once Style received confirmation that the bug in Schroeder's phone was active he was able to relax slightly. Although relaxed, Style was told by GRC that they would call him back as soon as possible with the results of Schroeder's phone calls. Fifteen minutes later the Global Response Center called Style to let him know there were only two-recorded telephone conversations, together the calls were made to the same mobile phone, and both calls were triangulated to the same address in Frankfurt, Germany. The telephone transcripts would be forwarded to his encrypted e-mail and the actual voice recordings would be sent to his voice mail on his mobile phone. Simultaneously, all information would be copied and forwarded to DiSciascio, in London. Within five minutes, Style was able to listen to both phone conversations Schroeder had with Ulrich Melmer. Obviously, this was no surprise to Style.

FIRST CONVERSATION

Melmer, this is Schroeder. This is critical information and I don't have much time. First, I would like to know how my family is doing, Melmer.

Melmer replied, your wife and children are safe and doing well. I need to caution you Schroeder about these phone calls. What do you have that required this call?

I just heard from a very reliable source, that the CIA is changing their planned action and movement in to Frankfurt to end of this week. I will call you back as soon as I get conformation of the day and the number of field agents that will be involved in the actual tactical plan and who is responsible for directing the CIA agents, MI6 and Interpol. The next time I call, I would like to speak with my wife.

I'm not sure I can do that, Schroeder.

Why not Melmer, is she hurt?

She is doing just fine, Schroeder.

Then Melmer, I expect the next time I call that I can speak with my wife.

Melmer replied, I will see what I can do.

SECOND CONSERVATION

Hello Melmer, this is Schroeder again.

What is the update, Schroeder?

First, I want to talk with my wife.

Hold on. When she gets on the telephone, you only have thirty seconds to talk, so make it quick. Those are the ground rules, Schroeder. Do you understand?

Yes, yes, of course. Let me talk with her now.

Hello dear, these people are animals, Hans.

How are the children doing?

They are doing okay, Hans, considering the harsh circumstances that we are being subjected to and the terrible conditions.

How do you mean, dear?

I don't know where we are, but the smell is terrible and so is the cold, wet mildew environment where we must sleep. Both girls are getting sick with colds.

Dear, how is your health and how are they treating you?

Why are they doing this, Hans? I don't understand why these terrorists are so mean to us. Do you have something they want? My health is better than the girls and most days my hands are tied. Also, they cover my eyes with a blind fold most of the day.

That is enough, Schroeder. What do you have for me?

First, promise you won't hurt my family, Melmer.

I won't hurt them. What is the fucking update, Schroeder?

The CIA has definitely delayed their strategic move to the end of the week because of the additional manpower of approximately three hundred men coming to Frankfurt. There is a combined force of at least seventy-five CIA agents, seventy-five to ninety MI6 British Intelligence agents and probably close to two hundred Interpol police."

What else is there, Schroeder? You had better not hold back anything or your family will die. Do you understand, Hans?

Yes I do, Melmer. That is all the information I have at this time.

You call me, Schroeder, if something changes. Do you understand?

Yes, completely.

Now remember Schroeder, this isn't a game. I will kill your family if you say something to the CIA. I hope you get the picture because I'm quite serious.

Yes, yes of course I won't say anything, Melmer.

Good bye Schroeder.

As soon Style finished listening to both conversations, he called DiSciascio for his input and interpretation.

"Style, I listened to both conversations a couple of times. I'm still trying my best to put my arms around the whole mess. My first reaction is we can't allow just one family's safety to interfere in the outcome of the entire strategic plan. There is simply too much at stake. There are literally thousands and thousands of potential innocent people going to be put at risk if we allow ourselves to make emotional decisions. For that reason and that reason only, we need to remain steadfast and on course. Do you understand, Style?"

"Yes I do boss, completely. May I suggest something for us to consider? With your permission, I would like an opportunity to first talk with Schroeder."

"Okay, I don't have a problem with that, Style. What do you have in mind?"

"First, I will confront Schroeder explaining that we are totally aware of his circumstances and specifically mention that we have the tape recordings of both his conversations with Melmer. Second, I will threaten to have him thrown in prison unless he's willing to cooperate with us and he'll never know what happens to his family unless he goes along with our plan and we work together. Third, I will tell him as a result of the phone conversations he had with Melmer, we were able to track the exact location of the terrorist's hideout in Frankfurt."

"Style, the fact is we do have the exact location and address of where Melmer received those phone calls. However, it is possible he's moving around. To be perfectly honest with you, Melmer is too smart to stay in one place after having made an open mobile telephone conversation. I would be shocked if he hasn't already moved somewhere else."

"DiSciascio, I have a gut instinct that he hasn't changed locations."

"As you know, Style, that isn't enough of a justification to allow us to deploy over three hundred agents to the triangulated address. I need concrete facts of where Melmer is located."

"Boss, I understand completely. Would you allow me and two other agents to go to Frankfurt and do an advanced search of the address we have on Melmer. Allow me just two days at most. If after two days, I'm not successful, we do it your way. What do you think?"

"To be fair, I will give your idea some consideration. However, I need to call Langley to get them to buy in to your proposal Style. I will try my very best because I emphatically trust your judgment, Style."

"That is fair enough. How long will that take, boss?"

"I will call Langley the moment I hang up and have a discussion on the merits of your proposal. I will call you back in no more than thirty minutes, Style."

"I will be waiting for your phone call, DiSciascio."

In the meantime, Style started to reflect on a number of recent events and relationships. First and foremost are his continuous reflections of Zosa. It seems as though Zosa has become a whimsical fairytale character when Style daydreams. The CIA psychological doctor Holmes, reminded Style his reflections and dreams of Zosa were normal and healthy. The other less important dream was going fly-fishing with his dad in Montana and, of course, his relationship with Schroeder. The first dream would simply remain a wonderful fantasy, whereas the second was a potential reality within the next eight months and the latter almost becoming a nightmare. What do I say to Schroeder if I receive the green light. Do I totally risk our friendship and put everything on the line. Obviously, I don't have much time for too many options. Approximately fifteen minutes later, Style received the anticipated phone call from DiSciascio.

"Style, this is DiSciascio, once more with a recommendation. After a conference call with the Director and Assistant Director, we have decided to go along with your suggestions. There are several provisos. They aren't complicated, but we need for you to agree to the stipulations."

"Okay, what are the terms, DiSciascio?"

"You won't need to write these down because they are very simple. First, you will be given the two days you requested. Second, we would prefer you take at least seven agents with you instead of two. Third condition is the moment you experience serious opposition, you contact me as soon as possible. Fourth, Schroeder will not be part of your team, and the fifth and final provision we highly recommend these field agents: Dave Robie, Richard Weiner, Ken Harvey, Robert Handwerker, David Clapp, Joseph Piccolo and Tom Colli. We encourage you to take Handwerker along because he's excellent in close quarters and hand-to-hand combat. Weiner, Harvey, Handwerker, Piccolo, Colli and Clapp are seasoned veterans and are the best in our craft. You already know how good Robie was on your trip to Dubai. Do you have any questions at this point, Style?"

"No boss. Thank you for this opportunity."

"There is an additional item that I need for you to be aware of just in case."

"Yes, DiSciascio, what is the additional consideration?"

"The following agents have been notified and are on their way to Cologne, Germany: Elaine Ann, Henry Cotteli, Joseph Hackett, MaryAnn McLaughlin, Thomas O'Brien, Janet Wilbur, Ashley Jones, Jennifer Christine, Sam Toy and John Quinn."

"DiSciascio, is there a reason for the additional agents at this point?"

"Yes, absolutely Style. This strategic move is just proactive and pre-cautionary. We want this mission to be successful, productive, positive, but also safe."

"I understand and I will be checking in with you as usual, boss."

"I get a little nervous when you call me boss, Style."

"There is one more important item to discuss, boss."

"Yes, what is it?"

"I will be talking with Schroeder momentarily and placing him under house arrest."

"Style, why are you arresting him?"

"I believe it is for his own safety and protection. Furthermore, I don't want him involved at this point because of his emotional condition."

"All right, I agree that is a good move."

"Good bye, DiSciascio. I will talk with you shortly."

"Be safe, Style."

33

The release of atom power has changed everything except
our way of thinking... the solution to this problem lies in the heart
of mankind. If only I had known, I should have become a watchmaker.
———Albert Einstein

Immediately after talking with DiSciascio, Style called Schroeder and suggested they get together before leaving for the training session. They arranged to meet for a quick cup of coffee in the Hyatt Hotel lobby bar.

"Good morning again, Style."

"Yes this will be a great day, Schroeder. Did I ever tell you anything about the town where I was raised in the state of Georgia?"

"No Style, you haven't."

"I'll be real quick. The town of Blue Ridge is located in the foothills of the Blue Ridge Mountains, all part of the Appalachian Mountain Range and one of the oldest mountains ranges in the world. The landscape is spectacular. Although I have a romantic love affair with the state of Montana and all of its magnificent beauty, I remain a steadfast Georgian. Sometimes I just wished that both states were neighbors instead of being over 2,000 miles apart. Most of the people, who live in the Blue Ridge part of Georgia, are hardworking farmers and blue-collar type folks. Many of the locals are very religious, and unfortunately, are branded rednecks. They are honest as the day is long and would give you their heart if you asked for it. My mom and dad are fifth generation farmers from this part of northwest Georgia. There are over 5,000 acres that my family farms and ranches. The land has been in the family since way before the Civil War. Obviously, my family's farm is nowhere the age of many of the farms and ranches in all of Switzerland but a wonderful place to have been raised as a boy. I have a beautiful, younger sister that I simply love and have nothing but the greatest respect for because of her accomplishments in her profession. Today, she is a pediatric physician, practicing her profession in our hometown of Blue Ridge. My dad and mom are the ones most responsible for my sister's success and education, as well as mine. We have never forgotten our roots and who guided us. My parents are magnificent. When we were young, my dad introduced my sister and me to hunting and fishing. Let me elaborate and state, not just fishing, but fly-fishing. There is a major distinction between the two. I will not go into any explanation but suffice to say fly-fishing treated with reverence. When my father introduced fly-fishing to us, he would take us to the local Toccoa River. Often, he would say, 'If fishing is a religion, fly fishing is high church.' In our early years my sister and I often joked about our dad's passion for fly-fishing, but soon we discovered why he had such a strong feeling and fervor of the sport."

"Style, where is this conversation headed and why now?"

"I will get to my point shortly. On my parent's farm, they raise corn, cattle, and chickens and have an apple orchard. The essence of sharing my personal life has more to do with values, ethics, truth, commitment and honesty. Until very recently, you and I have been very honest with one another."

"That hasn't changed, Style, whatsoever."

"Let me finish. Truth is a very delicate and often difficult word for people to understand. After all, truth is most often used to mean in accord with fact or reality or to a standard or ideal. The opposite of truth is falsehood, which correspondingly, can also take on a logical, factual or ethical meaning."

"My god, Style, is this a philosophy class? Get to the bottom line."

"You know as well as I do, Schroeder, what I'm talking about. You haven't been truthful with me recently and you know damn well what I'm talking about. I think I know why you can't be honest and I understand. Let me blunt and to the point. We, the team, are well aware of your family being held hostage and you are being black-mailed to become a double-agent for Ulrich Melmer's National Democratic Party and Al Qaeda."

"I can explain, Style."

"There is no reason to explain because there is no justification. However, we do understand your position and most of us would probably do the same thing. For that reason, I'm going to arrest you and put you in protective custody. In a few minutes, Interpol will be here to read to you your rights and take you into their custody. However, we, the CIA, will not be pressing formal charges. In addition, both British Intelligence MI6 and Interpol have also decided not to bring charges against you. Instead, you will be under house arrest for your own safety."

"How long have you known that I became a double agent?"

"When you returned home from your snow skiing trip, I noticed something had changed. Mainly it was your very short wire of patience. That pretty much summed up your sudden change of attitude and almost hostile behavior. Today, we were able to confirm our suspicion. We know for a fact you had two telephone conversations with Melmer this very morning and we are also aware that you talked with your wife."

"How did you know?"

"I can't provide any of the details. On the other hand, I can tell you we know exactly where Melmer is hiding your wife and children. Also, we feel confident that is where Melmer has a hideout, along with Al Qaeda."

"Style, I would like to go with you on this mission."

"Unfortunately, I can't allow you to assist. Remember, you are now under official house arrest."

"I understand, Style."

'I promise you Schroeder, we will do everything humanly possible to rescue your family so no one gets harmed."

"I believe you. I apologize for the way things have worked out."

"There is no need to apologize. We do understand completely. We will safely free your family."

"Your sense of truth and understanding is quite remarkable for a young man, Style. I do believe you when you say you will free my family. You truly have been a great friend. Thank you."

Everyone was milling around in the lobby of the hotel when Style finally showed up. "Team; there has been a temporary change of plans."

"How do you mean," asked DeFeo.

"Suffice it to say, initially only eight of us will be moving out and that will be later today instead of waiting another two days. Would the following agents meet with me for approximately an hour or so: David Robie, Richard Weiner, Ken Harvey, Robert Handwerker and David Clapp, Joseph Piccolo and Tom Colli? Everyone else, training will go on as planned. Susan Gross will lead the training and will assume lead until I return or meet up in Frankfurt. I can tell everyone briefly that there has been a minor change in the overall strategic plans. In addition, I would like to share with everyone; Hans Schroeder has been placed under house arrest for his own safety."

Enequist interrupted and asked, "What happened?"

"Schroeder's family has been kidnapped and held for ransom by Al Qaeda and National Democratic Organization."

"But why; what value could a finance guy provide Al Qaeda?" observed Handwerker.

Both Al Qaeda and NDO were hoping to squeeze Schroeder to become a double agent and to begin spying on us in order to keep his family safe. To be honest, Schroeder didn't have much choice but to go along with their demands or they would kill his family."

"When did all of this occur?" asked Colli.

"We arrested Schroeder just this morning. However, we, and that includes MI6, Interpol and the CIA, will not be pressing charges against him. As a direct result of this investigation, we were able to locate the exact location of Al Qaeda, NDO and Ulrich Melmer in Frankfurt. Our boss and Langley have decided initially a small contingent be deployed to confirm the exact location and to make certain all the bad guys are at this location. If necessary, we have been given the authority to use whatever force is necessary to perform our assignment."

"What about the hostages, Style?" asked Piccolo.

"Our first priority is to confirm the exact location. Once we accomplish the confirmation and report back, we then can determine what will be needed to rescue the Schroeder family."

Robie raised his hand and wanted to know, "Is the thirty-five billion dollars a priority?"

"Yes, the thirty-five billion is indeed our main goal along with the capture of key Al Qaeda personnel and Ulrich Melmer, along with his sidekick Karl Huber."

Capella asked a follow-up question. "What will happen to all of the military hardware that we have been training on?"

Style turned to Capella, "As far as I know, there are no changes anticipated in the weapons being used. I would anticipate that those weapons and the agents remaining behind would be deployed within two days, just as I said earlier. Are there any more questions at this time? If not, I hope to see all of you shortly. Will the seven team members I named earlier please join me in the restaurant?"

Once everyone was comfortably seated in the restaurant, Styled promptly convened his meeting with the seven-team members.

"Gentlemen, all of you have been highly recommended for this assignment. We are about to be engaged in one of the most important assignments in the recent history of the CIA. Initially, the intent is to engage with the enemy in a stealth manner. Al Qaeda and NDO are actually anticipating a very large contingency of force of over two hundred or more agents composed of the CIA, Interpol and MI6."

"How would they know the exact number and the composition of their enemy?" queried Weiner.

"We intentionally told Schroeder all the information earlier today. By the way, Schroeder wasn't aware that we already knew everything about his circumstances. We anticipated as soon as we told him, he would call Melmer and as a result, we were able to listen to their telephone conversation."

"The fact they already know we are coming, how can we be stealth and surprise them?" asked Harvey.

"Very simple," replied Style.

"I don't understand, Style?" asked a confused Clapp.

"Seven of us speak Arabic, and you Clapp, speak Farsi, correct?"

"Yes, that is right Style," said Clapp.

"Gentlemen we will be stealth as stealth can be."

"Okay, Style, what are you talking about?" remarked Weiner.

"All right gentlemen. Let me explain. We will all dress as Arabs in the traditional tharwb or long white robe. A professional makeup artist will be arriving this afternoon to provide makeup to all of us, so we will look just like traditional Arabs including any special effects. This will include plastic noses and beards. So get prepared for some dramatic changes. "Before we all leave, there are a couple of items we need to discuss in order to make this mission a success. One of the very few benefits of wearing the tharwbs is we can conceal our weapons without any detection. Also, we will blend in nicely to the Middle Eastern environment allowing us to move freely throughout the Arabic crowds."

"How do you know what the environment is like? Have we already received intelligence reports on the layout and the exact location?" observes Handwerker.

"Yes, we have the exact location and here are some recent photographs taken by an unmanned aerial vehicle (UAV) drone. These photos were taken late yesterday afternoon and early today. As you can see, most everyone in the photographs is wearing tharwbs. There are very few of the subjects wearing Western clothing. Take a careful look at photograph number four. It was taken at a higher altitude, providing an excellent layout and clarity, demonstrating the very large geographical size of this particular Arabic community residing on the northeast side in Frankfurt. Statisticians have indicated there are approximately two to three hundred people in photograph four, just walking in the streets. These same statisticians are suggesting there could be as many as two or three thousand Arabs living and working in this section of Frankfurt. As you can see, most of the facilities have just tin roofs or they are wooden shacks. The few brick buildings are located more in the center of what is called 'Little Tehran.' These buildings are the major focus of intelligence reports from Langley and the location of the placed phone calls earlier today. The reports strongly indicate this is where Ulrich Melmer, Karl Huber, Abu Alouni, Asif Zardari and the core of the militant terrorists are living. We also feel very confident that Schroeder's family is being held hostage in one of these brick buildings. Wiener you look a little perplexed; what is on your mind?"

"I believe the essence of this whole action is to retrieve the thirty-five billion dollars. Am I correct, Style?"

"Yes, partially that is correct, Weiner. That is our main objective but we are also delegated with the responsibility of apprehending the above known terrorists. Before I came down to meet with everyone, I was notified we would be also responsible for the rescue of Schroeder's family. I believe I mentioned that earlier from a question asked by Piccolo. Apparently, Langley feels this is a very high priority and I totally agree. Robie, do you have a question?"

"Yes, Style. Where do you think Melmer has hidden the money?"

"Personally, I have worked directly with Melmer for over a month. I think I know him well enough. As a result, I feel very confident all, or most, of the money is located in either his office or his bedroom. My gut instinct tells me his office would be the place. Now, let's talk about what weapons we will take with us. Since there are only eight of us on this initial operation, we will be limited. In addition, we will be using one of the assigned military trucks for transportation to the outskirts of Frankfurt. I have arranged for two large SUVs as transportation when we arrive at that location. Once we have settled and become familiar with the landscape of Little Tehran, we will then locate the exact address of where Langley has directed us to the triangulated target. At that point, we will set up a tactical operation center. The Counter Terrorism Center has just sent me a notification that we will be receiving surveillance and reconnaissance intelligence support from the U.S. Air Force epicenter 100th Strategic Reconnaissance Wing, based at Ramstein Air Base, Germany. Any questions so far?"

"Yes," asked Weiner, "The engagement that we are about to take on, is it considered overt?"

"No. As you probably are well aware, anytime the CIA is involved in a conflict, officially it is called covert. There is nothing else I can say. Let me continue with the report. Apparently, the U.S. Air Force has already launched several drones known as Ravens. The Ravens are specially designed and useful in urban warfare in order to discover insurgent's hideouts and potential ambushes within relative proximity of the immediate conflict or battle zone. In addition, some of these sons-of-bitching UAVs have become so small that they can be launched from one's hand and maneuvered through the streets. UAVs are especially useful because they can fly for days at a time. According to some reports, Al Qaeda terrorists and most insurgents are loathe to stay in the open for more than a few minutes at a time for fear of UAVs locating them. When we arrive in the target zone, I will download the latest intelligence and surveillance information. Before I get in to the subject of weapons inventory and tactics, does anyone else have a question?"

"Yes sir," answered Colli. "In most similar skirmishes, we use a team of snipers to provide advanced logistical analysis and to eliminate known visible bad guys. What is our status?"

"Colli, I'm so pleased you asked that important question. You raised that question, as if I had prompted you. We will need two snipers on adjacent roofs to the location in question. I understand you, Colli, and Piccolo are two of the best snipers in the agency. Is that correct?"

Colli was quick to respond by saying, "Not only are we the best snipers in the agency, but the best period."

"Now that is what I like, two Italians who are shy with no confidence," said Harvey.

"Colli and Piccolo, there is no need for you two guys to wear the tharwbs or get cosmetic makeup today. Our goal is to arrive just after sundown, so we can rapidly fit into the environment. Most likely, because of time restraints, we will arrive at our target at around nine o'clock. Now let me discuss what weapons and ammunition will be needed for this friendly visit today. Colli and Piccolo, I understand both of you have already selected two U.S. Army M24 SWS Sniper Weapon System, firing the 6.62x51mm NATO .308 Winchester round with the Redfield/ Leatherwood 3-9x automatic ranging telescope sight. Is that correct?"

Piccolo responded, "Yes, Style, that is absolutely correct. We will need one additional back-up M24 and at least one hundred rounds. For up close encounter protection, two M16A2 5.56mm and another one hundred rounds and two Benelli M4 super 90 shotgun and sixty rounds.

For sidearm protection, we will use our standard Sig Sauer P226, 9mm, with fifteen rounds, silencers and Siglite night-lights."

Style sarcastically said, "Hopefully, that satisfies the snipers in the crowd. Now for everyone else on my Santa Claus list. Don't forget, we will also have the new weapons we trained on this week. We will take one Manpackable killer drone and a backup unit. Remember, they are capable of seeking out and destroying targets up to a distance of ten thousand feet or two miles. I would like for Weiner, Harvey and Handwerker to team up and take on the drone. The backpackable system is lightweight weighing only six pounds and comparable to a smart mortar system. Remember, you guys, instead of launching up and then down on a sharp ballistic arc, the drone lofts into the air and will assist you searching for your tactical targets. The drone will attack your target when established. For close quarter backup and protection, you will have three M16A2s with one hundred fifty rounds and two Benelli M4 shotgun and sixty rounds. I expect you also have your Sig Sauers?"

"Yes sir," yelled Handwerker.

"Finally, there is Clapp, Robie and me. I will drive the truck to pick up the SUVs. In addition, Clapp will drive one of the SUVs and the other SUV will be driven by Piccolo. Does everyone understand their role? Any questions so far? Good, that makes things easy. Finally, here are the weapons for Clapp, Robie, and me. We will take three M16A2s with one hundred-fifty rounds and two Benelli M4 shotguns and sixty rounds. Naturally, we will also carry our Sig Sauers for side arms. Essential to this mission's success, we will also bring C-4 explosives, approximately eight pounds of M112 and more than enough blasting caps. Finally, everyone should have two percussion grenades in their inventory. I will take sixteen grenades for backup. Are there any questions or concerns at this point?"

"Yes", replied Harvey. "What time are we taking off for our vacation trip?"

"No later than four o'clock. It is just over two hundred kilometers from Cologne to Frankfurt. It should take no more than two hours to get to the northeast side of Frankfurt to pick-up the SUVs.

34

Never think that war, no matter how necessary,
nor how justified, is not a crime.
Ernest Hemingway

𝒪t looked almost comical as the guys were loading up their weapons and gear in to the back of the truck while wearing their tharwbs or white robes. Handwerker said, "How do women wear these god-damned dresses. I constantly trip and can't walk straight."

Harvey jumps in and says, "Handwerker, nothing has changed. You can't walk straight even with training shoes, on a six-foot wide white line, down the middle of the road, stone-cold sober!"

Initially, the general atmosphere was full of dread and accentuated because of the icy, bitter cold and foreboding late afternoon dark gray skies. At this point, everyone had trepidation and was excited at the same time. Fortunately, most every man had a great sense of humor in dealing with the pressure and seriousness of the moment. Precisely at four o'clock, they rolled out of the old foul smelling and decaying warehouse on their way to Frankfurt.

Just about two hours later, they arrived on the northern outskirts of Frankfurt. Without delay, they parked the large truck in the parking lot of the American Embassy but just prior, everyone had to produce their U.S. CIA identification in order to enter the embassy compound. Immediately, a U.S. Marine escorted Style and his team into the American Embassy. Waiting for Style, was a member of the diplomatic staff. The young staff member introduced herself as Ms. Susan Will, chief administrator for the American Ambassador. She provided Style with the keys for two large black SUVs. All that was required was his signature. After signing the necessary paperwork, Ms. Will mentioned that she had also arranged for a cosmetic artist to be at the American Embassy to meet with Style and his team at six-thirty p.m.

"Ms. Will, thank you for all of your assistance. Everything seems to be running like a clock."

"You are most welcome, Mr. Style"

Just as Style was sharing pleasantries with Ms. Will, another young woman walked in asking for Mr. Style.

"Miss, I'm John Style and thank you for being so prompt."

"My pleasure sir, but I didn't anticipate meeting someone wearing a long white robe."

"It's a long story Miss. In fact, a group of us are going to a costume party tonight and we need to be made to look just like Arabs. Do you think you can pull that off?"

"That will be no problem whatsoever, Sir. I will make you and the rest look like you just arrived from Saudi Arabia. How is that?"

"Just fine with me," Style replied. "Here comes the rest of the crew. How long will this take Miss? There are eight of us, but only six of us need to be made to look like Arabs."

"I would say thirty minutes each."

"We are late now; could you do it in less time, say around fifteen minutes each at most?"

"If you just require mustaches and beards with a little darkening of your face, perhaps I could do it in fifteen minutes, Mr. Style. There are two of you who have noses just like a Middle Eastern man."

"Who are the two men, out of curiosity?"

"The two men standing together, talking in front of the desk just across from you, Mr. Style."

"Oh, you mean Mr. Robie and Mr. Weiner. Just wait until I tell them the good news."

Within a matter of thirty minutes or so, the cosmetic artist had transformed five of the team members in to looking just like Arabs, as if they were going to prayer at the Islamic mosque in downtown Cairo.

Style reacted first and said, "My God, I could sit down with Abdullah bin Abdulaziz Al Saud, the King of Saudi Arabia and he would not know the difference. The rest of you guys look the same way, just like genuine Arabs."

Weiner and Robie both said simultaneously, "Our wives wouldn't know us."

Harvey puts in his two cents, "If I walked up to my wife and whispered in her ear, she would scream and call the cops. That is how genuinely Middle Eastern, I look. Damn, I do look like someone from Saudi Arabia or Iraq."

"Miss, you did an outstanding job and quick too. People at the party won't recognize any of us for certain."

"Thank you, Mr. Style."

"Have you been paid yet, Miss?"

"Yes, Mr. Style. Mrs. Will sent me a check to cover everything yesterday. I would like to thank you for your business."

As soon as the cosmetic artist left the embassy, Style gathered everyone up for a quick review. "Ms. Will, is there a conference room we could use for approximately fifteen minutes?"

"Yes, of course Mr. Style. There is a conference room available just down hall on the right hand side, titled the Georgia Room."

"How fitting, is the ambassador available, Ms. Will?"

"No, Mr. Style. He left for a trip to London yesterday. However, he left this envelope for you."

Style opened the envelope swiftly. The message was very brief.

Mr. John Style:

I would like to wish you success on this extremely important assignment and mission. May god look over you and your exceptional team."

Signed

Reed Robertson
United States Ambassador, Federal Republic of Germany

Style hastily offered the note to all of his team to read. "All right guys, let's go to the conference room down the hall on the right for a quick review and briefing. Before we go in to the conference room, let's take a piss break and get back here immediately."

Within minutes, everyone returned to the conference room and sat down around the large mahogany conference table. The room was very impressive with a large photograph of the current President of the United States, prominently displayed at the head of the table. On the wall behind the table, was the American flag and alongside, the flag of the United Republic of Germany.

"Let's get started, gentlemen. Are there any questions on what you need to do?"

"No question, Style. I would like to just say, let's kick ass tonight," added Piccolo.

"I have just one last thing to add before we depart, gentlemen. Please remember, this mission will literally save thousands and thousands of people around the world. These bastards need to be told, in no uncertain way, they are wrong, they are the devils, they are indeed the heathens and that God almighty is on our side. We are here for one reason and one reason only and that is to liberate the oppressed. We are here not to conquer but enable all people to understand the meaning of freedom no matter their religion, race or skin color. If there are no more questions and if you don't mind, I would like to say a quick prayer."

As soon as Style ended the prayer, the whole team walked out of the conference room and went directly to the lobby.

"Ms. Will, thank you for your assistance. You were most helpful."

"Mr. Style, may I extend to you and your team success and our best wishes for your safe return from this very dangerous mission."

"Once more thanks, Ms. Will."

"All right guys, we're on our way."

As soon as Style said his last thanks, the whole team was out of the embassy. They honestly did look like Arabs. They all loaded in to the SUVs and were on their way within minutes. The GPS display was a large portable unit, bright and accurate within a few meters. Once the triangulated coordinates were programmed in to the GPS unit, all the drivers had to do was simply follow the audio and display directions. The large GPS display provided a dramatic picture of where they were as they continued their journey in to the heart of Little Tehran. It all seemed so surreal because the team was now dealing with the reality of the situation. Finally, they arrived within one block of the target and the insurgent safe house.

It was getting late, just before nine o'clock. Most streets were relatively empty of people. Fortunately, there was no moon whatsoever. The sky was clear. However, it was damn cold and getting colder by the minute. The first to get out of the SUVs was Colli and Piccolo. Based on the latest intelligence information downloaded from aerial surveillance and communication reports, Colli and Piccolo had already predetermined ideal tactical locations on the roof of two adjacent buildings. Each would setup their U.S. Army sniper weapon system, including night sights. Both also had to zero their weapons, to adjust the scope so the bullet's point of impact is at the point of aim for a specific distance, and in this case it was approximately one hundred meters.

Ordinarily, they would work in a team with one shooter and one spotter. However, because of the manpower restraints, each man had to work separately. Each of them was almost on identical angles to their pre-determined target. The approximate distance to their respective targets was the same, just over three hundred feet. Since the most accurate position is prone, both men had already setup sandbags to support the stock and to enable a comfortable hold of the stock against their cheek. Both Colli and Piccolo were the consummate professionals and they understood the key to sniping is accuracy, which also applies to both the weapon and the shooter. To be effective and accomplish their respective mission, the weapon should be able to consistently place shots with tight tolerances. When both finished setting up their equipment, they called Style to notify him they were in the cradle and ready to go. At the same time, Weiner, Handwerker and Harvey were walking down one side of the street and Clapp, Robie and Style on the other side. Since they had already driven down these same streets earlier, several times, they were very familiar with the layout and topography. By now, everyone had become comfortable with their tharwbs, except Harvey. For whatever reason, his robe kept riding up his ass. Style was laughing because it reminded him of one of the fiercest and one of the best professional tennis players on ATP circuit, Rafael Nadal. He was always tugging and picking at his ass while he was playing a tennis match. Style was actually surprised there wasn't more activity on the streets. He kept on asking himself, is it possible that they already know we are here and everyone has been warned to stay off the streets? Immediately, he recognized it was just his imagination playing tricks on him at this point. As they approached their objective, they discovered there were a large number of Arabs with weapons walking in front of the targeted brick building. There were approximately twenty-five to thirty armed insurgents with AK-47s walking the grounds, all wearing tharwbs. The headdress that Style and everyone else on the team were wearing denoted they were peasants. One insurgent yelled out to stop. Style, Clapp and Robie all stopped immediately. Style acknowledged by replying in perfect classical Arabic a few pleasantries and said they were on their way home from the Mosque where they helped sweep and clean the floors. Style followed-up the conversation by telling the man he would pray for him tonight. The young Al Qaeda operative replied by saying, "Thank you and may God be good to you." The three continued on their way down the street until they got to the corner to meet up with Weiner, Handwerker and Harvey. There was an Arabic coffee shop still opened at the corner. Style suggested they go there and compare notes. They all sat down and ordered Middle Eastern coffee. Fortunately, they were the only customers in the café at the time and there was only one person working. He was young, preoccupied with cleaning the back storeroom and obviously in a hurry. He took everyone's order and returned at once with the espressos. Once the young man served the coffee, he hurriedly returned to the back room to finish cleaning up. As a result, Style wasn't too concerned about security in having a conversation with his team. Quietly, Style and the team were assessing the situation. Soon thereafter, Style decided to reveal he was going to change the tactics of the planned frontal attack on the target buildings.

"Gentlemen, a few minutes ago I received the newest intelligence data and as a direct result of the recent walk by of the target buildings, I decided to modify our tactical plans. My reason is very simple. If we were to perform the original frontal attack, there is no doubt we would be successful killing most all of the insurgents and arresting Ulrich Melmer and the rest of the fucking asshole terrorists. I also think it will not be much of a problem finding the thirty-five billion dollars. On the other hand, I don't think we would be successful in safely rescuing Schroeder's family. As a result, I've decided to go it alone on the rescue of the family."

Weiner was the first to express doubt and concern. "Style, I admire what you are thinking, but I don't agree with the change of plan. You actually would compromise the entire process and that would be very unfortunate."

"I'm inclined to agree with Weiner," said Clapp.

"Much too risky considering what is at stake, Style," added Harvey.

Handwerker said, "Frankly, I support and favor the unexpected change of plans. I think it would work without question."

Robie said, "I'll just wait until I hear all of the facts then make a decision."

Gentlemen, please listen to my strategy. If after presenting my approach, I still don't convince at least four of you, I will back down and go forward with our original plan. Do all of you agree? As you know, we don't have a lot of time. First, I will need to locate the family fast, but with the most recent reconnaissance photographs providing the details of the exact location of where they are being held hostage, most all of our speculation and theorizing is now over."

"I need to interrupt and ask why the speculation is over?" questioned Harvey.

"Do any of you remember the company NorthFlex and the new trial experimental systems they have been testing, primarily with U.S. Air Force? Most recently, U.S.A.F. and the CIA have agreed to a joint acceptance of the new synthetic aperture radar (SAR). As a result, today we are now utilizing this powerful new technology. In fact, the reports I just received are from the SAR and its long-range electro-optic infrared sensors. Apparently, the Global Response Center has been utilizing SAR to locate and digitally record and listen to all of Ulrich Melmer's most recent conversations.

"That is powerful shit," responded Clapp.

"Now, gentlemen, this is the best news. GRC has also managed to track and record the voices of Schroeder's wife and two daughters."

"How does GRC know the voices belong to the Schroeder family," queried Weiner.

"I don't have a lot of time to provide all of the technical details, however, the previous mobile phone conversation that we recorded of Hans Schroeder and his wife matched perfectly with the recent SAR recordings."

"All I can say is, WOW! That takes a lot of guess work out of the whole fucking problem,." comments Clapp.

Style further adds, "All of this is happening as we sit here having coffee. It is so technically advanced; SAR can track and listen to conversations of people in the deepest caves, secured buildings and even in the oceans as deep as two thousand feet."

"Style, now we understand completely why you wanted to change the tactical plans." observed Weiner and Robie.

"Let me share some of my concerns with you guys on the three women. Because they have been traumatized, there is certainly worry for their emotional stability, which in turn may compromise the rescue. Next, the second aspect would be to get them calmed down. Perhaps the most difficult and last consideration is to convince them I'm an American CIA agent sent in to rescue them dressed as an Arab. Now that everyone understands the circumstances, I would like to present the details of my tactical rescue plan."

Once Style completed his ten-minute presentation, he asked, "What do you think, and is there anything you would like to add?"

"Now, that I have listened to your idea in more detail, frankly I give it my absolute support and think it will work," said Weiner.

"Great news." said Style. "How about the rest of you guys; how do you feel?"

Handwerker said, "I still go along with your plan and I haven't changed my opinion, especially now with the recent intelligence report you just shared with us."

"What about you, Harvey?"

"I'm for it one-hundred per cent and I agree with Handwerker now that you know for certain the exact building that the Schroeder family is being held hostage."

"All right. Robie, what do you think at this point?"

"From what all you have shared, your change of plans makes a great deal of sense and I go along with all changes, Style."

"Thanks, Robie."

"That is four. To be fair, I need to hear Clapp and get his input."

"Well, after listening to your logical explanation, your tactical plan is extremely reasonable and I support your idea, Style, without any question."

"Okay. Now I need to contact Colli and Piccolo and let them know there has been a slight change in our tactical plans."

After briefing Colli and Piccolo about the change of plans, Style also told them that since everyone was wearing tharwbs and looked alike, including all of us, everyone would have multiple black Xs on the back of their tharwbs underneath their white sweaters and stand out so they would not be targeted and shot my mistake. Style turned to everyone and said, "As discussed in my presentation, I will need at least thirty-five to forty minutes to locate them in the building. Most likely, they will be in the basement because of the conversation I heard Hans Schroeder have with his wife. She specifically mentioned that it was dark, damp and cold. Once I successfully extract all three women from the building. I would like for you, Clapp, to be on standby in one of the SUVs, waiting for my return with the Schroeder family. Is that understood?"

"Yes it is, Style. I will be prepared and ready to go."

"Next. You will leave with the three women and immediately take them to the U.S. Embassy. The on-board GPS system, will guide you directly back to the embassy. Do you have any questions at this point, Clapp?"

"Just one question, sir."

"What is it?" asked Style.

"Once I get to the American Embassy and drop off the Schroeder family and they are safe, should I return here?"

"Yes. Absolutely we are shorthanded as it is. Return as fast as you can."

"I will return promptly, Style."

"When we leave this coffee shop, all of you must return to the SUVs to retrieve your weapons and put the Xs on the back of your robes. Does everyone understand?"

Robie said, "Speaking for everyone, we certainly understand completely; consider it done, boss." "Since there has been a major change in tactics, we need to discuss what happens now that we are one man short with Clapp driving the hostages back to the embassy. I'm still convinced that with total surprise, the Al Qaeda insurgents will be caught off guard and not be prepared initially for an assault."

"I believe you are right," observed Harvey.

"Gentlemen, catching them by total surprise will be a major advantage and will contribute to our successful operation."

Style and his team all felt confident that in the initial attack, they would kill or eliminate at least 20 insurgents. That meant Colli and Piccolo had to eliminate at least four to five each. There is no doubt that there would be an insurgent contingency force in place for backup support and it was anyone's guess how long they would take to respond. The estimated time of the initial attack should take no more than twenty minutes.

Finally, Style outlined the schedule of when everything would get started.

"Initially, at precisely ten o'clock, I will walk down to the backside of the building and enter through one of the back windows or by means of a basement door as shown in one of these enlarged photographs. I then will find the Schroeder family, and since one of the girls is relatively young, if necessary, I will administer to her a tranquilizer. Then, I will exit with them out the same entrance I used originally. Obviously, my goal is be as covert as possible and to avoid unnecessary confrontations.

If anyone has any questions or would like to make any changes to the plans, speak up now?"

"Weiner and Robie both added. "Again, I think we can speak for everyone else and say, success to you, Style."

"I would like to thank my great team for all of your hard work and sacrifice. I realize this mission is extremely dangerous but I have all the confidence in the world in every one of you. We will be successful and complete our assignment. Okay, finish your coffee and let's go do our job. Remember, there is no greater sensation, than to say, mission accomplished."

35

The CIA Hostage Rescue Team (HRT) was one of the critical crash courses that Style participated in when he first attended Langley. Now more than ever, all that training was beginning to pay dividends. If he remembered anything, it was the saying, "There is no greater mission we have than to save somebody's life." The HRT counter-terrorism and hostage rescue process, was specifically designed to become skilled at how to penetrate hostile environments without being detected or seen. The HRT's purpose is to serve as a domestic and international counter-terrorism action when high-risk law enforcement situations develop, such as terrorist taking the Schroeder women as hostages.

Once Style effectively penetrated the outer perimeter and avoided detection on the inner courtyard leading to the back of the building, he felt a surge of confidence. He remained in his tharwb only to get past the initial two hurdles, including the insurgents milling around in the courtyard. His disguise and superb Arabic enabled Style to get past several of the guards after he persuaded them he was there to help clean up the mess in the back kitchen. Somehow, his mention of the kitchen drew laughs from several Al Qaeda operatives, candidly complaining the dinner they were served tonight was burned and dreadful tasting. As a result, they all said the kitchen had to be a terrible mess, because the food must have been prepared on the floor. Once he was successful in getting beyond the second set of guards, Style removed the white robe and hid it under the stairs in the corner leading to the basement. Now he was dressed in all black head to toe, including a black bandana around his face. Because his face was darkened to look like an Arab, Style looked menacing and intimidating. As he descended the stairs to the basement, he encountered two more militants who were totally surprised and unprepared. He effectively neutralized them both with his silencer mounted Sig Sauer. He continued his search through the basement; suddenly, a lone insurgent carrying a couple of boxes confronted him. Unfortunately, for the man, his life was suddenly abbreviated. Hastily, Style continued his search, finally discovering several rooms containing hostages. There were young female voices emanating through the old wooden door. Clearly, they both were having a discussion in French. Style distinctly remembered Schroeder mentioning that both of his daughters spoke fluent French. Cautiously, he pinned his ear to the door and listened intently. Suddenly, he heard a man's voice, most likely an insurgent. Style, knocked on the door and the man responded in a very heavy Arabic voice, "Who is there?"

In his very best Arabic, Style replied, "I have a gift for the girls from Ulrich Melmer."

"What is the gift?" asks the man.

"I have no idea because the box is wrapped up just like a birthday gift."

After some hesitation, the man replies, "I will be there shortly."

Style then adds, "You better hurry, because I'm already late getting here and you should not piss off Melmer. You know what happens when he gets pissed."

"Okay, I'm coming."

Almost immediately, as the insurgent opened the door, his life was over with two shoots to the head. Both girls were temporarily traumatized. Immediately, Style calmed both girls down by telling them he worked with their dad at Clearstream, and he was there to rescue them and their mom. At first, they were extremely cautious, and then asked Style some questions. "How long have your worked with our father?" asked one of the girls.

"I'm an American and originally I was hired by an American company as a consultant to help finance DeSoto Industries, an American company. Your dad is the Executive Vice President of Finance and you have a home on the east side of Lake Zurich. Recently, your dad sent the two of you along with your mom to visit your grandmother on her farm located on the southwestern side of Switzerland on the border with France. Also, you dad just received a large amount of money and I understand all of you purchased lots of clothing."

"Yes sir, that is correct."

"Do either of you know what room your mother is being held captive? We need to hurry so we don't get caught"

"The last time we were together was early this morning. We were permitted to go outside for a quick walk with our mother in the courtyard. When we returned, she was escorted to a room just down the hall in that direction. I can show you the exact room."

"All right, you have to be extra quiet and not make any noise."

"We understand."

"Are you both ready?" The girls timidly shook their heads yes. "Okay, let's go."

Style and the two young girls walked quietly down the hall until one of the girls stopped in front of a room and whispered, "This is the one." There was loud Middle Eastern music coming through the cracks of the old wooden door. Style turned to the girls and told both of them, "Please stand over by the stairs in the corner and crouch down."

Immediately, Style knocked on the door and at first, there was no reply. He knocked on the door a second time with much more force. This time there was a response. The man sounded somewhat intoxicated. "What do you want?"

"I was sent down by Ulrich Melmer because there is too much noise."

"I will turn down the music and I will be much quieter."

"Melmer also asked me to make certain that the woman was okay."

"She is all right, go away. Who the hell are you?"

"I don't think you want Melmer to come down and check on her, do you?"

"You are a pain in the fuckin ass. I'll be right there."

The man hastily opened the door and before he had an opportunity to take another breath, he was shot dead between the eyes, hurtling him against the far wall like a leaf in a windstorm. Schroeder's wife was lying in the corner on an old torn cot, obviously physically abused in great discomfort and emotionally stressed. The room smelled appalling because of the excessive dampness and mildew hanging in the air. Style also recognized she was shivering with fright and decided the best thing to do was get her daughter's into the room as fast as possible to settle her down. Style went to the door and signaled for both girls to come down to help their mom. As soon as the girls walked in to the room, Schroeder's wife responded at once. They hugged for a moment until Style walked over and started to explain they needed to leave as soon as possible. She was now a little more relaxed and more cooperative. As they were leaving, he started to give an explanation quickly to the woman, who he was and why he was there. Speaking in his very best French, Style communicated unambiguously and distinctly in plain straightforward words. He managed to make clear the circumstances and the need to move fast and quietly. Style proceeded to take the same route out that he used initially to get in to the basement compound. The time was ten thirty-five. So far, Style's rescue was running according to the original schedule. Silently they made it to the top of the stairs and Style temporarily held the women back until he was able to get a better assessment of the courtyard. Suddenly, Style became conscious of two militants walking casually and slowly toward them. They were two minutes away at least, allowing him time to make a last minute desperate change. He managed to get all three women back into the corner under a tarp where they laid motionless. All four remained completely silent on the ground until both of the militants walked straight by, not realizing they were even there. It seemed like an eternity. Within a minute or so, Style managed to get all the women up and on the move. As they stepped closer into the courtyard, Style realized that most of the insurgents had left and there were only two men walking around. All of a sudden, he decided to retrieve the tharwb and put it on. As soon as he had put the white robe back on, he rushed out the door in to the courtyard. In the meantime, he had all three women hide in the doorway's dark shadows. There was only one insurgent in sight and he yelled to Style to stop. Style continued walking, pretending not to hear him. Before neutralizing the terrorist, he waited as long as possible until the insurgent was much closer. The young terrorist started running after Style and was within ten feet and suddenly Style whirled around getting off two rounds, one through the chest and other above the right eye, dropping the man in his tracks where he collapsed dead, not making a sound. He signaled for the women to run with him. At this point, they were almost home free with just about a hundred feet to go to the outer perimeter. It was dark and bone chilling cold as they continued running out the rear entrance without making a sound. In a short time, they were greeted by the large black SUV driven by David Clapp. Style hurriedly got the women in to the SUV and joined them for a few minutes of discussion. The moment he shared with them, he was able to find out some vital information about where they were kept hostage and something about the layout from the women. Style instructed Clapp to take the Schroeder family to the American Embassy immediately. They were gone in an instant.

Style finally realized that the rescue was over and he could now focus his primary attention on finding the thirty-five billion dollars and apprehending Ulrich Melmer and Abu Alouni. Immediately, he called Robie to let him know that the women were on their way to safety. He then asked Robie to call Piccolo and Colli to let them know everything was on schedule and be prepared for an encounter in a matter of minutes. After Robie completed his phone call to both of them, he joined Weiner, Harvey and Handwerker anxiously waiting at the front entrance hiding behind a large wooden framed old rundown house just off to the right of the brick buildings where Al Qaeda has been hiding out. Shortly, Style joined the four of them. Once more, they reviewed the tactical plan. Style specifically established that he was able to locate the exact office and bedroom of Ulrich Melmer. Schroeder's two daughters provided this essential information when he asked them when they last saw Melmer. They were able to provide the exact location and the room layouts. Schroeder's wife was able to confirm and verify what her daughters had told Style. In fact, the older of the two girls had been studying art before they were moved to live with their grandmother on the farm in Southwest Switzerland. She illustrated on a piece of paper the arrangement of the entire floor where Melmer, Karl Huber and Abu Alouni have shared offices and the precise location of their respective apartments. She was able to recall from memory a detailed outline of a very accurate and meticulous layout of the house, including where the doors and windows were placed along with the exits and entrances of the stairs. In fact, she had even memorized the number of steps from one floor to the next and finally how the furniture was placed in each room and in the large hallways connecting the many different rooms. The young artist also explained that one morning she had seen Melmer opening a very large wall size walk-in vault containing a lot of money with stacks and stacks of gold bars lining the right side of the vault. Style asked the young woman on what wall was the vault located. She quickly replied, the wall to the right, when you first walk in to Melmer's office. The young women illustrated on paper, the exact location of Melmer's desk and furniture. She also described that there were two insurgents with rifles standing guard twenty-four hours a day just outside of Ulrich Melmer's office. To determine the accuracy of what she was telling him, I asked her how many times she had visited with Melmer and for what reasons. She replied that she met with him more than a dozen times and was in the process of doing a drawing of Melmer. I asked her why so many times to draw a sketch of Melmer. She replied that Melmer liked the drawing so much, he made me return to start an oil painting of him and I wasn't far from finishing.

36

I have no doubt that we will be successful in harnessing the sun's energy....
If sunbeams were weapons of war, we would have had solar energy centuries ago.
Sir George Porter, The Observer, 1973

Style decided he had to share this information fast. "Everyone, we need to make this quick. DiSciascio just called me to let us know that Hans Schroeder called him to express his thanks for rescuing his family. However, the major reason he called was to let us know the terrorist were also believed to be in possession of a nuclear device. There is no way to confirm this information as fact. Nevertheless, I do believe Schroeder is telling the truth. He also expressed confidence that the nuclear device is somehow related with the vault in Melmer's office."

Robie was quick to observe, "I would bet their intent of using this nuclear device would depend on several factors. First, how serious a threat is being made against them. Second, what are their circumstances and how desperate are the conditions."

Style interjected. "I agree with Robie, and we don't have a lot of time. If there is a nuclear device, it would be armed and located in the vault to destroy all of the gold and money. We need to neutralize and disarm the bomb before we do anything else. Harvey, I understand you had nuclear weapons disarmament training in recent years; is that correct?"

"Yes sir," replied Harvey. "Approximately a year ago I went out to Los Alamos, New Mexico, for biological and chemical defense systems disarmament training. In addition, I was also trained to perform nuclear, biological, chemical weapons and conventional operational demobilization."

"You are the guy we need at this point," responds Style.

"I'm ready to go," said Harvey.

"There is one last question," asked Style.

"I'm ready, what is the question?"

"Harvey, there is a large walk-in vault where all the money is stored in safekeeping."

"You want to know if I can crack a safe, is that correct?"

"You read my mind, Harvey."

"Boss, the answer is yes. We will need to take at least four pounds of C-4 explosives with a small inventory of blasting caps."

"Damn, Harvey! I don't want to blow up the whole fucking building with us in it, just a vault."

"I understand. I will not be using all four pounds. Most likely just two pounds but just in case something goes wrong, I have the additional C-4, if necessary. The blast will be controlled and restricted to the immediate proximity of the vault door."

"What type of noise do you think will occur?"

"Because it will be controlled to explode inward, the blast will be muffled, but it will be heard in the building. I can't prevent that, Style."

"I understand Harvey. Now, I need to ask you, approximately how long do you think it will take to defuse the bomb?"

"That is a tough question Style. However, I will speculate and say no more than six minutes at most."

"I will remain with you, Harvey, for backup. Once you have defused the bomb, we both will take off running down this hall as shown on the map. Once we get to this location, just down the hall from Melmer's bedroom, I expect all hell to break loose. At this point, I'm confident we will have sufficient time to search for Melmer and prepare for a response from the insurgents. Are there any questions?"

"Terrific, that makes things a little easier," replied Harvey.

"Listen up team. Synchronize your watches. The time will be eleven-ten, in ten seconds. If I remember correctly, Ulrich Melmer mentioned time and again, he would go to bed by eleven and read for about ten minutes and go to sleep. Hopefully, tonight should be no different. We are going to break up in to two teams. First, Harvey and I will need to penetrate the offices of Melmer, neutralize the bomb if there is one, and secure the vault. The second team consists of Robie, Weiner and Handwerker. You guys will hold back until I contact you that we managed to infiltrate the terrorist safe house and have neutralized both guards in front of Melmer's office. Once we confirmed the location of the nuclear device, secured and deactivated it, I will call Robie. At that point, we will all converge onto the floor that contains the bedrooms and especially Melmer's bedroom. Robie here is another drawing I made of the layout of the house. We will then nullify as many of the Al Qaeda insurgents as necessary. Once we either apprehend or kill Melmer and most of these asshole terrorist, we will then search for Karl Huber, Abu Alouni and Asif Zardari. Frankly, my orders were to catch Melmer alive, if possible. However, I really don't give a fuck how we capture him. We can take him back to the embassy in a hundred separate bags as far as I'm concerned."

It was time to go. Harvey and Style remained dressed in their tharwbs. Both men walked casually together through the inner courtyard, having a discussion in Arabic. There were now just three insurgents walking about. Style made it a point to stop and acknowledge one of the terrorist by telling him in Arabic, "Melmer asked us to come clean up something he spilled in his room." The insurgent replied. "No problem."

Style turned back to continue his conversation with Harvey. Finally, they approached the stairway leading to the offices of Melmer. Once they were inside the building, Style removed the map to make certain they were headed in the right direction. Melmer's office was just around the corner. Style glanced quickly to see if both guards were on duty. He discovered that one of the guards was seated reading a book and the other one was gazing out the window. Style and Harvey continued speaking loudly in Arabic, as they turned the corner walking in the direction of both insurgents. Style and Harvey both bowed out of respect and once they started to rise up, out came both of their silencer mounted Sig Sauers, firing off three and four rounds respectively. Both of the insurgents dropped without ever having a chance to fire a shot.

Harvey turned to Style and said, "I don't think we need these handcuffs after we put two rounds in each of their foreheads."

"That is a great observation, Harvey."

Immediately, Style and Harvey dragged both bodies down the hallway and dumped them in to a closet. Without delay, they returned to Melmer's office to allow Harvey to pick the front door lock. Without much difficulty, they were in Melmer's office. It was eerily quiet, almost as if this night were pre-determined for something major to occur. The young woman's drawing was accurate enough, so most everything she described was exact to the last detail. As she indicated, the vault was on the right side. Harvey then sat on a chair in front of the vault door and quickly set down all of his tools just like a surgeon preparing for major surgery. Immediately, he started to place the C-4 plastic explosives into the tumbler combination lock, crevices, hinges and the cracks of the vault door. Style stepped outside the office door to keep guard. Harvey then took a long lead wire outside and joined Style. He triggered the detonator through the detonator cord to the blasting cap. There was a powerful shock wave but surprisingly very little noise. The explosion actually had two phases. The initial detonation inflicted the most damage, creating a very low-pressure area around the explosion's origins, blasting the massive metal door open and then created a partial vacuum. This was followed by a second, less-destructive inward energy wave. Style and Harvey moved back into the office fast discovering the vault door was now opened. They both stepped inside the vault and discovered in the corner was the bomb Schroeder referred to and described. Harvey straightway went to the corner, sat down and took out some tools. He started to talk to himself, more out of nervousness, and then he took a deep breath and exhaled. Harvey turned to Style and in a very low voice said, "This bomb looks similar to the nuclear bomb I had to de-fuse when I attended training at the nuclear weapons disarmament school in Los Alamos, New Mexico."

"Obviously, you were successful, Harvey?"

"Now, that is real funny, Style. There is one major difference," observed Harvey."

"Okay, what is the difference?"

"I had the benefit of using the 'The Little Beast,' a remote controlled robot that is equipped with a water-cannon. It can pick up the bomb, carry it to a specific location and ease it down. It also has a zoomable camera with image stabilization and an extremely dexterous mechanical arm that can navigate rough terrain and is controlled wirelessly from up to a half-mile away."

"Harvey, I have bad news for you. You are just one foot away and have no mechanical arm or camera. However, there is a jug of water and some straws on Melmer's desk."

"Boss, you are a comedian. Nevertheless, your humor is relaxing me. I'm just about finished dismantling this very complicated son-of-a-bitch nuclear bomb."

It was obvious that Harvey was under tremendous stress by the amount of sweat running off his forehead and dripping down his nose and chin. He was soaked with perspiration. Time was now becoming a critical factor. In the distance, Style was beginning to hear loud noises and people running. "One more minute," yelled Harvey.

"I understand, Harvey, I understand. There are insurgents coming and they will be here in sixty seconds or less."

"Finished at last and the bomb is defused and we are safe, momentarily, Style."

"Terrific, we need to get prepared."

Style called Robie to let him know the bomb was defused and they found all the gold and money in the safe. He told Robie to move fast. Robie in turn called Colli and Piccolo to get ready for action. In the meantime, Clapp managed to get back in time and was now in the back of the building, not too far from the courtyard, dressed in all black. As Style and Harvey worked their way down the hallway running toward Melmer's bedroom, they encountered several insurgents. Without hesitation, they both threw their grenades at the rushing insurgents, blasting four of them into the walls and one out the window. Out front, Colli and Piccolo were doing their job, picking off Al Qaeda as they ran from one building to another. Within less than two minutes, they both had already killed and seriously injured at least eight insurgents. Robie, Handwerker and Weiner worked their way up to join Style and Harvey. There seemed to be action everywhere. The scene looked like a battlefield, with soldiers fighting in the streets and on rooftops, moving under the cover of darkness and a moonless night. The evening was bitterly cold and it had started to snow; the wind began to pick-up, adding to the excitement of the spectacle. The air was filled with choking smoke while the deafening sound of gunfire, grenades and small arms fire all seemed to be going off at once. Clapp encountered three terrorists and used his shotgun to release several rounds at close range, snuffing out two instantly, and the other were badly wounded in the chest and shoulder. He finally made it to the stairs, cautiously taking leaps up stairs two and three at a time, navigating his way to join Style and the rest of the team. As soon as he entered the door leading to bedrooms, he confronted another militant. This time he was eyeball to eyeball with his adversary. He removed his 9mm, and pulled off three quick rounds, hitting the insurgent in the chest, neck and shoulder. Clapp was hit once in the side and fell to the side of the hallway. He dove for cover, rolling over and over. Although he was in pain and loosing blood, he managed to get back on his feet and continued moving. Robie, Handwerker and Weiner came across Clapp as they were running down the hall to join Style. Hurriedly, they provided some first aid, dragged him into a nearby vacant room and sat him down on the floor. No sooner had they left Clapp, they found themselves face to face with at least four insurgents rushing in their direction. Suddenly, running from behind the four terrorists, came Style and Harvey blasting their way and taking the terrorists by surprise. All four of the Islamic insurgents were gunned down without a chance of defending themselves. There was blood splattered all over the walls and floor. Gun smoke filled the air, choking everyone and making it difficult to see. Robie glanced out the window overlooking the courtyard and discovered there were several trucks pulling into the courtyard loaded with many reinforcements.

He called Colli and Piccolo and asked them to join in the fracas in the courtyard. Weiner then speedily removed one of the drones off the back of Handwerker and set it up on the outside stairway. At the same time, Robie configured the backup drone and moved to the open window. Style reminded them that they didn't need line of sight and they were capable of seeking out and destroying targets using the screen. Once it lofts into the air, it will assist you searching for your targets. When the target is marked, the drone will attack your target when established. We have a limit of six drones to be fired, including the backup. Weiner and Robie fired their first drones and immediately loaded up again. The first two hit their respective targets well before any of the insurgents had an opportunity to escape the trucks. Flames shot up instantly, creating a light spectacle in the night. Razor-sharp strips of shrapnel and ball bearings flew through the air stabbing and wounding the terrorist in horrendous ways. Many were decapitated and others lost limbs. Some were in shock and running aimlessly through the courtyard. The massive explosion blinded a few, setting all the trucks ablaze and sending a column of black smoke high above the five story brick buildings.

There were at least two dozen insurgents killed instantly. Human remains could be seen splattered all over the courtyard, as well as what remained of the vehicles. Apparently, one of the trucks contained a sizeable amount of ammunition and explosives. It soon erupted into the most horrific of sounds when it exploded. One terrorist was running with blood spilling into his eyes from a shrapnel gash to his forehead and severe wounds to his leg and torso. Although the squirting blood and smoke were a terrifying sight, the battle continued. All you heard for a period was, Boom. Boom. Boom. Successive blasts, each one seemed louder and more powerful. Screams could be heard everywhere. It was a frightening and terrifying sight to see such bloodshed. At this point, there were literally over a hundred militants down on the ground, bloodsoaked and gravely wounded or dead. There was another hundred fifty or so wounded in the massive explosions and many were in critical condition. Despite the overwhelming odds, the Americans were pounding and pummeling the insurgents under a moonless sky - eight against many. The constant presence of death was all around the American team and the courtyard had become witness to the carnage of men baptized with blood and the horrifying sight of corpses.

Twenty-minutes into the clash, there was a sudden quietness. Prior to the engagement, every one of the Americans was given photographs of Ulrich Melmer, Karl Uber, Abu Alouni and Asif Zardari. Style held up all the photographs of the group of insurgent leaders, and then asked, "Gentlemen, it seems our conflict is just about over. Has anyone seen any of these assholes?" No one responded.

"We are going to have to search every room, one at a time. Because these buildings are very old, they contain hidden and secret passageways. I understand they were built prior to the turn of Twentieth Century and somehow they managed to survive the Allies carpet-bombing in World War II. Check closets, bathrooms, storage rooms and look for secret rooms by tapping on the walls, looking behind paintings and check-ing floors for possible stairs. We know Melmer hasn't left because the clothing and shoes we believe he wore yesterday were piled on a chair in the corner. Consequently, we think even now, he's wearing his paja-mas. Earlier, I called MI6 and Interpol, requesting immediate support and backup. Both indicated they were on their way and would be here in a matter of minutes. Has anyone seen Colli and Piccolo, and how is Clapp doing?"

The first to reply was Robie. "No, I haven't seen either Colli or Piccolo. Clapp is holding on and should recover without complications."

"That is great news. Ordinarily, at this juncture I would give you guy's kudos. However, we haven't finished our mission until we have apprehended the four assholes."

Just as Style was finishing his discussion, Colli and Piccolo came slowly walking down the hallway. Colli was barely able to support his partner because of a minor gunshot to this his arm. Piccolo was notice-ably in severe pain from two wounds, both serious. They received their wounds when he and Colli had close quarter engagements with four insurgents at the entrance to the courtyard. Piccolo had one critical gunshot wound to his left thigh and the other was a life-threatening chest wound. He was completely covered in crimson red. Suddenly, he collapsed but remained conscious. Handwerker rushed to provide

Piccolo first aid. It was obvious that Piccolo was in bad shape and may
not survive because of all the blood loss. Handwerker decided to rest
him on the ground. Piccolo's condition was getting worse by the second;
soon he lost consciousness. Handwerker yelled out, "Is there a doctor
around this goddamned place." At last, a German medical team came
running down the hall and rapidly started to provide resuscitation and
medical treatment to Piccolo. Once they managed to stabilize him, the
medical team immediately put him on a stretcher and hurriedly rolled
him and Colli out. Finally, Interpol and MI6 arrived almost at the same
time. After a quick introduction and discussion, the commanding officer from Interpol volunteered thirty men to assist Style in the pursuit of
Melmer and the rest of the insurgents. They divided in to three teams
lead by Robie, Weiner and Style. Immediately all three teams dispersed
in different directions. Style and his team promptly returned to the
floor where Melmer had his apartment to begin a thorough search of
every room. Once Style arrived at Melmer's apartment, they started to
take it apart, room-by-room. Style focused his attention in Melmer's
bedroom. He inspected every wall and all the wooden floors, investi-
gated and tested the wall tiles in the bathroom for any possible hidden
button or switches. He removed all of the expensive art displayed on the
walls and found absolutely nothing. Next, he moved onto the first of two
closets. First, he checked the ceiling for a drop down ladder that would
lead to a hidden room. He kept asking himself, "How could these guys
disappear without a trace. There is nothing but dead ends." Finally, the
last closet remained. He removed all the clothing, luggage and a number of boxes until the closet was barren. He tapped and banged the walls
and ceiling. At this point, Style was getting frustrated and disappointed.
As he was leaving the closet, he discovered that the light switch moved
as he depressed it. At first, he thought it was his imagination until he
started to play with it. He took out a knife and removed the light switch
box. Just inside on the right was a button. He depressed it and magi-
cally the entire closet floor slid open to reveal a staircase. Silently he
navigated himself down the stairs. The room was void of light and made
the circumstances more mysterious and sinister. He took out his 9mm
weapon and attached the Siglite night-lights. He was now able to find his

way without stumbling in the pitch-blackness. As he walked slowly, he heard a couple of voices in the not too far distance. As he got closer, the voices became more distinct and clear. One of the voices he recognized belonged to Ulrich Melmer. As Style approached the door where the voices were coming from, both men were talking in German and saying something to the effect that they would split the money. All of a sudden without hesitation, Style crashed through the old weak wooden door and there sat Ulrich Melmer and Karl Uber. Both were shocked and stunned. Uber reached for his gun but Style managed to rapidly pull off three quick shots with his 9mm. All three shots were to the head, blowing away the back of Uber's head and spewing blood and brain tissue on to the wall behind. In the meantime, Melmer reached for his weapon but didn't quite get his revolver out quick enough, as Style turned and unloaded another three rounds into Melmer. One bullet entered just above the left temple and the other two were delivered to the chest. Both men were dead. Style couldn't control himself, yelling out loud, "justice served, finally, you sons of bitches and this is for Zosa."

Without hesitation, Style took possession of the money on the desk and departed. When he made his way back up to Melmer's apartment, most of the team had gathered in the den. The first thing he asked was, "How are Piccolo, Colli and Clapp doing?" Robie replied, "All three will survive. Piccolo will take a little longer, but will recover."

"Does anyone have any idea what happened to Abu Alouni and Asif Zardari?" Weiner responded and said, "We don't have to worry about them being sent to Guantanamo Bay military prison and having a trial. The American taxpayers have been saved millions of dollars because both of those assholes, and many Al Qaeda insurgents, are with their twenty-one virgins, wherever that may be. We did our job gentlemen." Harvey was quick to say, "Personally, I think all of them are in hell where they belong."

Style was staring out the window down into the courtyard where the carnage took place and observed. "This appears similar to downtown Beirut after a major battle. My God, this is such a waste of human kind. What is wrong with these people? I hope that the twenty-one virgins pay big dividends. We did indeed accomplish our mission, gentlemen."

The following morning when everyone was gathered at the American Embassy, Style received a phone call from DiSciascio.

"Style, I speak for the Director of the CIA and the President of the United States and congratulate you and your team for such a remarkable job well done. You have another four million dollars reward coming now that all the money has been recovered and accounted for to the last penny. Each of your team will also receive two million dollars."

"Thank you, DiSciascio, for the kind compliment and for the money."

"Before I forget, Schroeder would also like to say thank you for your trust and rescuing his family. He asked that you call him as soon as possible."

"Thank you for the message, DiSciascio."

"Would you like a couple of days off, Style?"

"Are you kidding? Just a couple of days? I need to start getting into condition because I have a major ATP tennis tournament in a few weeks."

"I understand; okay, how about three or four days because we have another important assignment waiting for you."

"I'm taking off for at least two, maybe three weeks, boss."

"I totally understand, Style; have a good time."

"I will."

As soon as Style ended his conversation with DiSciascio, he called Schroeder.

"Hello Schroeder, this is Style. How are your wife and daughters doing?"

"Style, I can't thank you enough for what you did. It was courageous and I'm lost for words. Thank you, thank you so much."

"Now, don't forget we have a date to go fly fishing out in Montana when you decide to visit the United States."

"That is confirmed. How about next summer?"

"Okay. That is confirmed. I will contact my dad and he'll make arrangements. But first, you must visit my family in Blue Ridge, Georgia."

"Consider it done. I have something I would like to share with you."

"Schroeder, do you mean some really exceptional French Bordeaux wine?"

"I will have that, too. I arranged for you to practice with Roger Federer at the upcoming Monte Carlo Rolex ATP Master Tennis tournament in Monte-Carlo, Monaco. He also said thank you for your bravery and for what you did for the Swiss people and most of Europe. He promised he would not discuss or reveal your other profession. I believe him. Thank you, Style."

"Good bye, Schroeder. I will be talking with you."

37

I know war as few other men now living know it,
and nothing to me is more revolting.
I have long advocated its complete abolition,
as its very destructiveness on both friend and foe
has rendered it useless as a method of settling international disputes.
General Douglas MacArthur

*M*EDITERRANEAN SEA, MONTE CARLO, MONACO
Five weeks later after the successful recovery of the approximately thirty-five billion dollars stolen by Ulrich Melmer and the capture or killing of Al Qaeda insurgents, Style managed to develop a daily tennis workout routine. He was now in southern France, near Cannes, on the Mediterranean Sea, where it was warm and very relaxing. Because of the ideal weather with warm sunny days and delightful evenings, Style managed to develop a daily workout that was demanding and exhausting, but was beginning to produce results. His injured leg was no longer a problem and he could run and move with agility and confidence. Style's twice a day tennis drills involved working out with two tennis-teaching professionals in two on one drills. Every day he ran five miles to build up his cardio vascular stamina. In addition,

he biked ten miles daily. He also hired a fitness coach and a nutritionist. Often, in the evening when Style was having his dinner on the veranda of one of the many excellent seaside restaurants, he would think of Zosa. It was obvious he couldn't forget her as often as he tried. He was in need of the companionship of a woman, especially with someone he could share and enjoy the beautiful scenery and exceptional French cuisine. Approximately a week after the dust settled in Frankfurt, Germany, Style's Orthopedic specialist advised him to postpone his comeback by at least one or two weeks. As a result, he optioned to notify the Associated Tennis Professional (ATP) that he couldn't participate in the Grand Prix Hassan, in Casablanca, Morocco, the first week of April. However, Style's physician did provide the green light to take part in the Rolex Monte Carlo ATP tournament in mid-April. Just recently, Style received an unexpected phone call from Roger Federer asking Style if he would be interested in going to Monaco a couple of days early and working out together in preparation for the upcoming Rolex Monte Carlo tournament. Federer indicated that he had reduced his ATP Tournament schedule and as a result, he was able to practice and workout more frequently. Of course, Style was elated and asked what date Federer had in mind to start a workout schedule. Federer suggested the second week of April, a full week before the tournament started. Style quickly responded that he would see him there. Before Style ended the phone call, he asked Federer what hotel he would be staying at for the week. Federer replied that his family and he like staying at the Fairmont Hotel, overlooking the Monte Carlo Tennis Country Club. They agreed to meet for a lite lunch at the Terraces at around noon and then workout for about two hours.

"Roger that sounds just about perfect. I will see you in a couple of weeks."

Style was thrilled and beside himself with excitement. The next few weeks went by swiftly. The day he was to meet with Roger Federer was a beautiful spring day. There were no clouds and the sun was shining brightly. Humidity was low and the temperature was ideal in the mid-seventies. Since the tournament didn't begin for another week, there were few tourists walking around, freeing up the streets and sidewalks. Style, arrived early at the Terraces, and was seated overlooking the tennis courts, offering a breathtaking view of the Mediterranean Sea as a back-drop to the well-manicured clay tennis courts. He ordered an ice tea and told the waiter he was at least fifteen minutes early and that he would wait until his guest arrived before ordering anything to eat. In the meantime, people started to arrive and were being seated at neighboring tables, all admiring the spectacular views. Style wasn't paying much attention when Roger Federer walked up to the table and said, "Hello, John Style."

"Good day to you, Roger. Where is your family?"

"It seems there has been a change of plans, John, and I hope you don't mind."

"Of course not, Roger. Hopefully nothing has happened to you or your family."

"No. They are just fine but I do have something I need to share with you."

"What is the problem, Roger? Can I help?"

"It seems we have a mutual friend in Hans Schroeder. Correct?"

"Is Hans okay?"

"Yes, of course, John. Two days ago, Hans Schroeder called me asking if I could help him with a favor and I simply asked him what was the favor?"

"You are keeping me in suspense now, Roger. What is going on?"

"Well, without further delay, there is a special person seated at a table, directly behind you."

"Do I know this person, Roger?"

"Yes, from what I understand, you know her extremely well."

Without further delay, Style turned around and discovered a vision walking toward him. Style thought he was hallucinating. It was Zosa Dena, his love. He thought she was killed months before in the horrific Zurich bombing. He couldn't believe what he was seeing and thought this was a fantasy. Style jumped up and hurriedly rushed toward her. He picked her up in his arms and swirled her around until both were in hysteria crying, releasing their emotions aloud so just about everyone within a hundred feet could hear their joy and happiness.

"Excuse me, John," interrupted Roger Federer. "I don't think today would be a good day to start practicing. I will call you in two days."

Style replied. "Thank you for understanding, Roger."

Zosa and Style finally sat down. Of course, both were confused and had a million questions. John asked first, "What happened and how did you survive that horrendous bombing. I was convinced that you were dead after a doctor pronounced you dead at the scene."

"Unfortunately, the person you thought was me was actually my sister Marie. Earlier in the afternoon, she came to my house to borrow my black dress you liked so well and the necklace you gave to me on our second date, John."

"Then what happened to you and where did you go, Zosa?"

"I suffered a broken arm and lacerations to my back, shoulder and thigh. In addition, I suffered a head injury that caused me to be unconscious for several days. They call it Post-traumatic stress disorder (PTSD). For approximately a month, I couldn't remember my name. I also would forget where I lived. Once I completed my medical treatment, the doctor suggested I needed a change of scenery for a short period. So my mom and dad took me to Majorca Island, in Southern Spain, where it was warm with beautiful beaches and a place where I could try to organize my life and heal. I miss my sister and her husband. They were made for each other and loved every waking moment they were together. My mom and dad also suffered considerably in Maria's death."

"Zosa, I don't know what to say. I'm lost for words."

"John, I understand you were hurt seriously and spent some time in Zurich Hospital."

"Yes, but my injuries were minor."

"I also understand you were a hero, John Style."

"How do you know all of this, Zosa?"

"A couple of weeks ago, your friend Hans Schroeder contacted the Hyatt Regency in Zurich, and requested information on my sister after reading an account of the bombing in a monthly Swiss news publication. He must be extremely important, because shortly thereafter, Interpol tracked us down on Majorca Island. When we returned to Zurich, we met and he shared the entire story with us. He was responsible for contacting Roger Federer and arranging today."

"Hans Schroeder has been a trusted and wonderful friend, Zosa."

"He also feels the same way about you, John."

"Zosa, it seems we made a bet and you challenged me to play a tennis match. Do you recall?"

"Well, yes, but I wasn't aware that you were a touring tennis professional at the time."

"I understand. How about if we play for lunch and your partner is Roger Federer and I play with Roger's wife. Now, you have to be easy on us because she is now pregnant with their third child."

"John, I play to win."

"Okay, then how about having lunch with me now and making arrangements to stay here with me for the next two weeks?

"Absolutely, John. I just hope I'm not too much of a distraction for you."

"Now there you go teasing me again Zosa...I love it."

Now this is not the end. It is not even the beginning of the end.
But it is, perhaps, the end of the beginning.
...Winston Churchill...